ESCAPE TO
ZION

OTHER BOOKS AND AUDIO BOOKS
BY JEAN HOLBROOK MATHEWS

The Light Above

ESCAPE TO
ZION

a novel

JEAN HOLBROOK MATHEWS

Covenant Communications, Inc.

Cover top image: *The Journey Together* © Daniel Gerhartz. For more information, go to www.danielgerhartz.com. Bottom Image: *Zion's March* © Glen S. Hopkinson. For more information, go to www.glenhopkinson.com

Cover design © 2010 by Covenant Communications, Inc.

Published by Covenant Communications, Inc.
American Fork, Utah

Printed in The United States of America
First Printing: May 2010

16 15 14 13 12 11 10   10 9 8 7 6 5 4 3 2 1

ISBN 13: 978-1-59811-956

To my husband, John, who has been my Hank
throughout many years of marriage.

Foreword

Historians have estimated that between AD 1650 and 1850, as many as one of every four immigrants to America arrived as an indentured servant. Many of them arrived at very young ages, and—because families were seldom, if ever, kept intact—as they matured, they had little or no memory of their cultural roots or family relationships. Though many were Irish, Scottish, Italian, English, or French, by far, the greatest number were ethnic Germans. How many of them were eventually sold as slaves by unscrupulous masters will never be known, but the fact that such things did happen is evidenced in the legal case of *Sally Miller vs. Belmondi* in New Orleans, which is referenced in this story.

Skin color was not the determining factor in slavery as is mistakenly believed by most Americans. All that was required was African blood to the sixth generation. Chief Justice Robinson of Kentucky wrote in 1835 in the case of *Gentry v. McMinnis:* "A white person of unmixed blood cannot be a slave . . . [But] a person apparently white may, nevertheless, have some African taint . . . sufficient to doom to slavery."

The author has attempted to portray the times and places in this story as accurately as possible. The details surrounding Sally Miller's legal fight for freedom are accurate, including the names of the attorneys involved and the quotes from the decisions in her case. Every attempt has been made to offer the reader an accurate description of New Orleans in 1846, including details such as the Urseline Convent, Madame Borgnette's school for girls, and the fact that Theophilis

Freeman was the biggest slave trader in New Orleans, a city with more than one hundred slave traders.

In LDS history, the members of The Church of Jesus Christ of Latter-day Saints from Monroe County, Mississippi, and the adjoining counties of Alabama are referred to as the Mississippi Saints. The names of those used in this story were actually part of this group. The primary characters of Maria, Hank, Karl, Minnie, and Lafayette Breaux are fictional and, thus, the interactions of these pioneers with Hank, Maria, and Karl as told here are, of necessity, fictional but plausible. The events that took place while the Saints were at Pueblo, where the Sick Company of the Mormon Battalion joined them, are reproduced as accurately as is practical, though certainly in no way can be considered all-inclusive.

The founding of Cottonwood, the second Mormon settlement in the Great Basin, and the hardships of the early years there are also based on historical accounts, but in no way is this book an attempt at a detailed history of that settlement.

The events of this book are placed in a historical matrix in an attempt to give the reader a glimpse of the world as those living at that time knew and experienced it. Any inaccuracies or mistakes are solely the fault of the author.

Jean Holbrook Mathews

CHAPTER 1
Escape!

Finding her way into the summer kitchen by the irregular flashes of lightning, Maria collapsed wearily on the dirt floor next to the fireplace. She picked up a large piece of sacking that lay crumpled next to the kindling box and wrapped it around her wet shoulders. Turning sideways, she leaned her head against the wall of the log structure and put her bare feet on the hearthstones to warm them with the residual heat from the previous night's fire. Her wet hair, made dark gold by the rain, clung to her head and lay against her shoulders, which were covered by only a thin cotton dress. She lifted her soaked apron and pulled it down over her knees as if it might offer some warmth. The dark kitchen brightened rhythmically with flashes of lightning while the thunder and hard rain pounded like fists on the roof.

She whispered to herself, "Please, dear God, just give me a few minutes of rest." And then she closed her gray-green eyes and drifted off into a restless sleep.

***

As the early-morning light struggled through the continuing rain, Bessie entered the summer kitchen, which stood about twenty feet behind the Franchot plantation house. The slave woman was almost as broad as she was tall and had rocked many babies, both black and white, against her generous bosom. Her hair was covered with a red bandana; her dress was covered by a wide, white apron. She placed the ten pound sack of rice she carried on the table.

Not seeing Maria in the shadows, she lit a candle and then stooped to fan flames from the banked coals with the small bellows that hung by the fireplace. She added several pieces of kindling and soon the flames were leaping higher. Maria stirred and opened her eyes. Startled, Bessie looked up to see the young woman huddled against the wall near the fireplace and said, "Maria, what you doing here? You run away?"

"Oh, Bessie, please don't tell anyone. I would rather die than go back to Mr. Breaux." She struggled to her feet, stiff from being huddled on the floor.

"Maria, child, I won't tell on you, but you got to know that my Lucinda will be here anytime. I let her sleep a bit late because the thunder kept her awake and in my bed most the night. And you know she can't ever keep her mouth still. She sees you, the whole world will know in ten minutes. Now you tell me why you running away." As Bessie talked, she poured water for grits into a pot that was hanging above the fire on a small, two-armed crane attached to the brick. As the water heated, she filled another pot with water for tea or coffee, whichever the master and his wife preferred that morning, and hung it on the other arm.

"Bessie, you know how some of the masters make babies with the pretty slave girls?" The kindly black woman simply nodded. Maria sat on the stool near the table where Bessie was working. "Mr. Breaux wants a baby by me."

Bessie did not stop her work but nodded as she mixed and kneaded the dough for the breakfast rolls. "Not surprising, child. With your white skin and pretty eyes, the only real surprise is you ain't had two or three already. You can't be surprised. Not really."

"Mr. Breaux came for me the last three nights. After everyone was asleep, he took me from the servants' quarters and forced me into his bed." She spat out the words as if they had a foul taste. "His wife went to visit her mother in New Orleans. I begged him to leave me alone, but he punched me and knocked me down. I tried to run away, so he hit me again and again until I couldn't stand up. When he was through with me, he sent me back to the servants' quarters, but he said he would give me ten lashes if I ever said anything or fought him again." She turned her face, and Bessie could see the blue bruise on her jaw and a red swelling on her forehead. As she studied the young woman, she noticed the darkening handprint on Maria's wrist and the bruises on her upper arms. "When he came for me the next night, he didn't wait for me to fight him. He hit me hard, put me over his shoulder, and carried me to his bedroom. When he was done with me, he pulled me to the doorway, and before he pushed me out into the hallway, he saw my locket and said, 'Where did you get that?' He pulled it off my neck and told me to get out. He put it on the table by the door when he pushed me out of the room." She dropped her head forward and lifted her hair. Bessie could see the red welt where the chain had cut the back of her neck when it was yanked off.

After a moment, Maria took a deep breath and continued, "Last night, his wife came home sooner than he expected, and when he opened the door and gave me a push, his wife was coming up the stairs. She saw me coming out of the bedroom. Oh, Bessie, she screamed at me. She screamed things I can't say. Then she went into the bedroom and screamed at him."

Caught up in the story, Bessie paused and asked, "What did she say to him?"

"She screamed, 'How can you take a slave into our bed?' Then I heard something break, a lamp, maybe. The door was still open, so I reached in and took my locket. I stepped back out into the hall so they wouldn't see me. While she was screaming at him, he started to talk. I wanted to hear what he had to say so I stood there by the open door and listened."

Bessie's eyes grew wide with alarm. "Child, you get caught listening like that and some masters will cut off your ear."

"I know, Bessie, but they were talking about me. I had to know what they were saying. He told her that I wasn't really a slave, that I was Dutch or German and as white as either of them, but since they had been married ten years and had no babies, he wanted one by me to give to her."

"What did she say then?" Bessie was hanging on every word.

"She was quiet for a second or two, but then she said loud enough for me to hear, 'Then you will sell her!' He said that he would sell me after the baby came. That way they could pass it off as their own."

She put her face in her hands and sobbed until Bessie wiped her hands on her apron, came around the table, and put her arms around the grieving young woman. "Bessie, no man will want me now. I am not who I was. I'm not clean anymore."

Wiping the tears of frustration and exhaustion with the back of her hand, she continued, "Bessie, you know I am not a slave. I came to this country as a redemptioner. Lafayette Breaux said he bought me as a slave, but he didn't tell me that until I turned eighteen and asked him for my freedom. He said he has papers proving that he owns me forever, but he wouldn't show them to me." Her voice grew intense and angry. "Bessie, I am a good Christian girl, and I am not a slave—but I don't know how to prove it." Fiercely, she whispered in her native German, "*Ich bin ein Baden geboren.* I am German. I was born in Baden." She put her elbows on the kitchen table and again covered her face with her hands. Her shoulders shook with renewed weeping.

"I believe you, child, but if you be really wanting to run away, you better get yourself away from here while it's raining." Bessie moved to the fireplace, ladled a helping of grits into a wooden bowl, and handed it to her. "You best eat this quick and get on your way. Mr. Breaux will have the dogs out after you soon as the rain stops. Get yourself over the river if you can, so the dogs can't follow you."

Trying to dull the hunger pains in her stomach, Maria ate the grits with a wooden spoon quickly, disregarding the heat that burned her tongue. Putting the bowl down on the table, she put her arms around Bessie and said, "Pray for me, Bessie. Pray that he doesn't find me."

The black woman patted Maria's back and answered, "I will, child, but I see Lucinda coming from the main house so you best get out the back window so she don't see you."

Maria climbed through the back window, further tearing her dress, and dropped to the sloping ground, seven feet below, twisting her ankle. She muffled the cry of pain that escaped her mouth. Limping, she made her way down the slope toward the Ouachita River about two miles away. She was grateful for the continuing rain, which she hoped would help confuse the dogs.

As she stumbled over the soft ground, the tree branches tangled themselves in her hair and scratched her arms and face.

She tried to protect her face from the stiff and brittle branches with a raised arm as she moved across the wooded hillside, favoring her injured ankle. Shortly after the rain had begun to ease, she heard the baying of the hounds echoing through the woods.

The ground was normally soft because the river was so close, but the rain had turned it into mire. To keep above the mud as much as possible, she tried to step from one tree root to another where they stretched over the surface of the ground, supporting herself with low-hanging branches. As the mire worsened, she knew she would run into the river soon, but she didn't know if she had the strength to get to it before the dogs found her. The rain stopped, and she paused to catch her breath. She could hear the baying growing louder and more excited.

"*Hunde von Helse*—hounds from Hell," she whispered in panic to herself as she neared the river, breathless from exertion. As the ground grew wetter, each step felt as though she had stepped into thick quicksand. The Ouachita River came into view between the trees, and she called on her fading strength to reach the bank. The hounds were closing on her fast, their baying increasing in volume.

After a quick look up and down the riverbank, she realized her hope of finding an abandoned canoe or raft was futile. She picked up a log about four feet long and a little more than a foot in circumference and dragged it to the river. As the fastest of the hounds spotted her, the baying became deafening. Added to the noise was the whinnying of Lafayette Breaux's high-strung stallion. She could hear his angry voice above the uproar of the animals, yelling, "Find her! Find her!"

She pushed the log out into the river, and praying under her breath for strength, she held on as the current took hold of it. The river was deep and fast at that point, and she and the log were pulled under the cold water for a few seconds. Her heart felt as if it would jump out of her chest with exhaustion and fear—fear of the water, Lafayette Breaux, the dogs, and the fact that she could not swim. Quickly, the log and its passenger were swept into the center of the current. Other logs and debris bobbed around her, occasionally scraping and bumping her hands, arms, and back.

The current slowed again enough that she could regain her senses and think of her safety. Knowing that if she let go of the log she would drown, she reached behind her back with one hand and pulled off her apron. Wrapping the sash around the log with her right arm, she managed to tie her left arm to it, holding one of the sashes in her teeth. Looking toward heaven, she cried, "God, do you know where I am? Please help me."

Gradually, the cold water and weariness took her captive, and the sound of the dogs and Breaux's angry shouts began to fade. She laid her head against the rough bark of the log, disregarding the water that intermittently swept over her face. She slipped into a dark pit of exhaustion. A dream enveloped her. In it, water extended as far as she could see, and the deck of the ship *Hope* tossed beneath her in the stormy sea.

"Mama, don't die. Don't leave me." Eight-year-old Maria Schumann knelt by her unconscious mother and held her limp hand. Her father lay next to her mother, his face white and glistening with sweat. "Papa, help me. Don't let Mama die. Tell me what to do."

Her father's words were so low she had to bend near him to hear. "I cannot help you, daughter. Your mother will soon go home to God. If I follow her, you must remember that God will not forget you. No matter what happens, God will not forget you. He will always know where you are." He was silent for a moment, his eyes closed. Then he added in a whisper, "Take the locket from your mother's neck. It is all we have to give you."

Her fingers shook so much she could hardly undo the clasp. She managed to fasten it around her neck, and then she put it under the top of her dress to hide it.

***

After the death of her parents on the voyage, Maria was sold as an indentured servant for sufficient money to pay the cost of the passage for the three of them, as the law required. When the ship docked in Baltimore in the late summer of 1834, a kindly, childless German couple by the name of Wentz attended the auction and purchased her for two hundred and fifty dollars, a large sum for a female indentured servant who was to gain her freedom at the age of eighteen. They had then taken the frightened child to a local notary where she was required to sign the contract, written in English—which she could not read—that bound her to servitude for the next ten years. In German, Mr. Wentz explained it to her, and she lowered her head and signed her name in her childish script.

Mrs. Wentz suffered from poor health, so Maria became her personal maid and companion for the next six years. Maria's education in Baden had been limited to learning to read the German Bible and signing her name, but Mrs. Wentz taught her to speak, read, and write in both English and German. She taught her from the great German and English classics, and she insisted that Maria strive to overcome any sign of an accent in her speech. "When you are free, I want you to sound like an educated American lady," her benefactor would often tell her. "Then you will marry a fine man and have many beautiful children." The speech she carefully taught Maria was laced with the soft sounds of Virginia. Additionally, she was also given lessons on the pianoforte, learning to play and love Beethoven.

When Mrs. Wentz died, Maria mourned as she had mourned for her own mother. Mr. Wentz, in his grief, neglected his mercantile store until it failed, and he became bankrupt. He was forced to sell Maria's services to a man from Arlington, Virginia, who wanted a domestic servant for his plantation house. Mr. Wentz and Maria both shed tears as she clung to him before her new master, Mr. Becker, pulled her away and forced her to climb into his wagon for the ride to his plantation. He did not speak to her the entire journey.

Gone was the affection and kindness of Mr. and Mrs. Wentz. Now only impatient orders and an occasional cuff when she did not move fast enough comprised her treatment each day. Often, as she climbed into bed, she whispered, "God, do you know where I am?"

For two years, she assisted in the kitchen, served at the table, washed, ironed, made candles and soap, and did anything else Mr. or Mrs. Becker or the cook ordered her to do. She slept in the servants' quarters with the slaves and was treated the same.

As she neared her sixteenth year, Maria began to bloom into a lithe and beautiful young woman. More and more often she would find Mr. Becker watching her as she served at the dining room table. Mrs. Becker watched Mr. Becker with her lips pressed into a thin line. One afternoon, when Maria was alone in the kitchen doing a tub of laundry, Mr. Becker entered the room, and taking her by the wrists, pushed her against the wall and pressed his body against hers. He started to kiss her neck, enveloping her in his brandy breath.

She struggled and begged him to leave her alone. "Let go of me," she cried out. He tightened his grip and laughed.

He did not see Mrs. Becker enter the kitchen and stand with her fists on her hips. With a grim expression, she picked up a frying pan from where it hung on a hook by the stove, stepped across the room, and hit him on the head. He staggered back and fell to the floor. Maria ran from the room and hid in the woods outside of the plantation grounds until dark. Then she slipped into the servants' quarters.

The next day, without explanation, Mr. and Mrs. Becker took her to the auction square in Arlington where she was sold to a slave dealer by the name of Freeman. He bought deck passage for her and ten other individuals of differing skin colors and bought cabin passage for himself. He took them down the Ohio and then the Mississippi by steamboat to the New Orleans auction behind the St. Louis Cathedral. It was there that Lafayette Breaux bought her.

Her new owner possessed a large plantation in Caldwell County, Louisiana, with a thousand acres of cotton and tobacco and hills forested with hardwoods. The plantation was nearly self-sufficient. There were flocks of poultry and cattle and hogs—even a few sheep for wool. Slaves combed and carded the wool, ginned the cotton, and wove the fabric that made the clothing for nearly everyone except the master and his wife. Slaves washed laundry in the river and then boiled it in a massive kettle over an open fire. They made soap from the ashes of the hardwoods combined with fat from the hogs. There was a very large vegetable garden and orchards of pecan and peach trees bordered by grape vines that hung on the lengthy fences. There, Maria learned to do whatever was needed, learning from and working beside the black women.

The man who had bought her services allowed nothing to stand in his way. Breaux saw himself as a sophisticated dandy, and, usually leaving the operation of the plantation to his overseer, Lem Pounder, he spent as much time in New Orleans as he could. He wore polished boots and a red silk coat made in France that was fitted at the waist with a skirt that was cut full to his knees. The polished buttons glinted in the sun in a double row down the front. He oiled his hair and carried a sword cane. When he walked the boardwalks of New Orleans, the younger women eyed him from under their parasols and giggled behind their fans. As much as he enjoyed the attention of the young women in New Orleans, he watched Maria as she continued to mature throughout the next two years; he spent more and more time each night as he lay in the large bed by his wife thinking about the lithe young woman with her gray-green eyes and blonde hair.

His wife, Bertha Breaux, was a tall, spare woman with no chin and narrow, pinched lips that seldom smiled. Her father's fortune had been the motivation for Breaux's marriage proposal. She was aware of that fact, and it was reflected in the coldness of their marriage.

On her eighteenth birthday, Maria had asked her owner when he was going to give her the document of her freedom. He'd laughed. "You will never be free, Maria. You're a slave. I bought you from Theophilis Freeman as a metif slave. Since that will never change, I recommend that you make the best of it." A few days later, after his wife left for New Orleans to visit her mother, he had come to her where she slept in the slaves' quarters and, taking her wrist, had pulled her to his bed.

CHAPTER 2
The Boatman

A tall, broad-shouldered young man with sun-bleached hair poking out from under a battered hat had been watching the log in the middle of the river for some time from where he stood in the stern of the small keelboat. Everywhere his buckskin outfit did not touch was deeply suntanned, and his eyes were so blue they were almost indigo. Moving the large oar mounted over the sternpost, he guided the boat toward the log. As he drew nearer, he could see what looked like the head of a woman, her hair in her face, leaning against the log with her eyes shut. He called out, "Hey, are you all right? Can you hear me?" There was no response from the figure holding onto the log. "Can you hear me? Are you alive?" he called out again.

He poled the boat closer, carefully trying to avoid hitting the woman. As the boat bumped the log, it began to bob past. Locking the oar in place, he stepped to the side and reached for her. He caught her hair in his right hand and tried to pull her closer to the boat. Then he saw that her arm was tied to the log. He pulled a bowie knife from its sheath on his right thigh and, with one stroke, cut the apron sash. She immediately began to sink.

As the water closed over her head, Maria heard a man's voice very far away saying, "Steady, I've got you. I've got you." The voice was confident and reassuring, but she no longer cared who was speaking.

Slipping the knife back into the sheath, Hank took hold of her arm with his left hand and pulled her closer. Using his right arm, he lifted her limp body into the boat. As he laid her down on the deck, she coughed and spit up river water. She rolled onto her side and coughed again.

"Well, at least you're alive, and you sure don't weigh much," he said. He took off his wide brimmed hat, scratched his head, and ruffled his hair. "What to do with you now," he muttered to himself.

He looked around the boat, which was loaded with a large heap of boxes, bags, trunks, and furniture, all lashed together and tied to the deck with rope. He stepped around the pile of freight and pulled out his knife. With its hilt, he broke the lock on the largest trunk. Opening it, he found what he was looking for—a large quilt. He pulled it out and covered the unconscious young woman with it. She was still breathing. He sheathed the knife and returned to the large oar at the rear of the boat. Never having had a sister and having lost his mother as a boy, he was not sure what else to do for her. *That's about all I can to do get her warm.* He studied her delicate features as she lay in the sun with her eyes closed and wondered, *What threat drove such a pretty young woman into the water? What kind of fear made her face drowning to escape?*

With the oar in one hand and a long pole in the other, he pushed the boat away from the bank, where it had drifted into the quiet water under the overhanging oak trees. As he did so, a large snake of more than five feet in length dropped from the branches of one of the trees. Its tail hit his left boot. Hank instinctively stepped away from it, though he had had enough experience with snakes just like it that it did not frighten him. It was marked with yellow scales that outlined brown and black diamond shapes the length of its body. In one motion, he pulled his knife and swiftly separated the snake's head from its body. He flipped the head of the eastern diamondback into the river, and picking up the body with the back of the blade, said, "Well, that's the first time I ever saw one of you fellows in a tree. I'll have to be a bit more watchful when I tie up near the riverbank in the future." Examining it further, he added, "At least we'll have some fresh meat for supper."

He continued to guide the keelboat down the middle of the river with the large oar at the stern, while glancing around the great heap of baggage and furniture to watch the unconscious woman who lay in the bow of the boat. He shook his head and said aloud, "Stray dogs have always liked me. Now I'm pulling stray women out of the river."

***

The April sun warmed Maria's face and body as she lay under the quilt. The flickering of the sun's rays as the boat moved through the light and shadows of the trees on the water gradually increased her awareness of her surroundings and enticed her to open her eyes.

As she did so, the young man said loudly from his position at the stern of the boat, "So, you're awake. That's good. I feared you might die on me."

She began to cough again and then sat up and looked around, thoroughly confused. Without thinking, she said, "*Danke*." After studying her situation, she looked up at him and said, "*Wie heissen Sie?*"

Reaching back into his memory, he brought up the German language he had not used in many years and answered, "My name is Hank Schroeder. What's yours?" She remained quiet so he added, "*Sprechen sie* English?"

She stared at him, startled, and said, "Of course I speak English. My name is Maria Schumann."

"Well, Maria Schumann, can you tell me how you ended up in the Ouachita River?" He pronounced the name of the river as *Washtaw*, as the locals did. She was silent so long that he began to wonder again if she really spoke English. He repeated his question and added, "How came you to be floating down the river tied to a log?"

Maria was too exhausted and weakened by her chilling experience in the river to attempt to fabricate a story. "I ran away." She swallowed and continued, "I ran away from the master who would not give me my freedom when I reached my eighteenth birthday. I am a redemptioner, but he was keeping me as a slave." She was quiet for a minute and then added, "Will you put me out for the reward he might offer?"

Hank smiled. After locking the oar in position, he stepped forward and offered his hand to help her stand up in the moving vessel. As she stood, he could not help but notice her graceful movements through the wet, clinging dress. "As I came to this country as a German redemptioner, like you, I don't think I'll be seeking that reward."

"I thank you," she said gratefully. Looking around at the riverbanks sliding by and the pile of mixed freight tied to the boat, she asked, "Where are you going? Are you working for your master?"

"Yes, I'm working for my master, and as I have been a free man for the last four years, I am my master. I'm taking this load of furniture and property to New Orleans for a rich man. When I get there and deliver these things to him, I will sell my keelboat for the wood in it, and make my way back upriver to the Bluff in Arkansas or some other place, as it suits me, and build another boat. That's how I make my living." He paused and looked at her ragged, wet dress. "I think it best that we get you covered in a dress that's not wet, torn, and stickin' to you."

Suddenly self-conscious, Maria picked up the quilt and put it around her shoulders for both modesty and warmth. "Where will we find another dress?"

"There's maybe one or two in the trunk where I got the quilt. I doubt the owner will resent the loan of one." He returned to the open trunk and lifted out a blue, flowered cotton dress with a full skirt. "I think if it fits, it will be only a small sin. This is the fourth load of property I have taken down the river for these folks. The first three loads had the things that were important to them. This load will probably be put in an attic. Mrs. Freeman, who is a large woman now, couldn't wear this dress even if she wanted to. She has so many dresses that she'll never even miss it." He handed it to her. "If she does, I will pay for it."

Looking at the dress, Maria said quietly, "I once knew a man by the name of Freeman. He lived in New Orleans. Do you suppose the man you are working for could be the same man?"

"I doubt it, as this man and his wife only relocated to New Orleans about two months ago."

She carefully made her way around the pile of furniture, bags, and trunks tied in the middle of the boat and returned to the bow where she stooped down so she was hidden from the boatman's view. She pulled off her ragged dress and slipped the blue dress over her head. When she stood up and returned to the stern of the boat where Hank held the oar, she smiled timidly. "Thank you," she said quietly.

Though Hank was very much aware of her youthful, slender beauty, he cleared his throat and said with a gruffness meant to cover his admiration, "Now you're presentable enough to take into town. The sleeves on that dress almost cover the bruises on your arms." Maria looked down self-consciously, crossed her arms, and tried to hide them with her hands. He added, "Can you do something with your hair?"

Maria was taken back by his sudden change of tone and tried to comb her wet, long hair out of her face with her fingers. "What town? I fear that Mr. Breaux will soon have handbills posted with a reward for me."

"We will just pull over to the bank and tie up tonight, but by tomorrow or the day after, I'll need to stop for supplies. If you think someone will be looking for you, you can stay with the boat. If anyone sees you, just tell them you're my wife." At that, Maria smiled shyly, and her face grew rosy with color.

That night, after the boat was tied to a large oak tree that hung over the water, Hank poked a stick up into the branches and made a loud noise beating them.

"What are you doing?" Maria asked curiously.

"Just making sure we don't have any belly walkers dropping out of this tree while we sleep. We're going to eat the last one that did, but if we were sleeping, one might want to turn the table on us." After settling in, he mixed up some batter for corn dodgers and cooked the snake meat over a fire.

As he offered her another piece of the roasted meat on the end of his knife, Hank asked, "How do you like it? Some people say it tastes like chicken."

She took her second piece and said, "It does *not* taste like any chicken I've ever eaten. I think it tastes like snake."

Hank threw his head back and laughed heartily. It was a sound Maria liked. As the evening darkened, they huddled a little closer to the fire but continued to talk. Hank shared his memories of childhood and his voyage from Amsterdam to America.

"My parents lived in Württemburg at the time of their marriage, but times were hard. Napoleon was conquering one country after another, and his armies were like locusts, eating everything the farmers could produce—cattle, grain, fruit, *everything*—as they moved across the continent. After he was defeated at Waterloo, there was a new hope that the farmers would finally be able to feed their families, but instead of getting better, everything got worse. Many of the people in the Old Countries nearly starved through the years without a summer."

"I remember my father telling me of that time."

Hank continued, "My father told me that in 1816, the summers grew cold for three years. The people believed it was the wrath of God, but in the years since, others have spoken of a great volcano on the other side of the world that had erupted and filled the air with so much dust that the sun couldn't warm the soil. The seeds rotted in the ground, and they were lucky to find enough acorns, berries, and roots to survive. They moved to my uncle's farm on the Rhine, near Düsseldorf, where I was born. After more hungry years, Papa was stricken with *auswanderungsfiebr,* immigration fever. Like so many others, he was determined to emigrate to America. He, Mama, my brother Karl, and I walked to Amsterdam to purchase passage to America. We were beaten and our money stolen on the way by highwaymen, so we were forced to sail as indentured servants to pay the cost of the voyage. Papa had promised us that we would be sold as a family—he said he would insist on that."

Hank grew silent for a moment, his lips pressed together in a tight, narrow line. He swallowed hard as he struggled to control the emotions that overtook him as his mind reeled with the painful memories. Though he had been only a young boy at the time, he remembered much of the voyage—the storms, the foul water and wormy bread, the death of his mother and her burial at sea.

"I will always remember the auction in Philadelphia where we were sold. My father's resolution to keep the family together was impossible to keep. After he had been sold, my father looked back at both Karl and me as though he knew it might be the last time he would see either of us. Then he climbed into the wagon of the man who had bought his services." Hank took a deep breath before he continued. "Karl was sold to a German named Schultz. After the final bid, he turned and put his arms around me and whispered, '*Mein Bruder, Geh' mit Gott—Auf Wiedersehen.*' Then, before he had even finished telling me to go with God, his new master took his arm, pulled him off the auction block, and pushed him toward a wagon. All Schultz said was, '*Komm mit mir*—Come with me.'

"Karl waved as he climbed into the wagon, and it started down the road. I don't know where either of them was taken. I was only ten and very frightened." He paused and took another deep breath to get past the pain of the memories. "I was sold to a man named O'Neal. My name is Hans, but my master called me Hank, and that's been my name ever since. My contract freed me when I turned twenty."

Maria was following his story closely, her eyes fixed on his face as he stared into the river. He continued, "Mr. and Mrs. O'Neal had bought a small farm in Mississippi, so we traveled by riverboat down the Ohio and the Mississippi Rivers. We finally arrived at Memphis and went overland to a small tobacco farm in Monroe County, Mississippi. The work was hard, but I was treated fairly, and when I turned twenty, Mr. O'Neal honored my contract and gave me my freedom and my freedom pay.

"In the years that Mr. O'Neal owned his tobacco farm, it never paid for itself. While he was my master, we took the tobacco down the Tombigbee River by flatboat to Mobile, but by the time we sold the flatboat for wood and paid for our passage back up the river by steamboat, he hardly had enough to get through the next growing season. One year, to save money, he decided we would go all the way to New Orleans where he could get more money for the crop and come home by foot up the Natchez Trace, but we were jumped by the John Murrel gang, and they took everything we had, even our shoes. That helped us understand how the Trace got its name—the devil's backbone. It seemed that Mr. O'Neal was never meant to be successful." He looked unseeingly out into the growing darkness.

After he was quiet for a minute or two, Maria asked, "What did he do then?"

Hank looked up at her as if, for a moment, he had forgotten her presence. Then he continued, "He sold the plantation and bought another one further west, near Natchez. He thought that it would pay for itself eventually because getting the tobacco downriver to New Orleans would be easier and faster on the Mississippi, and, at the time, it brought a better price there. But he never really got ahead. About the time I turned eighteen I went with him to buy a man at the auction that's held three times a week in the St. Louis Hotel in New Orleans." Hank pronounced the name of the city much like the residents—*Nawlins*.

"It made me remember how he bought me in Philadelphia. I could tell that every one of those men, women, and children were as scared as I was back then, and most of them would not be as lucky as I had been." He paused for a few seconds and changed position on the log where he sat.

"The black man's name was Cassius, but he must have been sick when O'Neal bought him because he died that first year. For the next two years, we made the float down the river, sold the tobacco, and came home on a steamboat. After I turned twenty and he had given me my freedom, I worked for him for another year. He could hardly afford to pay my wages, so after that, I moved to Natchez and became a boatman. I learned to build my own boats, and after taking three loads of tobacco to New Orleans for him and his neighbor, I decided that I could probably make a better living on the Ouachita."

"Did you ever look for your father or your brother?" Maria asked as she watched him stare into the fire.

Hank nodded. "I tried but had no luck. For the first few years of my servitude, I prayed every night that somehow God would help me find them, but as the time passed, I decided that it was not part of God's plan. They were to be freed several years before I was. Who knows where they are now—maybe dead of cholera or yellow fever." They sat in silence and watched the fire burn down. Finally, Hank asked, "What are you thinking?"

"That I am in unknown waters. Mrs. Wentz once had me memorize a poem that said, 'No man is an island, no man stands alone,' but I feel like a very lonely island right now. I'm frightened," she said quietly.

"I can tell. Your feelings show on your face like sunshine or rain through a window." They sat quietly for a few more minutes, and then Hank asked, "What is that gold thing around your neck? Is it a locket?"

Her hand went to cover the locket as if to protect it where it was exposed against the outside of the dress. She looked down at it and said, "It was my mother's. It is all that I have to remember her, except a few memories." Then she tucked it back inside the neck of the dress.

"It looks like the chain has a knot in it. Do you want me to untangle it for you?"

She answered quickly, "No, no. The chain was broken, and I had to tie the knot in it to keep it around my neck."

After the fire was reduced to embers, she returned to the boat and wrapped up in the quilt. She lay down on the hard deck and watched the boatman through half-closed eyes as he sat by the fire. Up to that time, she had felt unthreatened, but now she wondered if he might try to force himself on her while she slept. It was evident that he was a strong man, his muscles firm and well defined under his buckskin shirt. But after another hour, Hank poured water on the last of the coals and stepped onto the deck, stretching out near the stern, unaware of her nervousness. Maria finally closed her eyes. The rocking of the water brought dreams to her sleep—memories of a long and lonely voyage after her parents were buried at sea.

In the morning, as Hank hung a pot of water to boil grits over the fire on the bank of the river, Maria said, "You said you make your boats. Did you make this one?"

"Yes, it's just a small keelboat, not much more than a flatboat. I designed it myself after making the trip downriver in a flatboat with a couple of hired hands. After they tried to steal everything I had, including the boat, I decided to build my own boat and make it small enough that I could handle it without help. That's why it's less than half as long and not as wide as most keelboats." He laughed and added, "The design isn't perfect yet, and I've been known to get myself into some trouble on the river now and then. But I'll break it up and sell the wood when I get to New Orleans, so I'll have a chance to try again on another one for my next trip down the river."

"Do you always break up the boat and sell it?"

"They're building walkways in Lafayette and in the Second Municipality to keep the ladies and their fancy dresses above the mud, so I usually get a fair price for the wood. If I can get my money's worth, I always sell the pieces."

As the boat moved with the current, Maria could feel the promise of spring against her skin in the soft air. Her hope in the future began to grow within her in some indefinable way as the breeze warmed her skin. She watched the hillsides that rose above the river slide by with their uncut forests that were so thick the sunlight only sprinkled the ground, hiding the plentiful bear and small deer that lived there.

Hank was content to watch Maria as she sat in the sun, occasionally closing her eyes. He wanted to talk, to get to know her, but his previous lack of association with girls or women seemed to tie his tongue. But, he decided, since their association was likely to be brief, the silence between them was fine as far as he was concerned. *Too much talking with a woman might give her the idea that there was a future relationship in store,* he mused. *A boatman should keep his mind on the river and forget about women.* He made an effort to turn his attention back to the river when he felt he had watched her too long.

Maria studied Hank's movements when he was busy handling the boat. As he worked to control the keel in the strong current, she thought, *He saved my life. Was it luck or did God send him? Perhaps I'll never know, but I am grateful. He is such a quiet man. I guess I'll never get the chance to know him very well. He lives on the river and seems to have no roots.* Her thoughts turned to her future. *Where will I go? What will I do?* A fear almost as deep as what she had felt as she ran from Breaux returned to chill her. She was cheered by the thought: *Hank knows New Orleans. Maybe he will help me.* It helped chase away her fear.

The next day was quiet, both of them involved with their own thoughts. In the late afternoon, Hank tied up at a pier that extended into the river and said, "This is Riverton. I won't be long. You stay here with the boat."

While she waited, Maria vacillated between pacing and sitting in the stern. She tried to sit low enough that it would be hard to see her from the riverbank. After two hours, she felt the boat shift as someone stepped onto it. It was nearly dark now, and she couldn't see the figure clearly. He was just a dark figure against the lighter gray of the dusk. She stood and nervously called out, "Hank, is that you?" The man didn't answer, so she asked again, "Hank, is that you?"

The man looked up at her from under his battered hat brim, clearly startled. He was unshaven, his clothing was filthy, and the smell of whisky reached her as she said, "If you have come to see Mr. Schroeder, you will have to wait. He will be here shortly."

"Well, sweetie, I really didn't 'spect to find anyone here, but since you are, I guess I come to see you." He leered at her and grinned, exposing tobacco stained teeth. As he moved toward where she stood in the stern, she backed away from him, moving around the far side of the pile of bags and furniture.

Panicked, she whispered under her breath, "Hank, where are you?" She called out to the man in a shaky voice, "Get away from me. Get off the boat." She looked around, hoping to see Hank's familiar figure. "I told you that Hank . . . my husband," she added, "will be back in a few minutes." When she had circled the pile and was near the pier, she jumped out and started to run, but the bearded man leaped after her and grabbed her by the wrist, pulling her back into the boat. He shoved her down hard, and while he held her down with his knee, he started to untie the rope Hank had used to tie the boat to the pier. She screamed and struggled to push him off, so he paused for a moment and looked closely at her, and then he laughed. "Well, ain't you a pretty thing with lots of yeller hair, jes' like that metif slave in that handbill somebody gave me in town. I'll bet you're her, that runaway slave they're lookin' for. You got green eyes, girl?"

"No, no, my eyes are blue." Her panic almost choked off her voice as she lied. In the darkness she hoped he couldn't see the color of her eyes. She continued to fight him, and when she couldn't push his knee off her chest, she started to pound on his thigh with her fists. "Get off me. Leave me alone." She tried to scream but couldn't get her breath as he leaned harder on her.

"I think I got me a runaway slave. Yep, you sure 'nough fit the description. You're gonna make me rich. I'm gonna take you in." He laughed as he labored with the knot.

Hank suddenly appeared on the path and dropped the bags of supplies he was carrying as he ran at the man, hitting him with his full body weight behind his shoulder and knocking him off Maria. As the ruffian tried to rise, Hank jumped astride his back.

"Maria, are you all right?" Hank called out.

"Yes. Yes, I'm all right," she answered breathlessly as she rolled away from the struggling men.

Both men crumpled to the bottom of the boat. They rolled and kicked in the limited space, making the boat rock and the water churn. After a few minutes, Hank came up on top, pulled his bowie knife from its sheath, and put it to the man's throat. Panting with exertion he said, "Tell me why I shouldn't kill you for trying to steal the boat, the freight—and the woman."

Ceasing to struggle, the man said, "'Cause I can tell you how to get five hundred dollars for her."

Hank pulled the man to his feet and pushed him toward the pier. "Get yourself off my boat and away from us, or I may give in to the temptation to use the knife." The man climbed onto the pier and began to run with a shuffling step, yelling over his shoulder as he went, "You won't get far with that runaway, and I'm gonna tell them where she is and get the money for her."

Without saying a word, Hank stepped out of the boat, retrieved the supplies he had dropped, and set the bags in the bow. He quickly finished untying the knot that had stymied the drunken man and pushed the boat out into the current.

"Thank God you came back when you did," Maria said, trying to control the tears of relief that were threatening to overflow. "How did that man know I was a runaway?"

After the boat began to move with the current, he held the tiller in his right hand. "Someone has been down the river ahead of us. They must have floated all night while we were sleeping." Reaching into his pocket, he pulled out a paper. In the moonlight she could see that it was a handbill. She held it close to her face and read:

Runaway: a metif slave named Maria. She is as white as any white woman, with straight light hair and green eyes, and can pass herself for a white woman. She is very intelligent; can read and write,

and speaks fluent German, having been owned by a German couple in Virginia. She was last seen wearing a yellow cotton dress. She is of great value to me, and I will give five hundred dollars for her return.
—*Lafayette Breaux, Caldwell County, Louisiana*

Maria's face took on a look of dismay as she read the notice. "Are you sure you do not want the reward? It would make you rich," she asked, biting her lip to keep it from quivering.

Hank quietly shook his head and replied, "I don't believe money gained by taking another person's freedom can bring satisfaction." Then he turned and looked at her and said, "Where is it that you were going when I pulled you from the river?"

"Anywhere away from Lafayette Breaux's plantation. Now I think I must go anywhere you will take me."

CHAPTER 3
The River

After a few quiet minutes, Hank said, "I'm going another six or seven days down the river to New Orleans. When we get there, I think we can try one or two places to find a home for you. One is the Urseline Convent. They often take in homeless girls and women. The other is a girls' school in Chartres Street run by old Madame Borgnette and her daughter. I know of it because they often use German redemptioners as maids and cooks. Perhaps you can find a position there."

In her panic, Maria had never thought about a destination, only escape. Now she had to face the reality that she might find it difficult to find a haven at the end of her flight. She suddenly felt as frightened as she did that day when, as a small child, she had been put on the auction block in Baltimore.

"I hope and pray you're right," she whispered.

After another hour on the river, Hank poled the boat over to a stand of trees that leaned out over the water, and while he tied the bowline to the nearest tree, Maria lay wrapped in the quilt, watching him through half-closed eyes as he made the boat ready for the night. She quietly smiled to herself. *I think he is a trustworthy man. Maybe God did send him to save me.*

The following day, Hank showed her how to steer using the large oar in the middle of the stern so she could steady it when he had to use the pole to push off from the occasional sand bars in the wider, slower parts of the river. When she gave the oar over to him, she wiped the perspiration that the effort had raised from her forehead and said, "Being a boatman is very hard work. Do you expect to do this kind of work all your life?"

As he pointed the boat into the swiftest part of the current, he answered, "Honorable work is usually hard, whether it's being a farmer or a blacksmith or a sailor. The Lord gave us work to make us strong. He told Adam that by the sweat of his brow he would eat his bread all the days of his life."

Maria's feelings of the night before were confirmed. As she sat quietly, she thought, *He is a man who knows the scriptures, who is willing to work hard all the days of his life. A man who would pull a stranger from a river. He is a good man.*

As the days passed, their self-consciousness melted away, and they began to talk more, opening up to one another and sharing their thoughts and experiences. Maria talked about her years with her first owners. "Mr. and Mrs. Wentz were wealthy when they came from Hamburg. They brought many books with them, and she taught me to read to her from the writings of Johann Goethe, sometimes in the German. Then she helped me translate what I had read into English. I read the poetry of John Milton, William Wordsworth, and John Donne." She paused for a few seconds and then asked, "Do you believe that 'God is our home,' as Wordsworth wrote?"

Hank was quiet for a full minute before he shook his head a little and answered, "I don't really know the answer to such a question. I don't have an education equal to that of my father, but my parents taught me that God's greatest creation is an honest man. My father often quoted the philosophy that guided his life. 'Noble be man, helpful and good! For that alone sets him apart from every other creature on earth.'"

Maria laughed and clapped her hands together in pleasure, "Perhaps you have a better education than you know. Your father also knew the works of Goethe! I once translated those words for Mrs. Wentz."

Hank laughed, responding to the lilting sound of her laugh. As he looked at her, he felt his breath come short, and he was suddenly aware of her presence in a manner he had not been aware of previously. *She's a remarkable young woman, beautiful and well-spoken. Any man would look at her twice—or more, even a man as rough as a cob, like me. But I'm not even a marrying kind of man, so why am I watching her?* Giving his head a shake, he focused on the water ahead of the boat and tried to push speculation about Maria from his mind.

As the days passed, the Ouachita turned into the Black River, and the Black joined the Red River, and on the fourth day, the keelboat was finally spit out into the muddy Mississippi. There, the steamboats moving up and down the broad, twisting river left wakes that tossed the boat about like a piece of flotsam. The Mississippi was deep and swift in places and required Hank to give it his full attention to avoid the logs and other floating detritus upon which they might become entangled.

As the next days passed, much of the time Maria sat with her knees drawn up under her skirt, enjoying the sun on her face. Hank noticed how her long, golden hair glistened in the sunlight. He studied her long-fingered, delicate hands. Even her feet were small and, he took note, obviously needed shoes. He admitted to himself that he had never seen gray-green eyes like hers. They enticed him into their depths like a cool pond on a hot day. He fully understood now why Lafayette Breaux was willing to pay such a large amount to get her back.

The bruises on her arms and on her jaw were beginning to turn pale green. They did not go unnoticed, but he assumed that she had received them while drifting in the river. After a quiet morning, she asked, "How many times have you been to New Orleans?"

Embarrassed that she may have noticed him looking at her, he looked down for a moment, trying to regain his composure. Then he answered, "I think about eight or nine times, maybe more."

"Do you like this kind of life?"

"It's fine for a man without a family. If I settle down someday, I guess I'll have to become a farmer and grow cotton, sugar cane, or tobacco. But I don't really want to do that."

"Why?"

He answered thoughtfully, "Because to be successful, I would have to own slaves. Being a redemptioner taught me something about being owned by someone else, even though my master was a good man."

Maria grew quiet again. As the boat slipped southward with the river current, they could occasionally see a plantation of cotton fields stretching from either riverbank where, for a few minutes, they could watch a white overseer on a horse supervising the black men, women, and children who were working in the fields. Maria whispered with a voice filled with anger, "I think God must hate slavery."

Hank responded with equal intensity, "I'm sure He hates it." Then he added, "And this nation will have to pay a terrible price someday for permitting it to continue."

The villages and towns slid by. They stopped briefly next to a few tied-up steamboats at a settlement called Bayou Sara for water. Every evening they tied up in a quiet place on the river to sleep, nowhere near a town. When they passed Baton Rouge without stopping, Maria asked, "Are you afraid for me to be seen in a town as big as that one?"

Hank nodded and said, "We don't know how far down the river Breaux has sent those handbills or if he put a reward in the newspapers. It will be easier to hide you in New Orleans, in the German community there."

In the early afternoon of the eighth day of the journey, they could see a dark smudge across the sky to the southeast. Hank pointed to it and said, "That's the sky above New Orleans. You can see how the smoke from the coal stoves and the funnels of the steamboats blackens the sky."

"What is the city like? When I was taken there to be sold, I was so frightened that I don't remember much about it."

With wonder in his voice and a shake of his head, he said, "It's the most unexpected and unexplainable place in all of this country. Of every four souls there, one is white, another is Creole or Cajun, the third is an African slave, and the fourth—it's often impossible to tell."

"What do you mean, some are impossible to tell?"

"There are skins of every color in New Orleans, and many of them are white or nearly as white as you and I, but because they were born of a slave mother with some African blood, they are as much a slave as those with the blackest skin. That was why Breaux was able to tell people that you were a slave, and they believed him."

"I heard him tell people that I was a metif, but I didn't really understand what he meant."

Hank explained, "In New Orleans there are mulatto slaves, who are half African; quadroons, from a white father and a mulatto mother; metif slaves, from a white father and quadroon mother; meamelouc, who are one sixteenth; and sang-melee, who are one-thirty-second African. As long as they are born of a mother with African blood who was a slave at the time of their birth, they are born to slavery, as well. If they are born of a free woman, no matter how much African blood flows in her veins or how black their skin, they are free."

He continued in a thoughtful manner as if he were trying to explain the culture of the city to himself, "In New Orleans, cotton is king. On the waterfront, the bales of cotton are three deep and sometimes stretch down the levee for a mile while they are being loaded on steamboats and ships to be taken up the river to St. Louis or up the Ohio or to Europe, Britain, France—everywhere and anywhere. Anything a man could want, good or bad, can be found in New Orleans." He paused, and then added, "New Orleans is big, the biggest city in this part of the country, maybe half a million people. Some people call it Crescent City, but others, who know it better, call it Sin City."

When he grew quiet, Maria asked, "Is it safe there? Is everyone rich there?"

"There are rich Frenchmen and Creoles who live on the Vieux Carrè and rich Americans in the Second Municipality, which is on the north side, but there is great poverty in other areas, such as Faubourg Tremè where the free Africans live. The worst place is Girod Street on the waterfront at night, or the area they call the Swamp on the south side of the city.

"It's a city of contradictions—a place where Catholic cathedrals point their steeples toward the sky, but the streets below are often full of prostitutes and women who practice voodoo in the back alleys. There are places of learning—schools and libraries—but most of the people live in ignorance and superstition."

Giving Maria a side-glance as a warning, he continued, "No man goes about in New Orleans without a weapon. Every man carries a broad sword or a rapier, a cane sword, a knife, or a pistol. That is why I carry this." He pulled the knife with the ten-inch blade from its sheath on his right thigh and turned the blade to catch the sunlight as he examined it. "I made the mistake of going alone into New Orleans without a weapon after I was freed, and the money I'd been paid for the load of tobacco I'd brought down the river was stolen by two ruffians. Since then, I've learned to handle a bowie knife just about as good as a Kaintuck, and they're some of the best fighters on the river."

"Where did you get such a fearsome knife?" Maria asked, unconsciously pushing herself a few inches away from him.

"A smithy by the name of Jim Black made it for me in Washington, Arkansas, just a few miles from Bluff. He earns his living making knives like this."

"Have you ever killed a man?' she asked, her eyes filled with fearful curiosity.

"On my last trip to New Orleans, a man attacked me. I fought back and wounded him, but I guess I'll never know if he died. I didn't wait around to find out." Maria looked at him with increased nervousness.

CHAPTER 4
New Orleans

Maria was shocked by the sights and sounds of New Orleans. As Hank guided the keelboat to the pier, she studied the jumble of warehouses and piers, and the steamboats that were coming, going, or tied at the levee while being loaded or unloaded. Wagons, carts, and teams of horses on the cobblestone streets created more noise than she had ever heard. On the great wharves were kegs of nails from New England, shoes from Massachusetts, coffee beans from Cuba, crockery from England, tea chests from China, boxes of bottled wine from France, and bags of sugar from Cuba, in addition to the great bales of cotton and stacks of dried tobacco, all being loaded or unloaded on the levee. The seething tumult of streets frightened but also fascinated her. The different corners of the world seemed to converge in this city: French, Creole, Cajun, Indian, German, Irish, Haitian, English, frontiersmen, riverboat gamblers, nuns, and priests.

Hank tied up at a pier where other smaller vessels were docked: flatboats, keelboats, even a few large canoes called *piroques*. He walked the levee until he found a small black, barefoot boy of about ten who was willing to run an errand for a coin or two.

"What do they call you, boy?"

"They call me Wash, but my name's George Washington Whitesides."

"Wash, I want you to take this note to Mr. Demosthenes Freeman who lives with his brother, Theophilis Freeman, in a big house across from the St. Louis Hotel on the Vieux Carrè. Do you know where that is?"

The lad nodded but suddenly looked very frightened. He began to back away from Hank, so Hank took hold of his thin arm above the elbow and, holding him, asked, "Why are you so scared? Don't you want to earn some coins? If you run this errand for me, I'll give you a picayune or two."

The boy grew more frightened and looked down at Hank's hand where he held him. "Yes, sir, I'm scared. Mr. Theophilis Freeman be the biggest slave trader in this city. Maybe he will take and sell me."

Hank looked at Maria and then back at the boy. "If he wants to sell you, you tell him that you already have a master."

"But I don't have a master. My ma be given her freedom 'afore I was born. Maybe he take me and sell me anyway."

"If he wants to sell you, you tell him that your master is Hank Schroeder—that's me—and that you have to hurry back to me."

"But you ain't my master."

"Until you finish the errand I have just given you, I am. Do you understand me?"

The boy grinned slowly and nodded. "Yes, sir. I understand."

"Then hurry. And when you get the note delivered, wait for him to send a note back to me. When you get back, I'll pay you." Hank let go of the boy, and the boy nodded vigorously and ran down the street into the French Quarter of the city.

As the boy disappeared among the carts, wagons, and carriages, Maria said, "Hank, Theophilis Freeman will know me by sight. He will want to take me back to Mr. Breaux."

"He isn't likely to even see you. We have about two hours before the boy will be back. We must wait with the boat to make sure nothing is stolen. After I have been paid and he has his property, we'll go to the Urseline Convent and see if you can find a home there."

Maria nodded but moved to the stern of the boat with her back to the town to avoid inquisitive eyes. There she watched the other boats on the river until the boy returned. Nearly two hours later, a panting Wash returned with a note, which he proudly gave to Hank. As he did so, he said, "That man ask me who my master was and, like you told me, I said, 'Hank Schroeder be my master.' He didn't look very happy." Wash grinned up at Hank, his white teeth showing against his sweaty, ebony skin.

Hank patted him on the shoulder and read the note:

Mr. Schroeder, I will send my brother's man, Thomas, within the hour with a wagon to collect my possessions. If you choose to, you may ride back with him and collect your pay at that time. —Demosthenes Freeman

"Thanks, Wash." Hank dropped two coins into the small, outstretched hand. The boy bobbed his head and said, "I always be here at the pier, Mister Schroeder. I be glad to help you anytime."

"Do you have a brother or a friend I could hire to watch my boat while I go to get my money?"

"I could do that, Mister Schroeder," the boy said earnestly.

"Wash, I need a bigger boy or even a man to see that my boat doesn't get stolen."

"I'll find somebody." He darted away, with the precious coins clutched in his hand. He was back within ten minutes with a taller, older boy. "This here be my friend, Jim. Is he big enough to watch the boat?"

Hank smiled and said, "Between the two of you, my boat should be safe. I'll pay you both when I get back in two or three hours."

Maria stepped up to Hank and said quietly, "What should I do, Hank? I'm afraid to go with you and afraid to stay here without you."

"You can ride with me in the wagon. Mr. Freeman won't even see you, as he'll just send my pay out with one of the servants. That's what he did before. After I get my pay, we'll ride the omnibus to the convent and see if they will take you in."

Maria said nothing but nodded hesitantly. She hoped that the Urseline sisters would take her in, but at the same time, she feared they might. She did not want to see Hank walk out of her life. Even though he frightened her at times, or perhaps because of it, with him, she felt safe.

Thomas arrived with the wagon and introduced himself. "I'm Thomas, Mr. Freeman's man." He was a tall, well-spoken black man in red livery. Without any further comment, he followed

Hank's pointing finger and began the process of transferring the bags, boxes, and furniture from the boat to the wagon. When he had filled the wagon bed, he asked, "Is the lady going with us back to Mr. Freeman's house?"

When Hank nodded, Thomas took a large carpetbag off the seat of the rocking chair he had taken from the boat and offered the chair to Maria. Hank helped her climb into the back of the wagon, where she sat in the chair and smiled nervously.

As the team of horses pulled the wagon through the waterfront streets lined with shanties and hovels, Maria noticed the rough-looking men sitting lazily in front of the cabarets, which were little more than a few chairs and tables in a small, shabby room open to the street, where they drank from battered coffee cups or whisky bottles. Some of the women on the street hurried to the wagon, offering to sell sweet biscuits or rolls. Thomas raised his hand as a signal that they were not welcome, and they backed away. Painted women approached the wagon as if to speak to Hank. Maria recognized by their dress and manners that they were selling more than biscuits. Hank paid them no heed. By the time they had reached the mansion of Theophilis Freeman, Maria was feeling a complicated mix of equal parts wonder and contempt for the city.

Hank was proven right when another large black man came out of the front door of the mansion and handed him his pay of thirty dollars for bringing the possessions of his master's brother down the river. Hank assisted Maria down from the wagon and nodded in the direction he wanted to walk. As they walked, Maria noted that the ladies all wore skirts held wide by crinolines. Only servants or slaves wore dresses that fell straightly to the ground as the one she was wearing did. After they had walked a few blocks, Hank paused and looked at her bare feet, and then turned in a different direction. They walked past several small shops before he found what he wanted—a boot maker's shop.

He ushered her in without saying anything but said to the man behind the counter who was nailing the heel onto a man's boot, "Do you have any shoes for ladies?"

The man put his spectacles up on his forehead and looked at Maria's bare feet. She wanted to hide her embarrassment at being barefooted, but the man said in a matter-of-fact manner, "I think

I might have something to fit the lady." Looking at Maria, he asked, "How much heel do you want, ma'am?"

Maria was not sure what he meant, so Hank quickly said, to cover her hesitancy, "Something not too high, I think."

The man rose from his work counter and entered the back room. He reemerged with three pairs of ladies' black-leather, high-topped shoes. He pulled up a keg and said, "If the lady will be seated, I will help her try these on."

Maria had never had another individual wait on her, aside from the small courtesies Hank had shown her. Burning warmth crept up into her face, but she raised her foot, and the boot maker took it in hand. She struggled to fit her foot into the first shoe, which was too small, but the second pair, made of soft calfskin, fit nicely. The boot maker laced them and stood up. "I hope your lady . . ." There he paused and raised an eyebrow as he looked at Hank. "I hope the lady likes the shoes."

Hank answered firmly, "I am sure my sister will enjoy the shoes very much. Thank you for your service. What do I owe you?" Hank paid the man the three dollars he requested, took Maria's arm, and led her from the shop.

They walked two blocks down the street before Maria asked, "Why did the boot maker look at you so strangely and hesitate when he called me a lady?"

"He thought you might be my mistress, my *placeé* as they are called around here."

"Oh!" Maria's face turned a deep red. After a few minutes, she asked, "Why would he think that?"

"Because many men in New Orleans have entered into what is called a 'left-handed marriage' with an attractive quadroon or metif woman. It's an accepted custom among the Creoles and Frenchmen. Some of the Americans indulge in it, as well."

"Do I look like that kind of woman?"

"There is no way to identify a woman of that kind. The only requirement is that she be very beautiful and know how to act in a refined manner. Perhaps it was an unusual compliment on his part to assume that you were one of those women."

"I am not complimented," Maria said quietly but firmly. Then she added, "But I thank you for defending me by calling me your sister."

Hank smiled at her concern and wondered why it mattered to her what the boot maker thought. The two of them waited at a corner, and in a few minutes the horse-drawn omnibus lumbered down the road. They boarded by simply stepping up and taking a seat. The half-full vehicle was little more than a long wagon without sides. It had a fabric cover to help block out the sun and benches back to back that ran its length. The horses pulled it down Bourbon Street and onto Esplanade Avenue. After almost an hour of a very jolting ride, Maria recognized the convent, which was surrounded on three sides by a high wall, as if to protect it from the filth and clutter of the city around it.

Hank stepped off as the omnibus slowed and took Maria's hand, helping her step down. They walked toward the large double doors of the two-story, square building. Maria swallowed hard as Hank lifted the round, heavy iron door knocker. When he brought it down against the door, the sound echoed through the building. After a few minutes, a tall, thin nun in a black and white habit opened the door only about six inches, as if to keep the world out, and asked, "How may we serve you?"

Hank took off his hat and held it in both hands. "This young lady is in great need of a place to stay. She is a good Christian woman but has no place to live in this sinful city. Can you take her in?"

The sister shook her head. "We have more young girls and women than we can care for properly at the present." Looking at Maria she said, "If you are Catholic and desire to take vows, we might be able to find a place for you in a few months."

Maria dropped her head and said quietly, "I am not Catholic, Sister."

"Then we can be of no service to you, child. May God bless you in your search," she said as she closed the door.

Maria was surprised by her sudden feelings of relief. She looked up at Hank's face and whispered, "Now where shall I go?"

Looking at her new shoes, he asked, "Do your feet hurt?"

"No."

"Then we will walk to the Vieux Carré to see if old Madame Borgnette can use you at her girls' school." As they walked, Maria began to ask questions about many of the people and things she saw. Hank seemed to know so many things.

As they passed a small cabaret, the man standing in front handed Hank a handbill. Having seen her name on one some days earlier, she asked to see it. She quickly handed it back to him. It read:

Come and see three hounds kill a full grown bear. Best cock fighting in the South nightly. All bets welcome. Only four bits or 50 cents per gentleman. Ladies half price. River end of Girod Street every night at 8:00 PM.

"This is considered entertainment by some people, Maria. Others prefer the American Theater on Camp Street, where they can see one of the plays offered to the population of the city. As I told you, a man can get anything he wants in this city." He added with grim emphasis, "Anything."

As they walked, Maria's head drooped like a wilted rose as she avoided the eyes of those they passed. Hank stopped, turned her to face him, and put his finger under her chin. "Look at me, Maria." She looked into his face. She turned a rosy shade of pink as he talked to her. He continued, "You must never drop your head in the presence of others. No matter who they are, you are their equal. Only a slave looks at the floor or the ground in the presence of others. You must look every person you meet in the eyes. Do you understand me?"

She hesitatingly nodded, and they began their walk once more. Nervously, she took his hand as they hurried across a busy street, but neither of them let go when they reached the other side.

When they arrived at the School for Excellent Young Ladies, they found a three-story building set back from the dusty street behind a six-foot wall. The double wrought-iron gate stood open. They entered the tree-shaded grounds and knocked on the eight-foot-high wooden door. The door opened, and they were invited in by a young, neatly dressed black girl with braided hair. She looked about twelve. They were shown into the parlor, where Madame Borgnette invited them to be seated across from her. Her gray hair was piled high on her head, and the cuffs of her once-elegant purple silk dress were slightly worn.

The room was full of heavy claw-footed furniture. Ornate kerosene lamps sat on end tables of mahogany. The fabric of the chairs was worn but had been elegant many years earlier. After offering them a cup of tea or chocolate, which they politely refused, Madame asked, "What brings you here, Mr. Schroeder? It has been a long while since we last saw you."

Introducing Maria, he said, "This young lady is a redemptioner, as I was, and as many of those you have hired once were. We have come here in the hope that you may be able to find a situation for her."

"Are you free, my dear?" she asked.

Looking from Hank to the school mistress, she nodded. "The contract I signed freed me on my eighteenth birthday. Now I need a way to support myself."

"Your master gave you no freedom pay?"

"No, Madame. His wife was unwilling to see me take anything away with me."

"Well, I do need a girl in the kitchen who can serve properly in the dining room. Have you had experience serving, Maria?"

"Yes, Madame, I have done much serving."

"On your recommendation, Mr. Schroeder, I will hire her. Can you begin immediately?"

Her head started to droop, but after taking a deep breath, Maria looked up at Madame Borgnette and said with more confidence than she felt, "Yes, of course, Madame."

"You may bid Mr. Schroeder farewell while I get Bridget from the kitchen so she can show you what will be expected of you."

As the school mistress left the room, Hank stood and put his hands on Maria's shoulders, smiling at her. "I think you are in good hands now, Maria. I wish you well."

Maria fought to keep back the tears that stung her eyes, and she smiled a quivering little smile. "Mr. Schroeder, you have been as kind to me as a brother or a father could have been. I shall never forget your kindness . . . or you." As he turned to go, she said quickly, to put off his good-bye. "Where will you be going now? Will you be going back up the river soon?"

"I will spend a few days with some friends who live in Lafayette. The Kopps were friends of my parents in Württemburg many years ago and as they are growing old, I try to visit them when I am in the city. Perhaps in a fortnight, or sooner if I find a commission, I will buy my passage on a steamboat going up the river so I can bring another load of goods or freight back down to New Orleans." Before leaving, he stepped closer to Maria and leaned over to whisper in her ear. The warmth of his breath made her skin tingle. "Do not speak German while you are here. Let everyone think that you have forgotten your childhood language."

He straightened, and Maria's forehead wrinkled as she looked at him with a question in her eyes. He continued, "Remember the handbill from Breaux." With sudden understanding, she nodded.

"Good-bye, Maria." He took her hand and bent over it briefly, and then he put his hat on his head. As the young girl at the door closed it behind him, Maria felt that she had lost her only friend, a man who had entered her life unexpectedly and whom she was suddenly devastated to see go. The words of her father came back to her. *What cannot be changed must be endured.*

Madame Borgnette entered the room, "Oh, Mr. Schroeder has left. Well, he never stays for very long." Pointing at the young woman who had followed her into the room, she said, "Maria, please follow Bridget. She will show you to your room. We will expect you to serve at dinner. Bridget will train you in all your duties."

Maria followed the freckled, red-haired Bridget into the kitchen. At the first landing, on the narrow stairway at the back of the kitchen, Bridget opened a door. The room was small with only two narrow beds and a two-drawer dresser on which sat an oil lamp, a pitcher, and a washbasin. "This is my room. Now it is yours, as well. Madame said you are a redemptioner like me, but I will not be free for another year." Bridget sat down on one of the beds and chattered as though she had not had someone to talk to for a long time. "Tell me what it is like to be free."

Maria sat on the other bed and looked at her hands in her lap. "It's frightening. I am so scared." At that, she could hold the tears back no longer. As her shoulders shook with her weeping, Bridget moved over to sit by her and put her arm around her.

"Don't cry. This is a good place to live, and we will become friends."

Maria wiped her eyes and smiled weakly at Bridget. "Yes, I'm sure we will become good friends."

"Do you have any other things? Do you have another dress? There is a peg on the wall that you can use."

Maria shook her head.

"Well, no matter. It is time for us to help Cook get dinner. Come with me, and I will find you an apron. You will like Cook. She is a good German woman who was also a redemptioner many years ago."

That evening Bridget and Maria served dinner to the young female students and the teachers. As they carried out their assignments, they were apparently invisible. There were twelve young women and three instructors at the school, in addition to Madame Borgnette and her daughter. The long table could have seated twenty.

"Francine, do cut your meat into smaller pieces," Madame Borgnette said firmly.

"Hannah, do not talk or laugh with your mouth full," Mistress Beatrice Borgnette corrected another young lady. Madame Borgnette's daughter was a spinster of nearly thirty years of age, and though she could be called well groomed, no one would have described her as attractive. A nose too long and a jaw too firm ruined the symmetry of her face. She compensated by correcting the prettier girls more harshly than the others. "Janette, do cover your mouth when you laugh, and remember, a lady does not laugh like a man. You are much too boisterous."

After the meal, the young women retired to the study or the music room to continue their studies.

After the dishes in the dining room had been cleared away, the servants ate in the kitchen, their meal made up of leftovers from the dinner. No one went hungry, as Cook had fixed an ample meal—it fed Cook; Maria; Bridget; Clara, who was twelve years old; and the gardener, a young man by the name of Pierre. After the kitchen was cleaned, Bridget led Maria on a tour of the school, which included two school rooms with desks; the music room, which they only peeked into because some of the girls were continuing their music lessons; a study; and the dormitory room, which had sixteen beds, only twelve of which were being used.

Bridget also introduced Maria to the three Irish girls they had met earlier in the stairwell.

As they made their way back to the little room the two of them would share, Bridget said, "Betty, Eliza, and Jan are good and kind girls. Their fathers are Irish merchants, so they don't think they are better than the servants," she explained. "The Creole and French girls will not speak to us. If one of us should touch Francine as we pass, she would go wash as if she had been soiled."

As they prepared for bed, which for Maria meant sleeping in a borrowed night dress, Bridget said, "Breakfast must be ready by seven o'clock in the morning, so we will need to be awake and dressed by six o'clock. Don't worry, I will wake you."

Despite her anxiousness, Maria was soon overtaken by exhaustion, and sleep submerged her as if it were a deep and dark pool. In her dreams she was a small girl again, calling to her parents to come and get her. Then she called to Hank to come back, but when he came, he had the bowie knife in his hand, and she ran away. When Bridget shook her awake in the morning, she felt as if she had not slept at all.

The day was busy as Maria and Bridget helped in the kitchen and served in the dining room. After Cook had started the midday meal preparations, she told the two young women, "Bridget, take Maria around the gardens and enjoy the sunshine for a few minutes. I can do without you for a bit."

As Bridget passed the kitchen table, she picked up two carrots not yet prepared for the stew. As she did so, Cook said, "If you are going to feed them to Blackwell, don't plan on doing it every day. That animal eats twice as much as any of us."

Bridget giggled as she went out the kitchen doorway. The door stood open to let in the fresh air, which was only slightly cooler than the inside of the kitchen. As they started down the path, she said, "Cook says that to me every time I take a carrot for Blackwell."

"Who is Blackwell?" Maria asked.

"Follow me, and I will introduce you to him." As they walked toward a small stable at the back of the grounds, Maria noticed Pierre, who was kneeling over the azaleas that bordered the path at the side of the building. He had stopped what he was doing to watch the two young women.

Bridget lifted the bar that held the stable door closed and pulled the door open. It took a minute for their eyes to adjust to the darkness inside. Then Maria could see a small carriage near the back of the building and a large black horse in a nearby stall. It had turned from its hay to watch them enter.

"Here, Maria, offer him one of the carrots." Bridget pushed Maria closer to the animal. "He won't bite. Just hold it out so he can reach it."

Maria tentatively offered the carrot to the horse. Bridget gave her another gentle push. Laughing, she added, "You have to be close enough for him to reach it."

Maria stepped closer, and the animal moved its soft lips over the carrot and across her fingers. It snorted quietly before taking the carrot from her hand. As he chewed, Maria asked, "Why is he named Blackwell?"

"He's named after Madame Borgnette's husband."

"Why would she name a horse after her husband?" Maria asked as she turned to look at Bridget.

"Madame didn't name him. Her daughter named him that. Her father ran away with a pretty Creole student of Madame's about fifteen years ago, so she named the horse after him." Bridget laughed and added, "Here, give him the other carrot, too. Then he will always be your friend."

After the young women had rubbed the horse's face and neck, they left the stable and sat on a bench under a blooming magnolia tree. Maria said quietly, "It's beautiful here, inside these walls. The trees and bushes make it as pretty here as heaven must be." They looked around at the splashes of lavender made by the blooming red-bud trees and the pale pink of the tulip trees. The azalea bushes where Pierre was working were beginning to bloom a deep pink. Lavender wisteria blossoms hung from vines growing up the trellises that leaned against the walls.

Bridget nodded and said, "Tell Pete that you like the yard. It's his work."

"Why do you call him Pete? His name is Pierre, isn't it?

Bridget twisted her lips into a wry smile and answered, "Yes, but since he never looks at me the way he looked at you at supper last night, I call him Pete. If he ever looks at me that way, then I will call him Pierre."

"How did he look at me last night?"

"As if he had never seen a pretty woman before." Bridget laughed. When they reached the gardener, who was kneeling as he spaded horse dung into the azalea plants, Bridget said, "Pete, Maria says the yard inside the wall looks like heaven."

The young man stood up, removed his battered straw hat, and nodded at the women. "*Merci*, Maria. I am glad you like my work." The young man smiled broadly.

Then Bridget took Maria's hand and pulled her away. "We must get back to the kitchen to help Cook." Maria smiled at Pierre, and the two young women made their way back toward the kitchen door.

"Does Cook have a real name?" Maria asked.

"Of course she does. I just don't know it."

The rest of the day was full of meal preparations, serving, and cleaning. In the afternoon, Maria helped Bridget change the linens on the beds in the dormitory. By the time the servants' supper was cleared off the kitchen table, Maria was as exhausted as she had been the night before. As she lay down to sleep and closed her eyes, Hank's face appeared. One last thought remained as sleep submerged her. *Hank, will I ever see you again?*

CHAPTER 5
The Kopps of Lafayette

Once Hank had bid Maria good-bye, he walked swiftly up the street, telling himself that it was good to be unencumbered by the young woman. Now he would be able to go where and do what he wanted. But he could not forget the look in her eyes, gray with worry.

He climbed aboard the next passing omnibus and rode it for an hour back to the waterfront, where he gave Jim and Wash each a coin for watching the boat. Then he poled it out into the water and guided it across the river where it looped past the settlement of Gretna, where he knew he would find a sawmill. There he poled the boat onto the levee. He walked the short distance to the mill office and found the owner. "What can you give me for my boat?"

"Like last time, I'll give you four dollars for it."

"Done." Hank put out his hand, and the two men shook on the deal. After Hank received the money for the boat, he threw his small bag over his shoulder and walked to the ferry, where he paid ten cents to be ferried across the river and back to New Orleans.

Taking the omnibus again, he made his way to the home of Mr. and Mrs. Walter Kopp in Lafayette, at the corner of Jersey and Jackson Streets. By the time he arrived, the street lights had been lit in the riverside community. He was greeted like a long-lost family member and ushered into the parlor. They set another place for him at the dining-room table.

The dinner conversation was filled with talk of a slave by the name of Sally Miller who was believed to be a redemptioner from

Langensoultzbach in Alsace. A rotund Mrs. Kopp leaned across the table and put her hand on Hank's, saying in an excited voice, "A fine lawyer has taken her case and is determined to prove her a free woman. You must meet him. He has been such a friend to the German community here."

Hank gave her his total attention. "Lawyers cost money. How is he being paid?"

She continued enthusiastically, "The entire German community has come together to raise the money to defend her in court and have her declared a free woman."

"Wouldn't it be easier if you simply bought her from her master and set her free?" he asked.

Mr. Kopp interjected, "We asked Mr. Upton about that, but he said that Louisiana law, as it stands today, would require she leave the state forever if we freed her in that manner. We don't want that. We are sure that she is the daughter of Daniel and Dorothea Muller. Dorothea was my wife's sister, and they traveled together to America on the ship *Juffer Johanna* in 1818. She is family. We simply have to find a way to prove her to be a white woman mistakenly or maliciously sold as a slave."

Hank asked thoughtfully, "How can you know she is family? How old was she when she arrived in America?"

Here, Mrs. Kopp answered forcefully, "Oh, she is the image of my sister, her mother. Even though she was only about four or five years old when we arrived in New Orleans, there can be no mistake. We will fight as long as it requires for us to see her declared a free, white woman by the court."

Hank was thoughtful for the rest of the evening. After he had been shown to the little bedroom he often used when he visited the Kopps, he lay awake, fully dressed on the bed that was too short for his long frame, thinking about what he had heard about Sally Miller and her situation. Then, telling himself that the matter was no longer his business, he turned over and determined to go to sleep, but his thoughts strayed back to Maria and her gray-green eyes, which had been so troubled when he left her.

The next day Hank spent several hours moving about the city, trying to locate a merchant who might give him a commission to bring whatever was wanted down the river. He found none ready to hire his services. He returned to the Kopps' home by late afternoon, where he discovered that they had contacted as many members of the German community as they were able and invited them to a fine dinner that evening so Hank could meet Wheelock S. Upton, esquire, and his client, Sally Miller.

It was as fine a meal as had been seen in the German community in many months, with bratwurst, meatballs, and strudel, among other dishes, but Hank was more interested in the special guests. Sally Miller was a quiet, olive-skinned woman with long, brown curls. She spoke only when spoken to, but her lawyer filled the void. He spoke at length of the nobleness of his cause, the obstacles in his way, and the sureness of his eventual victory. He had even brought newspaper clippings of the case, which had appeared in the *Louisiana Gazette* and the *Courier*.

Eva Kopp spoke of how her friend, Madame Carl Rouff, had found Sally sitting on the stoop of a miserable little cabaret owned and run by Mr. Belmonti, the man who claimed to own Sally. "Madame Rouff went back the next day and coaxed Sally away for a few hours. She showed her to several of the members of the German community who had traveled on the same ship as Daniel and Dorothea Muller, and they all saw the family resemblance." Mrs. Kopp sat back and folded her hands in her lap as if she had just proven the point at issue.

Mr. Kopp took up the narrative, "She even has two small moles—birthmarks we know she had as a child. This is a cause we will support until we win."

As Wheelock S. Upton, esquire, prepared to leave with his client after the meal, Hank spoke to him as he shook hands in farewell. "Mr. Upton, where is your office? I would like to speak to you about another matter, if I could."

Mr. Upton swelled with importance and handed Hank his business card. "Mr. Schroeder, I would be pleased to speak with you on any matter you might bring to my attention." He put his hat on his head and, offering her his arm, escorted Sally to his carriage.

Eva Kopp stood at the door thanking her guests for their attendance, and as they departed she said to each one of them, "You will remember your pledge to the fund to free Sally, will you not?" Each guest reassured her of their dependable intentions.

After spending the following day approaching merchants and other businessmen regarding a commission, Hank returned to the Kopps by early evening. He was tired but not surprised to find that a young, unmarried German woman by the name of Elsie Freudenthal and her parents were the guests of honor at dinner. For the past year, Eva Kopp had made it her personal mission to see Hank married. He made a sincere effort at conversation but soon found that he had little in common with either the girl or her parents.

On the fifth day, he entered a butcher shop in Lafayette where he found a copy of the *Louisiana Gazette* on the counter. The butcher was busy, so Hank sat on a small keg and, through the smudges of animal blood and grease left by previous readers, read of the search of Mr. Lafayette Breaux of Caldwell County for a young metif slave by the name of Maria, who was believed to have run away to New Orleans or Baton Rouge. One particular line jumped out at him. *If identified, this slave should be taken directly to the Cabildo, where she will be held until her master can retrieve her.* The Cabildo, a small stone prison next to the courthouse near Lafayette Square, was little more than a hole where rats were companions to the prisoners, and many became ill in the damp and mildewed cells.

Her description was given, and the article ended by saying that anyone with information as to her whereabouts could give that information to Theophilis Freeman at his office on Bourbon Street, where they could apply for the reward.

Hank sat for a full minute as still as if he had been stricken with rigor mortis, and then he stood and strode from the shop without speaking with the butcher. He made his way back to the home of Mr. and Mrs. Kopp and hurried up the stairs to the small bedroom he was using. He quickly located the business card of Wheelock S. Upton, esquire, on the dresser. He descended the stairs and almost knocked his hostess off her feet as she stepped out of the drawing room.

"Mr. Schroeder, what is causing you such distress? You are hurrying as if the town is on fire."

He put his hand on her shoulder and said, "Forgive me, madame, if I do not take the time to explain." Then he literally lifted her aside and hurried out the doorway.

He was breathless by the time he reached the office of the lawyer. He hardly noticed that the man sat alone in the single room with a desk more covered with newspapers than legal documents. Upton stood as Hank entered and, after shaking his hand, urged him to take a seat. "Mr. Schroeder, what brings you to my office in such a hurried manner?"

Hank sat down and made an effort to control his hard breathing. Then he said, "From what I understand of your case on behalf of Sally Miller, you may be knowledgeable in obtaining the freedom of redemptioners held by their masters longer than their contract states, thus preventing them from obtaining their rightful freedom."

Upton sat back in his chair in disappointment. He had hoped for a simple, straightforward case, such as retrieving a stolen horse or a bankruptcy. The last thing he wanted was another case as complex and time consuming as the one dealing with Sally Miller.

"You flatter me, Mr. Schroeder, to consider me knowledgeable in any particular matter," he said modestly, "but I must tell you that at this time, I could not consider taking a similar case. Cases such as these are convoluted and challenging but, most of all, extremely time consuming."

"Can you refer me to someone else who might be willing to consider such a case?"

The lawyer narrowed his eyes as he thought and then said, "Christian Roselius might be of assistance, if he is so inclined. His office is on Customhouse Street. He was the state's attorney general not so long ago and is looking to build up his practice. With him you may have an advantage, as he is German by birth."

Hank rose to shake Upton's hand and then made his way out of the office and over to Customhouse Street. The office of Christian Roselius, esquire, was entirely different from Upton's. It held law books in floor-to-ceiling bookshelves, many in French, Latin, or German. Others were piled about the room, almost obscuring the red carpet. He motioned Hank to sit on the only chair in the room not filled with a pile of legal documents.

Hank put before him Maria's situation without mentioning her name. Roselius responded, "Ah, yes, could this be the young woman named Maria? The one mentioned in the ads for runaways that appeared in the newspapers today?" Hank nodded. The attorney sat back and rubbed his chin between his thumb and forefinger for so long that Hank began to hope he was considering taking the case.

His response was a disappointment. "I am afraid that I must resist the temptation to take your case, sir. You surely know that a similar case of a woman called Sally Miller is in the courts right now, and an excess of speculation among the citizens of this city fills dinner conversations at every table. If I were to take the case you offer before that one has a final determination, the outcome for all involved in both cases might be disastrous. Surely you understand my position?"

Hank did not for one moment understand the lawyer's position, but, accepting the rejection, he rose, put on his hat, and thanked the man for his time before he left the office. As he returned to the residence of Mr. and Mrs. Kopp, he turned the situation over in his mind. *What are my choices here?* Neither lawyer would take her case, so he saw no way she could obtain her freedom through the courts. Once more he tried to tell himself that her fate was not his concern, but he could not convince himself. He could not deny the pull of his feelings for her.

CHAPTER 6
The School for Young Ladies

A week passed and the days were full, but despite the tasks both had to complete, Maria and Bridget's friendship grew. Bridget was seldom quiet. As they washed midday meal dishes, she chattered away about each of the girls who attended the school. She was a remarkable gossip. "I told you that the Irish girls were nice, but the others walk with their noses in the air. Lucy and Suzette are Creole sisters from Attakapas. They live down on the Atchafalaya River where there are lots of poor Creoles and Cajuns, but here in New Orleans, they each act like royalty. And then there's Francine Freeman. Her father is the biggest slave trader in New Orleans. She thinks she's as good as the Queen of France, but some people think her father is the devil himself." Bridget continued to talk about the other girls, but upon hearing Francine's last name, Maria heard no more. She stood frozen with fear.

After another few minutes of talking, Bridget finally realized that Maria had become silent and was not listening. "Maria, what's the matter? You're white as a ghost."

"Oh, nothing, nothing," she excused herself. "I am just a little bit tired. Do you think Cook would mind if I go out into the garden and sit for a few minutes?"

"No, she won't mind. I'll come with you if you like."

"No. No, I think I would like to be alone for a little while."

Maria sat on the little bench beneath the magnolia tree and tried to control her fear. *What if she discovers who I am? What if she tells her father? If he ever sees me, he'll know who I am. He'll tell Lafayette Breaux so he can get the reward.* The thoughts tumbled about in her mind like a cup of marbles spilled by a child. She could not hold back a tear that made its way down her cheek. *Oh, dear God, show me what to do.* As she wiped the tear away with the back of her hand, Pierre approached her and asked, "Maria, what makes you cry? May I help?"

Startled, she looked up and covered her quivering mouth. She ran back into the kitchen and up the stairs to the little room she shared with Bridget, threw herself down upon her bed, and gave in to her tears. After half an hour, she arose and washed her face with the water in the washbasin. She combed her hair with the comb Bridget had given her and tried to smile at the tired and frightened face looking back at her in the mirror. Then she returned to the kitchen to assist in the preparation of the evening meal.

Maria regained her composure by the time she was called upon to serve in the dining room. After she began to remove the dirty dishes and goblets from the table, three of the girls began to whisper and giggle among themselves. Madame Borgnette tapped her goblet with her teaspoon and said, "Suzette, Lucy, Francine, what are you giggling about? It is rude not to share what you are talking about with the rest of us."

Two of the girls looked at Francine, who smiled innocently and said, "We understand that our new serving girl, Maria, speaks fluent German. Won't you demonstrate your German language skills for us? Perhaps she could even assist Mr. Walters in our language class."

Madame Borgnette looked at Maria, who was standing near the end of the table with a full tray of dirty dishes, and asked with a smile, "Is that true, Maria? Do you speak German?"

Maria suddenly felt sick and dizzy. She took a deep breath and, remembering what Hank had told her, responded, "Oh, Madame, I have been in this country so long that I have forgotten my native language. I would be of no use in a classroom. I am so sorry."

She made a small curtsey and hurried into the kitchen. She set the tray down hard on the old wooden kitchen table and stood still while taking several deep breaths to control the heartbeat pounding in her ears. Cook looked at her. Seeing Maria's white face, she asked, "Are you all right, Maria?"

Maria answered with a quivering voice, "I'm fine, Cook. I'm all right." Taking another deep breath, she returned to the now-empty dining room and continued to collect dirty dishes. That evening as the girls were pushing themselves away from the table in the parlor where some had been playing whist, Maria began removing the glasses they had used for lemonade. Francine waited until Maria reached for her glass and then said, "*Guten abend*, Maria."

Hesitating slightly in her task, Maria smiled and said, "I beg your pardon, Miss Freeman, did you say something?"

"Yes, Maria. I said, '*Guten abend*.'"

"I'm sorry, Francine. You will have to speak English if you desire a response from me." Trying her hardest to smile, she moved to the kitchen with her tray of dishes. As she washed the glasses with Bridget, she hardly heard her companion's chatter. By the time she had removed her apron, she had made up her mind. Somehow she had to leave the school—and soon. She stepped out into the warm night air and walked the paths between the azalea bushes as she tried to form a plan.

She jumped when Pierre spoke to her. He had stepped up to her side without being noticed. "Miss Maria, you are troubled? You have been walking in the garden for an hour. It will soon be time for the lights to be out. You will be in trouble if Madame learns you are out here."

She turned and looked at the young man. "Pierre, are you my friend?"

"*Oui*—I mean, yes, Maria. Yes, I am your friend."

"Then help me. Please help me," she said intensely.

"I will help you any way I can. Tell me what or who makes you cry."

She turned toward the stable and said, "Walk with me back to the stable where we can talk without anyone hearing us." When they were inside, he lit a kerosene lantern, and as they both stroked Blackwell, she stated, "Pierre, you are a redemptioner. You will be free according to your contract very soon, won't you?"

"In one year, when I am twenty-one."

"What would you do if Madame Borgnette refused to give you your freedom?"

"I would run away. I am not a slave, so she would have no right to refuse to give me my freedom."

Suddenly, Maria felt a sense of relief. "That is what I have done. When I was sold as a redemptioner in Baltimore, I was to be given my freedom when I reached eighteen, but my last master, Lafayette Breaux, told me that he bought me from Theophilis Freeman as a metif slave and refused to give me my freedom when I reached my eighteenth birthday."

"So you ran away? Why are you afraid? Does someone here know who you are?"

"Theophilis Freeman is Francine's father." He could hear the tension in her voice. "Somehow she knows who I am, or at least she suspects. She spoke to me in German. Mr. Breaux knows I speak German, and he put that in the handbill, offering to pay five hundred dollars to anyone who finds me and takes me back to him. Francine's father is the biggest slave trader in New Orleans. Somehow she has guessed—or perhaps she saw something in the newspaper." She paused and said, "Pierre, I don't know what to do. I must get away from here before her father comes to take me back to Mr. Breaux for the reward."

"Do you know anyone in New Orleans who can help you?"

"I know only one man, Hank Schroeder, the man who brought me here. He told me he was going to stay with friends in Lafayette by the name of Kopp, but I do not know where they live. I don't know how to find him. I am sure Lafayette is a large place."

"I know Lafayette well. It is near the river. I was a gardener to a German family there before my services were sold to Madame. I will take Blackwell after the lights are out and try to find him for you. When I find him, I will tell him to come immediately to get you."

"Pierre, I don't want to get you in trouble. If Madame Borgnette can prove you have broken the law by helping me, she could keep you for another year."

"I will be back before daylight, and she will never know that I have gone. Now you must go to bed as though this night is no different than any other, but when the moon is high, watch for me from a window." He lifted the bridle from the nail where it was hanging and opened the stall. He slipped the bit into the horse's mouth as Maria turned and ran back to the kitchen door.

The door was locked, so she frantically knocked, but not too loudly, hoping that her knock would be heard in the kitchen but nowhere else in the building. She knocked again, and after a few minutes, Cook opened the door. She was in her nightdress with a dust cap on her head. "Maria, what are you doing out after curfew? Madame will be angry if she finds you out of bed."

"Please, please, do not tell her. I will go up to bed right now."

"Young Frenchmen are handsome, Maria, but you must remember that Pierre's time belongs to Madame, and he cannot marry until he is free," Cook said very seriously.

"Oh, Cook, he is only a friend. You need not worry about me in that matter." Embarrassed by the implication, Maria hurried up the stairs.

As she entered the little bedroom, Bridget sat up in bed and whispered, "Maria, where have you been? I hunted all over for you when it was time to go to bed. Madame Borgnette wanted to speak to you. When I could not find you, I told her you were feeling ill."

"And Bridget, you are so right. I am feeling ill."

"What do you mean? Tell me what has you so upset."

Instead of answering her friend's question, Maria stepped to the window and lifted the curtain. She watched the figure of Pierre as he led the horse through the shadows in the garden to the main gate, carefully and silently closing it behind them. Then he mounted and rode down the street, keeping to the darkest shadows. Maria slipped into bed, still in her dress, and would not answer Bridget's questions. Finally, to get Bridget to leave her alone, she said, "Bridget, I cannot tell you anything. That way, if I get into trouble, I will not bring it upon you."

Bridget was hurt at being kept out of the secret, so she turned to face the wall and pretended to go to sleep. Maria slipped out of bed and knelt, whispering a fervent prayer, "God, if you know where I am, please keep me from Lafayette Breaux and Theophilis Freeman. Please, please help me." She lay back down on the bed, looking at the ceiling in the weak moonlight that filtered through the curtains. Though she did not meant to, she eventually drifted off to sleep.

She was not sure how long she had been asleep when Bridget shook her awake. "Maria, Cook wants you to come to the kitchen. Pierre is there and wants to see you. Put on your shoes and hurry."

When they entered the kitchen, Maria stopped and stared. By the light of the candle on the table, she could see Hank. To her relief, everyone else in the room briefly faded away. She actually felt warm in his presence, as if she were standing near a fire. Her gratitude and relief almost made her speechless.

Pierre turned and spoke, "Mr. Schroeder has come to get you, Maria."

"Do you have anything to take with you?" Hank asked.

Maria shook her head. The only thing she owned in addition to the dress she wore was the comb given her by Bridget, which was in her pocket. Hank said, "Then come with me now. We have a long way to go before it gets light, and we will not have the use of the horse."

Maria quickly gave a hug to Bridget and said, "You are my friend, and I will always remember you. And you, Pierre, and Cook, we have only known each other a few days, but you are true friends." At that, Hank took her wrist and began to pull her out of the kitchen door into the darkness.

They walked as fast as Maria could. Hank's long strides forced her to take three steps to every two of his, but he would not let her pause or rest for the first mile. He was silent as they walked in the darkness until they were deep into the French Quarter. Many of the bordellos and gambling houses were still bright with lights, and loud laughter spilled out into the street. She begged him to pause so she could get her breath. "How did Pierre find you?"

Hank answered almost absentmindedly as he looked up and down the street, "He went to the local police kiosk and asked the policeman there if he knew the Kopp family. He did, and he directed Pierre to their house. It took him several minutes to wake the household. Pierre insisted that I ride back with him. Blackwell is a fine animal, but the two of us were nearly more than he could carry. It will take him a day or two to recover."

"What time is it now?"

"It must be long after midnight. We can't linger any longer. Can you continue?"

"Yes. Where are we going?" Maria asked breathlessly as once more she hurried to keep up with him.

"For now, we're going to the Kopps, but we cannot stay there long. The police know that Pierre was looking for their house. That could help someone who might be trying to find you."

"Surely no one at the school would tell them. Only Pierre knows."

"News travels on its own legs in this city. There are many ears and eyes that report what is believed to be secret."

"Do you think that Mr. Freeman has that kind of power?"

"Probably." As they walked past a well-lit gambling house, an overdressed man, very unsteady on his feet, pushed his way out of the swinging half door and past them, bumping into Maria and knocking her down. As Hank bent to help her up, he said to the man, "Sir, you seem a bit unsteady on your feet. I suggest that you take greater care. You need to offer the lady an apology."

The man replied contemptuously, slurring his words, "I did not run into the lady, sir, she ran into me. She owes me the apology—as do you."

Hank quietly insisted, "Sir, your manner is rude and ungracious. A simple apology will suffice."

With a twisted snarl, he said, "I will make no apology to your *placeé*—your lady of the night," he sneered, "or to you. We will find it more appropriate to meet on the field of honor." The man stepped so close to Hank that a cloud of whisky fumes enveloped both men. The man put his hand on the handle of his broadsword and pulled it from its scabbard, waving it drunkenly in the air. He continued pompously, "I challenge you to weapons of your choice at sunrise behind the St. Louis Cathedral."

"Why wait until sunrise? You seem determined to appeal to the custom of the *duello,* so let's settle this matter here and now." Hank pushed him against the building wall and pulled the bowie knife from its sheath, placing it against the man's throat. With his left hand, he gripped the wrist of the man's hand that held the sword and said, "Now, you will offer the lady a brief apology."

"Y-you ha—you have my deepest apology, madame," the man said.

After returning the knife to its sheath, Hank used both hands to uncurl the man's fingers from the handle of the sword.

Removing it from his grip, he said, "I will find an appropriate repository for this. Perhaps you can get it returned if you put a notice in the newspaper."

The man did not move until they had walked about thirty feet farther down the street. Then he ran the other way as fast as his wobbly legs would take him. About a half mile farther, Hank put the sword into a rain barrel at the side of a butcher shop.

CHAPTER 7
Flight

When they reached the Kopp residence, a two-story frame house painted the color of oxblood with dark green shutters, Hank knocked on the door. Despite the late hour, it was quickly opened by Mr. Kopp. "We have been waiting for you. Come in, come in." Mrs. Kopp, who had evidently been sleeping in the rocking chair, patted her hair and straightened her dress as she stood to greet her guests.

Hank introduced Maria to the German couple and explained the difficulty of her situation. Eva Kopp, her face lit with a bright smile, embraced Maria and said, "We must raise the money to fight for your freedom, my dear, just as we are doing for Sally Miller. Surely, Mr. Upton will accept your case, too."

Hank shook his head and explained, "I have spoken to both Mr. Upton and Mr. Roselius about the matter, and both have explained that the public outcry about the Sally Miller case is such that neither of them will consider taking a similar case, lest it threaten the outcome of the Miller case."

"Oh, that is a disappointment." Mrs. Kopp slumped in the rocking chair again in a thoroughly unhappy posture.

Mr. Kopp asked with a thoughtful tone, "Then what are your plans?"

Maria sat quietly as she looked at her hands, which were folded in her lap. Though surprised that Hank had already been to two different lawyers in her behalf, she raised her eyes and looked anxiously from Hank to Mr. Kopp. "Mr. Schroeder has no obligation to continue assisting me. He was kind enough to save me from the Ouachita River and bring me to New Orleans, but I have no right to continue to burden him. I cannot expect him to alter his plans so that he might continue to protect me."

Hank was slow to speak but, looking at Mr. Kopp, finally said, "It seems the Lord has made me responsible for Maria. He asked this of me when I saw her nearly drowning in the river. If she will continue to accept my services, I am willing to continue to try and help her."

Maria dropped her head. "That is very kind of you," she responded quietly. She had felt herself growing attracted to him from the time they were on the river, so she was disappointed that Hank's reason for aiding her seemed so dispassionate. *I have let my emotions run away with me. I should have tried to control my feelings after he left me at the school. He evidently doesn't feel the same for me as I do for him.* She lifted her head and looked at him. *But then, why did he return for me?* She dropped her head again to look at her hands in her lap. *I think he would have offered the same consideration to a homeless puppy.*

What Hank did not mention was his quiet but powerful attraction to the young woman, which had been steadily increasing since he'd pulled her from the water. He felt it would be entirely improper for him to admit such feelings, considering her dependence upon him. He was, after all, offering to be her protector. She must not be made to feel that he might try to take advantage of her situation. He shifted his position in the heavy, carved wooden chair and continued, "I think we need to take passage on a steamboat up the river to Memphis, and from there we will make our way to Monroe County, Mississippi, where I have friends. It could take as long as a week."

"Why don't you go by steamboat to Mobile and then up the Tombigbee River to Monroe County?" Walter Kopp asked. "Wouldn't it be faster?"

Hank was quiet for a few seconds, and then responded, "I realize we could go much faster that way, but that will be substantially more costly, and we would be exposed to more people, some of whom might be aware of Breaux's search for Maria. I believe we ought to avoid any unnecessary expenses and mingle with as few people as possible." He rubbed his eyebrow for a moment and then added, "I think we will need to travel as husband and wife, if Maria is not offended by the suggestion. This arrangement would be in name only, of course." He looked at Mr. and Mrs. Kopp and then at Maria to watch the reaction of each of them.

Mrs. Kopp said to her husband with sweet innocence, "Walter, why don't they actually get married? Hank has been in need of a wife for some time, and Maria is a good German girl in need of a protector. They would make a lovely couple." She sat back with a benign smile, sure that she had found a solution.

Maria watched Hank's face to see his reaction. His jaw tightened, but he said nothing. She couldn't tell what he was thinking. Walter Kopp was more realistic than his wife. "My dear, as long as Maria is under suspicion of being a slave, the marriage would not be considered valid in Louisiana or Mississippi."

"Oh," she said in disappointment, "and I had such a nice solution for the problem." She spoke with a slight pout, as though such a law existed simply to vex her personally. "Well, for now we need to feed you and see that you get some rest. We will think more on this problem in the morning." She rose and made her way to the kitchen.

Walter rose and began to pace the parlor. His natural German efficiency had taken over. "I think we need to have your steamboat tickets in hand as soon as possible. Do you agree, Hank?"

Hank nodded and asked, "Do you have a trustworthy servant who could go to the waterfront and purchase two cabin tickets to Memphis in the name of Mr. and Mrs. Hanks? I have the funds with me."

"Yes, that would be the thing to do. As soon as it is daylight, I will send my gardener to purchase the tickets on a boat that leaves in the afternoon. I'm sure there will be two or three going north today."

***

When the girls and the instructors sat down at the long breakfast table and only Bridget served, Madame Borgnette asked her sharply, "Bridget, where is Maria? Is she still feeling unwell?"

Bridget straightened up and said bravely, "She is gone, Madame."

"Gone? What do you mean?"

"She is no longer here, Madame. She left in the night and left no note to tell us where she was going."

"Was she unhappy here?"

"I do not know, Madame."

Madame was most upset with the situation but said no more. Francine giggled and leaned over to the girl at her left and whispered something. When Madame looked sternly at her, she sat up and became quiet.

About ten o'clock in the morning, the carriage of Theophilis Freeman stopped at the front gate. His man, Thomas, again dressed in red livery, sat in the high front seat holding the reins. A pair of chestnut horses pulled the open landau. Clara opened the door for him, and he strode past her and into the parlor.

Madame hurried to greet him, flustered and apologetic. "Oh, Mr. Freeman, we did not expect you today. How can we serve you? Are you here to see Francine? Oh, of course you are. Clara, go and fetch Francine for her father."

He raised his hand to stop her nervous chatter and said, "Of course I will see my daughter before I leave, but I am here on another matter. Please bring your new servant girl to me, the one by the name of Maria."

Madame looked even more upset. "I am afraid that she is not here, Mr. Freeman. She left sometime during the night without telling anyone why or where she was going."

Francine entered and gave her father a curtsey. "Father, it is good to see you."

Without acknowledging his daughter's greeting, he demanded, "Where is she, Francine? Where is the servant you spoke of in your note to me?"

"They say she has run away, Father."

"Does anyone know where she has gone?"

At this point Madame answered, "She told no one that she was going or where. She left before any of the servants normally arise to begin breakfast."

"Did anyone help her?"

"We have no way of knowing, Mr. Freeman," Madame answered, nervously twisting her lace handkerchief. "May I ask why you are seeking her?"

"I believe her to be a runaway slave—a metif. There is a substantial reward for her. I came to take her back to her master."

Madame began to defend herself. "She said she was an indentured servant who had fulfilled her contract, Mr. Freeman. How was I to know any differently?"

Theophilis Freeman abruptly put his silk hat on his head, nodded perfunctorily to his daughter, turned on his heel, and left. After he was seated in the carriage, he spoke to Thomas, who then flicked his whip. The carriage moved rapidly down the street.

Madame Borgnette turned and looked at Francine after her father had left. "What do you know of this matter, Francine?"

"Nothing, Madame," was the pious answer she received.

Madame pursed her mouth in skepticism. "Well, return to your studies."

***

The gardener returned with the tickets for cabin passage on the steamship *Southern Belle* before the midday meal. It was scheduled to depart from New Orleans at three o'clock. Mrs. Kopp ordered her cook to fix a large basket of fruit, bread, and slices of ham and cheese that Hank and Maria could take with them. Then she took Mr. Kopp's best carpetbag and went to her bedroom, inviting Maria to join her. While Maria watched from the straight-backed chair where she was seated, Eva Kopp began to stuff the bag with Hank's few belongings and some things Maria would need. As she did so, she paused and said, "Maria, you are such a quiet young lady that we have been guilty of a grave discourtesy to you. We have not asked if you are in agreement with these plans." She paused with a yellow shawl in her hand and turned from the bed where the carpetbag sat half full. "Do you approve of the actions we are taking?"

"Mrs. Kopp, I believe you were sent by God to help me. I will never be able to repay you or your husband—or Mr. Schroeder. You have inconvenienced yourselves greatly on my behalf."

"I am so glad our actions meet with your approval." Eva Kopp seemed as excited as if she were packing her own bag for a long-anticipated trip. "I have obtained a lavender dress for you from my maid, Beth, as she is about your size. I will give her another to replace it. And I have put in here a brush, a shawl, two pairs of stockings, a chemise, a pair of Beth's knickers, a small hand mirror, and one of my nightdresses." She smiled and added, "It will be too large, I am sure, but Beth had only one. I could not borrow one from her." She paused and inspected Maria's dress. "I think you had best put on the dress I got from Beth for the trip. Someone may have a description of the blue dress you are wearing."

As soon as Maria had changed into the lavender dress and tucked the blue one into the carpetbag, Mrs. Kopp turned her around and took a long, critical look at her. "I need to put your hair in a chignon and find you a bonnet," she said matter of factly. "Then you will be ready to travel."

With her hair pinned in a twist at the back of her neck and hidden under a wide-brimmed bonnet, Maria looked at herself in the mirror. *Perhaps I can fool someone looking for me.* Her benefactress said, "Now you must be on your way quickly. Time is passing."

At the door, Maria set aside her natural reserve and embraced Mrs. Kopp. She then bobbed a small curtsey to Mr. Kopp and said, "I am in your debt. I know of no way to repay you."

Mr. Kopp replied, "To repay us, you only have to secure your freedom. May God aid you in your journey. Now take your husband's arm"—at that he smiled—"and remember to call him 'dear,' rather than 'Mr. Schroeder.'"

Hank shook his host's hand and then bent to give his hostess a peck on the cheek. "You have been my friends and friends of my parents for a long time. If our paths are never meant to cross again, know that you will always be remembered with gratitude." Hank turned, picked up the carpetbag, and handed the basket of food to Maria. He smiled formally and said to her, "Well, Mrs. Hanks, we must be on our way."

They walked three blocks and found a small cabaret on the corner where they could sit and watch for the omnibus as it approached. Hank ordered two cups of tea to keep the establishment's owner happy. Maria's hands shook slightly as she lifted her cup, so she quickly set it down. Glancing around and noting that there was no one near enough to overhear her, she asked Hank, "Why are you doing this for me? You owe me nothing. It is I who owe you."

Hank rubbed his chin as he weighed his words and tried to articulate a philosophy that he had never previously been asked to put into words. "My parents tried to teach me that whenever God placed a choice before a man, that man should make the choice that would be of greatest benefit to those around him." He was quiet for a moment and then continued, "My father often said that it was a poorly lived life that did not leave the world a better place than it found it."

"Oh, I see," Maria said. *I am simply an assignment from God to Mr. Schroeder—an object of compassion,* she thought to herself. She was grateful but disappointed. She sipped her tea for a few minutes until Hank pushed away from the table. Seeing the omnibus approaching, she stood and took his offered arm in a manner she hoped made them look like husband and wife.

As they waited to board the steamboat, she held on to his arm tightly and turned her face away from a man who stood near the gangplank holding a handbill and examining those boarding the vessel. To get her to turn to him, he asked her, "Miss, is this man your husband?"

Maria turned and said, "Why would that concern you, sir?"

"Just wanted to make sure you weren't bein' taken anywhere against your will, miss." But he had accomplished what he wanted. He had seen her gray-green eyes.

His only sign of any form of authority was the dented badge pinned to his worn shirt. She did not see him write a brief note on the handbill. As they climbed the gangplank, the purser took their tickets and allowed them to board. A porter took the carpetbag and showed them to a cabin on the upper deck.

When the door was closed, a relieved Maria asked, "How long will it take to get to Memphis?"

"At least two days. Maybe three, since we are going up the river rather than down. Depends somewhat on the weather and the currents." He lifted the napkin from the basket top. "If you are as hungry as I am, I think it's time to see what is in this basket."

As they ate, Maria looked around the cabin. It had a low, well-worn settee, a dresser on one wall, and a large bed with a worn red velvet coverlet. The two of them sat at a small desk at one end of the room on the only two chairs available as they ate their impromptu meal of ham wrapped in a slice of bread. Out of the corner of her eye, she watched Hank's strong hands. Though it was evident he was hungry, he remained alert, listening closely to the sound of anyone moving along the deck past the cabin door.

The boat trip up the river was quiet that first day. Maria and Hank thought it best that she not leave the cabin, except at night. After remaining in the cabin all day, Maria stood at the rail of the second deck and studied the night sky. When Hank stood next to her and asked what she was thinking, she was aware of the warmth she could feel from his hand where it rested near hers on the railing. She answered, "I was wondering if God knows where I am."

Hank had a sudden urge to pull her to him and tell her that God certainly did know where she was and had sent him to protect her, but he suppressed the impulse. They continued to stand at the railing near each other in the mild night air, each unwilling to end the quiet nearness to the other.

Hank arranged to have all their meals delivered to their cabin. In the evening he stepped out while Maria changed into the night dress given her by Mrs. Kopp. She lay down, feeling guilty but at the same time enjoying the luxury of the large bed. When Hank reentered the cabin, he took off his boots and took one of the two blankets off the bed and then stretched out on the rag rug.

Before Maria awakened in the morning, Hank had left the cabin. He returned an hour later, after Maria had dressed. He had in his hand a day-old copy of the *Louisiana Gazette*. He sat down at the desk and read aloud,

Wanted, a runaway female metif slave by the name of Maria. Has light hair and green eyes and skin as white as any white woman.

Hank thought that he had never read such an inadequate description—her skin was the color of thick, creamy milk, more beautiful than any woman he had ever seen, and her eyes weren't just green. They seemed to look into his soul, making him wonder if she could read his feelings. He cleared his throat and continued,

"Eighteen years of age. Speaks fluent German. Wearing a blue dress when last seen in New Orleans. Reward of five hundred dollars for her return. Contact Mr. Lafayette Breaux of Caldwell County, Louisiana or Mr. Theophilis Freeman of New Orleans."

Hank put the paper down. "I think this information has or will appear in every paper from New Orleans to Baton Rouge, maybe even as far north as Memphis. I'm sure it's best if you continue to stay in the cabin throughout the journey. If I'm asked why you haven't left the cabin, I will tell them you are not feeling well."

"And if they ask if I have something contagious?"

"I will tell them you are in a family way."

Maria's complexion grew red with embarrassment, but she nodded in agreement.

***

As Hank and Maria and the other passengers boarded the *Southern Belle* in New Orleans, the unshaven deputy watching the passengers made notes on the handbill he carried in his hand. He scrawled, *Young woman in lavender dress and bonnet, on the arm of man in buckskin. Has green eyes. Might be her.* A few minutes later, he wrote below that, *Young woman in dark blue dress accompanied by two other women.* After watching another thirty-five passengers board, he wrote, *Young woman with yellow hair in black dress. Could be her.*

When the warning whistle sounded, he boarded the boat and found the captain. "Captain, you have three young women on this boat, and one of them may be a runaway slave. I need to know where they're going."

The captain, looking startled, responded defensively, "I have only one passenger who has brought a slave on board, and that is the servant of a large plantation owner who is traveling to Natchez. I am well acquainted with the gentleman and his man."

"The woman we are looking for is as white as any woman you will ever meet and has light hair and green eyes. She's about eighteen or nineteen years of age, and her master says she's a metif. There's a substantial reward for her capture. I'm sure Mr. Freeman will pay you well for information as to the destination of the three women in question so he can determine if one of them is the woman he wants."

After hearing the description, the captain answered, "The young woman in the blue dress is traveling to Vicksburg with her mother and sister. They've made the trip before, so I can verify that she is not the woman you are seeking. The young woman in black is from Memphis and was in the city for the funeral of a relative. The husband of the young woman in lavender introduced them as Mr. and Mrs. Hanks. Her husband has the appearance of a Kaintuck and carries a bowie knife." The captain rubbed his chin for a moment and finally said, "If memory serves me correctly, they bought tickets to Memphis, but I'm not holding up the boat to give you time to go poking into the business of my passengers." The captain gave the signal to the crew to take in the gangplank.

The man wearing the deputy badge turned on his heel, stepping quickly down the gangplank, and left the boat. He walked briskly down the levee and out of sight. Four crewmen lifted the gangplank onto the deck while a man on the levee freed the ropes that held the boat in place. The captain moved to the pilot house and pulled on the chain, making the steam whistle sound again. The paddlewheel began to turn in reverse, pulling the boat out into the river. After it had cleared the other vessels tied up at the levee, the great wheel paused as the crew shifted the gear levers. Then it began its forward rotation, pushing the boat up the river against the current.

The deputy hurried to the French Quarter where he located the Freeman mansion across from the St. Louis Hotel. There he was ushered in by a black servant and offered a chair in the ornate parlor. Twenty minutes later, he left with several silver pieces in his hand, some of which were meant for the captain of the *Southern Belle,* but the captain would never see them.

Less than an hour later, two large, rough-looking men arrived at the Freeman mansion in response to a note carried to them by one of the household servants. One was muscled and dark haired, the other shorter and sandy haired with a scar above his left eye. Like the deputy, they were invited in. Within less than twenty minutes, they left with money in hand and instructions to take the next boat upriver to Memphis and locate the young woman called Mrs. Hanks, thought to be the runaway slave called Maria. The next boat left in four hours.

CHAPTER 8

The Journey Upriver

As Hank wrapped up in a blanket and lay down on the floor the second evening, Maria expressed concern for his comfort. "Hank, how can you sleep like that?"

He laughed and answered, "I've spent many nights for the last four years sleeping on the deck of one of my boats. This isn't much different."

As she prepared to blow out the flame in the lamp, Maria paused and studied his face after he had closed his eyes. He had a strong jaw, and when he closed his deep blue eyes, it seemed that he had drawn shades over the windows of his soul. She blew out the lamp and lay back on the bed.

The next morning, after they ate breakfast in the cabin, Hank left and returned with a day-old copy of the *Louisiana Courier*. Sitting down at the desk, he said, "Here's an article of interest. Its headline reads:

> *Case of Sally Miller before State Supreme Court.*
> *Having lost her case before the Second District Court in New Orleans, the plaintiff, a young woman called Sally Miller, has appealed her case to the State Supreme Court. It will be heard by Chief Justice Francois-Xavier Martin, sitting in concert with four additional justices. She has been seeking to establish that she is not a slave but rather a former redemptioner from Germany who arrived in this country as a small child. She continues to be represented by Mr. Christian Roselius and Mr. Wheelock S. Upton, who were engaged by and their fees paid by members of the German community.*
> *The respondents in the case are Mr. Louis Belmondi and Mr. John Fitz Miller, who continue to be represented by prominent New*

Orleans attorney John Randolph Grymes, best known for his defense of the gentleman buccaneer Jean Lafitte and his brother, Pierre, on charges of piracy some years ago.

Sally Miller was recently held for a week in the Cabildo, as her present owner, Mr. Belmonti, has accused her of being a runaway. She was released under a thousand-dollar bond posted by Mr. Francis Schuber, a prominent member of the German community. She has been residing with Mr. and Mrs. Schuber since her case was first filed before the court.

The article continued, and Maria sat very still as she listened. When Hank had finished reading, she spoke quietly, "I wish her success."

Hank put the paper down on the desk and said, "I spoke at length with the captain, who has agreed for a small sum to take us beyond Memphis to a small settlement at the mouth of the Hatchie River. He does not normally stop there, but there is a pier large enough to accommodate the *Southern Belle*. He said that there we can get a small shallow-draught steamboat that will take us up the Hatchie to Bolivar, Tennessee. From there, the river grows too shallow for a steamboat, but we can get a flatboat to take us farther upriver to Rienzi, Mississippi. It's only a few miles overland from there to the East Fork of the Tombigbee River where we will hire another flatboat to take us downriver to Aberdeen in Monroe County. I am sorry that it will be a journey of some inconvenience."

"You have traveled that way before?" Maria asked.

"Yes, a few years ago."

When the steamboat reached Memphis, Hank walked the length of the levee and found a small shop that sold newspapers as well as baked goods. He obtained a paper and read it carefully, finding what he had hoped would not be there. It contained an ad much as the other papers had, offering five hundred dollars for the return of Maria to Lafayette Breaux. He sat on a barrel on the pier for an hour, weighing the possible choices he and Maria could make. After an hour, the captain pulled the cord on the steam whistle that announced the *Southern Belle*'s imminent departure. He rose and boarded the boat with long strides, returning to the cabin certain that they had made the best choice.

"You were gone a long while. Is something the matter?" Maria asked nervously from where she sat by the desk.

"I left the boat to find a copy of the local newspaper." He handed her the paper, folded open to the ad placed by Lafayette Breaux, offering the reward for her return.

As she read it, her face blanched. "He follows us everywhere. Maybe I will never get away from him." The fear and frustration in her voice made her words choke off in her throat.

Not quite sure what to do, Hank rose from the old chair and paced the cabin as he spoke. "I have a plan that might help put this behind us."

She sat up and wiped her eyes with the back of her hand. "What can we do?"

"Do you have another name? I remember many of the German girls I knew had three names or more. Do you?"

"My Christian name is Maria Elizabetha Caroline Marguerite Schumann."

"Did anyone else know your full name?"

"Only Mr. and Mrs. Wentz. I was sold as Maria Schumann to my second master, and Lafayette Breaux insisted that I was sold to him simply as Maria."

Hank nodded and said, "For the present, you will be Caroline—or would you rather be Elizabeth?"

"No, Caroline is a beautiful name and not heard so often as Elizabeth. I will be glad to be called Caroline."

The steamboat reached the settlement in northern Arkansas across the Mississippi River from the mouth of the Hatchie River the next day, two hours before the midday meal. Maria, whom Hank now called Caroline, was relieved to leave the confines of the cabin.

Hank nodded to the captain, and Maria dropped a small curtsey as they thanked him for a smooth journey. He solicitously asked Maria, "Are you feeling better, ma'am? I know when my wife was in a family way, she felt right peaked for weeks." She nodded her thanks at his concern and colored slightly but said nothing.

He pointed out a two-story frame building on the single street of the little settlement and said, "The boat on the Hatchie may not follow a regular schedule, so you will need to get a room at the boarding house down the street until it arrives." He tipped his captain's cap and offered his hand to help Maria as she stepped onto the gangplank.

The short, rotund landlady, Mrs. Wilson, was as thrilled to see her guests as she would be if they were long-lost relatives. "Come in, come in. You may have any room in the house, as I have no other guests at this time. When would you like supper? I'll take you up to the best room in the house." Without waiting for an answer she led them up the stairs to a bedroom at the front of the second floor of the weathered clapboard building. "Supper is usually at about six o'clock in the evening, but if you're hungry, I can have it ready earlier—or later if you prefer." Then she asked, "What are your names? I will need them for my registration book." Then she coughed modestly and added, "The room with supper and breakfast is seventy-five cents a night."

Hank answered and said, "I am Mr. Hanks and this is my wife, Caroline, and seventy-five cents is surely a reasonable amount to pay for your hospitality."

At the dinner table that night, Hank asked, "Do you have any idea when the boat that goes up the Hatchie to Bolivar will be here?"

"Well, could be tomorrow or might be two or three days after that. Captain O'Reily doesn't keep a very regular schedule. Do you have kin in Bolivar? Not much reason for traveling upriver to that little town unless you got kin there." The landlady seldom waited long enough for her questions to be answered, so Hank made no attempt. She continued, "I don't get much company, so forgive me if I talk too much. 'Bout the only way my guests can keep me quiet is to have me play my pump organ in the parlor. Would you like me to play for you?"

Maria spoke for the first time since they had arrived. "I would love to hear you play the organ. That would be a special kindness on your part."

Leaving the dishes on the table, the landlady led them into the parlor, and for a half hour she pumped vigorously with both feet and played Irish melodies on the wheezy instrument. When she grew tired, Maria asked, "Could I play a little? Some years ago I played the pianoforte."

"Of course, my dear. I would like to hear you play."

Hank's face wore a somewhat surprised look as Maria sat down hesitantly on the little stool. She seemed afraid that this old acquaintance, to whom she was being reintroduced, might not know her. Then she began to pump with her feet, just as the landlady had done. Cautiously, her fingers moved over the keys, slowly and then increasing in familiarity. After she finished, she sat without moving, looking at the keyboard of the organ as if she had just learned that her old friend still knew and loved her.

Hank said gently, "Please, play some more."

For a half hour more, Maria played familiar German folk songs and finally finished with one of Beethoven's emotional sonatas. Only occasionally did her fingers miss the right notes. She played as though she had only been away from the keyboard for a few days, rather than many years. Then she said quietly, "The music is so comforting." She turned to the landlady and said, "Thank you. Now I hope you will forgive me, but I am very tired. I think I would like to go to our room. We do thank you for your hospitality."

When Hank closed the door behind them, he said, "It was a pleasure to listen to you play."

She answered simply, "Things learned in childhood seem to stay with us for a lifetime. I have not touched an instrument since I left the household of Mr. and Mrs. Wentz."

Hank again stretched out on the floor, and after he closed his eyes, many thoughts tumbled through his mind. *I would love to have such music fill the home I hope to own someday. How wonderful it would be if it were Maria who played that music.* He realized that the thought of spending his life as a boatman had lost its appeal. He smiled at the thought and promised himself that if the time ever came when it was within his power, he would obtain an organ or a pianoforte for her.

By this time, Maria had closed her eyes and was asleep. She was no longer nervous about his presence in the room as they slept—it had actually become quite comforting to her.

CHAPTER 9
The Shasta

The next morning, Hank and Maria came down the stairs to find four large men eating breakfast in the dining room. One wore a well-worn captain's uniform and gray chin whiskers. The other three were muscled, bearded crewmen. The landlady made introductions. "This is Captain O'Reily and the crew members of the steamboat *Shasta*. These good men arrived last evening after you retired and are determined to leave before midday today on their return trip up the Hatchie. I hope that meets with your approval, Mr. Hanks," the landlady said as she motioned Hank and Maria to seats at the table.

"We couldn't be more pleased. Captain, do you have room for two passengers?" Hank asked.

"Aye, and glad to have ye both," he responded, the sound of Ireland in his speech. "If ye will meet us down at the pier before the sun gets too high in the sky, we'll load yer bags and trunks. How far up the river do ye expect to go?"

"All the way to Bolivar on your boat. Then we hope to hire a flatboat to take us all the way to Rienzi. Do you know anyone who will do that?"

"Aye, my sister's husband is a good boatman. We can get ye both to Rienzi." After he swallowed a mouthful of sausage and eggs, he continued, "The *Shasta* is a small boat, so we don't have the niceties of the big boats. Ye'll need to have the landlady here pack ye a basket with food for at least three days, or ye'll be mighty hungry by the time we get to Bolivar. We do have a small stove, so ye can bring grits or eggs or things like that to cook."

For a dollar the landlady was glad to pack the basket that Maria and Hank had brought from New Orleans. Carrying it and the carpetbag, Hank and Maria walked down to the pier. The boat was much smaller than the *Southern Belle,* about fifty feet long, eighteen feet in the beam, and only a single deck. It was badly in need of paint, and it was evident that the paddlewheel in the stern had been repaired several times.

The captain approached Hank where he and Maria stood and said, "We need every strong man to help us load wood for the boiler. From the look of yer buckskin clothes, I'd guess that ye're no stranger to hard work."

After an hour of loading wood from a large pile that had been cut and stacked near the pier, the crew had the fire under the boiler hot enough that the sound of the steam whistle resonated across the river. The paddle wheel began to turn, and both Hank and Maria stood on the deck and watched the scenery as the steamboat made its way up the mouth of the Hatchie River.

The captain left the wheelhouse and stood near Hank, lighting a corncob pipe. "Right now, she doesn't seem to be makin' much headway, but as the boiler gets a better head of steam, we'll move a bit faster." He took a long draw on the pipe and continued, "Ye ever been this way before?"

"Not for a few years," Hank answered.

"Well, come with me, and I'll show ye both to the cabin." The cabin was small, with one straight-backed chair, a narrow bed, and a worn rag rug on the floor.

After Hank put the carpetbag on the bed, Maria asked the captain, "Could you show us where the stove is so I can fix us something to eat?"

"Aye, lass, I'm glad to do that." The small wood-burning stove was bolted to the floor in a little room behind the wheelhouse. A few battered pans and tin plates hung from hooks on the wall, and a worn, tobacco-stained table took up half the room. "Make yerself at home. There's the wood box. Feel free to build a fire in the stove. When ye're done, just wash the pans with river water." He added as an afterthought, "There's usually a poker game in here about eight o'clock each evening, so I recommend that ye get yer supper cooking done well before that. Mr. Hanks, ye're welcome to join the game." He then nodded and moved through the doorway to the wheelhouse, leaving them alone to fix their meal.

Maria boiled some grits and added some chunks of ham the landlady had furnished. It was a simple meal but adequate. They were the only passengers on the little steamboat. The crates and barrels of freight roped to the deck near the stern appeared to be the main purpose of the trip up the river.

A continuing series of oxbows and switchbacks slowed their travel on the river. Eventually, the water lost its brown color as the silt it carried lessened. Willows and oak trees hung over the water, with clumps of needle palms nearly hiding the banks on both sides. Hank brought the straight-backed chair from the cabin onto the deck and invited Maria to sit in it. Then he moved a barrel from the stern and put it next to the chair. He sat next to her, and the two of them were quiet as they watched the trees slide by, comfortable in the silence.

As the shadows lengthened, a mist like thin and tattered linen began to form over the water, reaching out as if to wrap the vessel in a soft blanket. The captain stepped out of the wheelhouse and tapped his pipe on the rail, knocking the dottle out of the bowl and into the water. He pulled a tobacco pouch from his vest pocket and started to fill the pipe again, pressing the loose tobacco in with his thumb.

Trying to hide her nervousness, Maria asked, "How will you pilot the boat if the mist gets thicker?"

"Lass, I have been up and down this river so many times I could do it in my sleep. Don't worry yer pretty head about it." After standing with them for a few minutes, he returned to the wheelhouse, leaving a backwash of pipe smoke and confidence.

But Maria did worry, and though Hank did not say anything about his doubts, if he had been asked, he would have admitted his concern. After Maria had climbed into bed, they felt the vibrations from the engine stop, so she arose and pattered with bare feet to the door. The mist had become thick enough that she could see neither the bow nor the stern. The boat engine was quiet, and the vessel had been tied to the trunk of a large hickory tree that leaned out over the river. The gentle tug of the current was all either of them could feel. The hoot of an owl floated across the water.

Hank rose from his blanket on the floor and stood behind Maria. "I think the captain has met his match in this fog. This is thick enough to stuff a pillow." Maria was very much aware of his presence behind her. The dampness of the mist had begun to penetrate her night dress, and she began to shiver.

Putting his hand on her right arm and gently pulling her away from the doorway, Hank said, "You had better get out of the doorway. The fog and night air will give you a chill." For several minutes after she had obediently climbed back into bed, she could feel the touch of his hand where it had warmed her skin.

The gauzy morning sunlight melted the fog into ragged tendrils moving with the current above the water. The fires were stoked under the boiler, and once more the *Shasta* pushed its way up the river.

The captain left the piloting of the boat to one of the crew and joined Hank and Maria at the rail again. After some casual comments, he said, "Now is a good time for ye to be fixin' breakfast. The water gets a bit rougher about an hour up the river."

Late in the afternoon of the third day, the little steamboat docked at Bolivar. The captain insisted on taking his passengers home to his wife to spend the night. "We don't have a hotel in Bolivar, but we do have a spare bedroom," he said, laughing. After dinner, he invited his brother-in-law, Jack Gibbs, to meet them. The evening ended when Hank shook hands with Jack, who had agreed to take them the rest of the way to Rienzi by flatboat.

The next morning the basket was filled with bread, cheese, cured ham, boiled eggs, and a few apples from the previous season's crop, kindly furnished by the captain's wife for seventy-five cents. Hank, Maria, Jack Gibbs, and Jack's fifteen-year-old son, Josh, climbed into the flatboat. It was a small boat, about twelve feet long and six feet wide. Jack handed Hank a long pole and said, "Since we are going against the current, it will be slow going for a while, and we will have to pole the boat the whole distance, but that's no problem when we get upriver to where it widens and slows. When we get tired, we'll tie up to rest."

As Jack poled the boat out into the river, he said, "You and Josh will pole from the left, and I'll pole the right. Just put your pole in the mud of the river bottom and walk your way to the stern, and then do it all over again." With a steady rhythm, they alternated. Hank started, and when he had reached the middle of the boat, Jack put his pole into the river.

After three hours, Jack tied up to rest for a half hour in the shade of a cluster of spruce trees. The Queen Anne's Lace blossoms on the banks bobbed in the light breeze, and the faint scent of honeysuckle wafted on the breeze.

Maria sat on the carpetbag. As the boat rose and fell gently in the water, she reached into the basket and offered each of the men something to eat. "How long will it take before we reach Rienzi, Mr. Gibbs?"

"At the rate we are going, tomorrow night. The current lessens farther upriver, and we will make better time this afternoon and tomorrow."

Hesitantly, Maria asked, "Where will we spend the night?"

"When it gets near dark, we will tie up in a quiet place where the river widens and sleep like babies in a rocking cradle."

"Oh."

Mr. Gibbs rose and brushed off the few crumbs of the bread he had eaten, as if that would make his rumpled, sweaty clothing more presentable. "Well, it's time to get moving," he said. So the three men began to pole the boat again with a steady and monotonous rhythm, the task growing easier as the river widened and the current slowed.

That evening the mist began to form over the water, imperceptibly at first, but before the twilight had turned to darkness, it hung around them like steam above warm water in a cold room. Jack and his son laid down in the boat and within a minute were asleep.

Maria tried to settle herself with her back against the side of the boat, but she could not hide the fact that she was shivering from the cool dampness. Hank sat down next to her and said, "Do you have a shawl or something in the carpetbag to keep you warm?" Glad to be reminded, she rummaged around in the bag, finally pulling out the yellow shawl.

Hank helped her put it around her shoulders and then said with unexpected tenderness, "A wife should be able to use her husband's shoulder as a place to put her head." Then he cleared his throat as if he had embarrassed himself. Gratefully, Maria smiled, and he gently put his arm around her to help keep her warm. Within a few minutes she had stopped shivering and both were asleep, his head leaning lightly against the top of hers.

In the morning, as the color of the sunrise faded, both Maria and Hank stood, carefully stretching stiff muscles but avoiding each other's eyes. Both were somewhat embarrassed by the intimacy of the night as they had slept leaning against each other. As the last remnants of the mist melted away, Maria handed out a simple breakfast. The rhythm of the day began again, but the river had widened into a slow-moving wetland, a natural reflecting pool with an almost indiscernible current. Clumps of willows and an occasional shaggy-barked cyprus tree made little islands that rose above the water. Bunches of giant blue irises grew on the heaps of soil surrounded by the water, as though an artist had made them bloom with a brush too full of paint.

Maria watched the egrets and herons as their stiltlike legs took them from one small island to another. The grebes, so ungainly on land, swam a water ballet both on top of and below the water.

"It's beautiful here," Maria said quietly, as if she did not want to disturb the stillness of the air and water or alarm the warblers singing in the morning sun.

"You're right; it's pretty," Jack said as he studied the river, "but for all that, we have to watch out for snags and shifting sand bars—and snakes. We're getting close to the village of Pocahontas. When we see it, we'll know we're almost at the Mississippi-Tennessee line."

That evening as the twilight faded, the lights of Rienzi appeared. After they tied up the boat to the pier, Jack Gibbs pointed out the only boarding house in the little community. As Hank paid him, Jack said, "Best of luck to you, Mr. Hanks, and to you, Mrs. Hanks." He touched the brim of his hat and put his hand on his son's shoulder. They walked over to the public house on the single dusty main street without looking back.

As they sat at supper in the boarding house dining room, Hank asked the two other guests and the landlord if they knew of someone who would help them go overland to the headwaters of the East Fork of the Tombigbee River. The landlord, who was standing at the doorway to the kitchen with his arms folded across his broad middle, answered, "Sam Jackson's boy can do that for you. Sam runs the pub across the street. He would probably want a fair amount, maybe as much as three or four dollars, but he's just about the only man around here who would do it."

Hank raised one eyebrow and asked, "Why is he the only man who would do it? Is it dangerous?"

"Nah, everybody else has to earn a living. Sam's Boy don't know what regular work is."

"How old is he? Is he just a boy?"

"Nah, he must be near forty, but sometimes a nickname sticks. He's always been Sam's Boy."

After Hank and Maria were shown to a room on the second floor, Hank walked over to the public house and asked for Sam's Boy. The older man behind the bar, who was evidently Sam, pointed out an unshaven man with a shock of black hair sitting at a table playing poker. Hank approached him and asked, "I need someone to lead me overland to the East Fork of the Tombigbee where I can get a flatboat."

He was obviously unhappy about being interrupted but finally laid his cards face down and pushed his chair away from the table. He stood up and faced Hank. "Yeah, I can take you there. Why should I?"

The bargain was struck for four dollars.

"It's a long walk, so bring enough food for a couple of days and meet me here in the morning."

"What time?"

"Sunrise." With that, Sam's Boy returned to the poker game.

***

When their boat arrived at Memphis, the ruffians disembarked and began a search for Mr. and Mrs. Hanks. After interrogating the desk clerk at each of the four hotels in the city, they started to visit the boarding houses. After a full day of searching, they concluded that in all likelihood Hank and Maria had not left the boat in Memphis, so they bought passage on a northbound steamship to Caruthersville, the next regular stop on the river. There, they searched the two hotels, paying the desk clerks to permit them to see the registration books. Returning to the Caruthersville Hotel, they rented a room and ordered dinner.

The biggest man struck up a conversation with the desk clerk. "Are there any other places a steamboat could stop to board passengers or let them off between here and Memphis?" As he talked, he played with several gold coins, dropping them one by one from his right hand into his left. The young clerk's eyes were on the gold coins.

"I, uh, I heard that the *Southern Belle* stopped down at Wilson, the little settlement across the river from the mouth of the Hatchie, two, maybe three days ago. The big boats don't usually stop there."

"When will the next boat stop here on its way south?"

"In the morning, sometime before noon."

The big man flipped a coin at the young man and grinned at his partner. As the young man walked away, he said, "I think we got 'em, Dag."

"I think you may be right, Lodder." The two men ate dinner with enthusiasm.

When they boarded the steamboat the next morning, Lodder found the captain and offered him a substantial sum of money, obtaining the desired promise that he would make the extra stop at the dock in the little settlement of Wilson. They drank hard and long into the night in celebration of their good luck. The porter had to bang on the cabin door to wake them in the morning when the steamboat docked.

When they left the boat, both ruffians walked carefully to the boarding house, as though their heads were full of broken glass. There they spent two hours sleeping away their intoxication. At lunchtime, Dag interrogated the landlady. "Any guests here lately, other than folks you know?"

She nodded as she set a platter of chicken on the table. As they ate, he pursued the matter. "A husband and wife been here lately? She's a pretty thing with light hair. He looks like a Kaintuck, in buckskins."

The landlady paused and answered, "Why, yes, I think you must be describing Mr. and Mrs. Hanks. Such a nice young couple. Do you know them?"

He answered, "Yes, she's . . . uh—she's my sister."

The landlady looked at him for a moment and said, "Well, there certainly isn't much family resemblance."

When she returned to the dining room with a slice of pound cake for each man for dessert, she added, "I'm sure you can catch up with them at Bolivar. They took the *Shasta* up the Hatchie River a couple of days ago. I think Mr. Hanks might have family or friends there."

The two men waited impatiently for another day before the *Shasta* returned. Then they purchased passage to Bolivar. The mate commented to the captain, "Seems that we're seein' more passengers in the last week than we usually see in a month."

The captain removed the pipe from his mouth and said, "But I like the looks of these two a whole lot less than the two we had a few days ago. I wonder what the sudden attraction is in Bolivar."

CHAPTER 10
Traveling Companions

Sam's Boy, whose name was actually Sam Jackson Junior, walked hard and fast as he led Hank and Maria through the thick woods of northern Mississippi. The hills, though not steep, were demanding at the speed they were moving.

The previous evening Hank and Sam had settled on a payment of two dollars when they began and two more dollars when they reached the Tombigbee River. They left at sunrise, anticipating that with luck they might reach the East Fork at about dark.

They had paused to eat something at midday when Sam suddenly sprang to his feet and whispered, "There's a deer— maybe I can catch us some venison." He grabbed his rifle and disappeared into the trees. He was gone for some time, so Maria took the two canteens the men had been carrying and made her way to the nearby stream to fill them. She climbed the little rise that separated the shady place where they had sat on the ground to eat and the stream that tumbled down the other side. After she filled the canteens, she sat down and removed her shoes. Taking off the precious pair of stockings given her by Mrs. Kopp, she put her feet in the water, lay back on the pine-needle-covered ground, and put her arm over her eyes.

She was not sure how long she had been asleep when she felt a man's hands on her body and his breath on her neck. Awakening, she fought to push him away and tried to pull his hands off her body. Sam's voice whispered threateningly in her ear, "Just give me a kiss, and shut up and enjoy it." He tried to press his mouth to hers. She threw her head back and screamed. As she scratched at his face, he put his hand over her mouth and said in her ear, "Shut up or I'll hurt you." She bit his fingers hard, forcing him to pull his hand away. She screamed again and tried to rise to her feet. He took hold of her arm, spun her around, and punched her. She dropped, stunned.

Hank roared like a lion. Out of nowhere, he seemed to fly through the air, impacting Sam like a boulder off a mountainside. As the men wrestled on the ground, Maria sat up and looked around. She could see Sam's rifle lying about ten feet from her. Crawling over to it, she picked it up.

"I should cut your throat, you animal," Hank yelled at Sam, who was pinned to the ground by Hank's knee on his chest. The knife was at Sam's throat.

"No, no, Hank. Don't kill him," Maria screamed. "Please let him go. Don't hurt him on my account."

Hank paused for a minute, his knee still pressing Sam's chest hard, took a breath, and then stood up and returned the knife to the sheath. He pulled Sam up by the front of his shirt and had a tight grip on his arm. "Consider yourself a lucky man. I should leave your body here for the hawks to clean up." Hank pushed him ahead of them until they reached the spot where they had eaten an hour earlier. Hank took the rifle from Maria and emptied the cartridges from it. Then he searched the pouch Sam had worn over his shoulder. Removing the cartridges he found in it, he put them in his pocket. "Get out. Get back to your pa's bar where a barfly like you feels at home. We'll find our own way." He threw the rifle at Sam and waited for him to move. With a hate-filled face, the beaten man turned and started back down the trail.

When he had disappeared in the trees, Maria said quietly, "I think we have made an unforgiving enemy."

"You're right about that. We may come to regret that I didn't kill him when I could have." Still trying to control his anger, Hank said, "Follow me. We'll continue southeast until we find the river. We can do it from here without him." The trail, though not well marked, was sufficiently visible. Hank was still seething inside. The entire incident had forced him to confront his increasing feelings for Maria, and the thought of that base and crude man putting his hands on her made him want to strike out.

He couldn't bear the thought of another man taking Maria from him.

When they sat down to rest in the late June afternoon heat and humidity, Maria said quietly, "I have not thanked you, Hank, for saving me. I am grateful. I know I can never repay you. It seems that I continue to get further and further into your debt." She paused and added, "Thank you for not killing Sam. I could not stand it if you took the sin of murder upon your soul for me."

Hank was not sure what to say, so he said nothing. He thought to himself that if ever there were a man deserving of being removed from the face of the earth, it was Sam's Boy, but seeing the gratitude in Maria's eyes, he was glad he had not killed him.

She continued almost as if she were talking to herself. "The future seems so dark, as if it's somehow shrouded in fog. I don't know where I'm going or if I will ever be really free." She paused for a moment and looked at something in the distance only she could see and then added, "I wonder if God knows where I am."

Hank mused, "All is light to God, but sometimes he lets us walk in the shadows for a while. Sometimes that is how we must learn His will." Hank continued firmly but almost in a whisper, "He knows where you are." He stood, giving the signal that it was time to move on.

As the sun was setting, they found a cabin with a light in the window. When Hank knocked, an old man's voice said nervously, "Who are you, and what do you want?"

"My name is Hank Schroeder, and I'm trying to get to Aberdeen to locate friends by the name of Crosby or Smithson. Do you know where I can get a flatboat?"

A man opened the door and said, "I got a flatboat. In the morning I can take you down the river for a dollar or two. I can't offer you much hospitality tonight, but your lady can sleep with my woman and you can have the floor."

***

When Hank and Maria got off the boat in Aberdeen, Maria held on to his arm tightly with both hands and said, "Do you know people here who will help us?"

"It's been a few years, but I think there will be some who remember me."

A variety of boats of all sizes were tied up at the wharf, bringing cotton and tobacco for shipment farther down the river. Aberdeen was a large and prosperous city in the middle of cotton and tobacco country with many two-story, well-built frame homes and mercantile shops. The population appeared to be evenly divided between black and white.

They started down the main street and occasionally asked someone where they could find a hotel. The third man Hank spoke to stopped and looked at him and then said, "Well, if it isn't Hank Schroeder." He reached out, and as they shook hands, the man said, "It's me, Allen Smithson. Don't you remember me?"

"Allen! Of course, I remember you."

"Is this beautiful young lady by any chance your wife?" Without waiting for an answer, he added, "You will both come home with me for supper. It's good to see you again. I would be in big trouble with Letitia if I didn't bring you home to be fed."

As the three of them walked toward West Jefferson Street where the Smithsons lived, the men talked and laughed, neither apparently noticing Maria's nervous silence. She was wondering just how long the charade would have to continue.

CHAPTER 11
Friends

All the way up the Hatchie River on the *Shasta* Dag and Lodder laughed boisterously, and one or the other consistently beat the other crew members at the evening game of poker. They were suspected of cheating, but no one could catch them at it. The captain loathed both men in a very short while and regretted ever admitting to them that Mr. and Mrs. Hanks had traveled on his boat to Bolivar. Though Dag claimed to be related to the young wife, he sensed that they meant no good. He refused to reveal any more information to the two ruffians.

When the boat docked in Bolivar, they prowled the town and finally found Jack Gibbs, who was willing to take them farther up the river to Rienzi. Hesitantly, he answered the questions for the rough-looking men. "Yeah, I took a young couple upriver to Rienzi. You say that's where you want to go?"

In Rienzi they asked around for a guide until they found Sam's Boy in his father's saloon. What the captain of the *Shasta* would not reveal, Sam's Boy was glad to tell them. By the next morning, they had hired him to take them to the East Fork of the Tombigbee.

As they hiked the hills, Sam's Boy said, "You better take him from behind or he'll cut your throat with that Arkansas toothpick he carries." Then he tried to make a bargain with the two men. "If you'll promise me an hour with the woman, I'll stay and help you take him down when you find him." His offer was brushed aside.

When they reached the river, Lodder and Dag sent Sam's Boy to find them someone to take them down the river in a flatboat. After finding the only flatboat on the river for a mile in any direction, they offered to pay the owner five dollars to take them as far as the couple that had hired him a week earlier had traveled.

"Well, that will be all the way to Aberdeen," the man responded.

***

When the Smithson family sat down to eat dinner, Hank introduced Maria. Both he and Maria felt more comfortable using her first name now that the journey was complete.

"How long are you going to stay, Hank? What are you going to do?" Letitia asked.

"Well, I'm hoping to find a farmer who needs a strong back. Do you think I can get a job here in Aberdeen?" he responded.

The conversation went on until late in the evening, and as they finished their dessert and the children left the table to help their mother with the dishes, Allen made an offer, "I know you could get a position on one of the big cotton plantations around here, Hank. There is always a need for a good overseer. But I think you and Maria would be happier here in town. If you are willing to run my mercantile, you can live above it and attend church with us, and your children can grow up with ours."

Maria colored a bright pink. The two men shook hands on the deal. Letitia Smithson spoke as she came back into the room, "I've moved the three girls out of their room so you can stay with us tonight."

Hank slept on the floor again, and in the morning at breakfast, Allen said, "As soon as you're finished eating, we'll go down to the store."

The mercantile was just four blocks from the Smithson home. It had three small, dusty rooms on the second floor that were used for storage. There were a few pieces of unused furniture. Allen said, "I think we can fix these rooms up for you and make you comfortable. I've been trying to run the store and the farm and haven't done much of a job at either. You will be a blessing."

Mr. and Mrs. Schroeder, as they were known, slipped quickly into the rhythm of life as citizens of Aberdeen, Mississippi. Hank took to wrapping himself in a quilt and sleeping on the rag rug on the floor of the little apartment's sitting room. Neither of them said anything, but both seemed to be in quiet agreement that since there was another room, it was more appropriate for him to leave the bedroom for Maria's use.

Former acquaintances came by the store to shake Hank's hand and meet the woman they believed was his attractive young wife.

Absalom Dowdle and his wife, Sarah, lived just over the state line in Alabama, but Ab came by to introduce her when they were in town doing some shopping. George Gibson came to shake Hank's hand and then tried to hire him away to run his plantation. Hank responded, "I appreciate your offer, Mr. Gibson, but I don't think I want to do work where I must oversee slaves or redemptioners. A man's freedom is a precious thing."

George responded, "You be careful how you talk, Hank. Folks might get the idea that you're an abolitionist." To break the tension in the air, Hank slapped George on the back and laughed heartily until George laughed, too.

On Sunday Allen and Letitia sent their son Johnny with the wagon to bring Hank and his wife to the church meeting at ten o'clock that morning, if they chose to attend. As Hank helped Maria into the wagon, he said, "I don't believe I've ever been inside a church. This will be something new."

Hank still didn't get to attend a meeting in a church because this one was held in the large plantation house of Mother Elizabeth Crosby, who had been widowed two years earlier. Her son, William, was an old acquaintance of Hank's. He ran his mother's plantation, and he and his wife lived there with his mother and their young son. The house had a large parlor and an adjoining dining room, which allowed the men who addressed the group to stand at the foot of the central staircase and be heard by all. The French doors in each room opened onto a veranda, which ran along the sides of the house, permitting the breeze to push the warm air out.

The meeting was under the direction of Abraham O. Smoot, who had been sent from Nauvoo, Illinois, in February of that year to lead the Church members in that area. About sixty-five men, women, and children gathered for the religious services, and though they sang familiar songs, the doctrine taught was remarkably new to Hank and Maria.

When the two-hour meeting ended, Hank pulled Allen aside and asked, "What church is this? I've never been taught that God is my personal friend and that I can pray to Him without a priest or minister as an intermediary. And if I can get a copy of that Book of Mormon that some of the speakers taught from, I'd be in your debt."

Allen laughed and answered, "Of course. We'll be pleased to give you a copy." He continued, "This is The Church of Jesus Christ of Latter-day Saints. This religion was brought to us in 1841 by John Brown. He's a Tennessee man who came down from Illinois, where he was converted. He preached up a storm about this religion.

"We believe that you can't fix what was broken, as some religions have tried to do, so this religion was restored by God through a young man by the name of Joseph Smith. This is the religion that was taught in the primitive Church by the Savior without all the trappings added by man over the last two millennia." Allen was warming to his subject.

"Brother Brown liked Monroe County so much that he came back and married Elizabeth Crosby's daughter Betsy last year. I think he must have baptized at least sixty or seventy people in this area, both black and white. There are so many folks here in Monroe County that are kith or kin that the numbers keep growing."

Allen continued, "You met Mother Crosby's sons-in-law this morning before the meeting began—John Brown, Dan Thomas, John Bankhead, and Billy Lay. They just got back from Nauvoo a few days ago. They were up there for three months helping to finish the temple and defend the Saints. After the Prophet Joseph was murdered last year, the Illinois legislature repealed the city charter, so they no longer have an official police force. When he got back, Brother Brown told us about the Whistling and Whittling Brigade that the men organized to protect the city before the Prophet Joseph's death. They would work on the temple during the day and whistle and whittle in groups on the streets at night. I hear that the city was never safer than when they were on patrol." Allen laughed heartily. Then he continued, "I hear that John and some of the others are going to pack up and take their families back to Nauvoo in a couple of weeks to rejoin the Saints."

"So you folks call yourselves 'Saints'? All of you look like just regular folks to me." Hank chuckled.

"Well, none of us pretend that we're ready for sainthood, but we do call ourselves Saints because there are some who insist on calling us Mormonites. We would rather be known as Latter-day Saints. As you can see, we're just regular folks trying to live what the scriptures teach." Then he laughed and added, "And some are doing better than others in that regard."

For the next five weeks, Hank and Maria attended religious meetings on Sunday at Mother Crosby's plantation house and a midweek scripture study meeting at the Smithson home. Mother Crosby was always pleased to extend her hospitality to the members of the little church that she, her son William, and four of her five daughters and their husbands had joined. Hank always found his curiosity stimulated, and he and Maria would discuss everything they had heard Sunday afternoons when they arrived back at the little apartment above the store.

Hank took to reading the Book of Mormon with such a fascination and curiosity that Maria could hardly get him to attend to the customers who came into the store. As the days passed, Hank grew more and more comfortable as he ran the little store, and Maria began to relax enough to smile or laugh at the little jokes Hank or the others made. Hank loved her laugh. She didn't titter or giggle. She had a full, rich laugh, and it showed her white teeth in a full smile.

Twice a week she stood in the doorway of the little store and watched for the young man who brought copies of the biweekly *Aberdeen Daily Spectator* to sell. The continuing story of Sally Miller's legal fight for freedom always appeared on the front page. In the edition delivered the second week of July, Maria read that Mr. Wheelock S. Upton, Sally's lawyer, had based his appeal of the lower court decision upon an old case decided in 1810, *Adelle v. Beauregard.* That case dealt with a young mulatto woman who had been sent to New York by her owner to be educated and taught the ways of a young lady, but upon her return, she resisted the pressure to revert to her ways as a dutiful servant. She ran away and filed suit against her master, Monsieur Beauregard, seeking her freedom. At the trial in 1810, Adelle's lawyer had demanded that her master show proof that she was his slave. This he would not or could not do. The writer of the article speculated that perhaps Monsieur Beauregard was the girl's father and did not want that fact revealed.

Monsieur Beauregard's attorney insisted that if Adelle wanted to be set at liberty, it was her responsibility to prove that she had been born free or had been given her freedom at some point in her life.

The Superior Court of the Territory of Orleans had decided in Adelle's favor. The decision stated:

Persons of color may have descended from Indians on both sides, from a white parent, or mulatto parents in possession of their freedom. Considering how much probability there is in favor of the liberty of those persons, they ought not to be deprived of it upon mere presumption, more especially as the right of holding them in slavery, if it exists, is in most instances, capable of being satisfactorily proved.

Maria quietly put the newspaper article on Hank's plate so he could read it at supper that evening. Looking up at her as he finished the article, he said, "This is of great interest. It is an old case, but surely any court in the land would have to pay attention to it." He continued to eat for another few minutes and then said, as his fork paused between plate and mouth, "Does Lafayette Breaux have papers stating that you are a metif slave?"

"On my eighteenth birthday, when I asked him if he was going to honor my contract that said I would be free at that age, he laughed. But even though I asked to see the papers that he claimed made me a slave, he never permitted me to see them." Looking at Hank, she said quietly, "It occurred to me that perhaps he has no such papers." Hank continued to eat as he reread the article. As he put down the paper, he noticed that Maria had eaten little of her food. She finally rose and put most of the food on her plate in the trash.

"Is something the matter, Maria? You didn't eat very much supper last night, either."

"I just don't feel very well right now. I'm sure it will pass."

***

While Hank and Maria made friends among the Monroe County Saints and rapidly grew comfortable in the three rooms above the mercantile, Dag and Lodder made their way around the city asking for Mr. and Mrs. Hanks.

CHAPTER 12
Heartbreak and Comfort

Seven weeks after their arrival in Aberdeen, as Hank and Maria sat at Sunday dinner in the Smithson's two-story white clapboard house, Hank could not help but notice that a normally reserved Maria was unusually silent and did not smile or speak during the entire meal. When they returned to the little store, Hank took his time to make sure everything was secure before he came up the stairs to the little apartment. There, he found her sitting in the old rocking chair, her shoulders rounded and her hands in her lap, crying with sobs that shook her frame uncontrollably. For a moment, he wasn't sure what to do. He had seen Maria cry on a few previous occasions but never with such anguish.

"Maria, what troubles you?" She made no response to his question. He knelt beside the rocking chair so he could look into her face, but she turned away from him. He reached out and put his hand under her chin, turning her face to him. "Maria, tell me what troubles you."

She leaned over, putting her head against his shoulder, and cried with renewed grief. Between sobs, she said, "If God knows where I am, I hope He will take me home. I want to die."

Hank was not sure he had understood her. He said firmly, "Maria, tell me what is wrong. What is it that makes you grieve like this?"

She brushed away some of her tears with the back of her hand, sat up straight, and looked at him with eyes that began to overflow again. Taking a deep breath, she said, "I cannot deny my condition. I fear that I am with child."

Hank sat back on the floor as if he had been struck. After nearly a full minute, he exhaled a great breath and asked quietly, "How can you be with child? I have not touched you."

"I am with child by Lafayette Breaux." As she spoke, she pounded her knee with her fist. "I would rather be dead."

He rose from the floor and began to pace the room. "How can you know?"

"It has been ten weeks since he took me to his room and forced himself on me. I know."

Hank stopped pacing and said, "He forced himself on you." His jaw tightened and he whispered, "If I had known, I would have hunted him . . ." There he stopped and said no more.

She nodded and answered, "That was why I ran away and tried to cross the river. If you hadn't found me, I would have drowned." She added bitterly, "That would have been better for me." Both were quiet for a few minutes.

When she spoke again, her voice was flat. "I've tried to put away the memory of those nights. I've told myself over and over that he could not touch the freedom of my mind, that I would not allow what he did to me to change who I am—to wound me." She paused as she wiped away the tears on her cheeks and added, "But he not only wounded me—he took my hope, my future. If he finds me, not only will I have to go with him, but my child will, as well."

Hank remained quiet. He paused by the window that looked out upon the street where he stared unseeingly at the wagons and riders that passed in the growing darkness. After a few minutes, he reached a decision. In a quiet voice, he said, "We will be married as soon as possible. The child must have a name and a father, and you must have a husband."

Looking up at him, her voice still flat and hopeless, she said, "But you do not love me. No man should be shackled to a wife he does not love and who is carrying another man's child." She turned away from him. Her shoulders began to shake once more as she was racked by silent sobs.

Hank returned to where she sat, and, taking both her hands, he pulled her gently up out of the rocker. Looking into her gray-green eyes, he said tenderly, "Is my love of no value?" He paused.

"Do you think I could have aided you these past weeks without falling in love with you? I have loved you from the first time I saw you lying on the deck of my keelboat, nearly drowned. I felt then that God had sent me to love and rescue you. I am even more sure of that now." He paused again and then continued hesitantly, "I fear that you do not love me."

She put her arms around him just above his waist, and, laying her cheek against his chest, pulled him tightly to her. Her tears soaked the front of his shirt. "Oh, Hank, I do love you, and I have loved you since you saved me from the river. But how will you love me when I am big with a child that is not your own? No man could love a woman in that situation."

Wrapping her in his arms, he spoke quietly in her ear, "I know of one who did."

Leaning away from him to look up into his face, she said doubtfully, "Who was that?"

"A man called Joseph." Slowly the light of understanding lit her eyes, and she smiled with a quivering lower lip.

He pulled her to him again and held her. Her arms circled his neck. He kissed her, and she kissed him. As they clung to each other, she whispered, "Thank you, thank you." After they had stood together a little while, wrapped in each other's arms, she looked into his face and said with alarm, "If Lafayette Breaux finds out that I am with child, he will be even more determined to find me. The child will belong to him, if I can't prove that I am a free woman."

"He can't take you or the child if you belong to another man. We will take a boat down to Pickens in Alabama. It's on the river. There we can rent a wagon and go over to the county seat at Carrollton. There must be a minister or a justice of the peace who can marry us there. We'll go in the morning."

"Will such a marriage be legal?"

Looking down at her, he said firmly, "Yes. It is legal for two redemptioners who have gained their freedom to be married. Will you trust me in this matter?"

"I have trusted you this far. I have no reason not to continue to trust you."

That night Hank went downstairs, and, despite the fact that it was the Sabbath, he energetically cleaned and straightened the store until midnight. As his hands worked, so did his mind. A dozen questions formed in his mind as he stacked the bags of feed and reorganized the barrels. *Should we leave Aberdeen? Would we be better off to move east into Alabama or north into Tennessee? There's still undeveloped territory there, with only a few Creek or Cherokee Indians still around. Maybe we could go downriver to Mobile.* He immediately discounted that alternative, as that would take them farther into the Deep South with its customs of slavery. *No, we need to go north and eventually get out of these slave states.*

Maria lay in the bed, listening to the sounds below as Hank worked off his agitation. She wondered if what they had talked about would solve any of her problems or just make them more complicated. *Did I really feel his arms around me? Does he really love me—or does he only pity me?* With mingled thoughts of pleasure and pain, she finally drifted off to sleep.

Only after Maria had fallen into an exhausted sleep did Hank come up the stairs, wrap himself in a blanket, and lie down on the braided rag rug in the sitting room where he had slept for so many weeks. His thoughts kept him awake. He felt that he could be a good husband to Maria. He had been living that role for the last several weeks, but he wondered, *Am I ready to be a father to a child that is not my own? Can I forget that and put it behind me? Will Breaux continue to search for her? Can I protect her?* He silently vowed, *With God's help, I will be the kind of man I will need to be.*

In the morning, Hank rose early and walked to the Smithson's house to tell them that he needed to close the store for two days so he and Maria could take a short trip.

"Allen needs a day or two out of the sun," Letitia said. "He can watch the store for that long." Looking at Hank's concerned expression, she asked with a question in her voice, "Is there some problem we can help you with?"

Hank tipped his battered hat and said, "It is a matter of some importance. When we return, perhaps we can tell you about it." While Hank was gone, Maria packed the basket and the carpetbag that had made past journeys with them. As soon as he returned, they walked briskly to the waterfront, where they found a southbound steamboat leaving before noon.

In Pickens they found a stable, where they rented a team and wagon and made their way to Carrollton, a few miles east. There, they found the county courthouse and obtained a marriage license. With the guidance of the court clerk, they located a Methodist minister who was willing to leave his supper to perform the ceremony in the front room of his small frame home. While his wife played the pump organ and his next door neighbors served as witnesses, Pastor Williamson, still in his shirtsleeves, united Hans Martin Schroeder and Maria Elizabetha Caroline Marguerite Schumann in holy matrimony. When he said, "You may now kiss the bride," Hank took her in his arms, caressed her face, and gave her a long, tender kiss. When he released her, his bride's complexion was a bright pink, but her smile brightened the entire room.

When they returned to Pickens, they learned that the last boat of the day had left, so they found the only hotel in the small settlement and rented a room for the night. That evening after supper, they sat next to one another on the veranda and watched as the stars began to unveil themselves in the sky. Maria said quietly, "Look, there is the evening star. Milton called it 'love's harbinger.'"

When the hotel manager began to put out the lamps in the dining room, they climbed the stairs to their room, and for the first time, Hank lay next to Maria. She put her head on his shoulder as he put his arm around her. He made no attempt to offer any more intimacy than she invited.

He spoke quietly, "I have been accused of being a man of few words, but these words you can always know are true. I will love and protect you all of your life, whether in life or in death, in this life or the next. Of that you can be sure." He smiled and kissed the top of her head. But his smile faded as he lay quietly for the next hour dealing with the thoughts that streamed through his mind, worries about Breaux's possible continued search and the potential difficulty of proving Maria's right to claim her freedom.

As Maria drifted off to sleep, a thought formed in her mind, *Hank Schroeder, I do love you—and with you, I am safe.*

During the night, a rainstorm washed the world clean, and in the morning the sun set the water droplets on the trees and shrubs sparkling like a thousand gems in a golden light. A touch of coolness from a westerly breeze relieved the heat of the morning.

As they sat in the dining room of the hotel waiting for breakfast to be served, a small black boy entered, selling newspapers. Hank purchased one for four cents and then noted that it was the *Mobile Examiner* and was three days old. He chuckled and said, "Well, in a place as small as Pickens, maybe a three-day-old paper is the best we can do."

The major story on the front page told of the Louisiana Supreme Court's decision in the case of Sally Miller. He read a portion of it aloud to Maria, while they waited for breakfast to be served.

Ever since the case of Adelle v. Beauregard, in the Superior Court, as early as 1810, it had been settled doctrine here that persons of color are presumed to be free. Slavery itself is an exception to the conditions of the great mass of mankind, and, except as to Africans in the slave-holding States, the presumption is in favor of freedom, and the burden of proof is upon him who claims the colored person as a slave . . .

Hank fell silent while he continued to read. As he neared the end of the article, he said, "Here are the final words of the judge's decision." Then he read slowly and with emphasis,

After the most mature consideration of the case, we are of the opinion that the plaintiff is free and that the judgment of the District Court be reversed; and ours is, that the plaintiff be released from the bonds of slavery.

"Oh, Hank, those are beautiful words, perhaps the most beautiful in the whole world." She paused and then added with a shy smile, "Next to the words 'I love you.'" When they arose from the table, Hank carefully folded the newspaper and put it in his pocket.

By late afternoon of the next day, Mr. and Mrs. Schroeder had disembarked from a steamboat at the Aberdeen pier. Their next task was to purchase a small gold wedding band from the largest mercantile store in the city. When they returned to Allen's little store, they thanked him for giving them the two days away but offered no explanation for their absence.

Instead of leaving, Allen pulled up one of the two chairs in the store and turned it around so he could put the seat between his legs and rest his arms on the back. "I had an unusual conversation yesterday with a coarse and vulgar man by the name of Lodder. He came into the store and told me he was searching for a runaway slave woman, a white-skinned metif slave by the name of Maria. He said he had followed her and the man she is traveling with all the way from New Orleans. Maybe it is a coincidence, but the description fits the two of you."

Maria put her hand over her mouth and ran through the narrow store and out the back door. She leaned with her left hand against the back wall and violently threw up what little she had eaten that day. Wiping her mouth with her skirt, she sat down on the top step of the little stoop and put her arms around herself as if she were cold. As she began to rock back and forth, under her breath she whispered, "He's found me; he's found me."

Leaving Allen startled and alone, Hank followed her and, stooping beside her, brushed her hair out of her face gently and said, "Please, dear Maria, go up to the bedroom and lie down until you feel better. I will come up as soon as I can. Do not let this upset you." With a hand on each of her arms, he guided her into the back of the store to the stairs. "Can you make it by yourself?" She nodded.

By this time Allen was aware of what had happened, but he'd only heard what Hank had said to Maria. He said apologetically, "I'm sorry if I have upset your wife, Hank."

Putting his hand on Allen's shoulder, he guided him back to the two chairs that were not far from the front door. Hank moved to the door and locked it. Then he motioned for Allen to sit back down while he sat across from him. "The world is not as we would have it, Allen, but I've always known you to be a fair man, and I am going to have to trust your sense of fairness." For the next thirty minutes, Hank told the story, from his pulling Maria out of the Ouachita River to their arrival in Aberdeen and the wedding ceremony in Alabama the day before. He explained in detail how she had come to America as a redemptioner but had been sold to Lafayette Breaux, who insisted that she was a metif slave.

When he finished, the two men sat in silence for several seconds. Then Allen spoke, "I did not say anything to those men about knowing anyone that matched that description, but others might."

"What do you think we should do?"

"Well, I can think of two things to do right away. Let's get you out of those buckskins and into some city clothes. Hide that bowie knife, even if you have to wear a vest in this heat."

"That's easy enough. What is the second thing?"

"Have you thought about becoming a member of our church? Are you ready to be baptized? If you are one of us, there will be a greater willingness on the part of the other members to believe and protect the two of you from these strangers and their false charges."

"I have no opposition to going into the water. In fact, I have wondered if you folks would have me. No one had yet asked if I was willing."

"I think many thought you were already a member. Do you think your wife would be inclined to join us, as well?"

"Oh, yes. She has only been waiting to be asked. She has embraced this religion wholeheartedly. Two days ago she burned the bread because she was engrossed in reading the Book of Mormon." The memory made him smile.

"Then tomorrow night we'll meet at Mormon Spring and make you official members of our faith. Surely, no one will connect Mr. and Mrs. Schroeder, the 'Mormons' of Monroe County, with Mr. and Mrs. Hanks of New Orleans.

In the late afternoon the next day, after the store was closed, two wagonloads of members of the fledgling Church cheerfully made their way to Mormon Spring, which was located near the crossing of Wolf and Splunge Roads. There was only one habitation within sight. For centuries the spring had been fed by good mineral water that bubbled up from the ground as well as by a stream that flowed down the hill. Four years earlier, it had been enlarged and deepened so that it could comfortably hold two adults with room to spare, and after the first baptisms conducted there by John Brown, it was dubbed "Mormon Spring."

The sunlight filtered through the dogwood, pine, and sycamore trees that grew around it, and the ground was covered by ferns and Cherokee roses. As the wagons came to a stop and silence filled the area for a few moments, Maria said in whispered awe, "What a beautiful place to make a covenant with God."

Hank and Allen Smithson entered the water, and Allen immersed Hank as Abraham Smoot oversaw the simple ceremony. As he stepped out of the water, his wet clothes glistened in the sunlight. Maria was invited to step in. She rose from the water, her face beaming with the thrill of a feeling that this was a new start for her life, and things would never be quite the same again. She was wrapped in a quilt for the ride home, but Hank refused the offer of a quilt, enjoying his cool, wet clothing as they rode in the July sunshine.

After they had climbed into bed that night and Maria put her head on Hank's shoulder, she said quietly, "Now I think God knows where I am." With that, she drifted off to sleep. Hank lay awake for a long time stroking her hair and thinking about the new life they had chosen. *Would there be more children? Should they stay in Monroe County?* He wanted to be more than a hired storekeeper. *Should we go west and homestead?* But he didn't find any answers before sleep claimed him.

CHAPTER *13*
Discovered!

Maria spent the next several days cutting and sewing a blue cotton shirt and a pair of trousers out of a sturdy twill fabric so Hank would no longer need to wear his buckskins. The heat of July had grown oppressive, but each day Hank wore the vest she had made. While most men carried a rifle or a pistol when away from home, Hank continued to favor the bowie knife, the sheath of which was tucked into the back of the waistband of his pants, under his vest.

Rain had fallen every afternoon for three days, making the air sticky and almost too heavy to breathe, enticing some of the women to remove most of their under slips, creating the immodest slenderness of a dress with a straight silhouette. The laundry the women put on the clotheslines hung limp and damp for days at a time, rinsed repeatedly by the rain. On this day, the clouds were nearly black in the southwest.

While Hank was stacking bags of flour in the store, a rough-looking man entered. After spitting tobacco somewhere in the direction of the spittoon, he said, "I hear you may know something about a woman named Maria, a pretty, white-skinned metif slave from Caldwell County, Louisiana."

Hank paused for the tiniest fraction of a second, and then said impassively, "What makes you think that?"

"Two, maybe three people have said that you just might know more than you're willing to say. Ya know there's a sizable reward for her."

"I don't know who you are, mister, but I think it would be a good idea if you left my store. We don't know anything about any white-skinned slave women around here. As you can see, the slaves in this town are black, and they work the land."

Lodder kept Hank busy talking as Dag located the back door of the store from the outside and slipped in. He was carefully making his way up the stairs to the apartment on the second level when one of the stair treads creaked under his weight. Hank looked back at the stairs, and Lodder sprang at him. Bending at the waist, Hank flipped him over his head, dropping the man on his back. Lodder immediately rolled over to his hands and knees and pulled a knife as he rose to his feet. Hank reached behind his back and pulled the bowie knife from its sheath. The men moved in a circle, bent at the waist and facing each other but making no move toward each other.

Then Maria screamed. Dag had pushed his way into the little sitting room and, taking Maria by the waist, began to pull her down the stairs. The scream shocked Hank into action, and he leaped on Lodder, forcing him down. With his knife at his throat, Hank yelled at the man holding Maria, "Let her go, or your partner's dead."

Dag put his hand over Maria's mouth and continued down the stairs, carrying her around the waist like a rag doll. "He can take care of hisself," he yelled back with a bark of a laugh.

Reaching for a cast-iron skillet above him, Hank grabbed the handle and hit Lodder hard on the head. Then he leaped for Dag, who had reached the bottom of the stairs, and pulled Maria from his grip. He twisted the left arm of the man behind his back and, bending him backward, walked him out of the store. He gave him a shove, and Dag went flying out into the street.

"If you ever come here and threaten us again, I'll be forced to kill you both," Hank yelled. He lifted Lodder by his belt and shirt collar and tossed him out of the door and onto his companion.

Dag pulled Lodder out of the way of an oncoming wagon and dropped him. He stood and waved his fist at Hank, yelling something lost in the sound of the passing wagon. The two men limped away. Lodder was holding his head where the skillet had left its mark.

Maria ran to the doorway. Standing with Hank, she asked, "What should we do now they've found us?"

"We will continue our lives as we have been. I'll go to the sheriff and charge them with trying to kidnap my wife. Basically, they're cowards. If I swear out an arrest warrant for them, I think they'll leave town."

"But they'll tell him I am a runaway slave."

"And I will tell him you're my German-born wife. It will be my word against theirs. They have no evidence of their claim."

George Gibson walked into the store and said, "Hank, what was all that ruckus about? I saw you toss two rough-looking men out into the street and threaten them. What's going on?"

Hank began to straighten the store while he talked. "While one of them tried to keep me busy here in the store, the other thought he could make his way upstairs to my rooms and have his way with my wife. I put a stop to that in a hurry."

George put out his hand to shake Hank's and said, "You'll be the hero of the town, Hank. There isn't a man in Aberdeen wouldn't have done the same thing." He pulled a list of items he had come to purchase from his pocket and handed it to Hank. Hank's hands were still shaking from the stress and exertion of his struggle with the two men, so he had some difficulty pouring the sugar into the bowl on the scale.

Hank locked the store early, and he and Maria walked to the Smithson's home where he asked to borrow a horse to ride to Sheriff Corbett's office. Maria remained with Letitia. When they told Allen what had happened, he said, "I'll saddle up and ride with you." Maria stood at the parlor window and anxiously watched the two men ride down the street.

The men were back in an hour. Hank told Maria in a relieved voice, "The sheriff has sworn out an arrest warrant for attempted kidnapping, and we gave him a good description of both men. I think we can sleep better tonight."

Maria looked up into his face and asked quietly, "Hank, will God ever free us from Breaux and his men?"

"If we do our part, the Lord will do His."

Allen insisted on hitching the two horses to his carriage so he could give the couple a ride from his home back to the store. As they rode, Maria said uneasily, "There's a wind starting to blow, and I can't see a star in the sky. Everything feels strange."

Hank just patted her hand and said, "It's been a hard day. Maybe you're just upset."

Allen shook his head and said, "She's right, Hank. There's something different in the air tonight. If the wind begins to blow, you two had better get out of the second floor and down into the root cellar behind the store."

"You think this could be a bad blow?"

As they pulled up in front of the store, Allen nodded once and said, "It could be. Sometimes we get those around here."

Hank lit a lamp, and as he and Maria climbed the stairs to the rooms above the store, the rain began to fall with the sound of great waves hitting the shore. "Hank, I've never heard rain like this." The branches of the large maple tree near the store tapped on the window of the bedroom, reflecting each gust of wind.

"There's nothing to worry about. The wind isn't too bad yet." But as he spoke, the wind began to howl around the building, banging the unsecured shutters.

Alarmed, Maria said, "I think it's getting bad. Let's go down to the root cellar."

"The root cellar won't be very comfortable. I think we ought to wait and see if it gets worse before we do that. The sound of a door banged downstairs, startling Maria and making her jump. Hank said, "Don't worry, the wind just got a hold of the door and blew it open. I'll go downstairs and lock it. You light another lamp." He stood and held the lamp high so she could make her way across the room to find another lamp. As she struck a lucifer and put it under the glass chimney, Hank turned and started back down the stairs.

As she set the lamp down, she heard a thump, as though something heavy had been dropped. She ran to the top of the stairs and, holding the lamp high, she could see Hank lying in a crumpled heap at the foot of the stairs. Where the lamp had fallen to the floor near him, flames were burning among the broken pieces of glass. "Hank, Hank, what's wrong?" she called frantically as she lifted her skirt enough to hurry down the stairs.

As she bent over him, an arm went around her waist, and a voice yelled above the sound of the storm, "I gotcha now, missy. You're worth a lot to us, so come along without a fight so I won't have to hurt you." And he lifted her off her feet.

Maria screamed, "Let me go! What have you done to Hank?" Lodder put his hand over her mouth to silence her, even though she could hardly have been heard above the noise of the wind and rain. Carrying her out into the howling storm, Lodder half lifted and half threw her into the back of an open wagon and jumped in after her. Dag whipped the horses into a hard, nervous gallop.

Sick to her soul with rage, helplessness, and worry for Hank, Maria huddled in the back of the wagon, knowing she could not throw herself from it to escape without injuring the baby.

Hank staggered to his feet. Looking around at the flames, he called out, "Maria, where are you?" He leaped through the increasing flames. Reaching the street, he could see the wagon in the flashes of lightning moving toward the river.

He ran to the Smithson's home, his hands doubled into angry fists. He yelled, pounded on the front door, and rattled the doorknob, but the noise of the storm was too much for them to hear him. Dashing around the house to the stable in the rear, he lifted the bar across the stable door and entered. In the flashes of lightening, he was able to locate a bridle hanging on the wall, which he put on the large bay that shifted nervously in the storm.

Throwing his leg over the back of the animal, he pulled its head around, and with his heel, he urged it out of the stable. It did not want to go, so he had to prod it with another kick in the flanks. As man and horse flew down the street through the increasing sea of mud and rain, he urged the animal in the direction the wagon had been traveling. He knew the likelihood was greatest that the men had hurried to the levee, where they might get down the river on a steamboat.

When he arrived at the wharf, he pulled the horse to a skidding, stiff-legged halt. The rain and wind were making it impossible to see more than twenty-five feet ahead, but he could see the empty wagon near the pier. It was apparent that only one boat had steam rising from its funnels. One man was undoing the lines that held it to the pier. The other boats were secured by multiple lines, and the crews had taken shelter in the warehouses on the wharf.

Hank dismounted and ran to the man who had finished untying the lines. "Did two men take a woman with child onto this boat?" he yelled above the noise of the storm.

"Aye, sir, they did. One had a gun, and she didn't want to go aboard. Something wrong there."

Hank yelled over his shoulder, "Get the sheriff!" as he made a running jump across the six feet of open water, landing on the wet deck. His words were lost in the uproar of the storm. When he landed, he slid into the bulkhead. Rising to his feet, he made his way toward a light that turned out to be the boiler room, where he could see Dag holding a gun on two men who were stoking the boiler with wood.

He turned without being seen and located the stairway to the second deck. From there, searched for the stairs to the third deck, where he made his way carefully to the wheelhouse. There, in the light of a kerosene lantern swinging from the ceiling, he saw Maria, wet and huddled on the floor, and Lodder holding a gun on the captain. Not waiting to be exposed by the lightning flashes, he leaped into the small cabin and brought his interlocked fists up hard under Lodder's gun, knocking it out of his hand. Maria quickly crawled over to where it had fallen and picked it up, holding it with shaking hands.

As Hank and Lodder struggled in the confined space, the captain was finally able to put his arm around Lodder's neck and pull him off Hank. As Lodder turned on the captain with a knife in his hand, Hank grabbed his arm and twisted it until he dropped the blade. Taking the man by his belt and his arm, which was still twisted behind his back, Hank ran him out onto the narrow deck around the wheelhouse and lifted him over the railing. As he dropped him, he yelled, "I hope you can swim." Lodder hit the railing below and was catapulted into the swirling river.

Maria rose to her feet. Without saying anything, she handed the gun to Hank. He gave her a quick embrace and asked, "Are you all right?" She nodded. At first she had been too frightened, but now she was too angry at her kidnappers to speak. "Stay here," he ordered. With the gun in his hand, he made his way back down to the lowest deck, where he followed the glow of the fire to the boiler room. He sprang in, and as Dag turned and pointed his gun at him, Hank fired. The bullet knocked Dag back into the bulkhead. He dropped the gun and grabbed his shoulder.

The two men who had been stoking the boiler straightened and put their hands up, not knowing if Hank was friend or foe. Hank put the gun into his belt and dragged Dag out of the boiler room. The boat had begun to pitch from side to side as the storm churned and roiled the river water. Hank pulled the wounded man onto his feet and then tossed him overboard into the roar of the wind and the river.

The captain appeared in the boiler room and yelled at the top of his lungs, "Can you men tie us up to the pier?"

They yelled in response to his question, "We're too far out into the river."

The captain motioned for the two men to return to stoking the boiler. He put the paddlewheel in gear and then climbed back to the wheelhouse. Using the flashes of lightning as a guide, he steered the boat out into the middle of the river, and for the rest of the night, he pointed the boat's bow upstream and tried to match the speed of the paddlewheel to the speed of the current. Occasionally, they could hear a great thump, followed by a great shudder that ran through the vessel as a tree trunk floating with the current struck the hull.

During the long night, Hank and Maria sat in a cabin on the lower deck, where he held her closely to keep her warm. "You will see no more of those two," he promised her.

"Oh, Hank, I fear that Breaux will never leave us alone until either he or I am dead," she whispered. Wrapped in a quilt and his arms, she finally fell asleep.

As daylight arrived and patches of blue sky began to show through the scudding clouds, the roar of the wind and rain eased, but the lashing trees continued to drop branches into the river. The unwilling passengers on the steamboat could see that two of the boats that had been tied up at the pier had been battered by the storm until they were taking on water and likely to sink.

The captain carefully navigated the boat back to the pier and had the two crewmen tie it up. All he said was, "That made for a long and wild night. I'm a lucky man. My boat doesn't seem to be too badly damaged." Then he shook Hank's hand and said, "Now that we can be heard above the storm, can you tell me who those two men were and why they wanted to steal my boat?"

"The sheriff has an arrest warrant out on both of them for the attempted kidnapping of my wife. They tried to take her earlier today but came back and took her during the storm. I think they hoped to take her down to Mobile on your boat."

"When they put a gun in my face as we were trying to tie the boat to the pier, I knew I was in trouble." Deep creases formed between his eyebrows. "I'll tell the sheriff what happened before we leave Aberdeen. Stealing a steamboat is an act of piracy, and that's a hangin' offense."

As he and Maria waited for the crewmen to put down the gangplank, Hank said, "If you could just give the sheriff your side of the story, it would be appreciated." Maria took Hank's arm, and they made their way down the gangplank and onto the pier. The rain had finally stopped, and the sun was melting the remaining clouds. Allen's horse was gone.

As they walked through the city in wet clothing, they could see homes and businesses without roofs and trees that were twisted, split, and broken. Several buildings were in near ruins, as though stepped on by a giant. They made their way to the sheriff's office and told him of their experience the night before.

As the young couple continued through the city, they were often forced to walk around the debris in the street. Men and women labored to salvage what the storm had not ruined, some in tears. Others called out cheerfully, "We came through it safe enough. Everything else can be replaced."

Hank said, "I don't expect that we will find anything left of the store. I couldn't stop to put out the flames last night. If I had, I would have missed the steamboat and lost you. I did what I had to do."

Pressing her face against his arm as she held onto it, she said, "I am glad you didn't wait. I was terrified when they took me, but by the time they pushed me down on the floor of the wheelhouse and pointed the gun at the captain to make him take us to Mobile, I was so angry that when I got the gun, I almost shot the man you were fighting."

Hank suddenly laughed, "I'm very grateful that you didn't. You might have put a bullet in me by accident." She laughed a little nervously, knowing he was right.

Hank continued, "I sure hope Allen's horse made it back home in the storm. If it didn't, I'll have to work for him for a long time to pay for it."

As they walked westward from the river, the damage to the city lessened. When they arrived at the little store on West Jefferson Street, they were relieved and surprised to find that from the front, they could see no damage. When they entered, it became apparent that the fire damage was limited to the rear where the lamp had been dropped. The door that Dag had forced open had remained open, and the rain, driven by the wind, had put the flames out before they'd done much more than burn the floor and scorch a portion of one wall.

Maria breathed out a grateful prayer, "God be praised. There is little damage."

Within the hour, Allen had ridden over to the store and upon entering said, "One of my animals was outside the stable when I got up this morning. It was nervous and wet from the storm. Do you know anything about it?"

Hank smiled and answered, "I was forced to borrow your bay last night without your permission."

After Hank shared the experiences of the night, Allen said, "We underestimated those two. We can count our blessings that Maria was not hurt or killed."

The next morning Hank left the store to assist Allen in repairing the Smithson's roof. "Your boys are just about big enough to get in the way without helping much," Hank called out when he arrived. "Let me get up there with you so one of them doesn't break a leg."

Maria tended the store, and whenever there were no customers, she would stand in the doorway and watch the street, quietly waiting for Hank. He did not get home until it was nearly dark, and she hurried to meet him.

She embraced him, making him smile broadly. "You act like you missed me a little bit," he said.

"I did miss you. I have missed you this whole day like I would miss half my heart." She looked up at him with a smile that filled her eyes. They walked back to the store arm in arm.

Hank could not help but tease her a little. "I think maybe you have become accustomed to my presence."

She nodded and answered, "Yes, I have become accustomed to your presence and your smile and your indigo eyes and your laugh . . ."

As they stepped inside the store, he turned her to face him and gave her a tender kiss. "I'm so glad," was all he said as they stood together in each other's arms.

Over the next several days, the sound of saws and hammers echoed throughout the city. The major damage from the storm was limited to mainly the blocks near the river. Only two bodies were found, both of them pulled from the river, one with a bullet in his shoulder. The sheriff came by two days later and asked Hank and Maria to go with him to the undertaker to see if they recognized either one. When the mortician pulled the sheet back on the first, Hank heard a sharp intake of breath, and then Maria said, "Yes, that is one of them. I think his name was Lodder." When the other man was uncovered, she said, "That's the other one. His friend called him Dag."

The sheriff looked at Hank and said, "Do you know them?"

Hank answered, "Yes, those are the men who tried to take Maria two days ago. Allen Smithson told me he had met one of them, as well."

"Well, I'll have him come down and take a look at them, too. I thank you for your time, folks. Your willingness to identify them makes my job a whole lot easier."

As they walked back to the store, Hank took in a big breath and let it out slowly. "I've got to admit that I'm glad they're both dead, but in another way, I'm sorry, as that makes me responsible. But they didn't give me any choice in the matter." He took a few more steps, patting her hand where she held his arm. "Now you can rest, knowing that they can't cause us any more trouble."

She said worriedly, "I hope you are right, but if Lafayette Breaux sent them, he won't give up."

He tried to reassure her, but additional thoughts and worries pressed on his mind. He had killed two men, taken the lives God had given them. Surely he had broken the commandment. "Thou shalt not kill." While he would never put aside his concern for Maria's safety, he was deeply troubled about his own soul. He said nothing about it to her over the following weeks, but he worried about the deaths of the two men and struggled to understand the moral ramifications of his actions.

CHAPTER 14
The Search Renewed

Lafayette Breaux sat opposite the elaborately carved cherrywood desk of Theophilis Freeman in his Bourbon Street office, impatiently tapping his walking stick on the sole of his immaculately polished boot. "Sir, I commissioned you to locate the slave woman called Maria more than four months ago. I gave you a substantial sum to use in the process. Now you tell me that the two men you sent after her have not returned. It is obvious that they have taken the money, spent it on a gambling boat, and have no intention of returning."

Mr. Freeman cleared his throat and said defensively, "I promised them an additional sum upon their finding the woman. I am sure they will return to collect it. We need only to give them a little more time."

"They have had more than enough time. I am relieving you of the assignment and requesting that you return to me the balance of the deposit I gave you. I have hired two professional slave catchers to take over the task. They have already made their first report to me in this matter."

Mr. Freeman lifted his left eyebrow. "Mr. Breaux, if I may ask, what is it about this woman that makes her so valuable to you? Can any woman be of that much value? If she is just a slave, surely she can be replaced."

"It is highly unlikely that this woman can be replaced—and that is a matter for me to decide!"

"Well, if you will return in the morning, I will have the balance of your deposit for you."

Lafayette Breaux stood, put on his silk hat, and exited the office. He had no intention of explaining to Freeman that his determination to find Maria had doubled when one of the men he had hired previously brought him the news that when questioned, the captain of the *Southern Belle* had stated that the young Mrs. Hanks was apparently "in a family way" and for that reason had kept to her cabin.

Breaux made his way to the Vieux Carré and the small but nicely furnished home of his *Creole-mulatto placeé*, Lulu Francaville, and their four-year-old daughter, Missy. The child squealed with delight when she saw him. "Papa! Papa, did you bring me a present?" She put her arms out to be picked up. The child had dark brown hair that fell in loose ringlets, framing her smoky-skinned face with large brown eyes.

He took a peppermint from his pocket and gave it to her. As thanks she threw her arms around his neck. He spent the night in the arms of his mistress, and in the morning he returned to the walnut-paneled office of Theophilis Freeman and claimed his money before making his way back to his plantation.

***

The two coarse and greedy professional slave catchers Breaux hired, Sharp and Grabbinger, were instructed to go upriver to the little settlement across from the mouth of the Hatchie River where the captain of the *Southern Belle* remembered letting the young couple disembark. They had been ordered to retrace the journey taken by the young Mr. and Mrs. Hanks—and they were told that money was no object in their search.

Within five days, the men reached Rienzi and hired Sam's Boy to lead them overland to the Tombigbee. Full of hate for Hank, Sam's Boy led them at a pace that made them beg him to slow down and give them time to rest. Sharp asked him, "What makes you travel these hills like the devil himself is after you?"

"That's my problem. You just remember that you'll have to take that Arkansas toothpick away from him, or it will take more than the two of you to get the woman."

When Sam's Boy started moving up the trail again, Sharp looked skeptically at his partner and shook his head as if to mock the guide. By the time the three men reached the Tombigbee, they were ready for a night's sleep. In the morning, they hired the man with a flatboat to take them south, and Sam's Boy headed back to Rienzi.

As they left the boat in Aberdeen, Sharp said, "Well, this is quite a town."

"Yeah, I hear it's nearly as big as Mobile. It may take us a while here." Grabbinger laughed and continued, "And as Breaux said, money's no object." They proceeded to make their way through the city over the next two weeks, testing the drinks in every bar, public house, and hotel and asking about the woman and her companion.

By late September, while the foliage was still a deep green, the two men began to inquire in every store or shop. When they entered the Smithson Mercantile, they stopped short. Here was a tall young man with sandy hair and blue eyes who came close to fitting the description Sharp and Grabbinger had been given. Deciding to change his approach, Sharp cleared his throat and asked, "Would you know anybody in this town who might know where I can get a bowie knife? I'm lookin' to buy one and to have someone show me how to use it."

Put off more by his manner than his words, Hank answered cautiously, "I think you would have more luck finding something like that if you found a good blacksmith who can work with steel. Then you can order a knife made just the way you want."

At that point, Maria descended the stairs, and called out, "Hank, I'm going to see Letitia for a little while. I should be back . . ." She stopped, noticing the two men in the shop and the way they were looking at her. It was evident to both men, and anyone else who saw her, that she was expecting a child.

Sending her a signal of caution, Hank said, "Caroline, I think you may need to help me here in the store for the next little while. I'm expecting a big order to fill shortly."

"Oh, of course, dear. I can go to Letitia's later." She turned and climbed the stairs quickly. She could feel the two men watching her all the way up the stairs until she disappeared into the sitting room. She closed the door and leaned against it, her heart beating hard and fast for reasons she could not understand. There was something about the way those men looked at her that frightened her.

"Well, I think we best be on our way, Mr. . . . er, Mr.—what was your name?" Sharp asked.

Hank looked him directly in the eye and said in total innocence, "Henry Spoonheimer. My friends call me 'Spooney.'"

"But the lady, er, your wife called you 'Hank.'"

"She never liked my nickname." Hank smiled benignly and offered his hand. As the two men left the store, Hank called after them, "Hope you'll come by when you need supplies." But before the smile faded from his face, he reached back to feel for the handle of the bowie knife under his vest. His smile melted into a hard jaw and thin lips.

After Sharp and Grabbinger had walked a few hundred feet down the street, Sharp started to laugh and grabbed his partner by the arm. "We got her, you hear me? We got her!" he said in a strident whisper. "Tomorrow night or the next, we're going to make that five hundred dollars." They walked to the nearest public house and bought a bottle of whisky to celebrate.

***

Hank hurried up the stairs and entered the little sitting room. "We've got trouble with those two. I'll lock up the store, and then I'm going to go over to the sheriff to see what he knows about them. I'll walk you down to the Smithson's so you won't be alone. Don't leave there until I come for you." Maria nodded and put on her bonnet without saying anything.

Hank went straight to the sheriff's office after he dropped off Maria and explained the situation to the sheriff.

"Well, if you are sure these men are a threat to your wife, I suggest that you make arrangements to protect her. There isn't much I can do until they break the law."

"I think we can do that."

Hank loped back to the Smithson's home, his long stride quickly eating up the distance. When he got there, Letitia invited him in and insisted that the two of them stay for dinner.

Hank and Maria made an effort to smile and converse their way through the dinner in a normal fashion. When it was over, Hank took Allen aside and explained what had happened. "How much do you know about the Whistling and Whittling Brigade that John Brown was part of in Nauvoo?" Hank asked.

"Why? Is it something I can help with?"

Hank explained, "There are two men in town that I think might be here to take Maria. I need help protecting her, at least until we can discover their real intentions."

After the meal, Hank and Allen walked toward the home where Abraham Smoot was boarding. Hank explained the potential problems the two men could cause for him and Maria. "I think we may need our own Whistling and Whittling Brigade, at least until we can be sure these men are no longer a threat. Will you help us organize some men to give us some protection for the next while?" Brother Smoot just nodded and grinned at the idea.

CHAPTER 15
The Whistling and Whittling Brigade

That evening at the Smithson home, under the direction of Elder Smoot, they organized a plan, and word went out to eight family heads among the Saints who lived within a mile. Eight men and three sons in their late teens and early twenties met early the next morning, and for the next week each one agreed to give up a day or a night to be present in the mercantile store, where they would whittle and whistle the day away, watching for questionable men who might be a threat to Hank and Maria.

On the first evening, after the store had been closed, Jim Harmon heard something at the back door that sounded like scratching. Rising from his bed on the floor, he moved to the door and yelled through it, "I've got a gun, and you're a dead man if you come through that door." The noise stopped. Hank came down the stairs in his nightshirt to see what had happened. Opening the back door, he could make out the figure of a man hurrying away in the darkness.

The next night, while William Terrill was trying to get to sleep on his bedroll on the floor, he thought he heard someone working at the lock on the front door. He stood and lit the kerosene lamp in time to see a figure rush past the front window.

The third day, Hank sent a note to the sheriff, telling him of the attempts to break in. That night two more men came to spend the night in the store. Will Matthews and his sixteen-year-old son, Johnny, joined Allen Smithson, and each came into the store before closing through the door at the rear. The men lay down on the floor of the darkened store, and two slept fitfully while the third watched and listened. Upstairs, Hank sat in the old rocker, fully dressed.

About midnight, Johnny nudged his father and whispered, "There's someone at the back door."

Will whispered back, "Just keep quiet, but be ready to light the lamp. Let's see what happens."

After the scrabbling sound stopped, the bar across the back door scraped slightly as it rose, and then the door creaked, and the night air blew in, telling the waiting men that the door was open. Johnny Matthews counted to five and then lit the kerosene lamp. The men stood in unison and rushed the two figures, one still on the landing of the stairs at the back of the building and the other with his foot on the first stair of the staircase. As they fell in a heap on top of the first man, Hank descended the stairs and leaped over them to chase the second man, who had turned and run. Even Hank's long stride was not enough to catch up with Grabbinger, who made his escape.

By the time Hank returned to the store, Will Matthews had sent Johnny, with his long legs, for the sheriff. It was almost an hour before the sheriff arrived on his horse, with his hair uncombed and his nightshirt tucked badly into his pants. Without waiting for an explanation from Sharp, the sheriff tied his hands behind his back, and, with the help of the men, he walked Sharp behind his horse back to the jail. He locked him in a cell and returned to bed without having said more than ten words.

The "whistling and whittling" group shook one another's hands and slapped Hank on the back. Sure that the second man was not foolish enough to return, they headed for home.

The next day Sharp was arraigned before Justice of the Peace John Wise. As the Aberdeen Court House was still under construction, the process took place in his living room. A short man with white chin whiskers, Wise sat behind a small table with his gavel in hand. His wife hurried into the room just as he was getting ready to bring the meeting to order. She placed a wooden cutting board on the table, saying firmly, "Now, don't you damage my pretty table top. If you must use that little hammer thing, use it on my cutting board."

Wise tolerantly said to his wife, "I'll be careful, dear." Then, turning to the men gathered in the room, he changed moods as if he had changed hats. He brought the gavel down on the cutting board and said with an edge in his voice, "The Monroe County Court of Sessions is called to order."

He then started to read the charge against Sharp written out by the sheriff. "To wit, you and your accomplice are charged with breaking and entering the business of Mr. Hank Schroeder with intent to do harm. What say you to this charge?"

Sharp looked at Hank, his eyes slits of hate. He started his defense by stating, "We were commissioned by Mr. Lafayette Breaux of Louisiana to recapture one metif slave woman by the name of Maria who ran away from her master in Caldwell County five months ago. That gives us the right to take her back to Louisiana!" He paused and then looked at Hank. "That man has the woman. She's pretending to be his wife."

The eyebrows of the justice of the peace rose. As a slave holder himself, he would tolerate no runaway slaves in his county, white or black. He turned narrowed eyes at Hank. "How do you answer that charge, Mr. Schroeder?"

"I do not believe that I have to answer that charge, sir, as I do not believe that these men have any evidence to prove the charges that my wife is that woman."

Looking around the room, Wise said, "Why isn't the woman here?"

Hank responded, "The sheriff didn't seem to think her presence would be necessary."

Looking at the sheriff, Wise ordered, "Go get the woman. I want to see her."

The sheriff nodded and left the house. "While we wait for the sheriff to bring her back, let's hear what happened."

Hank recounted the events, and when he had finished, Wise looked at each man in the room and asked his name and if he agreed with the account as given by Hank. Each man, with the exception of Sharp, nodded or said respectfully, "Yes, sir."

Looking at the prisoner, Wise said, "Well, since I have a number of witnesses who agree that you forced your way into the store operated by Mr. Schroeder, you are guilty of breaking and entering, regardless of the status of the woman."

Sharp said with a sly smile, "I got money right here for a fine, judge. If you'll remove the ropes from my wrists so I can reach my billfold, I will pay any fine you order and be on my way." It was apparent to those in the room that Sharp thought the matter was nearly settled.

At that point, the sheriff arrived with Maria. Her face was drawn and white with concern. The sheriff pointed to a chair one of the men had vacated for her, and she silently sat down. Turning to her, Wise said, "This man has accused you of being a runaway slave. What have you to say for yourself? Now tell me the truth, woman."

She stood and glanced over at Hank. He started to move over to her, but Wise motioned for him to stay where he was. Taking a deep breath, Maria began with a voice that quivered slightly, "My name is Maria Elizabetha Caroline Marguerite Schumann Schroeder. I was born in Baden in 1826. I came to this country on the ship *Hope,* which landed in Baltimore when I was eight years old. My parents died on the voyage, so I was sold as a redemptioner to Mr. and Mrs. Wentz. My contract said that I was to be given my freedom when I reached eighteen. When I was fourteen years old, I was sold to Mr. Becker of Alexandria, Virginia. His wife made him sell me after I turned sixteen. They sold me to a man by the name of Theophilis Freeman, who sold me to Lafayette Breaux of Louisiana. When I asked Mr. Breaux for my freedom on my eighteenth birthday, he laughed at me and said he did not owe me my freedom. I begged him to show me the papers that said I was his slave, but he would not show them to me." She added forcefully, "I do not believe he had any such papers." When she finished, she continued to stand. The shaking in her hands had quieted.

Wise said, *"Sprechen sie Deutch?"*

Maria answered, *"Ja."*

Wise then asked her several questions in German, which she easily answered. Then he smiled condescendingly as he looked about the room and said, "My mother was from Westphalia." Then his mood became somber again, and he added, looking at her, "But do not think that I will show any bias on your behalf in this case."

Wise nodded at her as if to give her permission to sit, which she did, grateful to feel the firmness of the chair's arms under her hands. He turned to Sharp and said, "What proof do you have that this woman is a slave?" Sharp pulled the sheaf of papers from his vest pocket and handed them to Wise.

The justice of the peace looked through them, and when he came to the handbill that described Maria and specifically mentioned her ability to speak German, his eyebrows lowered and creased above his nose. "I see here a handbill seeking the return of a slave woman whose description fits that of this woman. I see a commission signed by Lafayette Breaux of Louisiana stating that two men have been authorized to capture and return her. And lastly, I have in my hand what appears to be a bill of sale for a slave called Maria, dated June of 1842, sold to one Lafayette Breaux of Caldwell County, Louisiana, by one Theophilis Freeman of New Orleans." He paused and rubbed his chin. "The bill of sale looks somewhat suspect, as the paper is not worn like the other documents, but I must take it on its face, at least until it is proven to be false."

CHAPTER 16
The Decision

Maria's face blanched, and Hank's face grew red with suppressed anger. Ignoring the scowl of Wise, he stepped over, bent, and whispered in her ear, "Don't be worried. A forged document will not hold up under examination." Hank turned a deadly look at the smirking Sharp.

Wise looked at Maria, and continued, "What is your defense, woman?"

She stood and said quietly, "May I see the documents that would send me back into unjust slavery?"

Wise did not move for several seconds as he thought the matter over and then said, "I suppose your . . . Mr. Schroeder may examine them. You realize as a suspected slave, you have no legal rights in this proceeding."

Hank stepped forward, and as he examined each document, Will Matthews and Allen Smithson looked over his shoulders. Each page was studied carefully. Will said nothing but pointed at something. Hank looked at him and back at the document. Will was pointing at the signature on the bill of sale. Without saying anything, he took the signed commission from Hank's hand and held the two documents together so the signatures could be compared. Will then took the documents and placed them before Wise. "If you will compare the signatures, your honor, I believe you will see that the one on the bill of sale is a poor copy of the one on the commission. The bill of sale appears to be a forgery."

"And what makes you an expert in this matter?" Wise asked.

"All I can claim is that I spent a little time as a school teacher, and much of my time was spent attempting to interpret signatures nearly as bad as that one." He pointed to the signature on the bill of sale, which lay before the justice of the peace. "You can see for yourself that the signature of Mr. Breaux on the commission is that of an educated man. The signature on the bill of sale looks like it was written by a crippled chicken." Some of the men in the room chuckled but were silenced by a look from Wise.

Wise was quiet a moment and then said, "If I were to take the bill of sale at its face value"—he paused and looked from Hank to Will and then back to Hank—"can you tell me why I should not let these two men take the woman at this time and allow any interested parties to contest the matter in a court in the State of Louisiana?"

Hank pulled a newspaper from his shirt pocket and said firmly, "I have here an article about a case in New Orleans involving the woman Sally Miller. Many of us in this room have followed that case. With your permission, I will read a portion of the argument on behalf of Sally Miller made by her lawyer, Wheelock S. Upton. He began to read:

> *Even if at the end of this appeal the court thinks that Sally Miller is a mulatto, rather than a German, this makes no difference—the onus is on Mr. Miller to show that she is a slave. If he cannot prove his title to her, then she must be released. This is what* Adelle v. Beauregard *stands for. Even if the court entirely believes Mr. Miller when he says that he acquired Sally Miller from Anthony Williams in 1822, this still doesn't prove that she is a slave. No one knows how Williams obtained her, so she must be released. Even if the court harbors doubts about her age, none of this is conclusive. It doesn't prove that she is a slave, so she has to be released.*

Then Hank said, "This forged bill of sale makes no reference as to where or how Mr. Freeman, the seller, obtained the woman named in the document. Under such circumstances, it seems to me that any woman in the South could be kidnapped by one man and sold to another as a slave."

"The argument is interesting, Mr. Schroeder."

Sharp spoke up, "There's a dozen reasons why that case he read about shouldn't be applied in this situation." Sharp had the attention of the entire group. He continued, "It can't be true in a slave-owning society that masters must show how they obtained their slaves. If the court follows Upton's reasoning, any slaves who aren't pure African could demand their freedom if their masters can't display a piece of paper showing title to them. The rights of ownership of thousands of slave owners in the South will be threatened if this reasoning is accepted." Waxing more enthusiastic as he talked, he continued, "It is vital to the health and well-being of the southern states that the rights of slave ownership be protected."

Wise looked at Hank and said, "What is your response to that, Mr. Schroeder?"

Hank pulled another, somewhat-worn page of a newspaper from his shirt pocket, and said, "Here's the answer, and it's the answer of the Louisiana Supreme Court brought down on June twenty-first of this year in the matter of Sally Miller." He read,

After the most mature consideration of the case, we are of the opinion that the plaintiff is free.

The men standing behind Hank let out a spontaneous cheer. The frowning justice of the peace brought down the gavel.

Hank continued reading,

It is, therefore, adjudged and decreed that the judgment of the District Court be reversed; and ours is, that the plaintiff be released from the bonds of slavery."

Wise said tersely, "Give me those newspapers." For the next few minutes, he read both of the extensive articles about Sally Miller and her appeal before the court. When he finished reading, he looked up at the faces of those in the room and said, "Here is my decision." He paused, rubbed his forehead, and then continued, "I believe that the bill of sale is of dubious authenticity, and in the face of the decision of the Louisiana Supreme Court, I am ruling that the woman before me known as Mrs. Maria Schroeder is free and cannot be removed from Monroe County or from any other portion of the state of Mississippi against her will." He brought down the gavel one more time.

Hank swept Maria up in his arms and turned her around. The other men present, with the exception of Sharp, cheered and slapped Hank on the back. The group poured out of the little house, leaving Hank and Maria behind to thank the justice of the peace. Hank also wanted to see what Wise was going to do with Sharp.

Wise turned to Sharp and said, "You will be bound without bail on charges of breaking and entering and attempted kidnapping. The circuit judge should be here within two weeks."

As Hank offered his hand to Wise, he said, "We thank you for your decision in this case."

Wise finally smiled briefly, as though it hurt a little, and said, "I'm glad the decision pleased you. But I suspect that his accomplice will continue to be a threat. Take precautions." He ushered them onto the porch and said, "I wish you a good day," as he closed the door behind them.

As Hank and Maria walked toward the store, Allen fell into step with them. "We were blessed, my friend. If you had not had those newspaper articles, we might not have had such a happy outcome. John Wise is not fond of 'Mormonites,' as he calls us. He might have ruled in a different manner."

"But he didn't, and we can go on with our lives."

"Just be careful. Don't let your wife go anywhere alone for the next few weeks."

CHAPTER 17
A Change of Plans

Sharp's trial on the charge of breaking and entering with intent to kidnap took place two weeks later. Justice of the Peace Wise had regretfully turned it over to the circuit judge. Sharp was convicted and sentenced to one year at hard labor.

The circuit judge explained as he passed sentence, "I could toss you in jail here for that length of time, but I think we would be better off sending you downriver to Columbus. They have a newer jail there." He brought down the gavel and ended the procedure.

On the boat trip down the Tombigbee River, Sharp was able to loosen the rope around his wrists while the sheriff was at dinner, and, without much difficulty, he took the gun away from his guard, eighteen-year-old Jack Nunley. Sharp hit Jack so hard on the head that he dropped in a heap, dead. When the sheriff returned to the cabin, Sharp hit him hard on the head as he came through the door, knocking him unconscious. Sharp left the boat at Demopolis, Alabama.

The sheriff returned to Aberdeen, where the news of the escape traveled throughout the city as quickly as a river flows downstream. Maria said quietly, "Do you think he will come back for me, Hank?"

"Even he can't be that foolish," Hank said with more confidence than he felt.

***

For Hank and Maria, life continued at a pleasant pace, though Maria occasionally wondered about Hank's increasing lack of sociability. He continued to attend Church meetings but was so taciturn that he seldom participated in the discussions the way he had previously. Maria grew large with the child everyone believed was Hank's, and friends happily anticipated its birth. By early December, when the magnolia leaves were brittle, the azaleas were bare clumps of sticks, and the autumn rains felt cold against the skin, Hank finally allowed Maria to occasionally go to the Smithson home unescorted.

In early January, John Brown, William Crosby, and several other families who had been temporarily living in Nauvoo left the piercing cold of an Illinois winter and returned to Monroe County with news of the increasing persecution of the Saints. Life in Monroe County had held little bias or bigotry for the Saints. Many citizens of the county had even gone so far as to express their sympathy when they learned of the death of Joseph Smith. But Brown and Crosby brought word that Brigham Young and the leaders of the Church in Nauvoo had announced the need to move west shortly after the temple was completed and dedicated.

During the rainy winter months, the meetings of the Tombigbee Branch of the Church continued to meet in the plantation house of Mother Crosby. At the last Sunday meeting in January, Brother Brown put forth the plan advocated by Church leaders. The Mississippi Saints were urged to leave in a timely manner that spring so they could unite with the advance exploratory company under Brigham Young somewhere along the Platte River in Indian territory.

George Gibson asked the question on everyone's mind. "But Brother Brown, why should we leave productive land and our homes to go west to a strange place we know nothing about? Life is good here, and our branch of the Church is steadily growing."

"The troubles the Saints are facing in Illinois will soon find you here. Some of you know of the hardships I faced both times I was sent as a missionary to the South in '41 and '43. I came near to being tarred and feathered in Tennessee and run out of town on a rail twice in Alabama."

He continued, "A few months before he was murdered, Brother Joseph prophesied that the Saints would find a place to dwell in peace in the Great Basin of the Rocky Mountains. Now

Brother Brigham has directed us to gather there, where we will be outside the United States, where we can establish our own cities and our own government, and, if necessary, our own army." As Brother Brown talked, some of the men shook their heads as if he were asking more than they were prepared to do.

CHAPTER *18*
A Dark‑Haired Baby

Maria's baby came in late January, a boy with strong and healthy lungs. They called him Martin, Hank's middle name. Betty Matthews, who helped with the delivery, had insisted that Maria drink an herbal tea made from black cohosh every day for two weeks before her labor pains began. "Oh, Hank," she whispered, as the pains came closer and closer in time, "I have such mixed feelings about this birth. I know the child is not guilty of the sins of the father, but what if he—or she—has the same bad blood?"

"We will love this child and raise him or her to love the Lord, and there will be no bad blood," Hank answered solemnly as Maria squeezed his hand. Though she said nothing, Maria still worried about why Hank had grown quiet and introspective since he had saved her from Dag and Lodder. The successful prosecution of Sharp did not seem to improve his sociability.

The baby had large blue eyes and a head of dark hair. Within five minutes of his birth, both Hank and Maria had given him their hearts. When Betty Matthews saw him, she laughed. "He looks like my Lizzie did when she was born. She had a head of black hair like that, but by the time she was two, it had come in as light as it is now. With parents as light as the two of you, I'm sure that will happen to little Marty." Maria simply looked at Hank with anxious eyes as Betty talked. They both knew that Martin would probably be a child with a head of black hair all his life.

As a gift for the new baby, Allen brought over a stray dog that had attached itself to his family. It was part terrier, and the rest of its family history was undetermined, but it was friendly and easily trained. When Allen pointed to Hank, who was sitting by Maria's bed where she held the baby, he said, "Stay, Buddy. This is your new home." Then he said to Hank, "Give him a pat on the head, and he will be your friend forever. That's why his name is Buddy. With a little training, he might make a good watchdog."

Maria was wondering if she really wanted a dog. A new baby was enough work, but then Hank said thoughtfully, "If we'd had Buddy last year, maybe those first two would have been less likely to try to kidnap Maria, and the last two would not have been able to cause us so much trouble. At least we would have had some warning." At that, Maria decided that a dog might be a good addition to the family.

In late February, John Brown came to talk with the young couple. Though he was an intimidating man in appearance, lean, with a thick black beard and dark eyes, those who knew him were aware of the tender heart any friend could count on. As he talked with Hank and Maria in the little sitting room, he said, "I know you have a young baby, but sometimes that works to everyone's benefit, as a babe in arms will not run off and get lost or fall into a stream as the group travels."

Hank asked, "Am I right in thinking that you've come to ask us to make plans to go west?"

Brown nodded. "We're hoping to have a group ready to leave by early April. As you folks have little property to sell, it seems that you would have fewer preparations than most to become part of our group. Have you given it any thought or prayer?"

Hank said evasively, "Frankly, we haven't."

"Will you think about it now?"

Hank clasped his hands between his knees and dropped his head. He was silent for so long that Brother Brown cleared his throat and looked at Maria with a question in his eyes. When Hank raised his head, he said quietly, "There's something that has been troubling me for the last few months, John. You see, I don't think I'm worthy to go with the Saints. The Saints can't build Zion with men like me among them."

Both men heard Maria's sharp intake of breath, but she said nothing.

Hank continued, "The Good Book says, 'Thou shalt not kill.' I'm responsible for the death of two men—and it troubles me greatly. I knew when I fired that gun that I was giving up my eternal soul, but I had no choice if I was to save Maria and the baby." Then he added quietly, "And I would do it again if I had to. How can the Lord forgive me with an unrepentant attitude like that?"

Maria put her hand over her mouth but said nothing. She suddenly understood why he had been so quiet and withdrawn.

Brown answered thoughtfully, "Hank, you're new in the gospel, and it's possible that you might benefit from increasing your understanding of what the Lord expects of us. I'll try to explain something to you. When we read the scriptures, we learn of many times and places when God's people had to protect themselves and those they had responsibility for. Moses killed an Egyptian to protect one of his kinsmen; Sampson killed the Philistines with the jawbone of an ass. Nephi was commanded to kill Laban to obtain the records to make sure that his people would not perish in ignorance."

Hank did not seem convinced, so John continued, "The Lord commanded the Hebrews to establish cities of refuge for those who had killed by accident, in self defense or in defense of others. They were to be protected from the penalty that was attached to the deliberate taking of a life." By this time Brown had risen and was pacing the floor in his earnest attempt to convince Hank of the justification for his act. Pausing, he turned and added, "And Ecclesiastes tells us that there is a time to live and a time to die, a time to kill, and a time to heal. If you have been hurting over this incident, it is time for you to heal. Here with the Saints, you have a place of refuge."

Hank looked at him and offered a wry half smile. "I'll give what you have said some thought, John, and let you know what we have decided in the morning." He stood and shook the other man's hand and walked him to the door. He said nothing for the rest of the evening, but as Maria put the baby to bed, she saw him take down the Bible and the Book of Mormon and sit in the old rocker. He read by the light of the kerosene lamp for most of the night.

When he climbed into bed with her two hours before the sunrise, she opened her eyes. He said quietly, "I think we will be going west with the Saints. Will that be all right with you?"

Maria smiled and said, "Yes, I'll be glad to leave this place. I still feel unsafe here. We will find a home with the Saints where Lafayette Breaux can't find me and will never again send anyone to take me or Marty away from you."

***

After Sharp had escaped and left the steamboat in Demopolis, he made his way carefully back to New Orleans, unwilling to give up his plans to collect the five-hundred-dollar reward. He took another steamboat up the river to Vicksburg and then crossed the river and went overland to the Breaux plantation. When he sat down in the parlor of the plantation house, he dispensed with the usual formalities. "Mr. Breaux, my partner has disappeared and I have been thrown in jail, all in the attempt to complete the commission you gave me to find your slave woman. I want my money now."

Breaux looked at him and snorted in contempt. "But you did not finish the task. I owe you nothing yet."

"You owe me plenty for what I been through." He scratched his nose and then continued in a more conciliatory tone, "If you still want the woman, I know how you might get her back."

Breaux stopped in the process of lighting his cigar, the flame of the lucifer burning his fingers. He shook it and dropped it onto the carpet. "Tell me, and I may be willing to pay you."

"The Mormonites are planning to leave Mississippi. I read in the Mobile newspaper and again in the *Courier* while I was passing through New Orleans that they're going to leave their city up in Illinois and go west. I heard the rumor that those Mormonites in Monroe County will be going to join them, for sure. If they follow the River Road up the Mississippi until they reach the Ohio and then go overland to the Oregon Trail, it won't be hard to locate them. If you'll extend my commission and pay me for my trouble to date, I'll go up to Memphis or Dyersburg and wait for them to pass through town. I can grab her and the child there."

"What makes you think you will have more luck this time than you did before?"

"Because I know now that I've got to kill the man before I take the woman."

Sharp left the Breaux mansion with three hundred dollars in his pocket and a promise of an equal amount, all of it his to keep, if he brought Maria and her child back unharmed. As he stood at the door on his way out, he asked, "If it's not too much for me to ask, why is this woman of such importance to you? You could buy ten slave women for what you are spending on trying to get her back."

Breaux stepped out of the house onto the porch and pulled the door closed behind them. With a scowl, he said in a fierce near-whisper as he put his face close to Sharp's, "Have you ever seen the woman I married?" He turned and paced a few steps and returned to add, "Do you know how few and far between really beautiful and educated white-skinned slave women are? Do you realize that they are nearly impossible to obtain?" With each question, Breaux's voice rose until it was nearly a shout, "Do you realize that this woman, Maria, also has my child—a child that my wife cannot give me? I will have that child! I will have an heir to inherit this plantation! Now get out there and earn your money!" He turned, reentered the mansion, and slammed the door. Sharp quickly descended the porch stairs and mounted his horse.

From inside his office, the plantation owner sent for his overseer. Breaux was sitting with his feet crossed on his desk, when a servant girl showed his overseer into the parlor. At about fifty years of age, the man was sunburned and leather skinned. He stood in his sweaty clothes, shifting his weight from one foot to the other, wondering why the plantation owner had sent for him.

"Lem, I seem to remember that you had a woman in Memphis that you wanted to marry—your dead wife's sister or some similar relative. Did I remember that right?" Lem Pounder wondered why Breaux suddenly seemed concerned about his marital happiness.

"Yes, sir, you remembered right." Lem turned his sweat-stained hat in his hands uncomfortably.

"Well, I have a little job for you. I'm sending you to Memphis. If you bring back a wife when you return, that's fine with me." He continued, "I want you to go to Memphis and stay until you learn about a wagon train of Mormonites from Mississippi. I hear they will most likely be going through Memphis on the River Road, headed north. The minute you hear about them, I want you to hightail it back here and let me know. I want to know how many wagons are in the company and who the wagon captain is. Do you understand?"

"Yes, sir."

With that, Breaux added, "I suppose you're wondering why I'm interested in the group. Well, you'll find out sooner or later that my white slave girl, Maria, is with them. You remember her?" He did not wait for confirmation from Lem. His voice grew louder, and his forehead began to wrinkle with anger. He dropped his feet to the floor and brought his fist down on the desk in front of him. "When she ran away last year, she was carrying my child, and I want her and the child back."

Lem again said, "Yes, sir. When do you want me to leave?"

"Right now, since you can't leave five minutes ago. Pack a few things, and take one of the good horses. Here's a hundred dollars. I'll expect to hear back from you sometime within the next two or three months. That will give you sufficient time to court and marry your woman and get a job until then. In the meantime, your son Jeremiah will take over your job here. He's got a wife and family, so I'm sure he'll appreciate the promotion." With a few simple preparations completed, Lem started the ride to the little settlement of Mound on the Mississippi River, where he would board a steamboat headed upriver to Memphis.

CHAPTER 19
Leaving Monroe County

By the first of April, a group of Monroe County families had gathered nineteen wagons, some of which were hitched to teams of oxen that had previously plowed the fertile fields of the area. Others were hitched to double teams of mules or horses. This group consisted largely of those who had little property or who had been able to dispose of land and homes easily.

"Oh, Hank, I'm so glad we will be traveling with friends." Maria had been contentedly humming as she gathered supplies for the wagon. From late January to April, Hank sold tents, twill cloth for wagon covers, tools, small wood-burning stoves, flour, cornmeal, molasses, guns, and the many other supplies that every family would need for the journey. While assisting others with their preparations for the trip, Hank had proudly purchased a .56-caliber Hawken rifle with money he had been saving for that purpose.

Additionally, he had purchased a cow and calf.

"Gertie will be such a blessing on this trip," Maria said as she fixed supper. "I hope she will be able to tolerate the long walk without going dry, and I hope her calf will tolerate the trip at least as well as her mother."

Allen told Hank, "I've sold the store, so you might as well take as much of the furniture as you can fit in your wagon. You'll be able to use it, I'm sure."

"Allen, you're a true friend," Hank said as he shook Allen's hand.

The company was unofficially headed up by William Crosby and his brother-in-law, John Brown. Billy Lay and George

Bankhead decided to join the group. John Holladay from across the state line in Alabama chose to join the other married men temporarily leaving families behind, as well. All five men left instructions that their families were to be ready to join the second company when they returned in the fall.

Others in the company included George Gibson, his wife, and their large family as well as Dan Thomas and his wife. James Harmon and his family were quick to make up their minds and become part of what was, at that point in time, viewed as a great adventure. The company also included the Crow family, which had come down from Perry County, Illinois, with John Brown when he'd returned to Mississippi in January. There were others in the company, including old George Sparks and his wife, Lorena, Absalom and Sarah Dowdle with their infant daughter, and William Matthews and his wife, Betty, and their family. But Maria and Hank were especially pleased that they were able to pull their wagon behind Allen and Letitia Smithson.

Maria laughed when she discovered that nearly every family in the company was related in some way to several of the others. She told Hank, "I think that you and I are the only ones not related by blood or marriage to the other folks making this journey, but by the time we reach the Great Basin in the Rockies, I think we will all be family."

The shaking of hands and calls of farewell to those remaining behind went down the entire line of nineteen wagons. John Brown called out, "I'll be back again to lead another group out of Mississippi, hopefully later this year. Be ready to join me then." Shouts and good wishes filled the air as the company started to move northward, out of Monroe County.

As Hank slapped the reins against the rumps of the mules to get the wagon moving, Maria said, "I thought I would be glad to leave, but I have mixed feelings. It's true that we had some frightening times here, but we found friendship—and the gospel here, too." Then she looked up into Hank's face with a smile and added, "But we are taking both of those precious things with us, aren't we?" He smiled and nodded.

Martin was sleeping under a soft quilt in a small cradle they had tucked between two sacks of flour that now steadied it. As the wagon began to move, Maria put her arm around her husband where they sat on the wagon seat and leaned on his shoulder.

"We are doing the right thing," she said.

The company made its way northward along the Tombigbee River until it reached the small settlement called Booneville. From there, it moved westward to the Mississippi River. Near the Mississippi, they turned northward onto a well-worn trail toward Memphis. As the company of people, wagons, oxen, cows, dogs, pigs, and a few sheep moved laboriously over the rutted trail, lurching over clumps of undergrowth and tree roots, families would come out of their cabins to stare. Men and women working in the fields and others using the same trail would pause to watch as the group passed by, staring at the wagon company in amazement. In an area where most traveled by steamboat, wagon companies were rare. Cheerfully and lightheartedly, Maria waved at the onlookers.

When the group reached Memphis, they paused for two days, long enough to purchase replacement supplies. While they camped there the second night, a stranger and his wife walked into the camp. Allen Smithson invited them to join the group as they prepared supper.

Lem Pounder introduced himself and his wife, Nancy, and as they sat on a log with several others, they were handed a tin plate of squirrel stew. Lem asked, "Who's your wagon master?"

Allen Smithson nodded toward the Crosby family where they were eating. "Well, I guess that would be Will Crosby. He's right over there, where the woman in the brown dress is passing around the biscuits."

After Lem and Nancy had finished the stew, Lem tipped his hat and walked over to the Crosby family, leaving his wife sitting on the log. Brother Crosby stood and offered his hand, which Lem shook. "What brings you into our camp tonight?" he asked.

Lem rubbed his unshaven chin for a moment and then said, "I think I need to talk to you," he cleared his throat, "confidentially, if I could."

The two men walked into the woods about twenty feet, where they stood silently for a few seconds. Finally, Lem spoke, "For the last couple of months I've been living in Memphis waiting for your wagon company to get here."

"How did you know we were coming?"

"I was ordered to come up from Louisiana by a man I've worked for for the past ten years. He told me to wait for your company to get here. Then I was told to hurry back and tell him when your group had arrived and who was leading it. I don't know how he knew about your plans."

"Why did he want to know when we arrived in Memphis?"

"He's looking for a woman, a white woman he insists belongs to him. He said he would pay me two hundred dollars if I could establish that she is part of your group. I'm guessing that he plans to send someone after her."

"Do you know her name?"

"Her name is Maria. Mr. Breaux says he bought her as a slave when she was sixteen."

"Do you know what she looks like?"

"Oh, yes, I know her. She's a pretty thing with yellow hair and green eyes. She always treated me with respect and kindness. She never seemed to be afraid of me the way some of the slaves usually were. She once told me that she was a redemptioner, not a slave."

"Do you plan on taking this information back to him?"

"I been thinking on that for the last month. I don't think Breaux realizes how much I've always hated him—him with his fancy clothes and mean-spirited wife. He likes to use the whip. He even used it on me once when I didn't answer him quick enough." He paused and pointed to a scar on his right cheek. Then he cleared his throat and continued, "I'm hoping you'll let me and my wife join with your company. I've outfitted a wagon, and I'm looking to join a company going west. Will you let us join you?" He paused. "What do you say?"

"You don't mind traveling with a group of Mormons?"

"Your religion don't bother me."

Captain Crosby pursed his lips as he considered the matter. Then he said, "Wait here." He was back within a few minutes with Hank. He introduced the two men and then said, "Tell Mr. Schroeder what you told me."

After Lem had recounted his story, Captain Crosby asked Hank, "Under these circumstances, would you and your wife be willing to allow Mr. and Mrs. Pounder to join our company?"

"Under the circumstances, I would rather they join us than return to Louisiana, that's for sure," Hank responded.

CHAPTER 20
The River Road

The next morning there were twenty wagons making their way up the River Road that meandered from settlement to settlement, out of the reach of the occasional floods of the Mississippi River. Hank explained the presence of Lem and his wife in the company to Maria. "How do you feel about them joining us?"

Maria answered thoughtfully, "I have no objection. He was always fair to me. I think it speaks well of him that he wants to get out of the employment of a man like Lafayette Breaux."

She nodded in recognition to Lem when they saw each other, but neither made any other sign that they were acquainted. At a steady pace, the wagons passed farms and cabins and an occasional small plantation. By the time they reached Dyersburg on the Deer River, two wagons needed repairs, so they camped outside the small community while a wagon axle was replaced on one of the Gibson wagons. About nine o'clock that night, Lem approached the Crosby tent and asked to speak to the unofficial captain of the company.

As Crosby lifted the tent flap and invited him in, Lem said, "We need to talk to Schroeder. There's trouble." Both men approached Hank and Maria's tent. They invited Hank to join them so they could speak quietly.

After they walked into the trees, Lem dropped his voice and said, "I saw a man by the name of Sharp in Dyersburg today. I've seen him before, at Lafayette Breaux's mansion. I'm sure he is here for the same reason I was sent to Memphis. I guess Breaux got tired of waiting to hear from me."

Crosby nodded and said thoughtfully, "So that's the weave of the wool," as he ran his hand through his hair. "What do you suggest we do?"

"Set up plenty of guards tonight, and every night, until we are free of him—and we had better keep Mrs. Schroeder out of sight." The first night, the men of the company each served shifts of four hours at guard duty, but several repeatedly asked why the sudden need for extra protection. Crosby remained tight-lipped.

Hank told Maria of Sharp's appearance. She responded, "I will remain in the wagon. Hank, you can make my excuses. Just tell people I am not feeling well, if anyone asks."

In the morning, Captain Crosby called the men together in small groups of four or five and explained the situation to them, asking them to keep the information confidential so as not to frighten the women and children. Several of the men were familiar with Sharp, remembering him from Aberdeen, but Lem told them, "He's got himself a red beard now, so he probably looks different than he did when you knew him."

The second evening, the guards again took their posts. About midnight, Buddy and the other dogs began to bark wildly, and shots were fired, rousing the entire camp. The men on guard, including Hank, ran toward the sound, finding that Will Matthews and George Gibson had a bearded man pinned to the ground and were pointing a gun at him. As they pulled him to his feet in the moonlight, they could see that the beard was black. As they began to question him, they heard a scream from the other side of the camp. Hank turned and ran toward the sound. There he found a gaping slit in his tent. Pushing into it, he found Ab Dowdle kneeling on a man, twisting his right arm behind his back.

Ab and Hank pulled him up onto his feet and pulled him outside the tent. Even with his beard, Hank recognized him. "What are you doing here, Sharp?" Hank stepped close to him in the bright moonlight, and as he did, Sharp pulled free from the men holding him and took a knife from his pocket. He made a swipe at Hank, cutting his left shoulder.

As Hank staggered back, holding the wound, Sharp yelled, "You know why I'm here! Give me the woman and the child!" He leaped at Hank again with the knife held above his head.

As the knife started to come down, Lem Pounder pulled a revolver from his belt and fired, dropping Sharp in a heap. The entire camp had been awakened and was noisy with the sound of children crying and dogs barking. Clutching Martin, Maria had rolled into a corner of the tent, where she was trying to protect the baby with her body.

As Hank offered his right hand to help her to her feet, she cried out, "Hank, you've been hurt. You're bleeding!"

While Letitia held Martin, Maria bound Hank's shoulder. "Is he dead?" she asked.

Ab Dowdle stepped over to where Hank was sitting on a log and answered her, "Yep. Lem got him in the heart. He dropped like a sack of potatoes. I think you can be done with being afraid of him."

Within the hour, the local sheriff had arrived, and, after talking to each of the men who had been on guard duty that night, as well as Ab Dowdle, he said, "Well, I guess I got to accept your story, even if I don't like it. I hope you're planning to leave in the morning. I hear that everywhere you Mormonites go, there's trouble." He paused and then added, "Mr. Pounder, you said something about knowing the dead man. Does he have any family to notify?"

"Not that I know about. The only man who might be interested in him is a plantation owner from Caldwell County, Louisiana, by the name of Breaux."

"Well, I'll put that in the record." Then the sheriff left the camp, leading the horse with Sharp's body over the saddle.

The man with the black beard, a suspected would-be horse thief, was allowed to leave, muttering under his breath, "Those Mormonites are all crazy."

After the sheriff left, Hank shook Lem's hand and thanked him for his alertness. Lem responded, "Didn't do anything that you wouldn't have done for me."

Maria couldn't sleep the rest of the night. She curled up next to Hank with her head on his uninjured shoulder, while she held Martin. As they sat together, Hank said, "The past has a way of intruding upon us, reminding us of what we least wish to remember."

"Hank, did you ever dream that you would have to face problems like these when you pulled me from the river?"

He kissed her on the top of her head. "Even if I had known what we would have to face or what we might yet still face, I would never have hesitated for a moment to pull you from that river, my love. I believe God brought us together."

Quoting Milton, she whispered, "'That power which erring men call chance.'"

The company continued northward. When they neared the confluence of the Mississippi and the Ohio, they could see the great bluffs called Iron Banks that stood prominently above the river. Ferrying the wagons across the river required two full days. There, in the little settlement of Belmont, Missouri, they purchased corn and wheat.

After the last wagon was pulled into the encampment, William Crosby called the company together. He explained that many of the rural citizens of Missouri were hostile to the Mormons. He instructed, "We think it best if we do not mention our religion while we are here in this state. We are headed for Independence, where the Oregon Trail begins. The Saints were persecuted and driven out of that area just a few years ago. Some folks here might think that Governor Boggs' extermination order is still in effect, so keep your children close and quiet. There's no reason for the folks here to suspect us of being Mormons, as nearly all of the Mormon wagon companies will be going west through the Iowa Territory, well north of here."

From Belmont, the company made its way in a general north-westerly direction through what was called Tywappity Bottom by the locals until it reached Charleston, a community with a large German population. Cultivated fields of corn, wheat, and cotton spread across the countryside, intermingled with forested hillsides of hardwood trees. Deer and waterfowl were plentiful, and the pink and white blooms of the dogwood and lavender red-bud trees sprinkled liberally throughout the wooded areas complimented the green of the new leaves on the hickory and ash trees.

Hank told Maria, "I'm going into town with some of the men. I need to get one of the harnesses for the mules repaired.

I'll be back before dark." In Charleston, he asked on the street if there was a leather shop in the settlement where he could get the work done.

One man answered, "Yep, up the way just a spit and a holler is a German who can do wonders with leather. His English ain't good, but if you can tell him or his master what you want, he can do it." The man pointed at a stable about a half mile up the street.

Hank made his way to the stable and, entering the half-open door, called out while his eyes adjusted to the darker interior, "Hey, can I have some help here?"

A man carrying a heavy hammer and dressed in worn clothing came out of the back room and answered, "Ja, how do I help you?" As he came nearer, Hank could see that he was not much older than himself. He had a scar that ran laterally across his cheek and his ear. Something about his voice and his eyes seemed familiar.

Raising the harness, Hank said, "I need some leather to reinforce the traces on this harness. Can you fix it for me?"

The German stood still and said, "Ja, I can fix it." He was openly staring at Hank. Hank returned his stare. Almost as if rousing from a nap as recognition increased, Hank spoke, "You sound like someone I knew a long time ago. What's your name?"

"My name is Karl, Karl Schroeder." His speech was full of the rhythm of a German dialect. He looked directly at Hank, and asked slowly, "Is your name Hans?"

Hank dropped the harness and stepped forward, putting his arms around his brother. He whispered, "*Mein Bruder, mein Bruder*. When we last saw each other, you prayed that God would go with me—and He has. He has led me to you."

Karl's eyes filled with tears as he stepped back and took Hank by the shoulders with calloused, worn hands and said, "When I was taken from the auction, I never believed I would see you again in this life. What brings you here?"

"My family and I are going west to begin a new life."

"You have a family? You are free?"

"I have a beautiful wife and a son, and I have been free since I was twenty. You are free, aren't you?"

"*Nein, nein*, my master has accused me of trying to run away many times, and the sheriff has made me stay two more years for each time he was told that I tried to run away. I will never be free of this man." He spoke the words with quiet fury.

He continued, "After the auction, he took me to a little town called Lancaster in Pennsylvania where he had a farm, but after his wife died and I turned eighteen, he sold the farm and brought me to Missouri. Everyone in Lancaster knew I was to be freed when I reached twenty-one. Here, they do not know that I should have been given my freedom years ago—and no one cares."

"You never tried to run away?"

"*Nein*, I have fulfilled my contract, even when he beat me for no good reason. I gave him what was owed—and more."

Hank sat quietly for a few seconds and then said, "You will come with us to the west where you will be free. Can you come right now?"

Karl looked up with a combination of hope and worry on his face. "Herr Schultz will be back soon. He will shoot me if I try to leave him."

Hank went to the stable door and looked out. "Come here. Is that him?"

Karl quickly glanced out and said, "That is him. He will be angry when he gets here if he finds you."

"He does not know who I am. I am just a man with a harness to repair."

Within a minute or two, Schultz entered the stable and yelled without even taking note of what Karl was doing, "Get back to work. Don't think that because I am gone, you can sit idle."

Hank spoke up and said with a sharpness he could not conceal, "This man is helping me repair my harness. Might I ask who you are, sir?"

"My name is Schultz, and I own this stable." His tone moderated when he discovered that there was a customer present. Speaking to Karl, he said in a more civil tone, "Well, don't just stand there. Help the man."

Karl motioned for Hank to follow him to the back room where the leather goods hung, and as he reinforced the worn traces of the harness, both men spoke in low voices so Schultz would not hear them, interspersed with louder statements for his benefit.

Hank said, "Where do you sleep?" More loudly he said, "That looks like a good piece of leather."

Karl answered quietly, "Here in the stable." More loudly he said, "I will fix it so it will hold a good long time."

"Where does Schultz sleep?" Hank whispered.

"He keeps a room in the hotel next door."

Loudly he asked, "Can you repair the other one in the same way?" More quietly he said, "When does he go to bed?"

"He goes to bed about ten o'clock, after it is too dark to work here in the stable any longer." Then louder, Karl answered, "If that pleases you, I will do the same for the other one."

Whispering again, Hank said, "I will come for you at midnight. Have everything ready to go. Will you do this?" Then louder, he added, "That looks like a good job. Thank you. What do I owe you?"

Karl answered loudly, "You will have to ask Herr Schultz. He will tell you what you owe." Then whispering he added, "I will be ready."

Hank paid Schultz two dollars for the repair on the harness, an exorbitant price, but considering that he had found his brother, Hank felt it was well worth it. After returning to the camp, he pulled Crosby aside and told him the situation with his brother.

"The sheriff may guess that the most likely way Karl could have escaped is if he left with us. Can we get an early start in the morning so we can put some miles between us and this town?"

Crosby nodded and said, "We will make the announcement at evening prayers that we will be leaving by five o'clock in the morning. Will that suit you?" Hank nodded appreciatively.

When Hank explained his plans to Maria, her eyes shone, and she said excitedly, "You have found your brother! Hank, oh, Hank, this is surely the hand of God." She paused and then said earnestly, "But please be careful when you go to get him."

At about midnight, carrying a shuttered lantern, Hank rode one of the mules bareback into the town, holding the reins of a second mule. He simply gave a low whistle, a signal they had used as boys. Karl opened the side door of the stable and put a roll of belongings under his arm. Making his way in the moonlight, he took the reins of the second mule and mounted. Without a word, they made their way out of the town in the darkness. After leaving the outskirts of the settlement, Hank opened the lantern and they rode the three miles to the camp by lantern light.

When they arrived, Maria embraced Karl as she welcomed him. Speaking quietly she said, "My husband has told me about you. Now you are a part of our family. Surely the hand of God is in this."

Karl responded quietly and skeptically, "Maybe."

CHAPTER 21
Additions to the Wagon Company

Maria had made a place for Karl to sleep in the wagon so he would not be seen and had laid out the bedroll for herself, Hank, and Martin under the wagon.

While Schultz was looking for Karl throughout the little town of Charleston, Karl rode in the wagon, despite the heat, lest anyone note the presence of a stranger. On the second day, after they had put some miles between them and the town, he climbed out at supper time, and Hank walked with him to each wagon and said to each family as they made supper, "This is my brother, Karl. He joined us at Charleston." Each man shook his hand to welcome him.

As the group traveled across southern Missouri, Hank and Karl became reacquainted. Hank worked to reacquire his nearly forgotten German language, and Karl labored to improve his English. During his years of indentured servitude, Schultz had made no effort to see that Karl learned proper English, believing that he was less likely to run away if he was not fluent in the language.

Hank could not help but notice that this brother, who was so near his age, appeared many years older. His skin was weathered, and his knuckles misshapen and swollen with hard labor. His sandy hair was shaggy, unkempt, and showing gray at the temples.

As Maria trimmed his hair with her scissors and the comb she had been given by Bridget so long before, she asked kindly, "Karl, how did you get that scar on you face?"

"Schultz struck me with his whip the first time he accused me of running away. The sheriff was there, and he made him stop, but I was told that I would have to stay another two years. Two years later, when the time for my freedom neared, he pointed the finger at me again. For four years I have served him, accused of trying to run away whenever my time for freedom was near."

"Why did he accuse you of running away—I mean, what reason did he give?"

"He would send me to Cape Girardeau to buy something we could not get in Charleston and a day or two before I could get back, he would go to the sheriff and tell him I had run away. He never gave me enough time to get back before he went to the sheriff. I began to understand that it was his way of keeping me in his service."

Each evening, after supper was completed, Hank would talk about the religion that was taking them to the West and to a new life. Karl listened but said little. Hank spoke of faith, baptism, repentance, and the need for the restoration of proper priesthood authority, but it was the principle of continuing revelation that most fascinated Karl. By the time they reached the Black River in south central Missouri, Karl said, as they made camp, "I think the thing that tells me that what you are teaching is true," he paused briefly so he could mentally order his words before continuing, "is that you tell me that God continues to talk to men. I think it is right to believe that He loves us as much as He loved the folks that lived during the time of Christ. It makes good sense that He should want to continue to talk to us. I think I would like to become part of this new religion."

While they were camped outside a small community called Poplar Bluff, the men found a deep place in the river where the current had swirled up against the bank, and Karl was baptized.

As the brothers stepped out of the water, Karl gave Hank a great embrace and said, "Now I am a new man. No more will I carry the burden of hate in my heart that I have carried for so long."

That night, after the camp had grown quiet, while they sat on a log near the dying fire, Hank and Maria talked with Karl about the difficulties they had faced as they'd fled the reach of Lafayette Breaux. When Hank spoke of the trip up the Hatchie River, he smiled and reminisced. "That was the only time I have ever heard

Maria play the organ. Karl, you would not believe how beautifully she plays. I would give more than I am ever likely to own to give her an organ or a pianoforte—but I don't suppose that will ever be possible." He reached out and affectionately put his arm around Maria's waist.

Karl sat quietly for a few minutes and then said thoughtfully, "I would have never believed that God would lead you to me, but He did. Perhaps it is my turn to teach you about faith. There are many surprises the future will yet bring us."

The travelers moved steadily along the base of the Ozark foothills until they reached the prairie of western Missouri. Rivers, lakes, and forested hillsides had been plentiful to that point. The journey across the rich Missouri lands allowed the cattle to feed well and remain strong. Gertie had plodded along, with milk enough for her calf and to spare. From that point on, water was plentiful, but the animals had to graze on the tough prairie grasses that were sprinkled with wildflowers as far as the prairie stretched.

Turning northward, they reached Independence on May twenty-sixth, having covered six hundred and forty miles. As the men crowded some of the mercantile and hardware stores to purchase additional supplies, they discovered that the city was rife with rumors that the Mormons had assassinated former Governor Lillburn Boggs. Several men urged Crosby to be wary of the wagon companies of Mormons that might be making their way west. "We ain't seen any Mormons for a long time, but you never can tell. If you run into any, you'd be wise to keep away from 'em, ya'll hear?" one well-wisher behind the counter urged.

That evening around the campfire, questions flew at Crosby. Raising his hand for quiet, he said, "I know what the rumors say, but I can tell you this: some of us knew Joseph and knew him well enough to know that he would never have ordered Porter to shoot Boggs. Joseph knew Boggs well enough to realize that the man had hundreds of enemies who would cheer to see him dead. He was a heavy-handed governor and hated by many. There are folks who will tell you that they have seen him alive and well in the last few days. The simple truth of the matter is that Joseph is dead, and Boggs is alive. Disregard what you are hearing from folks who want to justify their treatment of the Saints in Missouri by making slanderous charges against us now." With that, the women returned to preparing supper.

While the men replenished supplies and the animals rested, John Brown invited Hank to help him locate friends from Illinois who had made plans to meet the wagon company there in Independence. They moved from one wagon encampment to another, asking, "Anyone here know of the Kartchner family from Perry County, Illinois?" When they finally located George Kartchner, his wife, and infant daughter, they greeted them with pleasure and merged their wagon and animals into the company.

When the group gathered for morning prayer, an official organization meeting was called and the decision was unanimous to formally elect William Crosby to the position he had held in an unofficial capacity to that point—that of company captain, with Robert Crow and John Holladay as counselors of the wagon company, which was now officially setting out to meet and join the advance company under Brigham Young. Twenty-three wagons made up the expanded group that made its way to the rolling western prairie and the beginning of the Oregon Trail beyond the formal organization of the United States.

A small group of six wagons had paused there, the wagon master wondering if they should try to make the journey to Oregon alone or if they ought to join with another, larger group for safety. He approached Captain Crosby and said, "Seems both our outfits would benefit by joining together. How would you feel about that?"

Brother Crosby simply said, "Feel free to pull in behind our last wagon and join us."

***

Lafayette Breaux spent several nights of the last two weeks of June pacing the floor of his plantation office, dropping cigar ash on the expensive rug as he did so. His frustration at not having heard anything from Lem Pounder or Sharp increased almost hourly. On the morning of the first of July, he informed his wife that he was going on a lengthy trip and that he might be gone for some time.

As he moved around the bedroom deciding what he was going to take with him, his wife asked, "Where are you going, Lafe? Does this have something to do with those men you hired to find that girl, Maria? They haven't done their job, have they?"

Without answering, he pushed past her and down the stairs. In his office, he opened the drawers of his desk, removed a pistol, and put it in one pocket. He stuffed a large fistful of money in another. Speaking more to himself than to her, he muttered, "If a man wants something done right, he had better do it himself!" He put his hat on his head and stormed out of the plantation house.

His wife followed him out and called after him, "Lafe, when will you be coming home?"

"Don't look for me until you see me," he called back over his shoulder. He strode over to a chestnut gelding that Jeremiah Pounder held by the reins and took a moment to attach the carpetbag to the back of the saddle by two leather straps. Then he mounted. He leaned over and said to Jeremiah through tight lips, "If I find that your pa joined up with those Mormons or warned them about me, I'll kill him." Jeremiah was startled at the harsh words but, knowing Lafayette Breaux, did not doubt that he meant them.

As Lafayette turned his horse, his wife called out angrily, "Lafe, where are you going?"

"As far as I have to," he tossed over his shoulder as he rode away.

CHAPTER 22
The Oregon Trail

Maria and the other women in the company found that the heat of the prairie dried and burned their hair, skin, and lips. They saved animal fat to rub on their chapped and split lips and on their arms and hands, but it was a poor substitute for the French face cream many of them had used at home in Mississippi. As she lay down next to Hank one evening, Maria said, "Please forgive me if I smell like bacon grease, Hank. There is little else to use to protect my skin."

"I can forgive you for smelling like bacon grease, my dear, if you can forgive me for waking up much hungrier than usual." He laughed.

Arriving at the Platte River near Chimney Rock on July sixth, the company made camp. "I had really hoped we would find Brigham Young's group already here, but maybe that was too much to expect," Crosby commented to Hank.

The children of the smaller company of wagons had begun to play with the children of the Matthews and Smithson families as the days passed, but one evening one of the children said, "You know, if the Mormons catch you, they'll roast you over a fire and eat you. I know, 'cause that's what my pa said."

Little five-year-old Mary Matthews stood nose to nose with the six-year-old boy and responded, "No they won't. That's a lie!"

The belligerent boy responded, "How would you know? Do you know any Mormons?"

By this time six-year-old Johnny Smithson had stepped up behind Mary, and he said defensively over her shoulder, "Yes, we know lots of Mormons 'cause that's what we are."

The child's eyes grew wide, and he turned and ran back to his parents, yelling and crying, "Ma, these Mormons are gonna eat us."

The next morning, the six wagons of the smaller company pulled out before daylight, pushing the animals to a fast trot. When Captain Crosby discovered them gone, he shrugged and said, "That's their choice."

The following day, keeping their steady, even pace, the Mississippi company passed the smaller group of wagons, which had worn out their animals pushing them too hard the previous day. Realizing that they would fare better with the Mormons than with the Indians, the six wagons timidly pulled in behind the southern Saints again, but the smaller group made separate camp, and the children did not play together anymore.

As she began the evening meal, Maria said unhappily, "Oh, Hank, how I hate to use buffalo chips for cooking. It just offends the sensibilities of most of the women in camp. I wonder why the Lord didn't make more trees grow here on the prairie."

"Maybe we should thank Him for sending the buffalo to meet our needs." Hank chuckled. After supper, Maria spent two hours straining the muddy river water for cooking and drinking, as she did each evening so they could fill the water barrel on the side of the wagon.

That evening the men sat around the campfire and debated about the possible location of Brigham Young's company. Ab Dowdle suggested, "Let's just camp here. They'll surely be along in a few days, a week at the most."

Allen urged, "Let's move eastward and meet them as they come this way."

Gibson was adamant that the company travel westward. "They must be ahead of us. If we push the animals faster, we can catch up with them."

Captain Crosby said nothing until every man had voiced his opinion. Then he stood and said, "I think Brother Gibson may be right. I recommend that we move westward and keep a weather eye out for the smoke of their campfires." By majority vote, it was decided that the group would follow Crosby's decision, but several of the men expressed doubt about the choice. Several of the tired and sunburned wives talked quietly among themselves, expressing a desire to return home.

The next day the little company of six wagons separated from their "Mormon friends" and joined a passing group headed for Oregon. Lem Pounder approached a cluster of several of the men of the Mississippi company, and shaking their hands he said, "You folks been kind to us, but we're gonna join with this group headed to Oregon. My wife seems a bit inclined toward your religion, but frankly, I ain't ever had much religion in me, and I think we could be right happy settling in Oregon."

"We wish you well, Lem, and we hope you find Oregon to be just what you're looking for," Captain Crosby said as he shook his hand.

Hank added, "Lem, you've proven yourself to be a good friend, and we send our good wishes with you."

When Maria heard of Lem's plans, she hurried to his wagon and gave Nancy a hug and Lem a peck on the cheek. "May God bless and protect you both."

After following the Platte westward for five days, a group of the younger men set out to the north after camp had been made in the hope of finding deer or elk. They located a small buffalo herd. After dropping two of the animals, Johnny Matthews rode back to tell Captain Crosby, "We killed two buffalo. If you'll have some men unload one of the wagons and follow me, we can use your help to dress out the buffalo and bring the meat back to camp."

That day and the next, the company roasted buffalo meat, smoked buffalo meat, and dried buffalo meat. The plentiful buffalo meat almost quieted some of the complaints about the biting buffalo flies, the hot sun, and the muddy water of the Platte.

After evening prayer, Crosby spoke urgently to all those gathered within the wagon circle. "I have heard many complain that this is a hard journey. Are there any among you who think the Lord owes us an easy time? I warn you that the Lord can withdraw His protection if we do not express gratitude for all He has done to keep us safe thus far." Members of the company returned to their tents in a subdued manner.

After midnight, a strong wind began to blow, accompanied by a hard rain. As Maria held Martin and leaned against Hank in the tent, she said, "It sounds as if the heavens are emptying great floods upon us. Do you think that maybe this is what Captain Crosby meant about the Lord withdrawing His protection from us because of our ingratitude and complaints?"

"Before the night is over, I think we will know," he answered. Just then, a great gust of wind collapsed the tent on them. They struggled out of the tent with Hank carrying a crying Martin. All the wet and frightened travelers could do was climb into their wagons, crowded, soaked, and cold, to wait for the storm to blow itself out. The howl of the wind increased until it rocked the wagons and blew over the other tents. The crashing thunder and lightning seemed to shake the ground. The wind raged to a level that moved some of the wagons, making those inside hold on in fear. When daylight finally came, it was evident that the storm had been a small tornado. A large nearby tree with twisted and broken branches had been uprooted and two smaller wagons tipped over. The buckets and baskets normally hanging on the wagons were gone.

As Hank helped Maria out of the wagon, Karl saw a man trying to right one of the tipped wagons with only the help of his sons. Saying nothing, Karl hurried to the man's aid, and with his strength they quickly lifted and heaved the wagon onto its wheels. Then he helped the family put everything back in the wagon that had spilled out. *How like Karl,* Maria thought. *He seldom says much, but he is always there to help when he is needed.* When the Saints gathered together that morning, Captain Crosby offered a heartfelt morning prayer, with thanks for heavenly protection during the night.

After another week on the trail, a group of travelers going east from California met the Southerners. When asked if there were any other large groups of wagons to the west, particularly a group of Mormons, the leader of the group responded, "Nope. In the last three weeks, we sure ain't seen any more than a couple of small groups of wagons headed for Oregon."

By this time the company was well past Chimney Rock, which rose like a sentinel above the flat land. The company was much too far west to turn back. That night around the campfire, Gibson asked the question on everyone's mind, "Now what do we do?"

Several men had been swayed by their wives and suggested that maybe they ought to return home. They were sunburned and tired, their animals were nearly worn out, the food was monotonous, the water muddy, and the insects unrelenting.

Captain Crosby responded to their complaints, "Obedience is one of the great principles in heaven and on earth. Now, we must be prepared and willing to do the will of our Father in Heaven, who rules over all who love and fear Him. God will give us the strength to go and do what is asked of us." When he ended his remarks, he asked for a kneeling prayer and sought direction from the Lord in the matter. After they rose from their knees, he said, "By morning, we will know what the Lord wants us to do."

As Karl made preparations to lay down under the wagon, where he usually slept, he said quietly to Hank, "I cannot go back. I will not go back. I must go forward. There are too many bad memories behind me."

Thinking out loud, Hank mused, "I don't think the Lord will require that we go back. Somehow we got ahead of the company under President Young. Maybe they made a long-term camp before they got to the Platte."

Maria stated quietly, "I think we can trust Captain Crosby. The Lord will point him in the right direction by morning."

In the morning, a weather-beaten trio of long-haired trappers dressed in buckskin leggings and fringe, driving two ox teams, arrived in camp as breakfast was nearly finished. When they were invited to join the Southerners and have something to eat, the tall leader of the three bowed in a courtly manner, which somehow did not seem absurd, despite his buckskin clothing decorated with Indian beads and quillwork. His shoulder-length, curly black hair suggested some concern about his appearance, which bordered on vanity. He introduced himself as John Baptiste Reshaw.

As the Southerners and trappers became acquainted around the campfire, the Southerners learned that the American-born Reshaw spoke with a slight French accent acquired from his parents.

"We are well ahead of the main body of Saints moving west under Brigham Young, and we are not sure what we should do during the winter months," Captain Crosby said. "Do you think we ought to try to get through the winter at Fort Laramie?"

"I would not recommend such a plan. The winters here on the High Plains can be hard to endure, even for someone like me and my friends here," Reshaw responded, as he pointed to his two companions. "Folks from the South would not do well. I suggest that you follow us south to Fort Pueblo, where you can spend the winter more comfortably. *Mais oui?*"

When several people looked inquiringly at Captain Crosby, he smiled and responded, "I think we can take this to be the Lord's answer."

The wagons lined up and followed Reshaw south on a barely perceptible trail. On the way, they met several small groups of friendly Indians who wanted to trade. Reshaw suggested that they might purchase moccasins or deerskins from them with some of the smoked buffalo meat. "Some of you folks are lookin' pretty ragged, and the winters around here can be fearsome. Those deerskins can be made into warm clothes. You better take advantage of this chance."

An Indian man called Blue Feather stared openly at Maria as Hank bartered for a deer hide. After the trade was complete, the Indian began to point to Maria and, in his own language, talked excitedly with the other braves. Hank had a bad feeling about the situation. Maria's forehead wrinkled with worry as she held Hank's arm.

Calling Reshaw over, Hank asked what the Indian wanted. Reshaw spoke with him briefly and then explained, "He is offering you five horses for your wife. He thinks she would make a fine wife." The other Indians gathered around the young couple and the Indian man to watch what they thought would be a good trade.

Hank didn't know whether to laugh at the offer or to get angry. "Is he joking?"

"*Non, non,* he says he is not a poor man. He will treat her well."

Hank settled on anger. "You tell him that she is my wife, and his offer is a sin against God."

Reshaw put his hand on Hank's arm and said quietly, "Be careful, Mr. Schroeder. Do not offend the man. Do not make enemies of these Indians. There are more of them than of us." Reshaw turned and spoke to the Indian in his own language in a nonthreatening tone. The brave then grumbled and walked away, the other Indians following him.

"What did you tell him?" Hank asked.

"I explained that the Americans, like the Indians, do not like to sell their women to strangers. I reminded him that I had been among the Indians five years before they allowed me to take a wife from among their people. This seemed to satisfy him."

Hank pulled Maria to him. She looked up into his face and said with a relieved smile, "I think that maybe I should be flattered that he offered five horses. That sounds like a very good price."

A relieved Hank laughed and pulled her against his chest. "A thousand horses would not be enough for you, my love." He kissed her on the forehead.

CHAPTER 23
Life in Pueblo

After nearly three hundred miles and more than three additional weeks on the trail, the wagon company arrived at Pueblo, hot, dirty, and tired, on the seventh of August. At the confluence of the Arkansas River and Fountain Creek, about a dozen mountain men and their Spanish or Indian wives lived in a primitive adobe fort with four dilapidated mud walls. It consisted of a handful of small adobe cabins, a few struggling corn patches, and small vegetable gardens. Well-fed but nearly naked children played in the courtyard.

The river could hardly be called a river, as the late summer had left it little more than a few large scattered puddles. When they climbed off the wagon seat, Maria voiced the thoughts of many of the other women. "Oh, Hank, this can hardly be called a settlement. It's dirty and wretched, and there is almost no water in the river."

Hank agreed but responded cheerfully, "But it has a great view of the mountains."

Reshaw heard Maria's complaint and explained, "The water is still there, you just have to dig a bit. Make a hole, and the water fills it quickly. When the snow melts in the spring, the river will fill again."

Letitia Smithson, who had been standing near them, said quietly, "I can't imagine living here in these conditions. Hank, don't you think the men can find a better place for us to make a more permanent camp?"

"Well, Sister Smithson, I suspect that many of the other women feel the same. I'm sure we can get Brother Crosby's support in finding a better location."

As the Southerners and the trappers shared a supper that night, several of the trappers, who had traveled the length of the Platte and Missouri Rivers that year, shared information about the first company of Saints that had left Nauvoo. "That big bunch of Mormonites led by Brigham Young was forced to winter along the Missouri on Pottawattamie Indian land in the Iowa Territory. The United States government took more than five hundred of their men to help fight the war with Mexico. They ain't goin' nowhere without any men. They got no teamsters and no one to herd the cattle." The trapper spoke as though delivering bad news increased his self-importance.

After the trappers retired, Captain Crosby spoke to the men still gathered around the fire and voiced what most of them had already concluded. "Many of you are going to be greatly disappointed to learn that there is no way we can unite with the main body of the Saints this year. We are substantially farther west than they are, and it will be nearly a year before they come this direction." A few shook their heads in recognition of the fact. "We will need to winter here, so it is vital that we begin preparations to get us through the cold months. We have water from the Arkansas River and Fountain Creek and timber and grazing land for the cattle. I recommend that tomorrow we begin our efforts to build the necessary cabins to house our families."

In the morning, six of the men, including Hank, rode along the creek until they found a spot a few miles from the fort that met their needs. After returning to the group and giving their report, they led the wagons to a broad meadow that bordered Fountain Creek on one side and a thick stand of trees on the other. It was only a short distance from the river, and the creek carried a small but steady stream at that point.

"Brethren, let's get our axes and go to work. We should have some sturdy cabins built within a week or two." Soon the sound of axes and the falling of cottonwood trees filled the woods and the adjacent meadow as every able-bodied man took to the work. The men began to cut trees in the heavily wooded river bottom, and the women began to plant a garden with seeds they had brought with them. As Maria wiped the perspiration from her forehead with the sleeve of her shirt, she said to Letitia, "I wonder if the turnips, pumpkins, beans, and melons will have sufficient time to ripen before the fall frost sets in."

Letitia responded, "Let's put the matter in our prayers each night."

Each day after the first two or three hours of work, the men would take a few minutes to sit and rest on some of the felled trees, and they soon began a discussion on religion. As the men rested and caught their breath the first day, Jim Therlkill asked, "If there are three degrees of glory like Joseph taught, where do the wicked go after Judgment? It seems to me that the Lord has made provision for the good, but it looks to me like there are too many folks left over who won't deserve any glory." The discussion went on for an hour before they returned to work.

On August seventeenth, before the cabins were completed, Margaret Kartchner delivered a baby girl under a cottonwood tree. Several of the women in the camp hurried to tell the men when they returned to camp. "Hank," Maria called out, "can you get some of the men to finish the Kartchner's cabin so Margaret and baby Sarah will have a roof over their heads?" With the help of all the men in the camp, they swiftly completed the small, rough-hewn structure.

Within the next two weeks, they completed many more cabins, each like the next, with a dirt floor, a rock fireplace and a hole in the roof for the smoke, a small window cut in the wall for light, which had a wooden shutter to close out the cold, and a rough-hewn door.

As Maria stood with her hands on her hips in the newly finished cabin that Hank had just presented to her, she said, "Well, it isn't quite a palace, but we will be safe and warm here for a while. With the furniture in the wagon, we will get along just fine. I think it will be good to rest here in Pueblo for a few months."

Hank and Karl brought in the table and its legs, which they set about assembling. "Where do you want it?" Hank called out when it was finished. Then they brought in the big trunk, the two chairs, the churn, and the little wood stove. The two smaller clothing trunks would also serve as places to sit if company should come. As soon as the frame for the rope bed was complete, Hank and Karl set off to cut enough timber to add a small second room to the rear as a bedroom for Hank and Maria. Until then, Karl would continue to sleep in the wagon, and the nights were beginning to grow cold.

"Maybe I should build a cabin for myself, so you and Maria can have a home for the two of you," Karl said as they sat at the supper table, not long after the cabin had been completed.

Maria responded, "We are family, Karl. You will share our home. It is no imposition. Cooking for one more adds no more work." She was firm in her resolve.

After the extra room was finished, Hank entered the cabin the next evening, and said, "Well, those of us who thought we were finished with building now have another project. Captain Crosby has asked that we build a large cabin about twenty by thirty feet to serve as a chapel, school, social hall, and place for community meetings. He wants it built to face that wide wagon trail that most of us laughingly call Main Street."

As the large cabin rose, the trappers sometimes came to watch. Reshaw said what some of them were thinking, "These Mormons will soon put us to shame, boys. This much energy and industry makes me uncomfortable."

But the trappers were not too uncomfortable to attend the first dance in the big cabin. They were somewhat startled to find that a sermon preceded the dance. Reshaw put up his hand as some of the trappers started to leave and said, "Hold up. We can tolerate a sermon if that's what it takes to get to the physical exercises on the dance floor."

Maria was amazed at the awkward but enthusiastic efforts of the trappers as they moved around the floor, so much so that she stood with wide eyes and a hand over her mouth. Watching the trappers dance, Hank laughed so hard he had to wipe his eyes. "They might not know any dance steps, but they can sure eat up the distance around the room when they have a pretty Mississippi girl in their arms."

One of the Southerners played a violin, while a trapper joined in with a Spanish guitar and a Mississippi man kept time on a homemade drum. Before the evening ended, every trapper needed a new pair of moccasins, and several were marched home by an unhappy wife who scolded them in heated Spanish.

In late August, Hank announced to Maria, "I'm going out tomorrow to find us some meat. If I'm really lucky, maybe I'll get a buck—or even a bear. This time of year the bears will be getting ready for hibernation, so they'll be really good eating—and you can make soap with the fat. Wouldn't you like a bear rug?"

"Hank, you're not going alone, are you?" Maria was alarmed at the prospect.

"George Therlkill, Billy Lay, and I are going together. George is a good shot, and Billy's got the best dogs for tracking this side of the Mississippi. We'll take Buddy, too." Hank genuinely liked Billy and the quiet, loose-jointed George, who wore homespun clothing and looked like a forty-five-year-old boy who had never quit growing.

"Will Karl be going?"

"I think we need to teach Karl to use a gun before we take him hunting." Hank grinned at his brother, who was sitting by the kitchen table, whittling a small toy for Martin.

"So you're afraid I might shoot something that should not be shot," Karl good-naturedly responded.

Maria gave Hank a stern look. "A bear rug would be wonderful, but I would rather have a husband in one piece than a bear rug, so you be very careful," she said, putting her arms affectionately around his neck.

The next day, about a mile into the woods, the men spotted a large buck. Hank fired at the animal, wounding it in the shoulder. It struggled and dragged itself into the trees with the dogs chasing it. The men followed with Hank in the lead. All three had their knives out, ready to cut the deer's throat.

Suddenly, an eight-foot-tall grizzly reared up and roared. The woods shook with the sound. With one great paw, the bear struck out at Hank, knocking the knife from his hand and pulling the strap to his rifle from off his shoulder. Stunned, he staggered back, bumping into George and sending his knife flying through the air. Both men yelled in panic, turned, and bumped into Billy. Each one tried to get out of the bear's way as it lumbered toward them.

Therlkill raised his rifle and fired, but the huge animal did not hesitate. The dogs barked and leaped at the bear, adding to the sound of its roars, gunfire, and the yells of the men. Hank had crawled to his gun and got off a shot, but still, the bear came at them. By this time, all three men were trying to reload with shaking hands. The roars of the wounded bear were nearly deafening. Hank fired again, but the bear had reached George and with one great swipe it knocked him to the ground. Blood spurted from the great gashes on his face. Hank raised his rifle and fired, but with one more swipe, the bear knocked the gun from his hand.

The noise of the confrontation carried back to the settlement and brought several other men running as hard as they could. Several others came, riding bareback with rifles in hand. They arrived with enough firepower to finally drop the bear. They put George on one of the horses and took him back to the settlement where his wounds were sterilized with turpentine and wrapped with clean rags.

The bear meat made several good meals for the three families. Hank and Billy agreed that the Therlkills had earned the bear rug—the hard way. Sister Therlkill said as it was presented to her, "The rug will be nice, and I thank you for it." She added quietly, "But I think I would rather have my husband unscarred." Her husband would carry three great white scars across his face for the rest of his life.

On the last Sunday in August, John Brown stood to deliver a sermon in the social-hall-turned-chapel. At the end he announced, "We can all recognize the lateness of the season, and most of you know that some of us promised the other Saints back in Mississippi that we would return in the fall to lead the rest of them west. We will be starting on September first for Mississippi. In our absence, Robert Crow and Ab Dowdle will serve as leaders of the group here." The next morning the four brothers-in-law—William Crosby, John Brown, Billy Lay, and John Bankhead—set out with a few other men to return to Monroe County.

By late October, some of the crops began to reach maturity. As Maria carried Martin, who had become a very sturdy little toddler and was struggling to get down to pat the squash, Hank called out, "Maria, look!"

She looked up to see him pointing toward the south. Her eyes followed his arm. In the distance she could see a great dust cloud on the horizon. "What or who do you think that might be?" she asked.

CHAPTER 24
The Sick Detachment

Hank shaded his eyes from the sun. "It's a big group. I can see a few pack mules, one wagon, and a few men on horseback, but most all of them are on foot." By the time the great knot of exhausted, slow-moving bodies neared the settlement, almost everyone there was watching the group approach.

The man on horseback led the group, and ten other officers and a supply wagon accompanied the group of more than a hundred and fifty individuals. It included weak and sick members of the Mormon Battalion, more than twenty women, and a like number of children. Many walked on bleeding feet wrapped in rags and leaned on makeshift crutches. Others were supported by friends and were weakened by illness, heat, thirst, and hunger. Several men rode out to meet them and escort them back to the settlement.

As the group drew nearer, Maria cried out, "Oh, my goodness, there are small children among them." She and three other women ran to meet them, and each picked up a small and dirty child and carried him or her back to the settlement. The weary and grateful smiles of the sunburned and exhausted mothers thanked them.

Many of the other women ran to their cabins to get clean rags and buckets of water for drinking and soap to wash the wounds of the injured. As the weak and sick men and women reached the settlement, they were led to the big log cabin, where the stronger settlers spent the afternoon feeding them and bandaging their wounds and injuries. That night, the Mississippi Saints took the sick ones in by ones and twos. While the sick and exhausted soldiers, women, and children slept in their beds, many of the

Southerners made beds in their wagons or set up tents again. The strongest of the Battalion group were bedded down in the big log cabin on bedrolls on the floor.

Using a cold, wet cloth, Hank wiped the forehead of the young man Karl had carried to their cabin and put into his bed. Maria made a pot of soup that evening. "I'm sure you can eat some soup and corn bread before you sleep," Maria said to him as she stirred the pot over the fire.

"Thank you, ma'am. I'm sure I can, too. We ain't had a good meal for the past month—except what you folks fed us today when we got here. We've been so hungry that we've been eating those flat, prickly pear cactus leaves like the Indians do."

As he wrung out the cloth in cold water, Hank said, "I'm Hank Schroeder and that's my wife, Maria. The bed you're sleeping in belongs to my brother, Karl, who carried you here. What's your name?"

"James Earl's my name, but most folks call me Jim. And I'm real glad for your hospitality. I don't know what we would have done if you folks hadn't been here to take us in. What brought you to Pueblo at this time?"

Hank explained, "We managed to get ahead of the first group of Saints that left Nauvoo. We were supposed to meet up with them somewhere along the Platte River. We came out of Mississippi and ended up so much farther west that we were lucky to be invited to spend the winter here in Pueblo by the French trappers who use the fort."

Jim responded reverently, "Thank God you're here. Some of us couldn't have survived much longer without your help. A few men traveling east from here met up with some government teamsters at Bent's Fort, and we crossed paths with them. They told our commander that there were some folks here at Pueblo, so we separated from the main body at Cimarron Crossing and headed here."

Between sips of hot soup from a large tin cup, Jim continued, "The men in this group became sick and weak from bad water, heat, forced marches, and poor food, and the women and children, who had wanted to go on the march with their husbands and fathers, couldn't keep up, so they were sent with us. Our commander, a young lieutenant by the name of Andrew Jackson Smith, replaced James Allen early on, and he marched us every day until we dropped. I guess Lieutenant Smith hates Mormons, as he sure had it in for all of us." He took a big drink of the soup and then added, "And that military doctor— Sanderson—he treated us worse than animals. Some of the men called him 'Doctor Death.' No matter what was wrong with a man, Sanderson would feed him powdered calomel mixed with molasses followed by a dose of arsenic. And he used a rusty spoon. He didn't seem to care if we lived or died." He looked at Maria and tried to smile gratefully, despite his swollen and split lips. "I guess our numbers have suddenly expanded the population of your little settlement."

"We don't mind. We're very glad that we were here to help you folks." She smiled as she spoke and patted his arm.

Hank took the empty cup and said, "We've heard from Ab Dowdle that counting all of the members of your group, we have close to 200 of us here to get through the winter. I sure hope our gardens bring in a good harvest, or we may have to learn to eat a few prickly pear cacti like you did."

To open the first Sabbath meeting held in the big cabin after the arrival of the sick members of the Battalion, Dowdle offered a fervent prayer, "We see Thy hand in our travels, Lord, which have brought us here to meet and care for the sick members of the Mormon Battalion. We are grateful for Thy providence and guidance, and may we never doubt that Thy hand is over all."

Within the next few weeks, the men of the community, with the help of the few soldiers who were physically able, built an additional eighteen cabins for the sick Battalion members and their families. As the men regained their strength over the next two months, some of their sick beds were taken by a second group of seventeen Battalion members, who made their way to the fort from New Mexico in November. Then a third group of fifty-five sick and hungry Battalion members arrived in early December. Like the first group, many arrived with open wounds on their feet, legs, and faces, while others had trouble keeping food down.

Betty Matthews gave small sacks of elm bark to Maria and several of the other women and told each of them, "Boil it and strain it, and then bring it to me. While it is warm, we need to give it to the sickest of the soldiers." With Betty's nursing and good food, the vast majority of the men quickly regained their health and strength.

By December, the Battalion members, the Southerners, and the trappers made up a community of nearly two hundred and seventy-five. By Christmas, the dances on Saturday nights in the big cabin were overflowing with young men lined up to dance with the Southern girls, even those as young as thirteen. There were several trappers who would have asked the married women to dance, if the looks from their frowning, silent wives had not deterred them. Jim Earl had been a bugler in the Battalion, and he added his horn to the little group of music makers after his split, chapped lips had healed.

Karl sat quietly and watched. When encouraged to ask a girl to dance, he smiled and replied, "I do not dance so well. I might break a lady's toes."

CHAPTER 25
Saying Good-Bye to Friends

When Maria began to suffer with a stomach that would not hold anything she ate, Hank worried aloud, "Maybe you caught something from one of those sick soldiers."

Maria looked at him and smiled weakly. "No, Hank, this is not something that is catching."

"Then what is it that is making you so sick?"

"This won't last long, just a few weeks, and then, Husband, I will probably want to eat everything in sight. You see, I am going to have a baby next summer."

Hank put his arms around her. "I hope it is a girl—a girl just like her mother, and we will call her Caroline." Then he held her close.

Food for the winter months included cornmeal—used as payment by the trappers for services the Southerners gave them—and vegetables from their gardens, augmented with elk, deer, and smaller animals that were plentiful. Supplies from Bent's Fort about forty miles to the east kept them from getting excessively hungry.

Hank brought home two raccoons for supper in early January, so they invited the Kartchner and Dowdle families to join them, if Ab would agree to cook the meal. Maria gave Margaret Kartchner and Sarah Dowdle a hug as they arrived. She laughed as she said, "I've never eaten raccoon, but I know some folks from the South prefer it to other meals."

Ab Dowdle grinned and said, "You can bet your bottom dollar on that! All us Mississippi folks know just how to cook this dish." And he took over the preparation of the meal, for which Maria was very grateful.

After receiving his serving of the meat, served with roasted pine nuts and winter squash, Hank said, "You have done yourself proud, Ab."

The meal did not sit well with Maria, and, after the guests left, she spent the next two hours holding a dish pan as the meal came up the way it went down. "I will never eat raccoon again," she moaned.

By spring, seven new babies had enlarged the numbers of the Mississippi Saints. A similar number of deaths kept the numbers stable. Two weddings brightened the settlement. The trappers enjoyed the celebrating that accompanied the births and the weddings as much or more than the Southerners. Reshaw mused out loud, "These Mormonites sure know how to have a good time. I think this is a religion I just might consider joinin' up with." Two of the other trappers slapped him on the back and laughed long and loud at the thought of Reshaw "getting religion."

In early April, the Therlkill and Crow families made preparations for the trip to Fort Laramie, where they hoped to meet the advance exploratory company as it made its way toward the Great Basin. "Oh, we will miss them, but I am excited for them all the same. We will follow them later this summer, after the baby comes," Maria said confidently as she leaned against Hank with her arm around his waist. As she stood there, she felt the baby stir, and she unconsciously put her hand on her growing body. Though Hank said nothing to discourage her plans, he looked down at her and thought that they would make that decision after the baby came.

About three weeks later in Sabbath meeting, Ab Dowdle stood and announced, "Plans have been made for the rest of us who are able to make our way to the Valley. There is no reason for us to remain here in Pueblo now that the weather is warm." Very quickly, the remaining Southern Saints and the balance of the Battalion members began planning for the exodus.

"Oh, Hank, Letitia and Allen are going—and Will and Betty Matthews. Everyone is going. I don't want to be left here all alone." Maria's disappointment was evident in her voice.

As he hugged her to him and patted her shoulder, he said, "You know that Betty Matthews said that as sick as you were in the beginning, it would not be good for you to face that long journey. It could cost you the baby."

"But that means that we will have to travel nearly alone after the baby comes. I don't think that we will be safe."

"Karl will be with us, and the Lord will help us work it out."

The Saints, Battalion members, and some of the trappers had formed lifetime friendships. Excited cheers sent the wagons on their way northward. Maria called after them, "We'll see you in a few weeks." Turning back to their own cabin, they saw the other cabins of the once-flourishing settlement now standing empty. Trying to hide her disappointment at not going with them, she said, "How will we ever keep the gardens up by ourselves?"

Hank said gently, "Many folks did not even plant this spring. They knew they would be leaving, so there won't be much for us to keep up." A feeling of isolation closed around Maria.

CHAPTER 26
Renewed Pursuit

Lafayette Breaux spent less than a week in Memphis asking about the wagon company of Mississippi Mormons that had passed through the town some weeks earlier. Making his way to Dyersburg, the sheriff there told him of Sharp's death.

"And you let them go!" Breaux shouted.

"I had to. He tried to kill a man who was protecting his wife and child."

"That man is probably the man who stole the woman. They belong to me!" Breaux stopped pacing and turned on the sheriff and asked angrily, "Was the child a boy or a girl?"

"Seems to me it was a boy, too little to walk yet. Yeah, I remember now, it was a dark-haired boy. If they belong to you, how come you didn't know if it was a boy or a girl?" The sheriff's eyes narrowed. "How could she belong to you? She was white as my wife."

Breaux refused to explain but turned and stormed out of the office. The sheriff said in a puzzled tone to his deputy, "I don't think I've ever seen a man as mad as that one. Can't help but wonder what's really driving him."

By the third week of July, Breaux had reached St. Louis, and he steadily made his way across Missouri, by coach where possible and by horseback when he had to. When he reached Independence in mid-August, he began to ask if there were any wagon companies known to be composed of Mormons that might have left from that area during the summer months.

The Jackson County sheriff answered his inquiries. "Not many wagon companies of Mormons come through Missouri.

They got whipped good and driven out of here a few years ago. Now, they mostly go through the Iowa Territory. Why you interested in Mormons?"

"One of them stole a woman who belongs to me. I want her back," Breaux responded tersely.

"Well, you ought to think about waiting until next year to follow them. That's a journey you don't want to try to make in the winter months. It can snow in the Rockies as early as late August. We hear that those Mormons are planning to settle out in the Great Basin in territory belonging to Mexico. You'll be able to find them there in the spring."

Lafayette Breaux drank himself into a stupor that evening in the bar at the largest hotel in Independence. In the morning as his pounding head made war in his skull, he decided to return to his plantation for the winter. There, he spent every night drinking and pacing in his office, counting the days until spring, unresponsive to his wife's questions. He left the operation of the plantation completely in the hands of Jeremiah Pounder.

After the early spring rains had ended in May, he ordered five of his strongest male slaves be sold to give him money sufficient to last several months. He packed a large trunk and had his light spring carriage brought, with his four best horses hitched to it.

"Lafe, where are you going?" his angry and frustrated wife demanded from where she stood on the wide front veranda. "Why have you sold our best slaves? How long will you be gone?"

His response was terse. "Like I told you when I left last year, don't expect me until you see me. Just see that Jeremiah Pounder keeps the plantation running." He slapped the reins against the rumps of the horses, and the carriage moved rapidly down the road.

"We will do just fine without you, sir," she muttered under her breath. "You have been absolutely no help this entire winter. We will be just as well off if you never come back." With that, she turned and entered the large house, slamming the door.

Breaux paid to have the carriage and horses taken on board a steamship at the levee at Mound City, and he disembarked at St. Louis. It took him less than two weeks to cross Missouri, and when he reached Independence, he hired a Mexican-Indian guide with limited English-speaking skills by the name of Garcia to lead him to the Great Basin in the Rocky Mountains. While in Independence, he also traded his carriage and fine horses for a sturdy freight wagon and two teams of mules. He took a week to load it high with supplies—a sturdy twill tent and items meant for trading with hostile Indian tribes along the way, just in case he had to buy himself out of a difficult situation.

Even though it was heavily loaded, the wagon and its two passengers made good time. When travelers on horseback going east on the trail brought rumors of Indian raiding parties, Breaux and Garcia would attach themselves to a wagon company moving west, but when Breaux's impatience grew too great to tolerate the slow pace, they would separate from the wagons and move much faster along the trail by themselves. They reached Fort Laramie about the first of July.

He asked the manager of the fort, a man named Boudeau, "Any wagon companies of Mormons from Mississippi passed this way in the last while?"

The stout, barrel-chested manager told him, "Seems you're a mite late to catch up with them. Brigham Young's advance company arrived here on the first of June and left on the fourth. There was a small group of folks from Mississippi that had come up from Pueblo that joined up with that company."

With increased interest, Breaux asked, "Who were they? Did you learn any of their names?"

"Nah, don't remember any names. The ones I talked to said they met some trappers on the trail last fall and were invited down to Pueblo for the winter, as they were too far west of the company led by Brigham Young to link up with them. When the weather got warm this year, they left Pueblo and traveled here in time to meet Young and his company. Then they headed for the Great Basin." The man paused for a few seconds and scratched his head. Then he added, "There was another group that came up from Pueblo, too, just about three weeks later. Must have been more than two hundred of them. That group was a mix of Southerners and some Mormon Battalion members."

"You're sure of that?"

"Yes, sir, that I am."

"I'll want to head out in the morning," Breaux said. "I need supplies."

In the morning, Breaux and Garcia headed west on the Oregon Trail. When they arrived at the Platte River in view of the great ridge called Casper Mountain, a group of young men who had built and were operating a ferry on the river made their journey easier. As they ferried Breaux's wagon across the river for a fee of one dollar, he learned that they had been members of the advance company. They had been assigned by Brigham Young to remain behind and operate the ferry to raise money.

This information fed Breaux's determination to reach the Great Basin quickly, where he was sure he would find Maria and their son. He and Garcia reached Fort Bridger two weeks later. The fort hardly deserved the title, as it was little more than a cluster of cabins and a few Indian wikiups, with a corral for the animals. Breaux again asked about the two companies with the Southerners in them.

Jim Bridger remembered both groups well. "The first one under Young was a big group, and there were a few in it who talked like you do. I told Young that they wouldn't be able to grow a good crop there in the basin near that salt lake, as the frost comes too late in the spring and too early in the fall, but nobody changes Brigham Young's mind. I even offered him a thousand dollars for the first bushel of corn grown there. They left here just about two, maybe three weeks ago." Bridger added, "That other big group came through here a little more than a week later. About half of them talked like you."

"How easy is the trail to follow?" Breaux asked urgently.

Bridger responded, "With both those big groups passing through not long ago, a blind man can follow that trail."

It took Breaux awhile to make up his mind as to how he was going to explain his presence in the Mormon settlement. After nearly a week of following the rugged trail, Garcia insisted that they leave some boxes of trinkets they had brought for trading with the Indians by the trail. "Load too heavy. Wagon won't go over the trail or through the canyon," Garcia explained.

The wagon finally rumbled down out of Emigration Canyon and into what was little more than a very large camp of wagons and tents in the Great Salt Lake Valley. Breaux and Garcia were greeted with open and friendly waves from the men who were flooding a small creek so they could put a plow in the ground. There were several fields where it was evident that crops had been planted. A few women were drawing water from the stream for cooking and washing. Breaux muttered to Garcia, "These people must be crazy to think they can build a city here in this desert."

He had Garcia stop the wagon so he could speak to the men who had diverted the stream. "Can you tell me where I can find Brigham Young? I hear he's boss around here."

One of the men removed his hat and wiped his face with a dusty bandana. "Yes, I guess you could call President Young that. I think he's over in that tent where those men are gathered. He's been sick, but he might be able to see you. You got business with him?"

Without answering, Breaux pointed Garcia toward the tent where about six men were gathered around, talking. As the wagon arrived, a man of middle height and in his forties lifted the flap and stepped out. His complexion was sallow and his clothes hung loosely on him. "Well, stranger, I don't think I've met you. What brings you to this valley?" he asked.

"Mr. Young, can we talk in private? I have a matter of great importance to discuss with you."

Young nodded, and said wryly, "Just step into my office, and we can talk." He lifted the tent flap and offered the stranger a wooden box to sit on while he seated himself on a similar box facing him. "What is it that brings you out to this wilderness, Mr. . . . ?"

Breaux removed his hat and introduced himself, "I'm Lafayette Breaux from Louisiana." He then shared the story he had decided would get him the most cooperation. "I have followed my wife and child across this continent to bring her home. She has run off with another man, and I want her back. I have been told that she is part of the group that came from Mississippi."

"That's interesting, Mr. Breaux. We did have a large group made up of Battalion members and Southerners that arrived in the Valley a few days ago, and there were two families from Mississippi that joined my company at Fort Laramie. All of them had wintered over in Pueblo. I invite you to make your way among those that are here to see if you can find the woman and child that you say belong to you." Young paused and then looked directly at Breaux as if to make his next statement sink in and added, "If you find her and the child, you are to bring them to me. You will not remove them from the Valley without my express permission. Do you understand?"

Breaux responded in his most oily and accommodating voice, "Of course, Mr. Young. I would never think of handling the situation any other way."

As Breaux took his leave, both he and Young knew that he had no intention of doing as he had been asked to do. The Church leader said to a man standing outside the tent, "Find Port Rockwell for me and get him here as soon as possible."

When Rockwell appeared at President Young's tent, he was told about Lafayette Breaux and his professed reason for following the Saints to the Valley. "Port, I want you to meet this man and give me your opinion of him—and watch him. There's something not square about him."

Port said nothing but nodded and left the tent. He returned two days later and reported, "The man is a plantation owner from Louisiana. He had a couple of bottles of whiskey in his wagon, and while we shared one the other evening, I got him talking. By the time we reached the bottom of the second bottle . . ."

"Port, I've told you that you have got to give up liquor." President Young's voice was sharp. "The Lord is not pleased with your imbibing."

Porter paused for a moment and then said in a somewhat chagrined manner, "I know, I know, Brother Brigham, but this time it got what we were looking for—the real story. The man is trying to catch a woman he claims is a white slave who ran away from his plantation. He said that she tells everyone that she was an indentured servant, but he says that he bought her as a slave." He looked at President Young and raised an eyebrow. "He revealed what kind of man he really is when he told me that it doesn't matter to him if she's an indentured servant or not. He says he fathered her boy, and he wants the two of them back, as his wife has given him no children."

"You'll continue to watch him?"

"I will." Rockwell put on his hat and left the tent.

Over the next week, Breaux made his way through the settlement and checked at every wagon and every tent, asking every man he met if he knew of Maria or Hank. The guide, Garcia, sat near their tent and played solitaire with what was probably the only deck of cards in the entire Valley, using an excuse of poor English to avoid accompanying the plantation owner in his search.

During his next encounter with Rockwell at his campsite, an encounter which appeared to be entirely coincidental but wasn't, Porter took a bottle from his saddlebag and, as he offered it to Breaux, said, "Maybe the woman you're looking for, and the man with her, went on to California—or even Oregon. There's a lot of folks here who are wishing that President Young had decided to go to either of those places, rather than stopping here."

"You think so?"

"Yep, I think so."

"I don't know," Breaux said suspiciously. "It seemed to me that there are folks here who know more about the woman than they are willing to say."

Rockwell offered him the bottle again and said with a smile, "It's just that unwillingness on the part of us Mormons to talk to gentiles like you. You've got to realize that if they did choose to go on to California, they'd be in hot water with President Young, as he said that those who leave for California will be considered to have left the Church. But a few have done just that. They most likely would have gone on without letting very many people know of their plans."

"So you think I ought to go on to California?" By this time Breaux had located a corkscrew in his trunk and had opened the bottle. He filled a dirty tumbler with the dark liquid.

As Breaux emptied the glass, Rockwell said, "It sure seems like the best choice to me, unless you want to stay here and build an adobe house while you live in a tent and raise some corn and potatoes. And you said yourself that you have looked into every tent and wagon here and found no sign of them."

Breaux, who had poured a second glassful, offered the bottle to Rockwell, who declined it with a motion of his hand. "Well, I think that is just what I might do. Yes, I think I might just go on to California." He drained the glass again and poured a third. "If you were going to California, which route would you take?" he asked.

Rockwell answered, "The best route is to go north to Fort Hall and follow the Oregon Trail until it forks. Your guide, Garcia, shouldn't have any problem finding the way."

"I guess I can trust him. He says he's been there a couple of times," Breaux said as he threw the empty bottle against a large rock, where it broke. Then he slowly slumped against the trunk where the two men had been sitting while they drank. He patted the ground to signal that he wanted Rockwell to sit by him. "Tell me where to look when I get to California."

Rockwell began to tell him of the glories of the Yerba Buena area when Breaux began to nod and snore. Rockwell got up and sauntered away with a wide grin. In the morning, he drifted by on his horse and offered to help Breaux and Garcia load their wagon. He asked Garcia, "You know the trail to California from here?"

"*Si, si, señor.* I know the trail. We will follow the Oregon Trail until we meet with wagons going to California. Then we will follow the trail to the Humbolt River so we do not make the terrible mistake made by the Donner-Reed Company last winter. We will not take the Hastings Cutoff. We will go by the old trail."

Rockwell helped Garcia lift the tent into the wagon where Breaux was sitting, holding his head, and then he stepped back and waved his hat at the two men as Garcia slapped the reins against the horses' rumps, and the wagon headed toward Emigration Canyon. Porter then made his way directly to President Young's tent to give his report.

As he finished telling the president what had happened, the Church president said, "This slave issue is going to be a thorn in our sides, Port. I can see it coming. This is one issue that I sincerely wish we could have left behind us."

CHAPTER 27
Lost in the Snowstorm

The Schroeders, trappers, their wives, their children, and the daughter of George Gibson, who had married a trapper, were the only folks remaining in the area after the Saints and Battalion members left for Fort Laramie. The next evening Hank sat down with Maria and said, "Karl and I agree that we need to move into the fort for safety. We're too isolated out here. We need to pack up our things and ask Reshaw and the others if we can stay in the fort."

Maria nodded, glad to end their isolation, and in the morning they closed the door on the little cabin that they had considered home for nearly a year and turned the mules and the wagon toward the fort. They were welcomed and offered one of the adobe structures inside the wall. It was dirty and dusty living, but they felt safer there than alone in the settlement. Karl took the adobe next to theirs.

When the trappers left to take up their trade on the rivers, the number living in the fort dwindled even more.

One evening in late May at supper time, Maria could not find Martin. "Hank, Hank, where is Marty? I can't find him." She tried to keep the panic from her voice.

Hank left off repairing the wagon box and came quickly. "Where did you last see him?"

"He was playing with the water I was going to use to wash the dishes. He can't have gone far; he is so unsteady and his legs are so short."

Supper was put aside as several of the wives of the absent trappers helped Maria, Hank, and Karl search for the toddler.

"You know that wherever Marty is, Buddy will be there, too. He will keep Marty safe." Hank tried to calm Maria's fears.

Within a few minutes the searchers could hear a dog barking. They made their way toward the sound until they found the child playing near Fountain Creek, throwing small clods of dirt and rocks in the general direction of a rattlesnake, which had been warming itself on a flat rock near the bank. It had coiled itself into a round pile of tense muscle as its rattles shook a warning, and it bared its fangs. Buddy was barking wildly.

Hank called out, "Buddy, down, sit." The agitated dog sat but quivered with excitement. Hank took his bowie knife from its sheath and threw it at the snake. As it neatly severed the head, Karl leaped, taking three great steps, and scooped up Martin. The startled little boy cried loudly.

Maria took the child from his uncle and held him close. Buddy earned a pat on the head from Hank and a serving of rattlesnake meat for supper from Maria.

Maria hugged the struggling toddler to her that night, and as she tucked him into bed, she repeated over and over, "No snakes. Snakes are bad. When you see a snake you run and tell Mama and Papa. Do you understand?" Martin nodded, his eyes big with wonder but not understanding his mother's concern.

After Maria and Hank were in bed, Maria whispered, "Oh, Hank, what would we have done if he had been bitten by that snake? I couldn't live if anything happened to him."

***

Maria's baby came in early May, earlier than expected. Reshaw's wife, Iowae, was a capable midwife and assisted with the birth. As she wrapped the very little baby girl in a shawl and placed her in Maria's arms, Maria smiled weakly and said, "Look, Hank, we have a baby girl."

Hank smiled as he lifted the shawl away from her small face and said, "Hello, Caroline. Welcome to our family."

The baby's weak little cry sounded almost like a kitten. Maria looked at the tiny face that was losing the blue color she had been born with and was turning pink. "Oh, Hank, she is so little and weak. She can hardly grasp my finger. There is no way we can travel until she is stronger." Their plans to travel to the Valley that year were suspended.

The months passed, and Caroline grew slowly and gained little weight. "Hank, I am so worried. The baby is not thriving like Martin did at this age. I don't know what to do." Maria's face was clouded with worry.

Hank was quiet for a few seconds and then said, "Why don't you ask some of the wives of the trappers what they do for sickly babies?"

When asked, Iowae answered, "You must eat better so your milk will make the baby strong. I will bring you good medicine." Several of the other trapper's wives stood around the two women and nodded as Iowae talked. Within the hour, Iowae had returned with a bag full of what looked to Maria like dried berries. She said, "This good for you. Make your milk better. Boil and drink every day." She put the bag down and left.

Hank took some of the dried berries from the bag and after examining them said, "They look like black currants." He examined them more closely and added, "They can't hurt you and might even help." He put a pot full of water over the fire to boil. Every day thereafter, Iowae would come to visit and make sure that Maria drank a cup of the water from the boiled berries.

By December, Caroline was sitting up. "Hank, I think this is the bitterest potion I have ever had to drink, but I must admit that Caroline's strength and weight are much better."

In January, the food supply had shrunken, and the snow was too deep to make the trip to Bent's Fort, so Reshaw and Hank planned a hunting trip, hoping to locate a herd of deer or elk. Reshaw insisted that Hank attach a flat, woven web of willows set in a round birch frame to the bottom of his boots. "See, *mon ami*, shoes that walk on the snow." The trapper was proud of his invention. Hank found that walking with his feet spread apart was awkward, at best, but he did admit to the trapper that the "shoes that could walk on snow" were a clever tool that made getting around in deep snow easier.

Taking pockets filled with jerky and their rifles over their shoulders, the two men set out on foot in the early morning to

find game. Hank insisted that Karl remain behind to watch over
Maria and the children. Reshaw insisted that Buddy stay behind.
"That dog has a good nose, but his feet will freeze in the snow."

By the time the weak sun was ready to set late that afternoon,
Maria was pacing the floor, worried about their long absence.
Karl quietly whittled near the stove. When darkness came, he
patted Maria on the shoulder and said, "Call me when he gets
back." Then he quietly slipped out and returned to the adobe
cabin next door where he slept.

Maria put the children to bed but could only continue to
pace the floor. Every sound made her jump and rush to the door,
but still, Hank did not appear. Finally, she lay down on the bed
and spent the night looking at the ceiling of the cabin in the dark,
unable to close her eyes. The next morning, before the children
awoke, she made her way to Reshaw's adobe, and when Iowae
opened the door, she asked with a voice full of poorly contained
panic, "Why aren't they home yet? Has something happened to
them?"

Iowae answered, "Not to worry. Sometime Reshaw not come
home two, maybe three days. He take care of Hank." She opened
the door wider and added, "You come in?"

"No, but thank you. I must get back to the children." Maria
turned and ran back to her adobe. As she entered quietly, Marty
sat up in his little bed and asked, "Where's Papa?"

Maria picked him up and said, "He's gone to get us some
dinner. He will be home soon." She hoped her voice sounded
more convincing to him than it did to her.

Karl joined them for breakfast, and after he finished his
cornmeal mush, he pushed away from the table and said quietly,
"I should go and find them."

"No, Karl, you will get lost in the snow. Losing you will not
help Hank."

When Maria offered Martin a piece of corn bread for supper,
he grew petulant. He pushed it away and said, "Want Papa."

It was almost too much for Maria. She picked him up and
held him close. "I want Papa, too," she said.

She tried to wipe away a few tears without Marty seeing them,
but he pushed himself away from her and looked at her face.

"Mama cry?" She pulled him against her and tried to rock him some more, but he would have none of it. With great indignation, he pushed away again and demanded, "Why Mama cry?"

She wiped her eyes one more time and said, "Everything will be all right. Papa will be home soon. Mama won't cry anymore."

But despite her reassurances, Hank did not come home before the children were put to bed. Maria and Karl knelt by the chairs at the kitchen table and prayed for Hank's return. Kneeling by the side of the bed in the little bedroom, she tried to pray, but her fears stopped the words, and she woke an hour later with her head on the bed. She spent the rest of the night waiting—waiting for the sound of the familiar step that did not come. What did come was the sound of wind, carrying with it more snow. Even Buddy would not sleep. He paced the inside of the cabin, watching the door as if taking his cue from Maria.

The next morning when she opened the door, the snow had built a drift against it more than three feet deep. The thought of Hank out there in that storm almost made her heart stop. That day the sun rose and turned the world into glittering crystal. The trees were covered with glistening icicles, and a slight breeze made the limbs move to and fro in a silent dance. *If only Hank were here with me, it would be the most beautiful sight I have ever seen,* she thought. *But without him, it terrifies me.*

As she fixed cornmeal mush for the three of them, Marty asked again, "Papa come home?" His big blue eyes were wide with concern, and he looked at her like an interrogator who wanted the truth.

Taking a deep breath to help maintain her composure, she answered, "I don't know, Marty, but I hope it will be very soon." Forcing a cheerfulness she did not feel, Maria continued, "And when he comes, maybe he will bring us a rabbit or some venison for our supper."

Throughout the day, Marty played quietly near the stove with the wooden figures Karl had whittled for him. Caroline lay in her little bed and played with her toes. At every sound, Maria and Marty stopped what they were doing and hurried to the door to see if Hank had returned. Buddy lay by the door, unwilling to move. When Maria put Marty in his little homemade bed that evening, he said to her with a confidence and seriousness beyond his age, "I wake up, Papa come home."

Maria said, "I hope so," and kissed him on the forehead.

An hour after Marty had fallen asleep, Maria knelt by the bed again and offered a prayer of desperation. Hearing the door open, she hurried into the main room of the adobe. Karl was standing there. "I am going to find Hank," he said. Then he closed the door and started through the snow. She hurried to the door and opened it. She called out, "Karl, come back! You will never find him. You don't know where they went." The moon lit the snow almost like daylight.

She heard no response. In fear and frustration, she returned to her knees and offered a panicked prayer, "Dear God, please protect these good men. Please bring Hank home safely. He is the center of my world. Don't take him from me." She returned to pacing the floor for another hour. Wiping her eyes, she heard something scrabbling at the door. She pulled it open just in time to see a large form covered with snow topple into the room. Thinking it was a bear, she involuntarily stepped back but then realized it was Hank. She helped him stand upright. There was snow packed on his buckskin clothing, and ice had formed on his hair and ears and hung in icicles from his battered hat brim.

"Oh, Hank, you're back; you're back." She wrapped her arms around the snowy figure, almost knocking him off his feet.

He tried to speak but couldn't. Finally, he croaked, "Water—water."

She rushed to the table and poured water from the bucket into a cup. He drank it and put the cup out for more. When he emptied the second cup, she led him to the chair. Then she helped him remove the stiff, frozen clothing. She found herself talking a steady stream. "You're back, thank God. Karl went looking for you. I'm afraid he will get lost. Here, let me take your clothes. Sit down, and let me thaw your fingers and toes. Oh, Hank, we have been so worried." She tried to pull his boots off his feet, but they were too stiff with the cold.

"Be careful," he whispered. "My toes are frozen."

After some steady tugging, one of the boots finally came off. The hand-knit stocking was frozen to his flesh.

"Can you get me some more water? I'm so thirsty," he whispered.

She rushed to fill the tin cup again. She stood silently, watching as he drank it.

After tugging the other boot off, she hurried to fill the dishpan with water from the bucket. She helped him put one foot into it. He flinched with the pain and inhaled deeply, pressing his lips together to keep from crying out. After a few minutes, Maria was able to peel the thawed stocking off his foot.

When she looked at his toes, she caught her breath. "Hank, some of your toes are black."

"Yes, I thought so," was all he quietly said. "You said Karl went looking for me?"

"He went to look for you about an hour ago."

She helped him put the other foot into the cold water. After several minutes she peeled the stocking off the other foot. Three toes on that foot were black, and the forth and fifth were deep purple on the ends. "Hank, what are we going to do for your feet?"

Hank bent over and examined his feet. After a minute he said, "I'm sorry to ask this of you, my love, but some of the toes are going to have to come off."

Maria's face blanched. "What do you mean?"

CHAPTER 28
Frostbite

"You will need to get your sharpest knife." He looked into her frightened face and said, "Do it now. If we wait until I have more feeling in my feet, it will be much more difficult for both of us."

"If we wrap your feet up in a warm blanket, they'll surely get better."

"No, my dear. Reshaw explained that things will only get worse if we don't do something now. Get the knife."

With shaking hands, Maria located the big knife used for skinning and dressing the larger game animals.

"Get some rags," he instructed her. "Put them under my feet. Now take the knife and remove the little toe on my right foot. Try to leave a little skin flap on the bottom. You will need to sew it over the gap."

"Hank, I don't think I can do this," she whispered, so white-faced that she looked like she might faint.

"Of course you can, Maria. It has to be done."

"Can I go and get one of the trappers to do it?"

"I would rather have you do it. One of those rugged, old frontiersmen might not know when to quit and might just dress me out like a deer carcass." He smiled weakly at his joke, and then he put his hand over hers. "You can do it, my dear. Just take a big breath. Try to separate the joint as though you are cutting apart a chicken wing."

Maria sat down on the floor at his feet, and, holding her breath, she put the point of the knife against his toe. Then she dropped it, and put her face in her hands.

Hank's voice was weak, but, mustering all the strength he could, he said forcefully, "Maria, you can do this. You must do this, or I will lose my feet."

She sat up straight and, taking a big breath to steady her hand, said, "I will do my best." As she cut the flesh, Hank made no sound. She looked up at him and said, "Can you feel that?"

He shook his head but said, "Try to work as quickly as possible." Using the point of the knife, she easily separated the joint of the littlest toe from his foot. "Now get your sewing needle and some thread—quickly." With shaking hands, she located the needle and thread in her little sewing basket and returned to her place at his feet. Hank then instructed, "You've got to sew the open wound together to limit the bleeding when circulation returns."

Biting her lower lip, she poked the needle through the flesh and pulled the upper and lower flesh together. When she was through, she stood and turned away from him, holding her arms against her body and shaking from head to foot.

"You're not done. There's more to do." She took a deep breath, turned around, and again sat by his feet. "Now take off the next toe." She repeated the process as her hands continued to shake. Hank flinched.

She removed three toes on the right foot and two on the left foot and sewed together the flesh. As she looked at the mutilated feet, Maria said, "Some of the other toes don't look very good, Hank. Will they be all right?"

"I think so. They're not totally black, and there is some feeling in them. I hope in a day or two their color will get better. Do you have some clean rags to wrap my feet in?"

"Yes, of course." Maria took three clean dish towels and tore them into strips. Then she carefully wrapped his mangled feet.

When she finished the task, he said as he tried to stand, "Can you help me into bed? I'm a trifle tired."

Maria supported him as he made his way to the bed. There, he lay down so she could pull off his wet pants. Then she covered him with a quilt, and within a minute, he was asleep. She sat by the bed and watched him, just in case he wanted or needed something. He slept without moving, hardly breathing—but he slept, and for that she was grateful. After a little while, she knelt and prayed fervently, expressing her gratitude that he had returned and the hope that he would recover swiftly. Then she slipped into her nightdress and carefully climbed into the bed next to him to help warm his chilled body.

In the morning, Marty's voice awoke Maria. He had climbed out of his little bed and was pulling on Hank's hand. "Papa, wake up. You come home. You come home."

She climbed out of the bed and said to the just-barely two-year-old, "Papa's tired, let him sleep. We will fix some breakfast for him."

As she picked Marty up, he put one of his hands on either side of her face and turned her face to him. "Papa come home," he said simply.

She hugged him to her and said gratefully, "Yes, Papa came home, Marty. You were right." Hank slept the entire day, waking only briefly for another drink of water. As she worked in the cabin, she worried about Karl. He could be as lost as Hank had been, but she could not leave Hank to go look for him. Late that afternoon, Karl returned to the cabin, chilled and hungry.

As he entered, he said, "I can't find him, Maria. I'm sorry."

She pointed to the bed where Hank slept and said, "He got back not long after you left last night. Thank you for looking for him. I am so glad you are back. I was worried about you."

The next day two trappers came to the cabin with several large, frozen pieces of venison. One of them explained, "Reshaw and your husband shot three deer and then hung them high in a tree to keep them from the wolves. Reshaw asked us to find them and bring them back. We dressed one of them out for you and your family."

As she took some of the meat from them, she said gratefully, "Thank you so very much. How is Mr. Reshaw? Did he suffer any frostbite?"

"Not much. How is Mr. Schroeder?"

"He lost toes on both feet. He's still resting."

"I think Reshaw would have lost toes if he had any to lose, but he lost them years ago. He said that the two of them got lost in the snowstorm and ran out of matches, so they couldn't build a fire to melt snow or get warm. When the sun came out, they ended up snow blind. Reshaw is one very humiliated man because he got lost. Says that ain't never happened to him before. Well, ma'am, I hope you enjoy the venison." And then they were gone.

Maria washed the knife she had used on Hank's toes and cut a roast from one of the chunks of venison. She put it in the pot on the fire with a little water and put the lid on it. As she turned, she said to Martin, "Marty, now we will have a good supper for your papa when he wakes up."

That evening Hank ate his first real meal in four days. It was only venison and corn bread, but he relished every bite.

Spring came early, about the same time that Hank could finally walk without a crutch. As the weather warmed, they began to talk of leaving Pueblo and making their way to the Valley.

"We're going to need a guide. We really can't make the trip like blind men," Hank worried aloud. "I'm going to ask Reshaw if he or any of the other trappers would lead us at least as far as Fort Laramie." But the trappers were more interested in getting out on the Missouri and Arkansas Rivers, where they would find the animal pelts that furnished their living.

By April, Caroline was trying to stand alone, holding on to Hank's fingers as she bobbed up and down on her little legs like a puppet on a string. What little hair she had was like a halo of sunshine, and her laugh warmed her parents' hearts.

Reshaw and two of the other trappers set out eastward along the Arkansas River after the first spring thaw so they could trap the length of the river to its confluence with the Mississippi. They returned to Fort Pueblo in July with their pockets full of coins and folding money after having sold a full catch of beaver, fox, and bear pelts in St. Louis. Their wives cooked a fully dressed deer for all in the camp as a celebration. Reshaw stood importantly before the big fire and announced, "When we arrived in St. Louis, we got a hold of a newspaper that said . . ."

One of the other trappers interrupted him by calling out good-naturedly, "Now don't you go and tell us that you can read English, Reshaw. We know better."

Reshaw responded with a grin, "Well, I can have someone read English to me. That newspaper said that another big company of Mormonites, full of Southerners, had left the Council Bluffs area in the Nebraska Territory for the Great Basin about the end of June. They planned to be in Fort Laramie by August." Looking at Hank, he added, "Seems like the South is contributing a whole lot of folks to your new religion. Maybe everybody out in the Great Basin will talk with a Southern drawl." He laughed and then asked, "Do you suppose if we met them in Laramie, we could talk them into coming down to Pueblo so we could dance with some more of those pretty Mississippi girls again?"

Hank responded, "I wouldn't count on it, as I suspect that the word of your dancing has probably spread the length and breadth of this continent by now."

When they climbed into bed that evening, Maria said enthusiastically, "Oh, Hank, these are folks we know. Do you think we could meet them when they reach Fort Laramie?" Maria's face was bright with anticipation as she looked into his eyes for agreement.

"Now that Caroline is stronger and finally walking a little bit, it's time for us to be making our way to the Valley."

One more time, Hank asked Reshaw if he would consider leading them north to Fort Laramie. Reshaw finally agreed, saying, "After getting you lost in the snow and getting you frostbit, I guess I owe you something. *Oui*, I will lead you to Fort Laramie, and from there, I can trap the rivers west of the Rockies for what remains of the summer."

After they packed the wagon, they started northward. Two other rugged trappers accompanied Reshaw, all three on horseback and leading heavily loaded pack mules. As the trail wound along Fountain Creek, Maria said with anticipation, "Soon we will be in the Valley where we will have a permanent home and see our friends again."

CHAPTER 29
Bad News at Fort Laramie

The trail ran beside Fountain Creek until it reached the mouth of Monument Creek. Grass was plentiful for the animals, and the wooded creek bottom afforded plenty of wood for fires. As they moved north, Castle Rock came into sight, and for two days they moved north up East Plum Creek, watching the rock formation grow slowly larger. East Plum Creek connected with Plum Creek, which led the group to the South Platte. Either Hank or Karl drove the wagon, while the one not driving walked and carried Caroline. Maria walked with Martin, holding his hand—at least, as often as he would permit it—keeping him close to her despite his objections. The two of them gathered the blue columbine that grew along the streams and marveled at the great Rampart Range of mountains where Pike's Peak reared its head to the west.

After reaching the South Platte, they passed the ruins of Fort Vasquez, which had been abandoned seven years earlier, and were grateful to reach Crow Creek. They followed it northward until its course began to flow east to west. Finally, on August fifth, they reached Fort Laramie, which was located a few hundred yards west of the left bank of the Laramie River, about a mile and a half from its confluence with the Platte.

As the fifteen-foot mud-brick walls of the fort came into sight, the little group let out a cheer. As the wagon, horses, and mules moved through the open gate in the east wall, a few small children gathered to investigate these new arrivals. A bearded, balding man left what appeared to be an office built of the same mud brick as the walls. As the group paused in the central yard, he strode over to Reshaw, who was dismounting, and shook his hand vigorously. "Looks like you have brought me travelers, old friend."

Reshaw laughed and said, "*Mais oui*, I bring you the last of the folks who went with me to Pueblo two years ago. This is the Schroeder family, who are going to join with the Mormons in the Salt Lake Valley." Boudeau offered his hand to Hank.

Hank said, "We are hoping to join up with another company of folks out of the South headed this way. We haven't missed them, have we?"

"No, no, you're in luck. I just heard yesterday from some riders that came through here that there's a big company of Mormons led by Amasa Lyman about four days east of here with a bunch of folks from the Deep South. I imagine they'll be here before the end of the week."

As Boudeau talked, other men and women had ceased what they'd been doing and gathered around the little group. Sweeping his arm in a broad arc around the central yard of the fort in a proprietary manner, he added congenially, "There's plenty of room for you right now. Just pick a place and move in till your friends arrive. Just two bits a night."

The central yard of the fort was surrounded by one-room adobe buildings, each attached at the rear to the fort walls and to one another on each side. Some were occupied by the folks who had come to greet the little wagon company, but many were obviously empty. Each one had a rough-hewn door and one window facing the central yard.

When Maria stepped inside of one, she laughed and said, "I think this will feel like our little adobe in Pueblo."

While Marty played with the children of the permanent residents, Maria washed and cooked, Hank repaired the wagon, and Karl practiced shooting with a pistol he had obtained from one of the trappers. As Hank and Maria thanked the rugged frontiersmen before they left the next day, Maria gave Reshaw a little kiss on his whiskered cheek and whispered, "Thank you for bringing my husband back to me and for all your help these past two years."

"Well, ma'am, I just wish I could have brought him back to you through that snowstorm undamaged." After the farewells, the trappers started up the Laramie River, their traps dangling from the packs on the mules.

"I'm going to miss that old Frenchman," Hank mused as they watched them depart.

Four days later, late in the afternoon, Martin hurried to his parents from where he had been playing with some of the other children. "Mama, Papa, somebody coming. Come and see." He took his father's hand and pulled him to the large open gates in the wall of the fort. They could see the dust from a large wagon company rising in the distance. Soon, every person in the fort stood outside the great double gate and watched the group as it approached the fort. As the dust cloud grew closer, the folks in the fort began to whoop and holler and wave their hats. "There's business a'comin'," one man yelled excitedly.

The wagons pulled to a stop in the open area to the south of the fort where many others had camped before them. Then the women, children, and men who had been riding began to spill out. Those who had been walking simply asked the nearest person where they could get a cold drink of water. Among the more than two hundred and fifty hot and weary travelers, Hank recognized John Brown and his wife, Betsy. After they shook hands, John slapped Hank on the back and said, "You will never know how good it is to see some old friends like you—and to think you were here to meet us. Your faces couldn't be more beautiful if you were angels greeting us at the pearly gates!"

"This is the best present a man could have!" Hank responded. "Familiar faces are a gift from God. Look, Maria," he called out, "here's John and Betsy Brown and Billy and Sytha Lay!" William Crosby approached Hank and stuck out his hand. The men pumped hands up and down while Maria gave and received hugs from their wives. Each of them wanted to hold or play with Caroline, whom she hesitantly relinquished for a few minutes.

"Who else is here from the Mississippi church?" Hank asked.

Billy laughed and answered, "There's Jim Flake and his family." He paused and looked around. "And the Matthews family, and even Mother Crosby is here. If we only had her plantation house, we could have a church meeting just like old times."

That evening as the sky was lit by nearly a dozen large fires of sagebrush and buffalo chips outside the fort, the Southerners gathered around to talk about everything that had happened since the first group of Southern Saints had left Monroe County and the many things that lay ahead of them.

The second night, as Hank and Maria sat on logs near the campfire in the central yard, many of the members from the Lyman Company joined them. They and several of the permanent residents of the fort listened to stories of some of the many travelers who had stopped over the years at what Boudeau called "his fort." The fort manager particularly remembered the Donner-Reed party, made memorable by the sad circumstances that took the lives of so many of them in the High Sierras. When it grew late, Maria stood, carrying Caroline in one arm and holding a sleepy Martin's hand in the other, and said, "I think the three of us are going to bed, dear. I hope you will join us soon." Hank nodded but remained to hear a few more of the stories that Boudeau shared with those who sat near the fire.

After most of the others had retired, William Crosby called out, "Tell us about the most memorable person you have met here at the fort over the years, Mr. Boudeau."

"Well, I guess if I was to tell you about the most memorable traveler I've met here, I would have to tell you about the dandy from Louisiana with the Mexican guide. They came through here last year, and even out here in the dust and the heat, he was wearing a red silk coat with shiny buttons and a silk hat. He carried a sword cane and a derringer. His boots were even shined. I guess keeping them clean and shined was one of the jobs of his guide."

Boudeau shook his head at the memory of the pair and continued, "He said he was looking for a white slave woman and her child. He insisted that the Mormons had taken them. Now don't that take all!" He slapped his thigh.

As some of the others laughed, Hank sat without moving. Karl looked at him to watch his reaction. John Brown and William Crosby rose from where they were sitting and approached Hank. John cleared his throat and said quietly, "Do you think this is the man hunting for Maria?"

Hank answered tersely, "Sounds like it. Let's see if Boudeau got his name."

Boudeau was quiet for a minute after Hank asked him about the Louisiana dandy, and then he answered, "It seems to me his name was Beau or Breaux or something like that."

Hank ran his hand through his hair and looked thoughtfully at the ground. Shaking his head, he said under his breath, "Will we ever get away from this man? He follows us like the devil himself." Then he looked up at Boudeau and said, "And you say he came through last year?"

"Yeah, it was just a couple of weeks after that first company of Mormons under Brigham Young came through."

"What did you tell him?" Hank was trying to control his agitation.

"I told him about the group that came up here from Pueblo in May of last year and joined up with that first company that got here a couple of weeks later—less than twenty of them, if I remember right. Then I told him about the second group that arrived here about ten days or two weeks after that first company had left. That was a group of more than two hundred—about half of them were members of that Mormon Battalion, and the other half was Southerners."

"What did he do when you told him about them?"

"He bought supplies and lit out the next morning, headed west. Didn't say where he was going, but wherever it was, he was sure in a hurry."

Hank nodded his thanks to Boudeau, and then he, Brown, and Crosby stepped aside. Karl joined them. They stood silently for a few seconds, and then John said, "Look, Hank, we've left the slave states. I know that Mother Crosby, Billy Lay, and my family all brought several blacks with us, but nearly every one of them has been baptized and had the choice of coming with us or not. Even if Breaux finds you and Maria, he can't take her. We won't let him."

Crosby said thoughtfully, "A whole year can bring major changes, Hank. Chances are he looked the Valley over and didn't find her, so he returned to Louisiana."

Hank looked up and nodded in relief. "Maybe you're right, Brother Crosby. I sure hope you are. In the meantime, I'd appreciate it if you didn't mention any of this to Maria. No need to worry her."

CHAPTER 30
The Trail to the Valley

After the last crossing of the Platte, the company plodded westward toward the Sweetwater River. When they reached Independence Rock, a great granite formation that looked like a giant loaf of bread and stood a quarter of a mile long and one hundred and twenty feet high above the flat surrounding terrain, they held a celebration. The dancing lasted long into the night, with Martin clapping his hands as he sat with Karl, who held Caroline on his lap. Martin giggled as he watched his mother teach his father the Virginia Reel.

"Hank, I think we will sleep well tonight," Maria said as they collected the children from where they had been sitting with Uncle Karl. Caroline was asleep in his arms.

In the morning, Hank shook Martin awake and said, "Let's climb the big hill before we break camp." Hank carried Martin on his shoulders most of the way. On the way back down, they paused to carve their names in the rock.

"Pa, now everybody will see my name when they come here," Martin said happily.

At the first fording of the Sweetwater River, many of the children laughed and giggled as they held on to their mothers' hands and walked into the cold water fully clothed, but their clothing had hardly dried before they faced the second crossing.

By the time they reached the fifth crossing, Martin was complaining, "Ma, the water's too cold. Can I ride in the wagon?"

Maria looked at Hank and said, "Do you think it is safe for the children to stay in the wagon while you drive the team across?"

Hank said, "Let's wait and see if the other wagons make it."

"Can Buddy ride in the wagon, too?" Martin asked.

"Yes, Buddy can ride, too." Hank answered. They watched the other wagons from where they stood on the riverbank. After several had made it across safely with families riding inside, Hank said, "We ought to be all right. Marty, you hold on tight."

Karl insisted on walking beside the mules on the upstream side. "I can help keep them calm if I hold onto the harness." As the wagon started across the river, it became evident that the wheels of the previous wagons had churned up the riverbottom where the mud was dirtying the clear water. What had been a firm, rocky river bottom for the first wagons had become soft and muddy for the wagons in the rear of the company. Suddenly, Karl disappeared under the water, and Maria cried out involuntarily. Then, all but the heads of the mules went under. Karl came up coughing, but still holding on to the harness.

Hank called out, "Karl, the wagon is floating. Don't let go. Keep the mules calm, if you can. We will float downstream until the animals can feel the river bottom again." The current grew slower, and the river deepened. The wagon began to float sideways. With the mules acting like an anchor, the wagon was soon floating backwards with the mules being pulled rear-end-first behind it. Karl tried to calm the animals by talking to them as he kicked to keep himself on top of the water.

Suddenly, the wagon wheels hit the river bottom where it rose to form a hidden sand bar. The wagon teetered, nearly tipping over. Maria had been sitting on the seat, holding Caroline, but when the wagon stopped suddenly, she was pitched out into the current. Her scream stopped as she and Caroline went under the water. When she came up again, she found herself and her baby in the swiftest part of the water. She screamed, "Hank, help us!"

The current carried the mules around to where they could feel the sand bar under their feet. Leaving the wagon and animals where they were, Hank commanded, "Marty, stay in the wagon," and leaped into the water. Karl let go of the mules and followed. Sometimes floating feet first around the rocks, and other times stroking with strong arms through the deeper parts of the river, both men struggled to reach Maria and the child.

Caroline's screams pierced the air, filled with panic. Then suddenly, they would stop as she and her mother were pulled under the water again. Half a mile downstream, Hank finally reached out for them and caught Maria by her hair. Pulling her to him as they continued down the river, he heard a yell. Turning, he could see Karl within an arm's length.

"Give me the baby," Karl called out. But Maria was holding Caroline so tightly that Karl had to wait until the current pulled him closer. Then he reached out and took the child from her mother's arms. Caroline's eyes were no longer open, and she was beginning to turn blue. Looking around, he could see a low place in the riverbank about twenty-five feet away. He turned onto his back, and, holding the child above his head, he propelled himself through the water with his strong legs until he was able to stagger out and onto the bank.

While Hank and Maria struggled to follow him, he put the small child over his thigh and pressed on her back repeatedly until she spit up water and began to whimper. By the time Hank had helped an exhausted Maria out and onto the bank, Caroline was crying weakly. Her lips, hands, and feet were blue from the cold water.

Taking her from Karl's arms, Maria said repeatedly, "Karl, we can never repay you. We can never repay you for saving Caroline."

By this time, several riders on horseback had ridden down the riverbank, looking for the Schroeders. William Crosby dismounted and handed the reins of his horse to Hank. "Here, put your wife in the saddle while she holds the baby, and you can ride behind her on my horse. I'll ride double with Billy, and Karl can ride double with John Brown."

By the time they reached the fire that others had built to warm them, Maria was nearly frantic about Caroline. "Hank, her lips are blue, and she is so cold." Caroline had stopped crying and had grown sleepy even though her mother had held her against her body for warmth.

When they dismounted, several women hurried to them with quilts. While they wrapped them around Maria and Caroline, Captain Crosby called out, "Hank, Karl, your wagon is caught on a sandbar and is threatening to overturn. The mules are panicked. We've got to get them out of the river."

In their wet clothing, Hank and Karl reentered the cold river. Crosby ordered, "Unhitch the mules and get them out of the water. They're exhausted."

"Pa, Pa, is Ma all right?" Martin called from the wagon.

Hank answered him, "Yes, son. Your ma is all right." Then he called back to Crosby, "If we unhitch the mules, the wagon will overturn."

Crosby yelled, "Billy, unhitch your team and trade them for Hank's long enough to get his wagon out of the river."

Billy Lay unhitched his team and led them into the river. There he positioned them on the upstream side of Hank's animals. Jim Flake and three other men entered the water, and while Jim helped unhitch Hank's mules, the three men put their backs against the wagon to hold it in place against the current. Karl coaxed the tired and chilled mules up the riverbank. Billy and Hank then tried to hitch Billy's team to the wagon. Hank's hands were so stiff and cold that he was of no use. When Billy had gotten his team hitched to the wagon, he and Hank pulled on the halters, trying to get them moving.

Despite the mules' efforts, the wagon would not move. Billy dropped under the wagon, and when his head came up above the water, he yelled, "The wheels are mired in the sandbank. We need more men to lift it out."

Three more men entered the water, and with three on each side of the wagon and Karl in the rear, they lifted as Billy pulled the mules forward. Finally, the sandbar let go of the wagon wheels, and they dragged the wagon over to the bank where the mules struggled to pull it out of the water. As Karl lifted Martin out of the wagon, the boy worriedly asked, "Where's Buddy? He jumped out of the wagon."

Comfortingly Karl responded, "Dogs are good swimmers, Marty. I'm sure he is fine and will find his way back to camp. Don't worry about him."

As the cold and wet members of the company huddled around the campfire, several women heated a large pot of water to give Caroline a warm bath. Two of them carried the pot to Maria where she sat with the tiny girl, who was wrapped in a quilt. Maria said worriedly, "I'm afraid she will not survive the night if we don't get her warm." She placed Caroline in the warm water, and gradually the small child's alertness improved. After twenty minutes, her color grew normal, and they dried and wrapped her in a warm, dry blanket. She slept the rest of the night.

About midnight, a tired and bedraggled Buddy arrived in the camp. Hank woke Martin, and the boy sat up and gratefully put his arms around the neck of the wet, smelly dog. "I prayed he would come back. I prayed he would come back."

The company reached Pacific Creek on the western side of the Continental Divide the third week of September. "Hank, I never dreamed it could be so cold," Maria said as the wind drove the snow into small drifts against the tents.

The tents and wagons were poor protection against the wind and biting cold. Maria put all the clothing she had brought for the children on them in layers and then wrapped Caroline up in a shawl and held her close. Both children cried with the cold. Hank tried to hold Martin close enough under the thin blankets to keep him warm. Caroline coughed throughout the night.

The dark hours of the night passed slowly. "Oh, Hank, do you suppose it will be this cold in the Valley? I am so worried for Caroline. She's feverish." Maria's teeth were chattering.

"Brother Lyman says that the Valley is not so high, and the snow doesn't come so early there. Surely, it won't be so cold, and Caroline will get better." Caroline had been fevered and listless since she and her mother had nearly drowned in the Sweetwater.

The sun melted the sleet in the morning, but an increased urgency began to hurry the travelers. At Fort Bridger, what would have been snow at a higher altitude was cold rain, soaking everything in the wagons and chilling everyone walking or on horseback. Even though the mules were tired, Hank, Maria, and the children rode in the wagon to avoid the chilling wet. "Karl, please get in the wagon. You will catch your death of cold," Maria begged him.

"I am fine. I am fine. The mules are too tired to pull a heavier load."

When they reached the Bear River, the snow fell all day, driven by a hard wind, and by the time it was over, several inches of snow lay on the ground.

Amasa Lyman, John Holladay, and Jim Flake set out from the camp near the Pudding Rocks and traveled on horseback through Emigration Canyon to the Valley to recruit teams and drivers to help get the wagons over the steep portion of the trail, which yet remained to be covered. On their return, they met the chilled and weary company on the Weber River in Echo Canyon. There the wagons were double-teamed to get them over Big Mountain.

Karl drove the wagon while the others walked. "Why did the Lord leave the hardest part of the journey for the last when we are all so tired?" Maria said breathlessly as she walked beside him, carrying Caroline. He said nothing as he carried Martin on his shoulders. He was too tired to talk, and he knew she did not really expect an answer.

On the night of October sixteenth, the company wearily camped at the mouth of Emigration Canyon. In the morning, they could see in the distance the adobe walls that surrounded the fort where more than four hundred adobe cabins were located. A few farmhouses were built outside the walls, scattered to the south of the fort for about three miles.

Marty looked at the settlement in the distance that had been named Great Salt Lake City, growing to more than four thousand in the fourteen months of its existence. Looking at Hank, he asked, "Pa, we home now?"

"Almost, Marty, we're almost home."

The little boy leaned against Hank and said, "I'm glad. I'm tired." The exhaustion in his voice brought tears to his mother's eyes. Hank could hardly swallow around the lump in his throat.

"Oh, Marty, I'm tired, too." Maria stooped and gathered him in her arms. "It's hard to get excited when we are so tired, but we're nearly home, and when we have a home of our own, we will feel glad."

After breakfast, the company prepared to separate. William Crosby asked the Southerners to gather around the remnants of the campfire. With a raised voice, he stated, "Some of the wagons are going into Salt Lake City, but most of us Southerners are going to go south for about ten miles. There, we will join with some of our friends in the settlement we call Cottonwood, where there will be enough familiar faces to make us feel at home."

When they reached the cluster of cabins that comprised the settlement, it was evident that the previous year's arrivals had planted a few acres with wheat, corn, and potatoes and had built about twenty cabins near garden plots. When the wagons halted, Hank said to Maria, "Well, it looks like we will be starting over, Maria. Do you think we have the strength and will to begin again?"

She answered quietly, "I don't believe we have any choice." What pleasure Maria might have felt upon reaching the end of the journey was tempered by her worry for Caroline, who had been growing steadily weaker since the near drowning.

As they put up the tents and built fires to prepare the evening meal, many of the Southern families who had left Pueblo the previous year hurried to meet the new arrivals. With a broad smile Letitia Smithson hurried to embrace Maria. Allen laughed as he pumped Hank's hand. "We had begun to think that you folks were so content in Pueblo that you were never going to get here."

As Letitia put her arms out to take Caroline, Maria said worriedly, "Is Betty Matthews here? Caroline has been feverish and weak for the last two weeks. I need Betty's advice."

Letitia put her hand on the small child's forehead and said, "Yes, she is fevered. You are right to be concerned. I'll find Betty. You wait here." She handed the child back to her mother and hurriedly searched throughout the crowd that had gathered.

After a few minutes, she returned with Sister Matthews, who took the child and felt her hot little head. "We don't have much to use to help the sick here in Cottonwood, but we do have a few precious elm trees up in the canyons. I'll make some herbal tea with some of the elm bark I have. As soon as it is ready, I'll bring it to you. Where is your wagon?"

Maria pointed out the wagon and took the baby back. "Please hurry," was all she could say.

After they made camp that evening, Allen Smithson stood on a log and pointed out the landmarks to the new arrivals. As he pointed, he said, "There, to the east, is Big Cottonwood Canyon." Then he shifted his arm. "And there is Little Cottonwood Canyon. The streams that come out of those canyons flow year-round. You'll find that you need to go into the canyons several miles to find fully matured trees, so many of the Saints have built with adobe. But don't worry about that this evening. Tonight, we are going to celebrate."

The celebration lasted long into the night as old friendships were renewed, but Maria retired to the tent as soon as it was put up and tried to spoon the cooled herbal tea into a listless Caroline, without much success.

"Hank, can you put up the little stove and build a fire in it so I can put a pan of water on it to steam?" Maria asked. She wrapped the tiny little girl, not yet eighteen months old, in a harness made from a shawl that kept her little body against her mother for warmth.

In the chill of the next morning, Hank and many of the other men put their saws, hatchets, axes, and ropes into the wagon beds and turned their wagons toward Big Cottonwood Canyon to fell trees for the cabins that would house their families. At the end of the first day, exhausted for want of enough food, the men turned their wagons back to the camp, loaded with cut trees.

"Compared to the forested river bottoms of Pueblo, the trees are harder to reach and often up steep slopes," Hank told Maria as they sat in the tent, eating a supper of beans and corn bread. "We have to work in teams, at least two to a wagon and sometimes in groups of three and four, to get some of the bigger tree trunks into the wagon beds," he explained. With Karl's help, the Schroeder cabin walls were five feet high when the first snow hit in early December.

Even after the snow came, while some of the other families huddled in their tents around the small wood stoves they had brought with them, Hank, Karl, and some of the other men continued driving the wagons up the canyon to bring back logs, keeping warm only through their physical labor. On the ride back with the logs in the wagon bed, the bitter wind chilled the perspiration that had dampened their worn clothing. The cabin walls were soon ready for the roof.

To add to the hardships and challenges of building a new community, the company had arrived in the Valley in the midst of an epidemic of whooping cough. Weakened by the poor food and suffering from exhaustion, many of the children and some of the adults quickly became ill, including the infant son of John and Betsy Brown. Four days before Christmas, they buried their two-month-old baby boy, who had been born on the trail.

Two weeks later, little Caroline quit moving in the night where she lay next to her mother, and when Maria tried to wake her, she realized the body of her tiny girl was cold. "Oh, Hank, she's gone; our little girl is gone. What shall I do?" Maria whispered as she rocked the tiny body and wept.

Caroline was buried beside the grave of John and Betsy's baby. When Maria and Hank returned to the unfinished cabin, she suddenly cried out. "My locket! My locket is gone." Her desolation grew, and she sat on one of the trunks and wept inconsolably. From that time on, she grew silent. She could not stop the quiet tears that would start at unexpected times.

A few days after his sister was buried, Martin asked his father, "Pa, why does Ma cry so much? Why won't she talk?"

"She misses your sister, Marty. She misses her so much she just can't talk yet."

"But she still has us, doesn't she, Pa?"

"Yes, son, she still has us. She will get past this grief. Just give her time."

One morning when the sun was warm enough that much of the snow melted by midday, Martin disappeared for more than two hours. By the time Maria had a supper of corn bread and salted pork ready, she had begun to worry. "Hank, where has he gone? He is never away this long."

Just then the door swung open, and Marty stood in the doorway grinning and holding out his hand. "Look what I found, Ma." She put out her hand, and he dropped the locket into it. "I found it on Caroline's grave. I think it's yours."

Maria knelt and put her arms around the boy. "Yes, Marty. It is mine, and I'm so glad you found it."

"I'm sorry I couldn't find the chain."

She held him until he began to squirm. But even the finding of the locket did not seem to lift her spirits much.

By late January, the cabin was completed. For a roof, Hank and Karl split logs, putting them flat side up. Then they covered them with hard clay and willows from the streams, just as most other cabins had been roofed. As Maria entered the rough little cabin, she stood silently looking around.

Hank said quietly, "I'm sorry that it isn't fancier, but we will eventually add a room, and then it will be more comfortable."

She turned and put her arms around him. "I know you did your best. It's a nice little cabin, and I do appreciate it. I really do." She gave him a weak smile. They spent the next several days mixing mud, water, straw, or dried leaves to chink the gaps between the logs.

When they finished that task, Maria wiped her bitterly cold hands on her apron and said to Hank, as if to offer an apology for her lack of enthusiasm when he first presented her with the cabin, "Now we will be warm for the rest of this winter—and we will be happy here. I am sure of that." She tried to fill her voice with an enthusiasm she did not feel. Karl continued to sleep in the tent, and during the day the two brothers returned to cutting trees in the canyon so they could build a cabin for Karl.

Late in February, Mother Crosby passed away, and many of the Saints who had first heard the gospel in her plantation house gathered to bid her farewell as she was laid to rest next to the tiny graves of the children.

After they had returned to the cabin following the burial of Mother Crosby, Maria sat down on one of the trunks and looked unseeingly at her hands in her lap. She finally spoke, "We gave up everything to get to the Valley—even our little girl. And what have we found here? Cold, hunger, illness, backbreaking work—and death." She looked up into her husband's face. "Hank, what are we doing here? Was Brigham Young really inspired to lead us here? Tell me why we came," she pleaded.

He took her hands and lifted them until she stood. Taking her in his arms and holding her to him, he said, "Right now we are just trying to make it from day to day, but times will get better, Maria. I promise you that if we are patient with the Lord, times will get better."

She made no response.

CHAPTER 31
Courtship and Crickets

After the whooping cough epidemic ended and despite the snow, each family was encouraged to make the journey on Sunday mornings to attend worship services in the Bowery on Temple Square. As the Schroeders prepared to attend Sabbath meeting in late February, Maria called to Martin, who was preparing to climb into the wagon, "Don't forget your brick. It's here on the table." He hurried back into the cabin. He picked up the brick, which had been heating in the fireplace all night and was wrapped in rags so it would not be too hot to carry, and put it in the wagon in front of the seat where he would sit between his parents.

By the time Hank slapped the reins against the rumps of the mules, there were several hot bricks in front of the wagon seat to use as foot warmers. While Hank, Maria, and Martin rode on the wagon seat, Karl sat in the back, with a brick at his feet and a blanket around his shoulders.

When the sun was shining and the wind was still during the meeting, the weather was not too difficult to tolerate. There were two meetings, one at ten and another at two o'clock, and each lasted two hours. Most families brought hot bricks to warm their feet, but they had cooled by the afternoon meeting. They ate lunches of biscuits, buttermilk, and boiled eggs as they socialized between the meetings. Speakers were called upon from among the congregation, which was huddled together on the backless wooden benches under the roof of tree branches supported by tall, rough-hewn supports.

One of the bright spots on Sundays was Karl's courtship of a very quiet young woman with blonde braids, whose family had arrived from Holland in October. Between meetings, the two of them would sit together, somewhat removed from most of the others in attendance. They would laugh and talk—about what, Karl never revealed on the rides back to Cottonwood, but he always smiled most of the way home. It was not in Karl's nature to share his thoughts.

The snow melted in mid-March. They finally planted the seed corn, which had been so tempting to eat during the winter months when they were so hungry. Hank did the planting with Marty's help.

By April, the food shortage had become severe throughout the Valley. Maria would stand near the garden and watch for green shoots, wishing them from the ground. Hank shot two crows one afternoon, and when he brought them home, Maria looked at the carcasses of the birds and had to swallow hard before she could face the task of plucking and cooking them. "Mama, this tastes good," a hungry Martin said at supper. "But it's not big enough."

"You can have mine, Marty. I don't really want any," she responded, which was true. As he reached for another piece of one of the small birds, Maria added, "I'm not hungry," which was not true.

About midnight one evening, Buddy's wild barking woke them. Hank pulled on his pants and picked up his bowie knife and a rifle. As he opened the cabin door, Buddy rushed out into the night. Karl quickly followed. A pack of wolves had come into the settlement, trying to bring down one of the animals housed at night in Jim Flake's animal shed. By the time they reached the shed and could see the wolves in the moonlight, the animals were in a panic. Hank took aim and fired, killing one of the shadowy figures. Then another gun exploded in the darkness, and another wolf dropped with a yelp. The others turned and ran into the darkness. Allen Smithson was holding his rifle, standing near Hank, his nightshirt partially tucked into his pants. Karl arrived within a minute, and he dragged the carcass of one of the wolves back to Hank's cabin.

By the light of the moon and with Karl's help, Hank used his bowie knife to skin and clean the wolf. The next day as it boiled in the pot on the little wood stove, the cabin filled with a slightly wild smell, but when the meat had boiled long enough, it made a tolerable meal.

"We are eating things I never dreamed we would have to eat, even if we lived to be a hundred. How long can this go on?" Maria asked.

Hank laughed in an attempt to lift her spirits. "We're not only eating some strange things, but even more surprising, we also need to be grateful for these unusual additions to our diet."

Maria and Martin, with some of the other mothers and children, went out every day and walked the hillsides where the snow had melted, digging up sego lily bulbs and looking for wild onions, pigweed, and thistles, while Hank and the other men returned to the canyons to fell trees. When they became too hungry to keep digging, they would wipe the soil off the roots and eat them, pretending they were carrots. On one occasion, Maria reached out and stopped Martin from putting the root of a weed into his mouth. She said sharply, "Martin, don't eat that. It looks like a wild parsnip. It will make you very sick." He threw it away and picked up a thistle root.

"It tastes funny, Mama. The dirt feels crunchy on my teeth." The lump in her throat made it impossible for Maria to respond, so she just leaned over and kissed him on the head. In her mind she asked, *Dear Father in Heaven, when are we going to have enough food to feed the children?*

Hunger became such a problem that leather previously used as leggings and saddle bags was boiled for broth and for the sticky, greasy substance that rose to the surface of the pot.

"Mama, this is icky. I want some cornmeal mush." Martin was simply stating what everyone else was thinking.

"I know, Marty. When our crops begin to grow, we will have better things to eat."

A look of resolve passed over Karl's face, and without saying anything, he picked up the rifle and left the cabin. After four hours, he returned with a dead squirrel and a dead crow. "Thank you, Karl," Maria said. "But how did you kill them?"

"I am a better shot than you think," he said quietly with a smile.

In May, as the Saints left the bowery after Sabbath meeting and climbed into their wagons to return home, Hank called out to several men as they assisted their wives into the wagons or carriages, "Looks like it will be a good harvest."

As the Schroeder family rode south toward Cottonwood, Maria shaded her eyes from the sun and said, "Look, Hank. What is it that is covering the plants in some parts of some of the fields?" Perplexed, she wrinkled her forehead as she looked over the fields that stretched on either side of the dirt road.

"It looks like some kind of locust or cricket in great numbers." Hank stopped the mules, and he and Karl climbed out of the wagon and walked into a potato field. There they bent over for a moment. Both men hurried back to the wagon. As they climbed in, Hank said, "May heaven help us if they have reached our crops." He hurried the team toward Cottonwood.

As they rode, they could see hordes of black insects swarming over the plowed and planted fields like a dark, encroaching fog hugging the ground. In the distance, they could see moving black clouds settling on other green fields. The millions of crickets came like a black tide to consume the new green shoots—every green thing in their way. "It looks like a repeat of the infestation the Saints had last year. Some of the men told me about the problem, but I never dreamed it could be so—so overwhelming!" Hank said with alarm.

"Hank, will the trials never stop?" Maria wailed as she held Martin close to her, as if to keep him out of reach of the sea of black insects.

After the wagon reached the cabin in Cottonwood, they, along with their neighbors, took up sticks, shovels, and wet burlap bags to beat the insects off the green shoots in the garden and fields. Allen Smithson, who had survived the crickets the previous year, said breathlessly as they worked, "Just keep at it. This year isn't nearly as bad as last year. Surely, the Lord will send the gulls any day now."

Maria was consumed with an anger that drove her to stomp on the black insects until her shoes were sticky and heavy. She focused her rage on the crickets, but it was a reflection of the anger she was feeling toward a land that came so near to overwhelming those souls who were brave enough—or foolish enough—to try to tame it. Her jaw was hard, and her lips formed a tight, thin line. *What are we doing here? Why is God doing this to us?* Then a thought occurred to her that had not crossed her mind in a long time. Pausing and looking up, she cried aloud, "God, do you even know we are here?"

On the third day, clouds of great white seagulls darkened the sun and arrived by the thousands. They immediately began to gorge themselves on the crickets. Like starving men, they would eat more than they could contain. After filling their bellies, they would fly out to the irrigation ditches or the marshes near the lake and disgorge their meal so they could return and fill themselves again. Within a week, the plague that had proven to be a feast for the large white birds ended, and many of the gulls flew south, seeking similar meals. As Hank, Maria, Martin, and Karl knelt at the table before they ate a soup of weeds and boiled crow, Hank thanked the Lord for sending the gulls. As he finished the prayer, Maria added in a whisper, "And dear God, give us the strength to endure." Here she paused. "Or the willingness to go to our graves without complaint." The meals of sego lily bulbs, pigweed, wild onions, thistle roots, and an occasional crow continued.

The warmer weather brought more wagon companies. They arrived with nearly exhausted supplies and an increasing number of mouths to be fed. Maria wrapped herself in silence as a protection against the unrelenting hardships. Each night as they crawled between the thin blankets, Hank would repeat, "Things will get better, Maria. I know they will. We must be patient and have faith."

Sometimes she would respond wearily, "I'm trying, Hank. I'm trying."

For nearly a year, talk of gold found in California had occupied the conversations of the Saints. When many of the Mormon Battalion members had ended their months of military service in California, they returned with pouches filled with gold dust and nuggets. The men had been instructed to come home immediately upon their discharge and bring back as much gold as they were able so it could be turned over to the Church leaders to be used to benefit the hungry pioneers in the Valley. Their arrival fed the gold fever the hungry and impoverished Saints were experiencing.

One morning as Hank hitched the mules to the wagon, he noted that several of the men who had fallen in line each morning with their wagons and followed him up the canyon were not present. He climbed down and located the Jackson and Baxter cabins, which were side by side near his, and called out, "Brother Baxter, Brother Jackson, it's time to get rolling."

Sam Jackson stuck his head out of the doorway and said, "We ain't going up the canyon today—or any day. My wife has had enough of these starving times. We're packing up and heading to Sutter's Fort in California—and the Baxters are going with us."

Hank was not sure what to say, so he said nothing for a second. Then he responded, "Don't let the sound of easy riches take you away from the Valley. California will be just like Missouri—or Nauvoo. When the Saints became settled and prosperous there, our enemies coveted what they had and drove them out. The same thing will eventually happen in California."

"They don't have to know we're Mormons." It was evident that Sam had made up his mind. That day the number of men felling logs in the canyon was noticeably diminished. Hank and Karl returned that evening with half a wagonload of logs, and when Maria stepped out of the cabin and looked questioningly at the wagon, Hank answered her unasked question. "We only had about half the men we needed in the canyon today, so none of us was able to get a full wagonload." Then he told Maria what Sam had told him that morning.

She responded, "Hank, I think we should go, too. I'm sick of eating food hardly fit for the mules. Marty is so thin, and there seems to be no chance that he will ever get enough to eat in this desert. Let's go to California with the others."

Hank took Maria in his arms and said nothing for a minute. He could feel her stiff body resist his embrace. Then he took a deep breath and said, "I know things will get better if we have faith and patience with the Lord. Just hold on." He paused and then whispered in her ear, "Hold on to the log of your faith in this deep river of problems surrounding us. The Lord often pushes us to our limits before He rescues us."

Maria's composure broke, and she leaned against him and began to sob. Through the sobs, Hank could make out the words, "I don't think I have any more faith, and I'm all out of patience with the Lord. I think He has forgotten us. He doesn't seem to know where we are." When the sobs stopped, she said nothing more about leaving the Valley.

CHAPTER 32
Chickens and a Red Cape

Even though the crops recovered from most of the damage done by the crickets and the harvest was plentiful, the continuing stream of arriving wagon companies continued to stretch the food supplies throughout the Valley.

One evening, two brothers, Hyrum and George Curtis, arrived at the Schroeder's cabin, and as Maria was fixing supper, Hank stepped out and invited them inside. "Come in, come in."

George responded, "Only if you will accept a little gift and listen to our plans." Twenty-four-year-old George handed Hank five pounds of cornmeal. "That is some of what we got yesterday from a man headed to Yerba Buena and the gold fields. He wanted to trade us his team of worn-out horses for a fresh team of mules. To sweeten the trade he gave us a big bag of cornmeal."

Hearing that, Maria took the cornmeal with a grateful smile. "If you have time, I will be glad to make us some corn bread."

Nineteen-year-old Hyrum nodded his agreement, and as Maria made corn bread, Hank and Karl moved onto the trunks so the guests could sit in the two chairs. George Curtis cleared his throat and said, "I'm sure you noticed that there are plenty of folks all excited about going to California to get rich." Hank simply nodded. "Well, the official word is that President Young has warned everyone that if they rush off to get rich by panning for gold, they might lose their souls. He says that none of the Saints are to leave the Valley to go to California to settle unless they are assigned to go. That doesn't mean that there won't be some who will go, but Brother Brigham's words will discourage many of them."

Hyrum took up the conversation. "Since it looks like the Saints are not going to go to California, we need to bring some of what California has back to the Valley." Hank remained silent. "Don't you see the opportunity here?"

Hank slowly nodded but still said nothing.

"We're going to start a freight company." The conversation continued until the corn bread was ready, and as they ate, Maria joined them, sitting next to Hank on the trunk, her face filled with interest.

Hank finally responded, "I'm not prepared to leave my family for such a long period of time, and it's no journey for women and children. This is an enterprise for unmarried men. But if I can get an agreement to use one of the wagons that belongs to one of our neighbors while you are gone, I will lend my wagon and mules to Karl, and he can join you if he wants to."

The Curtis brothers looked at each other and then at Karl. Hyrum answered, "We will give you one-quarter of what we bring back for you and your brother to share. How's that for payment?" They agreed on the deal. For the next eight weeks, Hank borrowed one of Jim Flake's wagons to bring trees down from the canyons, dividing the loads in half with him as payment for the use of the wagon and the team.

As if to prove to her that times would get better, the day the Curtis brothers and Karl returned from California with wagons loaded with goods that would be in demand in the Valley, Hank presented Maria with six yards of red wool for a cape.

"Hank, it's beautiful. It will make the most beautiful cape in the whole world. I can hardly wait to wear it." Maria held the fabric up under her chin and turned as if she were dancing. "I've never seen anything more beautiful." She paused and looked at Hank with a sudden seriousness in her face. "I know it is vain of me to feel this way, and vanity is a sin, but I can't help it." Then she went back to twirling around with the fabric held up to her chin. It was the first time since they had buried Caroline that Hank had seen Maria happy.

"I hoped you would like it. I told Karl and the Curtis brothers not to come back until they had found some material just that color." Hank beamed because he was just as pleased as Maria.

From where he was watching the pleasure of Hank and Maria, Karl spoke, "There is something else in the wagon I have not told you about. I will need some help to bring it in. We will need Allen Smithson and Ab Dowdle to help us."

Maria stopped turning and looked at her brother-in-law. "What else did you bring, Karl?"

Karl pointed to one of the chairs and said, "You will sit down and wait until we bring it in. You agree?"

With a curious glint in her eye, she nodded. "Of course." She sat down as the two men left the cabin. She waited for the next twenty minutes, tempted to step to the cabin door to look outside but determined to keep her word and remain where she sat.

Martin had run outside, and when he came back in, he said, "It's something big, Mama, and it's covered with a canvas. I can't tell what it is."

After what seemed to be a very long time, Hank kicked open the door as the four men carried a very large and heavy item into the cabin. They struggled to set it down without catching their fingers underneath it. Then Karl pulled the canvas off, and Maria stood speechless. It was a pump organ.

As he held the rumpled canvas in his arms, Karl said quietly, "We found it sitting by the trail on the west side of the Sierra Nevada on our way home, where someone on their way to the gold fields had left it. I think it was too heavy for their animals to pull over the mountains. It is a little damaged, but I think it will play."

Maria gave Karl a peck on the cheek and wiped away a tear of joy. Then she sat down and began to play. The sound was wheezy, and after a few minutes, Hank said, "I think the bellows needs repair. I will find a way to fix it." Even the wheezy sound did not dampen Maria's pleasure.

As part of the payment for using Hank's wagon and team, Karl presented Hank and Maria with a hundred pounds of flour, thirty pounds of cornmeal, dried fruit, dried fish, ammunition, and a whetstone to sharpen Hank's bowie knife and ax. Karl pulled Hank aside, and with their backs to Maria, Karl dropped something into Hank's hand. They gave no explanation to Maria.

Hank mended the bellows for the organ with a piece of tanned leather, and thereafter, Maria played for nearly an hour each evening.

The Curtis brothers quickly sold the things they had brought back from California and were able to purchase an additional wagon and team so they could increase the amount of freight they could carry. The lateness of the season forced them to wait until spring to make another trip. Importantly, Charles Kinkead promised them he would buy anything they brought back for the mercantile he operated on Main Street with his partner, James Livingston. Both of these men were "gentiles," as those not members of the Church were called. Their establishment was the only source of manufactured goods in the Valley, aside from the goods sold or left by the side of the road by gold seekers who found their wagons too heavily loaded. Livingston and Kinkead did a thriving business.

Maria had enough red wool left after she had made her cape to make a similar cape for eleven-year-old Carlotty Flake to show her gratitude to her parents for allowing Hank to use the wagon. As thanks for the beautiful cape for her daughter, Agnes Flake gave Maria a rooster and two hens.

Maria hurried back to the cabin, carefully holding the makeshift pen the birds were in, calling out, "Hank, look! Look at this! We will have eggs!"

On a cold night in December, the three adults and Marty sat around the little stove that kept the cabin warm throughout the night. Hank and Karl talked about the journey and the voyage that had brought them to America.

"You never told me about this before, Pa." Marty turned to his mother and asked, "Did you come to America on a big ship, Ma?" When she nodded, he said, "Please tell me about it."

"Another night we will talk about it, Marty, but tonight is Christmas Eve, and we are going to read the Christmas story in the New Testament." She carefully took the Bible from the shelf—a Bible Hank had given her as a gift while they were in Monroe County—and read from the books of Luke and Matthew.

When she was through, Hank rose and took something out of the bottom of one of the chests, where it had been hidden.

It was wrapped in a twist of paper. He handed it to his wife and said, "Happy Christmas, my dear Maria."

She carefully opened the little package, and there in the firelight, a gold chain glistened. Hank said quietly, "It's from both Karl and me. He brought it back from California for me to give to you."

Tears began to stream down her cheeks as she closed her hand and held it against her breast. Then she stood and hurried to a small tin with a tight-fitting lid on the shelf near the stove and removed the locket. With trembling hands, she threaded the gold chain through it and said to Hank, "Can you hook the clasp?"

When he had finished, she stood and put her arms around him. "Thank you both. You are both good men. I will never take it off."

***

In the heat that came with the end of May, Hank and Karl completed Karl's cabin and then built a combination animal shed and henhouse. Early one evening, Martin burst into the cabin. "It's finished. Come and see it!" He took Maria by the hand and pulled her outside. The excited little boy pointed at the completed animal shed and henhouse. "See, now even Gertie has a house."

That night as Maria and Hank slid between the worn blankets on the bed, Maria snuggled up to Hank. The fire in the stove burned low. She mused, "I think that Zion is beginning to be home now. Even if the crickets come again, I have faith that the Lord will send the gulls. I'm glad that we didn't go to California after all. The Lord will take care of us here. I think He knows where we are now."

CHAPTER 33
Gold and Breaux

The spring had bloomed, and the Saints' self-sufficiency was gradually increasing. The crickets returned but in considerably fewer numbers than in previous years. In the evenings, Maria sat with Martin and helped him learn to read from the recently published weekly newspaper, the *Deseret News*, the first newspaper that most of the Saints had seen since they had come to the Valley.

By September, Maria was thrilled to be expecting again. The quiet grief that had burdened her heart since little Caroline's death lifted. She was contentedly humming under her breath and churning butter when Hank entered the cabin and said, "I'm going to have to hitch up the mules and take the wagon into Salt Lake City. I've broken my ax handle, and I'm never going to finish the fence without it. I really need to get it done to keep Gertie and her new calf out of the garden. Do you and Marty want to ride into Salt Lake City with me?"

"How will you pay for the ax handle?"

"Well, I was hoping that you had a dozen eggs I could trade for it."

Maria was quiet for a moment and then said, "I guess we can have custard another day." She left the churn and carefully lifted a wooden box lined with straw from a shelf. "Here's a dozen." As Hank took the eggs from her, she added, "I can finish the churning while you get Marty. He's shucking corn with Johnny Lay."

In a few minutes, Hank was back with Martin, and Maria had put on her cape and bonnet. "Let's take some of the vegetables from the garden to pay our tithing."

Hank selected three of the largest and best squash and a large pumpkin that he used to prop against the box of eggs in the wagon bed so it wouldn't slide around.

As the wagon reached the outskirts of Salt Lake City, it proceeded up Main Street, nearing the Kinkead and Livingston mercantile. Suddenly, Maria stiffened and grabbed Hank's right arm with a viselike grip. Her eyes were wide with alarm. "Are you all right? You look as if you have seen a ghost."

He followed her eyes and saw a wagon that had just stopped in front of the large store. A man in a red silk coat and polished black boots had climbed down and was lifting a very heavy carpetbag out of the wagon bed, while another man was tying the mules to the hitching post.

"Keep going, Hank. Don't stop," she whispered urgently. As they neared the rear of the wagon, the man in the silk coat looked up and his eyes met Maria's.

The expression on his face tightened, and a twisted smile of satisfaction formed on his lips. When they reached the corner, she whispered, "I've seen worse than a ghost. I've seen the devil himself. The man in the red silk coat." Her voice tightened and stopped in her throat for a moment. "That man is Lafayette Breaux. Hank, what could have brought him here, at this time, in this place?" A sob caught in her throat. "Hank, this is a nightmare!"

Hank turned and studied the dandy, who was still watching them. With an edge in his voice, he responded, "Do not let this disturb you. I won't let him harm you."

After they had turned the corner and proceeded another block east to the tithing office, he helped Maria climb out of the wagon. Martin climbed down and looked at his mother. "Who was that man, Mama? Why did he scare you?"

Hank answered, "That is a man your mother knew a long time ago. He caused her great pain, but we won't let him hurt her again, will we, Marty?"

"No, Pa, we won't," the little boy responded.

Hank put his arm around Maria and ushered her into the tithing office. Inside, they met Allen Smithson. Putting out his hand, Allen said, "Hank, how are you and your family? We haven't had time to talk in weeks."

Looking at Martin, Hank said, "Marty, will you go get the squash and bring them in here?" Martin nodded and darted back out of the door.

Without letting go of Maria, Hank put his left hand on Allen's arm and pulled him into a corner where they would not be overheard. "Allen, I know you will remember how Port Rockwell told some of us that he had talked Lafayette Breaux into going on to the gold fields a few weeks after the advance company reached the Valley?"

Allen nodded, looking perplexed. "Of course. We all laughed when we heard him tell how he had got Breaux drunk and sent him on to California."

Maria stepped close to Hank and looked into his face, demanding, "When did you learn of this, Hank? Why didn't you tell me?"

"What's the problem?" Allen asked.

Hank worriedly ran his hand through his hair. "We just saw him in front of the mercantile. He had a wagonload of supplies. He looked like he might be loaded with gold dust, as well." He rubbed his forehead with his left hand as if he had a sudden headache.

Allen was quick to see the danger in the situation. "Who else knows about this?"

"I don't have any way of knowing," Hank answered.

"Well, it looks like your worst nightmare is back." Speaking to them both, Allen said, "I recommend that you get back to Cottonwood and keep your family there."

"I will as soon as I get a new ax handle."

"You stay here, and I'll go over to the mercantile and get it for you. How were you going to pay for it?"

"I've got a dozen eggs in the wagon. I think that will be enough."

Allen said hurriedly, "You wait here, and I'll take your eggs and get that ax handle. At the same time, I'll check on what's happening where Breaux is concerned. I'll be back as quick as I can." Allen hurried out the doorway, retrieved the eggs, and climbed into his wagon. He hurried the mules to the mercantile a block and a half away.

***

It was a proud Lafayette Breaux who had ridden into Great Salt Lake City that day in October. His carpetbag was heavy with gold dust and nuggets. To make his entrance, he had put on his best silk coat and silk hat, both of which he had bought in San Francisco. Additionally, he had Garcia polish his boots. The wagon was piled high with the kind of things a desert community could use. Making his way along Emigration Road toward the city, he couldn't help but notice that in the two years he had been in California, the city had grown to a community of nearly eight thousand, spread out for several miles to the south and at least three or four miles east and west.

"One of the first things I want to do is find that guy named Rockwell and thank him for talking me into going to California. I'll bet he didn't know that I would come back a rich man," Breaux boasted as he lit a cigar.

Garcia just nodded, not wanting to encourage the dandy's conversation. As soon as he was paid, it would be for the last time. He intended to leave Breaux to find his own way, no matter where they were at the time.

As the wagon rolled up Main Street toward South Temple, he noted the mercantile establishment on the west side of the street and ordered Garcia to stop in front of it. As he climbed down from the wagon, he looked up at a passing wagon and for a fraction of a second stood unmoving. The face of the woman beside the man on the wagon seat—he knew it! He hadn't given any thought to that woman for more than a year, but there she was, with a small boy sitting beside her.

He knew he was right. He could see recognition in her eyes when they met his—and fear, too. Under his breath he muttered, "Well, hello there, missy. Here you are, the both of you." His lips formed a narrow line as he exultantly watched the wagon near South Temple Street. *The boy is mine! Look at that black head of hair. I will have a son and heir!* He watched the wagon make its way to South Temple Street and noted that the man turned to look long and hard at him. *They're here. I've got another chance to get her and the boy.* His jaw was hard with resolution.

He told Garcia to wait and watch the wagon. Then he entered the mercantile. Inside, he introduced himself to the owners and removed his hat. "I have a wagonload of goods from California in front of your establishment, any or all of which I think you may want to purchase."

Removing a cigar from his mouth, Livingston responded with a broad smile, "Yes, yes. Maybe we can do business. Come into the store office." For the next two hours, the three men grew acquainted as they tried to settle on the prices Breaux demanded and those that Livingston and Kinkead were willing to pay. No one was in a hurry. They sat with their feet on the desk, each smoking a cigar and holding a glass of brandy. These were men who understood each other.

The conversation covered many subjects. Unable to ignore Breaux's Southern drawl, Kinkead finally asked, "Where you from, Mr. Breaux? From your speech, I don't think you're a native Californian." Kinkead looked at Livingston and slapped his thigh as he laughed at his own joke.

"I've got a big plantation and a wife back in Louisiana." He took another sip of his brandy. "I left it in the hands of my overseer, so I expect that everything is running just fine back there. My wife will be on his back like an angry cat on a dog if he doesn't run things to her liking." He paused and inhaled the cigar. "I'm not in any hurry to go back, but I will—eventually."

As the conversation continued, Breaux brought the subject around to the few blacks he saw on the streets. "How many blacks are there here in the Valley?" he asked.

Livingston shrugged his shoulders and answered, "I think I heard that the group from Mississippi brought in as many as twenty-five or thirty. Most of them were baptized and are considered Mormons, just like everybody else."

"Are they still considered slaves?"

Kinkead dropped his feet from the desk to the floor, and as he poured more brandy into his glass, he answered, "There's been some question about that. The matter seems to be giving ol' Brigham Young some problems. There was one black girl who didn't like being told what to do by her owner after they arrived here, and when she refused to obey, he threatened to beat her. She ran to Brigham Young and took refuge there in his home. Now she's his problem." The man threw his head back and laughed boisterously.

Breaux asked, "Any other kind of slaves here?"

Livingston answered his question with one of his own, "What other kind is there?"

"Well, in the South sometimes we had light-skinned slaves, even white-skinned slaves. Any of those around here?"

"Not that we ever heard of, but you would need to talk with the Southerners that settled down in Cottonwood to know for sure."

At that suggestion, the expression of Breaux's face changed. He rubbed his chin and smiled with narrowed eyes. "Where is this place—Cottonwood?"

Kinkead answered, "About nine or ten miles south of here. When those folks from Mississippi and Alabama arrived in the Valley, they must have thought that they were better than the rest of the folks here as they went south to the mouth of Big Cottonwood Canyon and settled there."

The next day with his pockets full of cash from the sale of his freight to Livingston and Kinkead, Breaux paid Garcia. He stabled his mules and the wagon and bought himself the best-looking horse he could find in the city. With one of the saddles and bridles he had not sold to the mercantile owners, he set out for Cottonwood. He ordered Garcia, "Get a room at a hotel and wait for me."

Using the money he had been paid, Garcia retrieved the wagon and mules. He purchased supplies and loaded them in the wagon, which he then turned toward Emigration Canyon and California. He planned to be well on his journey before Breaux found him gone. The thought that stealing the wagon and team was a serious offense crossed his mind, but he brushed it away and muttered under his breath, "Two years with that man? He owes me."

CHAPTER 34

The Summons

After Allen had left to buy the ax handle, Maria looked at Hank, her eyes large with fear and concern that bordered on anger. "Hank, why didn't you tell me about Breaux?"

"I didn't want to worry you. He followed us when we left the States. Because we stopped in Pueblo, he arrived in the Valley ahead of us. He searched for us, and then Porter Rockwell convinced him that he should go on to California since he couldn't find us in the Valley. I didn't see any reason to worry you over the matter."

The conversation stopped when Martin approached his parents. After he'd turned in the three squash and the pumpkin for his parents' tithing, he'd started wandering about the tithing storehouse, looking at the vegetables, fruits, and animals that had been donated as tithing-in-kind. "Pa, there's a pig in the pen out back. The man told me it was tithing. How can a pig be tithing?"

Grateful for the distraction, Hank said, "If a sow has ten piglets, then the owner can donate one of them for tithing." With that, Martin wandered off to look at the pigs again.

When he was out of earshot, Hank said to Maria, "Let's not frighten him. When we get home, we will just encourage him to stay close."

Maria turned and put her hand to her forehead. "Oh, Hank, I would give anything to have that man leave us alone forever. Why does he have to haunt us and ruin our peace?"

Within half an hour, Allen was back with the new ax handle. "Breaux is having a good time sharing a drink with both Livingston and Kinkead. It looks like he is in no hurry to leave the city. I stopped at the Council House across the street to see President Young. He wasn't there, but I told Brother Bullock about Breaux. He said he would tell President Young about him and let Porter Rockwell know, too. For the time being, I think it would be a good idea if you folks headed back to Cottonwood and stayed out of the city for a while."

That evening after supper was finished, Hank put on his hat as he went out of the cabin. "I'll be back in a little while. If I'm late, don't wait up."

Hank headed for Allen Smithson's cabin. There, he asked Allen to go with him to the home of portly John Holladay, who had recently been appointed bishop of the Cottonwood settlement. They spent an hour by the fireplace talking with Bishop Holladay and his wife.

"I'm not sure what to do, Bishop. We don't have any kind of real law enforcement here in Cottonwood. Port Rockwell is the nearest thing we have to a sheriff anywhere in the Valley, and he's too far away to be of any real help here." Hank's concern showed in his face.

"As a bishop, I have some powers, but really my authority is limited to members of the Church. This situation isn't like requiring a fine because someone was driving his wagon too fast or using bad language."

The little group sat silently for a few moments, watching the dancing flames in the fireplace. Then Allen said thoughtfully, "This man Breaux has yet to commit a crime here in the Valley. The men he sent after Maria are dead—or gone—and cannot testify against him, so we really have no reason to have him arrested. I think that we need to organize another unofficial Whistling and Whittling Brigade here in Cottonwood to keep tabs on him, if he shows up."

Hank looked at Bishop Holladay to see if he liked the idea. He nodded his approval. "Let's keep this quiet and only involve the men who knew about your troubles back in Mississippi. They will need to know what Breaux looks like, as none of them ever saw him."

Hank said quietly, "I got a good look at him today. If I can get some help, we can talk to the folks throughout Cottonwood tomorrow to tell them what he looks like and what to do if anyone sees him. Can you help, Allen?"

"'Course I'll help, Hank. And we can probably get Dowdle, Brown, Lay, Bankhead, and Will Matthews to help."

Word came back from several men the next afternoon that a man fitting the description of Breaux was seen watching some of the boys as they were stick pulling with one another. Hank felt for the bowie knife under his vest and walked quickly toward the wide field the children used for their games. On the way, he met Allen Smithson. He waved his arm, and when Allen approached him, Hank said, "Come with me. Someone thinks they saw Breaux watching the boys play in the field."

They saw Ab Dowdle and waved to him to join them. The three men approached the field in time to see Breaux bending over, holding Martin's arm and talking to him. The other boys were nervously backing away from the pair. As the three men approached, they heard him say, "What's your name, boy? Where do you live?"

Martin was frightened by the intensity of the man who had grabbed his arm and wouldn't let go. Stammering, he answered, "My name's Marty, sir."

"What's your last name, son?" Though Breaux was trying to smile to ease the child's fear, he only made himself look more threatening. He shook Martin's arm as if to shake the answer out of him. Buddy, who had been watching, began to growl in his throat.

Hank and Allen reached Breaux, and Ab quickly joined them. From the rear, Hank put his hand on Breaux's shoulder and said firmly, "Let the boy go."

Breaux stood to his full height but did not let go. "And what's it to you, sir, if I interrogate the boy?"

"That is my son you are holding on to, and I am asking you once more to let go of him."

Looking from Hank to the other men who stood on either side of him, Breaux let go of Martin's arm. "So this is your boy. Your name Hanks, maybe, or Schroeder, by any chance?"

Hank said to Martin, "Run home to your mother—quickly." Then he turned to give Breaux his full attention. "My name is none of your business, and I recommend that you get back on your horse and remove yourself from our settlement—now." By this time, a small group had begun to gather, watching the confrontation. Martin ran only a few steps away before turning to watch.

"You can't chase me out of here. I have as much right to be here as any of you," Breaux's voice was getting louder.

Ab spoke up and said, "You don't live here, you don't own any property here, and it looked to some of us like you were trying to steal the boy. That gives us the right to tell you to get out."

Without saying anything more, Breaux turned, walked to this horse, and mounted. He wore a twisted smile on his face as he turned the animal and kicked it to get it moving.

"Glad to be rid of him," Allen said.

Hank responded, "We haven't heard the last of him. He's not a man to brook opposition. But I thank you men for your support." He shook the hand of both of them and started for home, taking Martin's hand when he reached him.

As they walked toward the cabin, Martin said, "Pa, that was the man we saw on Main Street in the city, the one that scared Ma."

"Yes, Marty, that was the same man."

Martin said quietly, "He scared me, too."

After they put Martin to bed and Hank and Maria were sure he was asleep, they talked long into the night about the situation but could find no real answers. Finally, they took one another's hands, and Hank quietly prayed for protection and wisdom. They both lay awake for a long time after they went to bed. On Sunday, Karl went into Salt Lake City alone to attend Church services in the Bowery.

Late on Monday afternoon, Buddy barked as a rider rode up to the cabin and dropped the reins of his horse to the ground. He dismounted and knocked on the rough-hewn door. When Maria opened it, she was startled at the unkempt appearance of the tall man. His age might have been not much more than forty, but his long black hair was streaked with gray and braided in two long braids, each tied with a leather thong. His beard was untrimmed and hung halfway down his chest, and he was dressed in buckskin. He removed his hat and said, "My name is Port Rockwell, ma'am, and President Young has sent me with a letter to be delivered to you and your husband."

Maria responded, "My husband isn't here. He's up the canyon cutting timber, but you are welcome to wait for him." She motioned for him to come inside the cabin, out of the brisk fall air.

Martin looked up at him from where he was sitting in front of the fireplace and asked, "You're Port Rockwell? Were you really a bodyguard for Joseph Smith?"

"I sure was, young man, and it was the saddest day of my life when I wasn't there to protect him in Carthage."

Martin was fascinated by the man. He stood and approached him. "I heard that you killed a hundred men."

Maria shook her head. "Marty, this man is our guest. You must not talk to company that way."

But Port threw his head back and laughed heartily. "I don't know who started that story. I never killed a man that wasn't trying to kill me or somebody else, but how the rumors do grow."

Maria interrupted the conversation and urged Rockwell to sit down. "Hank will be home in an hour, I expect. Will you take supper with us?"

"Yes, ma'am, I'd be right pleased to."

For the next hour, Martin interrogated Rockwell, getting him to talk freely about the years the Saints spent in Missouri and Nauvoo. "Did you really try to kill Governor Boggs, like some people say?"

"Young man, if I had tried to kill Lilburn W. Boggs, believe me, he would be dead. That's one man I wouldn't have missed. The only man I ever killed back there in Missouri or Illinois was Frank Worrell because he was trying to kill my friend, Sheriff Jake Backenstos. We were trying to help some of the Saints who had been burned out of their cabins near Nauvoo when Worrell and some of his cronies spotted Backenstos, who was riding alone. They chased him over a hill where they planned to shoot him if they caught up with him, but we surprised them. They didn't 'spect to find me and some other men there. When Worrell pulled his gun to shoot Jake, I let loose with my rifle and dropped him right out of his saddle. His friends stopped like they had hit a rock wall." Rockwell laughed again and shook his head. "They picked him up and rode out of there in a big hurry. I heard later that he died."

Maria said, "Marty, I think you need to help me put supper on the table and stop bothering Brother Rockwell."

"Oh, ma'am, he ain't bothering me. I like young 'uns."

Hank opened the door and walked into the house. Maria introduced him to Rockwell. Hank washed his hands, and they sat down to supper. After Hank offered grace, Martin wanted to ask more questions of Rockwell, but Maria would not permit it. At the end of the meal, Rockwell handed a letter from President Young to Hank, who opened it hesitantly. It read:

Dear Brother Schroeder,

You are asked to appear at ten o'clock on Tuesday morning in the office of President Brigham Young, which is in the Council House at South Temple and Main Street. You are asked to bring your wife and son with you. This is a matter of some importance.

Signed, Thomas Bullock, Clerk of the City and County of Great Salt Lake on behalf of President Brigham Young

CHAPTER 35
The Meeting

Rockwell returned to the city that night without any further explanation for the summons to President Young's office.

The two-hour wagon ride into Salt Lake City the next day seemed much longer than usual and hardly anyone spoke. Karl had asked if Hank thought he should come. Hank shook his head, so Karl stayed behind to work in the garden. Even Marty was quiet, sensing but not understanding his parents' nervousness. When they reached the not-yet-finished Council House, Hank tied the mules to the hitching post and helped Maria step down from the wagon. Her size was increasing and made her unsteady. They made their way up the five outside steps and pushed open the big door. Two men were covering the interior adobe walls with whitewash. Another man came through the door of a room at the far end of the building and said, "Brother and Sister Schroeder?"

"Yes, sir," Hank answered.

"I'm Thomas Bullock, President Young's clerk. Please follow me." He led them to the door he had come out of. As they stepped into the large room, Maria audibly caught her breath and stopped. Hank stopped behind her. There, sitting comfortably in a chair pulled near one end of the large desk that filled the center of the room, was Lafayette Breaux.

Bullock stepped around Hank and Maria and said, "Please take a chair."

Then he seated himself behind a smaller desk at the side of the room. They recognized the man who sat behind the imposing desk as Brigham Young. They had seen him many times when he had addressed the Saints in the Bowery at Sabbath meetings. He wore a black coat and vest, white shirt, and bow tie. Compared to the red silk coat Breaux wore, President Young looked plain and colorless. Breaux looked somewhat like a red-coated peacock. Young stepped around the desk and put out his hand. "I'm President Young. You have been wondering why I sent for you. Put your minds at ease and please take a chair. Thank you for responding to my request to meet with you."

The Church leader was a solidly built man with a leonine appearance, created by his black hair that was parted on the left and then swept back, falling almost like a mane to his shoulders. His piercing blue eyes appeared to look deep into the soul of any man with whom he shook hands. He motioned for them to be seated. "I understand that you are already acquainted with Mr. Breaux."

Hank nodded and stated tersely, "Yes, we are."

Young pointed to a small settee and a wingback chair near the opposite end of his desk, about four feet from the chair Breaux sat in. "Please be seated." Hank sat stiffly in the chair, and Maria looked as if she wanted to melt into the settee. Martin sat next to his mother and looked curiously around the room at the man in the red coat and at the man who had reseated himself behind the large desk.

"We will dispense with the usual courtesies, as it is apparent that all of you are wondering why I have called this meeting." Speaking to Hank and Maria, President Young said, "Mr. Breaux has come to me and asked that his property be returned to him. We are here to determine if the property he seeks is really his." President Young looked at his clerk. "Brother Bullock, would you take the boy down to the mercantile and buy him a peppermint stick?"

Bullock rose as if he had anticipated the request and motioned to Martin. Then he put on his hat and coat. "Let's do what President Young has asked us. Would you like a peppermint stick?"

Martin looked at his mother for her approval, and when she nodded, he slid off the settee and took Bullock's hand, and they exited the office together.

Young rose from his chair behind the desk and paced as he spoke. "Now we can speak freely. I had you bring the boy so I could see him, but he does not need to hear what we are going to discuss.

Mr. Breaux has come to me, in my capacity as governor of the Territory of Deseret, to insist that I permit him to take you, Sister Schroeder, and your son back to Louisiana. When he came through Salt Lake City two years ago, he told me that you were his wife, but he now insists that he purchased you as a white slave when you were sixteen and that you ran away from him two years later with the man who is now your husband. He also insists that your marriage has no validity because he did not give his permission for it."

He paused for what seemed a long time to all those present and studied the pattern in the carpet at his feet thoughtfully before continuing. "Additionally, Mr. Breaux claims that under the recently passed Federal Fugitive Slave Law—did I get that right, Mr. Breaux?" He continued without waiting for an answer, "All law enforcement officers and courts everywhere in the United States and its territories are obliged to assist in the recapture of runaway slaves. He has also informed me that anyone who assists a runaway slave faces a penalty of up to six months in jail and a one thousand dollar fine as well as a civil liability owed to the slave's owner of one thousand dollars for each fugitive." He paused and looked at Breaux. "He also claims the boy is his." As Young talked, Breaux smiled with a growing confidence. Turning to look directly at Maria, President Young said, "Would you share your side of the story with me?"

Hank took Maria's hand and said quietly, "Tell him everything."

Maria began hesitantly, but as she talked her voice filled with emotion, sometimes grief, and sometimes anger, as she spoke of the voyage to America, the death of her parents, and of Breaux's unwillingness to give her the freedom that was hers by right. She ended by sliding into German as she stood and said urgently and angrily, turning to look directly at Breaux, *"Ich bin ein Baden geboren!"* Then she turned to look at President Young but pointed at Breaux. "And he knows I was born in Baden! He knows he owed me my freedom on my eighteenth birthday, but he refused to honor my contract."

Hank patted the settee to get her to sit down again. Then he squeezed her hand and said encouragingly, "Tell him about Martin."

For a brief moment, Maria looked at Hank as if she did not want to say more, but trusting his judgment and regaining her self-control, she took up the story line again in a more normal voice. After she had explained the circumstances of her rape and the conception of Martin and how she had fled Breaux's plantation and was pulled from the river by Hank, President Young stood and turned his back on those in the room. He looked out of the office window, saying nothing for a few moments.

The room was silent except for the tick of the clock on the top shelf of the bookcase. "I have given the matter much thought since you came to me yesterday, Mr. Breaux. I have read the document you furnished me, but I find only a purchase contract for one female by the name of Maria, sold to you by Theophilis Freeman of New Orleans. There is nothing in the document to establish where or when Freeman obtained Maria or what her status was at that time. The document makes no reference to whether she was a slave or an indentured servant—only that her services were bought by you."

He paused and turned to look at Breaux, whose complexion had begun to grow almost as red as his silk coat. He continued, "I have the distinct impression that there may be other documentation you have not shown to me, which might specify that she was an indentured servant, rather than a slave." Breaux started to speak, but Young raised his hand to silence him. "Here in the Territory of Deseret, we consider ourselves well outside the conflict over slavery that continues within the States and hope to remain so—and until we declare differently, we do not recognize the right to sell, purchase, or capture slaves here. There are several Southern families who have brought their black servants with them, but at the present time those servants are free to leave if they so choose. We have no laws to enforce their continued servitude. Perhaps that will change in the future, but for now the only crime I find any evidence of here is the rape of Mrs. Schroeder, which took place in Louisiana, and"—there he paused—"I am sorry to say is beyond my authority to prosecute."

Breaux stood, scarlet with rage. His raised voice could be heard not only outside the office where the workmen were applying whitewash to the interior walls but also outside the building. "This matter is not settled. The woman and her child belong to me—and by law the one she carries belongs to me, as well!"

President Young spoke forcefully and directly to Breaux, "I urge you to leave the Valley, Mr. Breaux, and return to Louisiana. Your claims have been rejected, and if you make any attempt to remove either Mrs. Schroeder or her son from the Valley, you will be considered in violation of the law, and the full penalty of such a violation will be enforced." His voice had taken on a hard and somewhat threatening tone.

Breaux put his silk hat on his head and stormed out of the office, slamming the door behind him.

Hank stood and offered his hand. "Thank you, President Young. That man has tormented us for a long time. Your help in bringing that torment to an end is deeply appreciated."

As he shook Hank's outstretched hand, Young stated gravely, "Brother Schroeder, that is a prideful man, and he is consumed with determination. He will not be thwarted easily." Putting both hands behind his back, he continued thoughtfully, "This slavery issue will continue to trouble the Saints until there is a solution that frees the entire country from this awful burden. I recently wrote to William Crosby, who is again doing missionary work in the South, to tell him to discourage the immigration of slaves to the Territory. Joseph considered slavery abhorrent, as do most of the Saints, but if we are viewed as abolitionists, we will lose most of our Southern converts."

Taking a deep breath and letting it out slowly, as if he had suddenly become very tired, President Young shook his head. "This was one of the issues that caused the Saints great problems in Missouri." He straightened up and said with renewed determination, "I will have Port Rockwell keep an eye on Mr. Breaux, but you must do all you can to protect your family."

"I will, President Young. And again, we thank you."

Brother Bullock entered with Martin, who was sucking on a peppermint stick. Martin took the peppermint stick out of his mouth and said, "This is really good, Mama. I never had one before."

"Did you tell Brother Bullock thank you?"

"Yes, Ma, I sure did."

As Hank helped Maria descend the stairs in front of the building and step up into the wagon, Rockwell arrived. He had been watching and waiting for Breaux to leave the Council House, which he could see from the window of the saloon that was immediately north of the mercantile store. He tipped his hat to Maria without saying anything and entered the building.

Within a few days, life seemed to return to normal, and the people of Cottonwood ceased seeing every new face as a threat, but Martin was forbidden to leave the cabin unless in the company of his parents or Uncle Karl.

"I know Lafayette Breaux probably knows where we are," Maria said, "and it may seem foolish to you to continue to hide from him, but I would feel better if we did not go into Salt Lake City to attend Sunday meetings for the next few weeks. Karl can take the wagon and tell us of any news we need to know when he comes home." Maria remained frightened at the thought of going anywhere where they might run into Breaux.

"He has probably moved on by now, but if you would feel better avoiding the city for the next little while, I don't think anyone would judge us too harshly," Hank responded.

After three weeks of attending Church meetings alone, Karl openly began to speak of the young lady from Holland, whose name was Minnie Van Wooten. As they sat down to supper on a Sunday evening, Maria asked with a smile, "Should we be making plans to welcome this young woman into our family?"

Karl smiled and said simply, "We will see."

***

After leaving Young's office, Breaux climbed onto his horse and rode down Main Street to the Valley House Hotel. Rockwell found the task of keeping an eye on him easy, as over the next several days, he spent most of his waking hours in one or another of the saloons on Main Street. The saloons, founded by gentiles who had halted in their journeys west, found a ready clientele in the large numbers of gold-seeking wagon companies that stopped in the city to purchase supplies for the journey to California.

In early December, Rockwell watched a half-drunken Breaux as he apparently tried to recruit two men for some task. From across the room, Rockwell watched as Breaux pulled a large roll of bills from his pocket. Both men shook their heads and made their way out of the saloon. Port followed them. Out in the muddy street, he called out in a friendly manner, "Hey, either of you guys want to earn a dollar?"

They stopped and turned to look at him. "After what we been offered by that dandy inside, why do you think we would do anything for a dollar?"

"Tell me what that man inside wanted you to do."

One of the men raised an eyebrow and said, "Maybe what he said to us is worth more than that."

Rockwell responded with a new hardness in his voice as he rested his hand on the butt of his pistol, "And maybe it ain't. Now, what did he want you to do?"

"No reason to get upset, mister. He was half drunk. He won't even remember what he said in the morning. He wanted us to grab some little boy and take him back to Independence, Missouri, for him. He said if we took the boy's mother, too, he would double what he had offered for the boy."

"What did he offer for the boy?"

"Five hundred dollars, but we told him he was crazy. We don't want no part of that kind of thing."

The next morning Port set out by horseback toward Cottonwood with another letter for the Schroeder family from President Young.

CHAPTER 36
The Watcher

Hank offered Rockwell a seat when he appeared at their door and took the letter with curiosity. Maria put down the spoon with which she had been stirring the soup on the stove and stepped over to see the letter as Hank opened it. Hank read it and then handed it to Maria without saying anything.

She took it with hands that shook slightly and read aloud,

"Dear Brother and Sister Schroeder, I have been instructed by President Young to notify you that there will be a colonizing company leaving when the weather grows warmer, which will be traveling to Southern California to establish a community of Saints there. For your safety, he urges you to consider joining that company. Should you have any questions, Brother Rockwell will answer them.

Signed, Thomas Bullock, Clerk of the City and County of Great Salt Lake, on behalf of President Brigham Young"

Maria looked up from the letter. "Why are we being told to join the group going to Southern California? I thought President Young had admonished the Saints not to go to California."

"I understand why you're confused, Sister Schroeder. I hear that the president of these United States, Zachary Taylor, has talked of allowing the Saints to make part of Southern California a part of the State of Deseret, and he has encouraged President Young to send a colony of Saints down there. President Young wants the Saints to stay away from the gold fields and the evils that are found there. The starving times the Saints have experienced these past three winters have been hard on everybody.

Captain Jefferson Hunt of the Mormon Battalion has brought back word that there is land there where the Saints can establish a colony. If such a community is established, President Young hopes that it can be a source of fruit, vegetables, and beef for the Saints here in the Valley. He also wants it to serve as a gathering point for converts who are arriving in California by ship. Many of the Mississippi Saints are planning to go, as the winters here in the Valley are proving to be very hard on folks not accustomed to the cold."

Maria looked at him with a great question in her eyes and asked, "And this letter is telling us that he want us to be part of that group? There was a time when I wanted to go to California, but now we are settled in our own home. Our garden did well this summer. Hank built a henhouse and a shed for our animals." Her voice broke with distress. "We are finally happy here. Why should we have to move again?"

Maria's emotional words made Rockwell uncomfortable. He stood and cleared his throat and then, lowering his voice, answered as he shifted his weight from one foot to the other, "Ma'am, I don't want to scare you or the boy." He stopped to nod toward Martin, who was sitting by the fire trying to read some of the words in an old newspaper. "But that man, Breaux, has continued to hang around and recently tried to hire a couple of worthless types to take you and your son back to Independence. From there, I'm sure he would take you back to Louisiana. He offered them five hundred dollars for each of you. President Young is worried that you might not be safe here."

Maria put her hand to her throat. She sat down at the table, and when Hank stepped over and put his arm around her, she leaned against him. "Oh, I see," was all she could whisper.

Hank said, "When will the wagon company leave?"

"Probably about the time the snow is gone. I hear that President Young has picked Charles Rich and Amasa Lyman to lead the group, and Jefferson Hunt will be the official wagon boss. You'll be in good hands." With that, he put his hat on his head and said, "You will be hearing more as the time grows closer. If you don't have any more questions, I'll be taking my leave."

In early February, Maria's baby came. Vilate, the black midwife that Mother Crosby had previously owned but who had obtained her freedom when the Crosby family arrived in the Valley, delivered her. The little girl was strong and cried loudly, objecting to the world of light and cold she had been forced into. After she had been laid in her mother's arms, Hank and Martin were finally permitted to enter the bedroom. Hank bent over, gently brushed Maria's hair aside, and gave her a kiss on her forehead. "What shall we call her?"

"What would you like to name her?"

"I would like to name her Marguerite Caroline. Would that please you?" Hank asked.

Maria nodded. "And we will call her Maggie."

By the first of April, news came that the arrangements for the wagon company's journey to Southern California were almost finished. Many of those who planned to join the company were friends and neighbors of the Schroeders.

"We need to make a decision about joining the California group, Hank," Maria commented one evening as she rocked Maggie. "I am still wondering if we should go. I think the Harmons and Smithsons are the only families from Mississippi and Alabama that are not planning to go. It seems that so many of our friends here will be going that Cottonwood will nearly be a ghost town."

"We don't need to be concerned about that, my dear. The empty cabins they leave will fill quickly with some of the folks who will arrive in the Valley later this summer." Hank sat by the little stove where he had been reading the *Deseret News*. He put the newspaper down. "I am more concerned about little Maggie. She is doing well, but she is so young. I hear that the journey to Southern California is very hard, especially where it crosses the Mojave Desert. I think there will be other wagon companies making the journey later this year or next, and, for her sake, perhaps we need to wait until she is a bit older before deciding to make such a trip. How do you feel?"

Looking at the sleeping infant and remembering the death of her first daughter, Maria answered, "Yes, I think you are right—but what about Breaux? Some nights I can hardly sleep for worrying about him."

"We will need to be watchful."

The following Sunday evening when he arrived back in Cottonwood, Karl explained that he had asked Minnie to marry him.

"What did she say, Karl?" Maria asked excitedly.

"She said yes," Karl said with a wide smile. "It's time. The cabin is finished," he added pragmatically, but his pleasure was evident.

The following Friday the Schroeders and the Smithsons rode into Salt Lake City and met Minnie, her parents, and her sisters at the Council House, where Brigham Young united Karl and Minnie in marriage. The newlyweds were treated to a brief honeymoon of one night in the Valley House Hotel, and the next day when they returned to Cottonwood, Hank and Maria, with the help of Allen and Letitia, held a celebration for the couple.

***

Lafayette Breaux watched and listened to the news about the California-bound wagon train. For weeks, the large company that was headed for Southern California had been the talk of the Valley. When he heard that the wagon company was on its way, he sold his horse and changed into a buckskin shirt. Then he bought a wagon and a team of mules from the livery owner to replace the team and wagon Garcia had taken. He loaded the wagon with his possessions, added some jerky and hardtack, and filled a large canteen. Lastly, he tossed his derringer into a trunk and strapped on a gun belt and pistol. Then he climbed into the wagon and rode out to Cottonwood, arriving at dusk.

He stopped the youngest Smithson boy, who was carrying a bucket from the stream, and offered him a coin if he would point out the cabin where the Schroeders lived.

The little boy put down the bucket and pointed it out. "That one is Hank Schroeder's cabin, and the one over there is his brother's."

Breaux asked, "Did the Schroeders go to California with the others?"

Little Jimmy Smithson shook his head and answered, "No, sir. They stayed here, like us."

Offering another coin, Breaux asked, "Are there any empty cabins here I could maybe stay in?"

"Most all of them are empty around here, mister. Most folks in Cottonwood went to California."

He handed the coin to the child and patted him on the head. "Now be a good little fellow and run along. You don't need to say anything about where you got the money. Understand?" Breaux said innocently.

The boy nodded, picked up the bucket once more, and hurried home in the near dark. Breaux selected an empty cabin as far from Hank and Maria's cabin as possible but which still had a view of the front door and windows of the little cabin, where a fire in the fireplace and two candles made the windows bright. He could occasionally see Maria's shadow pass the window as she put supper on the table. Looking around to make sure no one was likely to see him, he parked his wagon behind the cabin he had selected and put the mules in an animal shed nearby. After he slipped inside, he lit a candle and looked around. Noting the rope bed in the corner, he spread out his bedroll on it, ate a piece of jerky, blew out the candle, and lay down.

CHAPTER 37
Confrontation!

Throughout the next day Breaux watched the Schroeder cabin from the window while he ate an occasional piece of jerky. He took note that there were very few inhabited cabins nearby. *The boy was right*, he thought. *Most of the settlers here must have headed to California.* During the day, he watched Hank and Maria work in the garden, and as the sun set, he watched Hank feed and water the animals. He waited until dark when he could see only a few cabins with light in the windows. He pulled his hat down far enough that it partially covered his face. With the mules hitched to the wagon again and standing near the cabin he had been using, he was ready to approach the Schroeder cabin. Taking his pistol in his right hand, he held it against his right leg to hide it from anyone who might see him. He stood for a minute at the cabin door and listened to the music of the organ that Maria was playing. Then he knocked on the door with his left hand. *Carefully, not too loud. Don't frighten the folks inside,* he thought to himself.

Maria left the organ and looked out of the little window. She saw only a figure in a buckskin shirt and a large felt hat pulled low over his face. "Who is it, Maria?" Hank asked from where he sat near the stove. Martin paused to look up from where he sat at the table, writing his letters on a board with charcoal.

"I think it may be Porter Rockwell." She opened the door.

Breaux pushed his way in and put the gun in her face. "Get the boy. If you give me any trouble, I'll hurt him." As she stepped backward into the room, Hank stood, toppling the chair he had been sitting in. Buddy rose from his place by the stove and growled with bared teeth.

Waving his gun at the dog, Breaux said, "Make the dog shut up, or I'll shoot it."

"Buddy, sit." Hank quieted the dog, which sat down but continued to growl in his throat.

Breaux waved the gun toward Maria. "I told you to get the boy—and get the baby, too. You're all coming with me." She looked at Hank, uncertain what to do.

He said quietly, "Just do what he wants, Maria, and he won't hurt you." Looking at Breaux, Hank said, "Let her get her cape and a coat for the boy. It's cold outside."

Waving the gun at the pegs on the back wall where the cape hung not far from the stove, Breaux said with satisfaction, "Hurry up. I'm in a hurry."

Maria stepped back to the rear of the cabin, reached up, and took the cape and Martin's coat from a peg. She turned and started for the open doorway. As she passed Hank, he snatched the cape from her hand and in one swift motion, pushed her down, and threw the cape at Breaux's head, as if he were a bullfighter and Breaux the bull. In the fraction of a second that Breaux's vision was blocked by the flying cape, Hank lunged at the man's gun, calling out, "Get down on the floor, Marty."

The men wrestled over the gun, the cape interfering with Breaux's attempts to push Hank away. As they fell to the floor and rolled about, Maria rushed to get Hank's rifle, where it was mounted high on the wall. As she took it down, she heard the explosion of gunfire from Breaux's pistol. As she swung the rifle around, she saw Hank stagger back and collapse on the floor, wounded in the foot. Breaux raised his pistol, and as he fired again at Hank, Maria aimed and fired. The roar of the rifle merged with the second pistol shot. Breaux's second shot hit Hank in the right thigh. Maria's shot hit Breaux high in the chest, and he staggered backward out of the doorway, where he fell dead in the dirt.

Maggie, who had been awakened by the shots, began to scream, terrified by the noise. Martin got up from the floor with a white face and cried out, "Ma, Ma! He shot Pa."

The boy ran to his father, where he lay with his right leg bleeding profusely. The sound of the shots had brought Karl and Allen Smithson at a run. Minnie arrived a few moments behind Karl and hurried to pick up the crying baby. Buddy had quit growling in his throat and was licking Hank's face, trying to get a response from his master. Within a few minutes, the few other men who still lived nearby gathered at the cabin door. Allen said to one of them, "Go, get a doctor. Hurry! And bring back Porter Rockwell!"

Martin tried to bravely stand by his mother as the men picked up his father and carried him into the little bedroom to place him on the bed. The boy looked up into his mother's face. "He won't die, will he?" The fear in her son's face hurt Maria almost as much as Hank's injuries.

Maria put her arm around the distraught boy and said, "Try not to worry. Someone has gone for the doctor."

It took two hours for the doctor to get to Cottonwood from the city, even though Dr. Andrews and the man sent for him almost rode their horses to death. During that time, Allen and Karl cut off the leg of Hank's pants and his shoe. Then they cut up a sheet into strips, and Maria wrapped his leg, trying to slow the profuse bleeding.

After she had bandaged Hank's leg, Maria knelt by the bed. "Allen, Karl, please ask the Lord to heal him," she asked.

The prayer was simple and pleading, and as Allen ended the prayer, he paused and then added, "But all things are in Thy hands, and Thy will be done."

When Dr. Andrews arrived, he quickly examined the wounds. He straightened up and said, "The bone in his left thigh is badly broken, and I think the artery is nicked. The wound is bleeding so much that I'm going to have to put a tourniquet on it." He continued giving directions. "I will need two long, straight pieces of wood to use as splints and some clean cloths to use as bandages. If you have any turpentine, get it. Hurry, so I can be finished before he wakes up."

While the doctor probed for the bullet in Hank's leg, Hank moaned but did not regain consciousness. After removing the bullet, the doctor wrapped the wounds tightly to stop the bleeding. When Hank's leg had been splinted, the doctor said, "That is about all I can do right now. I'll stay the night in case he needs me. If the pain gets too bad, I have some laudanum that will help."

Minnie had calmed the baby and put her back into her bed. Then she put her arms around Maria to offer her some additional strength and support.

The men who had been standing around the open doorway picked up Breaux's body and put it in his wagon, which they had located near the vacant cabin. Porter Rockwell arrived as they were finishing and asked each one of them to tell him what they knew of the situation. Two of the men had brought lanterns, and they held them high so Rockwell could examine the body. When he recognized Breaux in the wagon bed, he said wearily, "I feared it might come to something like this."

He stepped into the cabin and spoke to Karl, who stood with the two women. "Can you tell me what happened?"

"I don't know any more than anyone else. You need to ask Maria and Marty. The rest of us arrived after the shooting was over."

Maria said, "He knocked on the door, and I opened it. I thought it was you, Brother Rockwell. He pointed his gun at me and pushed his way in. He said he was going to take me and the children. Hank tried to take the gun from him, and Breaux shot him." She paused and put her hand over her quivering mouth for a moment. "When Hank fell on the floor, Breaux shot him again. By that time, I had the rifle, so I shot Breaux." She looked into Rockwell's face and asked, "Did I kill him?"

"Yes, ma'am, you sure did."

"Why did it have to come to this?" she whispered to no one in particular. Karl guided her to a chair.

"Well, I've learned all I need to know. I'll take his body and be on my way." Rockwell paused and spoke to Martin, "You're the man of the house right now, Marty. I know you will be a big help for your mother."

"Yes, sir, I'll try," the boy answered.

"Maria, you know that you can call on any of us if we can be of help in any way," Allen said as he ushered the men away.

"Do you want me to take the children?" Minnie asked Maria.

She nodded and answered quietly, "Thank you. I may need Marty, but it would help if you took Maggie for a day or two."

Minnie picked up the small child and returned to her cabin.

As the door closed, Hank moaned and opened his eyes. Maria rushed to his bedside and cried out, "Hank. Hank, thank God you're awake."

Marty joined her and asked, "Pa, how do you feel? Are you all right?"

He moaned again and closed his eyes. He did not stir for the next ten hours. The doctor slept in a chair next to the bed and woke several times during the night to briefly loosen the tourniquet. Maria sat in the rocking chair, watching her husband throughout the night, while Martin slept on a bedroll on the floor near his father's bed. Buddy lay next to him.

Oh, Hank, don't leave me. I need you—we need you! When I said I would give anything to be free of Breaux, I did not mean this. I did not mean this.

CHAPTER 38

Loss

In the morning, Hank regained consciousness and asked for water. Then he drifted into a delirium, a confusion of muttered words. Martin looked at his father and asked his mother in a worried voice, "Papa is hurt really bad, isn't he? Will he get better?"

All Maria could bring herself to answer in a near whisper was, "If it is God's will."

By noon, Hank was conscious, but in so much pain that Dr. Andrews helped him swallow some laudanum. Then the doctor sat quietly by the bed and waited for the drug to take effect. When his patient had slipped into a drugged sleep, he examined the leg again. The bandages were soaked with blood, and the leg was swollen. The flesh was purple and shiny around the wounds. The broken end of the tibia poked through the skin. The doctor removed the tourniquet and pulled on the right foot to lengthen the leg and reset the bone. Even in his drug-induced sleep, Hank moaned in pain. Then the doctor changed the bandages.

As the doctor straightened up, he said to Maria, who had been watching from where she stood behind him, "Don't let the bandages get too soaked with blood. Change them often. Otherwise, the blood will dry and stick to the wounds." He pulled the blanket up under Hank's chin and turned to face her. He added gravely, "I don't know if he will ever be able to walk on that leg again. If it gets infected, it will have to come off. I'm sorry I can't give you better news."

Maria's face blanched, and Martin cried out, "No, no, you have to make him better! You have to fix his leg." He had been standing behind his mother so quietly that neither she nor the doctor had known he was there. "Please, please, fix his leg," he pleaded.

"I'll do my best, Marty, but in this case, my best might not be enough." Then he said to Maria, "When he wakes, try to get some soup into him. I can't stay. I have two other very sick patients in the city to look after, but I'll be back in the morning." Hank remained unconscious for the next twelve hours.

The next morning, as the doctor pulled up in his wagon, Allen walked over to the cabin and spoke to Maria. "Maria, why don't you play for Hank while he is so sick? Maybe you can play him well."

"Play him well? What do you mean, Allen?"

"If you can play the organ like he said you can, I think it would help him to hear the music while he is so weak." Maria said nothing. She just looked at the organ as though she had forgotten its existence.

Dr. Andrews, who had arrived in time to hear Allen's suggestion, said to her, "Maria, it surely couldn't hurt, and who knows? It might help." As he followed Maria into the cabin, he asked, "Were you able to get him to eat or drink anything?" She shook her head.

Each morning for the next three days, the doctor came to check Hank's condition. Hank woke from his drugged sleep once or twice a day and drank a little broth from a cup Maria held. She sent Martin to Karl and Minnie's cabin for meals. She slept in the old rocker next to the bed, waiting to meet Hank's needs when he woke. She changed the bandages twice each day, washing out the old ones to use again.

On the fourth day, Hank woke and asked in a voice that croaked, "I think I'm hungry. Could I have some scrambled eggs?"

Maria flew into the other room to prepare some. When Martin came in the door and saw his mother cooking on the little stove and the bedroom door open, he asked, "Is Pa awake? Can I see him?"

"Yes, son. You can talk to him if you don't make him too tired." Instead of talking to his father, Marty stepped inside the bedroom and stood, watching silently as his father lay with closed eyes.

Maria returned and fed Hank the eggs until he said weakly, "No more. That's enough." He asked in his scratchy voice, "What happened? I remember Breaux forcing his way into the cabin, but I can't remember anything else."

After Maria explained what had happened, Hank said weakly, "At least he will never trouble us again." After a few minutes he said, "It would sure make me happy to hear you play, my dear."

Maria stood without moving for nearly a minute while she wrestled with the turmoil inside her heart. She was so exhausted, so emotionally drained. Finally, she said quietly, "I'll try. For you, I will try."

As she started to turn away from the bed, he took her hand, and said weakly, "Wherever or whenever you play, it will be for me. Remember that."

She let him hold her hand until he grew so weak that he had to let go. Then she went to the organ in the other room. Sitting down, she began to pump with legs that were weak with stress and lack of sleep. She put her fingers on the keys, and they sought a familiar melody as Martin sat down by the stove to listen. After a few tries, her fingers found the right keys and played a soothing melody by Beethoven.

As she finished, Martin coaxed, "Play some more, Mama. Play some more."

Hank called weakly from the bedroom, "Keep playing, Maria. The music eases the pain."

Despite the weakness in her legs, Maria played for another hour. By then, Hank appeared to be sleeping, and she was exhausted. Later that day as she entered the bedroom to change the bandages on his leg, the smell of putrefied flesh made the gorge rise in her throat. She could see he was feverish and almost incoherent with pain, despite the laudanum he had been given that morning. She called to Martin, "Marty, hurry to Smithson's cabin, and tell Allen to go get the doctor as fast as he can."

Allen saddled his horse and rode hard for the city. Halfway there, he met Dr. Andrews, who was coming by wagon for his regular visit. When told that he needed to hurry, he pushed his team to its limit to get to Cottonwood quickly. When he arrived, he examined Hank's leg and foot and said, "I'm sorry, Maria, but if I don't amputate, he will surely die. There's gangrene, and it's spreading."

Taking a deep breath, she said, "What do you need?"

Turning to Martin, he said, "Get Allen Smithson and your Uncle Karl, or any other two strong men. Tell them to come quickly." Again, without a word, Martin hurried out of the cabin.

The doctor continued, "Bring the biggest pot you have to catch the blood. Your kitchen table is too small to be of any help, so I will try to turn him so he is lying across the bed with his legs propped on chairs. Pull the rocking chair over here, and put his left leg on it. Now get two of the chairs from the other room, and we will put them under his right leg. Get sheets, as many as you have, and then get me a quilting needle with about a yard of quilting thread in it." His orders were coming as fast as Maria's heart was beating.

Hank roused enough to ask weakly, "What's going on?"

The doctor pulled the stopper out of a bottle of laudanum and put it to Hank's lips. "Here, drink this—all of it." Hank almost gagged as he tried to swallow it. Within a few minutes, it had taken effect.

Allen Smithson had waited near the cabin door to see if he was needed, and Karl was there within a few minutes. They knew what they had to do before Dr. Andrews could tell them. He just pointed to either side of Hank, who was moaning and muttering in pain. As Allen knelt on one side of him and Karl on the other, the doctor said, "Each of you must hold him down. Don't let him thrash about."

He took a large knife that he had sharpened to a fine edge and a meat saw from his large black bag and laid them next to the bottle of turpentine and the soft heap of cotton he had put near the sheets Maria had brought him. He said tersely, "Tear the sheet in strips about six inches wide and no more than a yard long."

The doctor put the pot between the bed and the two chairs that Hank's left leg rested upon. Then doctor applied the point of the knife above the wound in Hank's thigh and swiftly drew it around the leg, through the flesh to the bone. Hank moaned. Looking away, Maria saw Martin standing white-faced by the bedroom door. "You should not have to see this. Go over to Aunt Minnie's. I will come and get you when you can see your father."

He was almost mesmerized by the horror of the sight. His mother had to push him out of the room.

Taking the meat saw with experienced hands, Dr. Andrews pressed with his whole weight against the blade and drew it back and forth. Hank rose from the stupor he had been in, stiffened, and screamed. Then he slid into a merciful unconsciousness. The doctor made quick work of severing the bone, and then he pulled the skin over the gaping wound and began to stitch the flesh together with Maria's quilting needle. He poured turpentine over the stitches and then packed the cotton around the bleeding stump and wrapped it firmly.

Allen and Karl climbed off the bed and helped turn Hank's body until he lay straight in the bed once more. Then the doctor sat down in the rocker. His hands shook. No one said anything for a few minutes. When he was able to stand up, he said, "You need to keep his head cool and his body warm. When he wakes, have him drink as much as you can—broth, water, soup, anything to help him replace the blood he has lost. I'll be back in the morning." He stopped and turned to face Maria and said, "I would stay, but Sister Watson had a heart attack a few days ago, and I need to get back to her." He looked at Allen and Karl. "Help her clean up the room, if you will. She shouldn't have to face it alone." He put the tools and other things he had brought with him in his black bag, put his hat on his head, and left the cabin an exhausted man.

Karl said to Allen, "I think we need to bury the blood and the leg deep enough that animals don't bother it." He left the cabin to find a shovel. For what seemed a long time, Maria stood still and listened to the irregular breathing of her husband and the sound of the shovel against the earth as they dug a deep hole in the yard. She started to shake as though she had been chilled by a cold north wind. Minnie, who had seen the doctor depart, hurried to the cabin. She led Maria out of the bedroom and insisted that she sit on one of the trunks in the main room. She wrapped her in a shawl that hung by the door and sat with her arm around her sister-in-law to help calm her trembling.

After a few minutes Karl came through the cabin, and he and Allen left with the leg wrapped in a bloody sheet and the pot that was half full of blood. They buried both. Returning to the bedroom, they wiped up the blood and washed the bedroom floor with the other clean sheet. Allen carried the two chairs out of the bedroom. The woven seats had both been soaked with blood. "I'll take both of these home and reweave the seats so you can use them again." Maria nodded her thanks. As Allen paused at the door, he said, "I'll have Letitia wash the sheet, too, so you can use it again." Then he paused and said, "Call on us when you need us again."

Karl sat down on the big trunk across the room and said, "He'll get better, Maria. Dr. Andrews is a good man. He will do everything that can be done to see that Hank gets better."

Maria did not respond for a few seconds, but then she suddenly become aware of her surroundings. "Thank you, Karl. I thank God for you and Minnie. Please tell Marty that he can come in now."

While Karl sat in silence with Maria, Minnie hurried back to her cabin to check on the baby. An hour later, Minnie returned with a big pan of corn bread and a pot of beef stew. She put her arms around Maria, and Maria's self control melted. She wept on her sister-in-law's shoulder until there were no more tears. Then she straightened up and said, "Will you stay and have supper with us?"

"No, I brought the food for you, and I want you and Marty to eat. You haven't eaten in days." After supper, Martin lay down on the bedroll in the main room and said, "Mama, play the music again."

"Oh, Marty, I don't think I have enough strength to play tonight."

He responded quietly, "Pa would like it, Mama."

Maria nodded and stepped into the next room. Hank lay covered with the clammy perspiration of shock. As she entered, he raised his hand, and she took it in both of hers. "Marty said that I should play for you," she said gently. Then she lifted his head and put a cup of water to his lips. "Would that help you sleep, my dear?" She straightened the quilt and tucked it around his shoulders.

He whispered weakly, "Yes, my love, I would like to hear you play again, and whenever you play, I want you to remember that no matter where life takes us,"—he paused to breathe heavily—"I promised to love you and protect you, whether in life or in death. Now go and play for me. I will be listening."

Maria played for the next hour, until her legs shook with exhaustion. Then she folded her arms on the top of the organ and put her head on them to rest for a little while. Martin was asleep.

After she awoke, she raised her head and saw that twilight was wrapping the world in soft darkness. She rose from the organ stool and lit a candle from the lamp on the table, then slipped into the bedroom. Holding the candle above her head, she could see that the twisted look of pain had disappeared from Hank's face. It had been replaced by a peaceful and serene expression. She approached the bed and whispered, "Are you feeling better, dearest?"

Taking his hand, she could feel that it was growing cold. She dropped to her knees and put it against her cheek. She knelt, holding his hand for a long time, slowly grasping the fact that he was gone. Then she rose and tenderly put his hand beneath the quilt, as if to keep it warm.

Sitting down in the rocking chair by the bed, she said quietly, her voice breaking, "Yes, my beloved, you are feeling better now. Of that I am sure." For the rest of the night, she sat quietly near the bedside with quiet tears making their way down her cheeks. In the dark, the words of Johann Goethe took form in her mind—words that she had translated for Mrs. Wentz many years earlier. *"The sum which two married people owe to one another defies calculation. It is an infinite debt, which can only be discharged through all eternity."*

Please, dear God, give us a reunion someday so that I might have eternity to repay my debt to Hank.

CHAPTER 39
Called Home

A group of about thirty people gathered around the grave as Hank was laid to rest in the little Cottonwood cemetery next to the graves of Caroline, Mother Crosby, and John and Betsy Brown's baby. At the grave site, Maria stood in the sunshine and cold winter air, white-faced and holding a squirming Maggie in her arms, while Martin stood quietly at her side.

Allen gave the eulogy. "This is a man who withheld nothing that the Lord asked of him and never hesitated to go where the Lord directed. We have been promised in Isaiah that 'He will swallow up death in victory; and the Lord God shall wipe away tears from off all faces.' That promise is to be trusted. This good man, Hans Martin Schroeder, whom we all called Hank, shall stand with lifted head before that judgment bar to receive the approbation of God. He has earned the sure and certain promise of eternal life."

Maria hardly heard the words that were meant to bring comfort to her hurting heart. She only felt emptiness—total desolation deep inside. She cried out silently, *Dear God, how can I go on when someone who was such a part of me, so familiar and beloved, is gone—this man who was so fierce in my defense but so tender with me? How shall I go on?*

As people approached her to offer condolences and take their leave, she came to herself and stiffly tried to smile her thanks to each one. Letitia Smithson gave her an embrace and whispered in her ear, "Come over to our place for dinner on Sunday." Maria simply nodded.

That evening as Maria sat in the darkened main room of the cabin, after the last of those who had come to share her grief had finally left and Maggie had been put to bed, Martin sat down next to her. He leaned against her. "Ma, why did Heavenly Father take Pa? I miss him so much." He was too emotionally drained to cry. "I will always miss him."

Putting her arm around his drooping shoulders, she whispered, "So will I, Marty. So will I." After sitting that way for a little while, she inhaled deeply and said, "I think it is time for you to lie down and go to sleep."

"Will you be sleeping in the bedroom tonight?" he asked as he looked up into her face.

"No, not yet, Marty. I think I will sleep in this room again tonight, in the rocking chair."

"Would you play the organ while I try to go to sleep?"

She shook her head and said, "I don't think I can play the organ tonight."

"But Papa wanted you to play it. Will you play it for him, please? I think it would help me sleep. And wherever he is, I know he will hear it."

Unable to deny his request, she moved to the organ stool and played long into the night for both Hank and Martin. When her legs grew so weak she could not continue, she moved to the rocking chair to rest. Martin said quietly from where he was lying with closed eyes, "Thank you, Ma. I'm sure Pa liked it, too." As Maria sat in the chair that night, she felt only a smothering silence.

***

As spring planting time neared, Maria and Martin learned to hitch a mule to the plow, and they plowed and planted two acres in corn. While they labored at that task, Allen Smithson and Karl planted two acres in wheat and one in potatoes for her, knowing that the task was too great for her and her son.

The bright spot in the Schroeder's lives was Minnie's pregnancy. As she grew large with child, Karl grew more and more solicitous.

By July, Maria had received two proposals of marriage. She smiled wanly and thanked both suitors but shook her head. To both, she responded, "You would not want a wife whose heart is still owned by her dead husband." Both men went away muttering under their breath something about a foolish widow woman.

The passage of the months did little to heal the void inside Maria. As she washed her blistered hands and examined her sunburned face in the looking glass, she wondered if she would ever be whole again. As she lay in the bed where Hank had died—something that was ever present in her mind—she kept her tears locked inside. She had discovered when little Caroline had died that it was better to not permit herself to cry, as it became overwhelmingly difficult to stop. Each night after memories had worn their paths through her mind for more than an hour—wearing her emotional control thin—in a state of exhaustion, she would finally drift off toward sleep.

One evening after a long day of work in the garden, while in a state that was neither sleeping nor waking, she heard Hank's voice so plainly that she thought he stood in the room. *Remember, I told you that no matter where life takes us, I will love you and protect you, whether in life or in death. Do not fear, my dear Maria. I will be here watching and waiting for you.*

When she woke in the morning, she was sure that she had been dreaming, but the familiar sound of his voice had brought comfort, and she went about her responsibilities with a heart that hurt a little less.

When the wheat was ripe, Karl brought several men to harvest the crop. Most of the cabins that had been left empty when the Mississippi Saints left for Southern California had been taken over by new settlers, and many of the new folks assisted in harvesting Maria's crops. As the men gathered to get a drink of cold water after the harvesting was finished, Maria thanked them. "Your kindness means so much to me. I can never repay you."

Allen said quietly, "Hank would have done the same for any of us if the situation had been reversed. As Saints, we must care for one another."

When they had dug the potatoes, brought them in, and placed them in the newly dug root cellar, Allen straightened up and brushed off his hands. Then he spoke what had been on his mind for several weeks. "Maria, I don't think you are going to like hearing what I am going to say, but it needs to be said." He paused and rubbed his chin. "You know how much those of us who knew Hank respected him, but I have been urged to tell you that you need a husband and that there are at least three men in the settlement who would be willing to marry you and become a father to your children." He hurried to add, "A widow woman just can't provide for a family in this new country. It just takes too much physical labor. You're still an attractive woman. Don't look back. Make a new life for yourself."

Maria sat unmoving for a moment. Finally, she said, "I will give what you have said some thought, Allen. Please don't press me to make a decision tonight."

"Of course not. I don't mean to press you. You take your time, but remember that when it comes time for next year's harvest, you will need the help of a husband."

CHAPTER 40

Minnie's Baby

As her baby's due date neared, Minnie needed more rest. Maria had finally insisted that she stay with her. "Karl must tend the animals and the garden and finish harvesting your crops. You stay with me until the baby comes."

The baby was due in November, but in mid-October, Maria sent Karl for the doctor. Minnie's contractions had begun. There had been no midwife in Cottonwood since Vilate had married and moved to Salt Lake City.

Minnie's labor was long and hard. She lay in a cold sweat, biting on a clean cloth to muffle her cries. By twilight the baby had arrived, but his mother was failing. The baby was a big strong, healthy boy, and he cried loudly when he was laid in his mother's arms. "He is beautiful," Minnie said weakly.

When Karl and the doctor arrived, Martin ran out to meet them. "Uncle Karl, Minnie's baby came."

Karl hurried into the cabin, and by lamplight, he could see Minnie's white and clammy face. She lay in the bed, holding the baby. "Karl, it's a boy, and he is strong and healthy. You have a son." The pride was evident in Minnie's weak voice.

Maria spoke quietly with the doctor and explained that Minnie had lost a great deal of blood during the delivery. They had built a fire in the stove in an attempt to warm the cabin and alleviate Minnie's chills, but it did not seem to help. He felt her pulse and her forehead.

"I am so happy for you, Little Min." Karl knelt by the bed, his concern showing plainly in his face. "Yes, we have a fine, strong boy. Now you must get strong, too."

"I want you to name him Hans Karl Schroeder—and call him Hank. That would be a good name. We all loved Hank." Her voice was growing weaker.

Trying to comfort her, Karl knelt by the bed and agreed, "Yes, Hans Karl is a good name. Now you must rest so you can get your strength back."

She smiled weakly and whispered, "I'm afraid that I can't stay with you to help raise our son. But I know you will take good care of him—with Maria's help." She closed her eyes, and her hand slipped from his. The doctor stepped near her, feeling for her pulse again. Finding none, he shook his head.

Karl took her hand again and rubbed it, trying to bring the warmth back that was fleeing so quickly. "Minnie, we have a son. I can't raise him without you. Don't leave me," he whispered urgently.

Maria picked up the baby from Minnie's limp arm. Allen and Letitia knocked quietly on the door and entered without waiting for an invitation. Maria's head shake answered the question in their eyes.

Maria whispered to Letitia, "I don't have any milk for the baby. Gertie won't have her next calf for a week or two. Can you help?"

"One of our cows came in fresh a month ago. I will send you a quart of milk as soon as I get home."

"How will I feed the baby? Do you have a bottle and a rubber nipple a baby can use?"

"I'm sure I have one. I will bring it with the milk." Then she hurried back to her cabin.

Dr. Andrews picked up his bag, and, after stepping out of the room, he said, "Please tell Karl how sorry I am that we could not save Minnie. She was such a small woman, and the baby is so big." As he stepped out of the cabin, he added, "I know it is little consolation right now, but in time, he will come to realize what a comfort and a blessing the baby is." He mounted his horse and started back toward the city.

Maria held the crying infant as she paced outside the cabin. Within a few minutes, Allen and Letitia were back with a covered bucket of warm milk and a bottle for the baby.

"Thank you so much. I don't know what we would have done without your help."

After Allen had carried the bucket into the cabin for Maria and set it down, he motioned for her to step outside. "I'll get some men together, and we'll come over tomorrow morning to dig the grave. What time do you want the services?"

"Let folks know that the services will be at one o'clock tomorrow."

Allen nodded, and he and Letitia returned to their cabin. Maria reentered the cabin and touched Karl on the shoulder. He looked up at her from where he sat with crossed legs on the floor next to the bed. He still held Minnie's hand. Maria said gently, "Here, put out your arms. You need to hold your son." Karl carefully laid Minnie's hand on the bed and put out his arms like an obedient child.

While he held the baby, Maria poured some of the milk into the bottle. After struggling with the rubber nipple, she finally had the bottle ready for the baby. Karl lifted his son as if to offer him to Maria to feed, but she said, "No, Karl, he is your son. It is important that you feed him."

As the infant sucked hungrily on the bottle, Karl watched as if seeing his son for the first time. Everything else disappeared as he watched the baby. After a few minutes, he carefully stood and moved to sit on one of the big trunks. As the baby drifted off to sleep, Karl set the bottle down and continued to watch the infant as it slept. With a breaking voice, Karl said, "He is beautiful, Maria. How Minnie would have loved him." With a calloused hand, he brushed away a tear that slid down his weathered, sunburned cheek.

Maria slipped out to the animal shed and brought back a sturdy box meant to carry twenty pounds of potatoes. She folded a clean blanket into it and touched her brother-in-law's shoulder. "Here, Karl. This will make a good bed for the baby."

Karl looked up at her as if he had forgotten her presence. "I'll just hold him for a little while longer."

"Then you will need to sit in the rocking chair." Putting her hand on his elbow, she guided him to the rocking chair as if he were sleepwalking. He sat down and continued to watch the baby as it slept in his arms.

Maria placed her dish pan on the floor and then, taking both of her buckets, hurried to the stream a quarter of a mile away to fill them with water. When she got back to the cabin, she poured the cold mountain water into the dish pan. Then she set the bucket of fresh milk in it. She washed out the baby bottle and refilled it. She touched Karl to get his attention, pointed to the bottle, and set it near him. She stepped over to Minnie's body and pulled the quilt up to her chin, as if she were sleeping. Martin slept on a bedroll on the floor again, with

Maggie close by, and Maria kept watch from a chair in the corner throughout the night.

By seven o'clock that morning, Allen had gathered three other men to dig the grave. Another man brought a wagonload of precious milled wood to make the coffin. Minnie was laid to rest next to Hank in the little cemetery. After the eulogy, each adult offered his or her sympathy to Karl as they took their leave. He nodded his thanks at each one but said little.

That evening as Maria handed another bottle to Karl for the baby, he said, "Thank you, Maria, for letting me care for little Hank. A new baby must be God's greatest gift. It has helped me understand why he was so important to little Min. She told me not long after we were married that if God required her to lay down her life to have a baby that lived, she would gladly do it. I told her not to talk that way, but I think maybe she knew—knew that she would not live to raise a child." Maria said nothing. In her exhaustion, she did not know what to say.

He spoke again, as he laid the baby in the little wooden box to sleep. "Tomorrow I will go back to the canyon to cut more trees. We will need another room here." He seemed to feel that Maria fully understood what he was talking about.

"Karl, what do you mean?" As Maggie toddled unsteadily around the room, Martin watched his mother and Karl, listening closely.

"I cannot take care of the baby and plant and harvest and build—all the things a man needs to do to provide for a family. The best answer seems to be that we marry so my son can have a mother and your children can have a father—if you will have me."

Maria said nothing for a moment. She was not entirely surprised at his proposal, as his solution to their joint problem seemed practical—not romantic, but practical. She sat down on the big chest and said slowly, "Of course, I will have you, Karl. I know I am not and will never be your Minnie—and you are not my Hank, but we can be stronger together than separate. We will make a family and be a help to one another." She paused and then said, "But we must wait a respectful time before we marry. I will take care of the baby until you add another room to the cabin. When should we marry?"

Karl nodded and said simply, "Three months will be acceptable. Minnie would approve. Yes, that will be long enough."

CHAPTER 41
The Birthday Reunion

The years passed swiftly, as they always do when life is full of joys and hardships, growth and pain, light and dark. Maria often noted little things about Karl that reminded her of Hank. Sometimes it was the way he laughed or tossed his head to get wet hair out of his eyes that brought a nearly forgotten warmth flooding into her heart.

Maria milked Gertie night and morning. She made butter and cheese, preserves and pickles, soap and candles. She carded wool from the sheep they bought and spun and wove it—and on evenings when she was not too exhausted, she would play the organ that had meant so much to Hank. While she played, the memories and shadows of the years they had spent together filled and warmed her mind and heart.

During the summer months, farming a double plot of land used all of Karl's time and energy. He enjoyed working with Martin and teaching him how to make the ground produce. During the winter months, he often used his leather-working skills to mend harnesses and other leather goods for his neighbors. Some of his friends and neighbors urged him to open a leather shop, but he just shook his head. He loved the farm, and working with leather brought back too many painful memories he never talked about.

Karl and Martin threw themselves into the process of breaking the hard virgin soil, uprooting sagebrush and burning it, clearing away rocks, and chopping or pulling out cottonwood trees and willows to make way for plowing. Over time, they planted an orchard and dug a well and irrigation ditches. Karl kept the mules shod and sheared the sheep each spring.

Even though the work continued from dawn to dusk and often beyond, Karl and Maria never lost sight of the blessings the gospel brought into their home and the lives of their family. Despite his quiet personality and the German accent he never quite lost, Karl learned to deliver a good Sunday sermon with power and conviction when called upon in Church.

When the Utah Territorial Constitution was amended in 1867, giving the vote to every adult over the age of twenty-one, regardless of gender or race—the first state or territory to do so—the entire settlement celebrated, but Maria most of all. She baked a three-tiered cake and then wept tears of joy as she served it at the community picnic, much to the confusion of those who did not know her history.

The blended Schroeder family grew strong there in Cottonwood—one son tall, with hair as dark as coal dust, and the other one tall and lanky with straw-colored hair. Maggie grew to be as beautiful as her mother had been in her youth, with gray-green eyes and hair the color of corn silk. When the grandchildren came to visit, there were some with black hair and some with hair in shades of gold.

On Maria's seventy-forth birthday, as the century ended and another began, the family members gathered from as far south as Nephi and as far north as Ogden, filling to overflowing the little cabin that Karl had enlarged over the years to five rooms. He had put a wood floor in it and a porch that wrapped around three sides so in the summer they could eat breakfast as the sun rose or watch the sun set in the evenings.

After the birthday celebration, the children and grandchildren departed. As the sun slid below the Oquirrh Mountains to the west, Maria and Karl sat near each other in rocking chairs on the porch to watch the changing colors in the clouds. Karl sat with the Book of Mormon open on his lap. His eyes had grown so dim that though he often opened it, he had to read from memory.

As they sat there in the soft twilight, he asked, "I have often wondered, Maria, if your faith was strengthened by the pain and hardships of your life."

She was startled by the question. Karl had always been a quiet man who seldom initiated a conversation except to deal with the necessities of life. She weighed her words before she spoke. "I cannot deny that life has been hard at times, but at other times it has been good." She was quiet for a minute. "Sometimes it has been hard and good at the same time—or perhaps it is that time polishes the hard edges off our memories and makes them shine."

"Was there anything you would change—if you could?"

"I refuse to look back in regret, because nothing can be changed. If any of it had been easier, I would never have grown strong, and the Lord wants us to be strong. Easy times make for a weak people." She paused and added thoughtfully, "I sometimes worry about the grandchildren. I wonder if they will be robbed by a life too full of ease."

Karl chuckled for a moment and then added, "I think the influence of their grandmother has been enough in their lives to keep them strong."

She continued, "There were times after we arrived in the Valley when I thought that my faith was gone, that I had no more strength. At those times, I leaned on Hank. All that I felt then was fear, anger, or despair, but looking back, each hardship, each grief, was another stone in the foundation of my faith." She looked at her husband and asked, "Was it the same with you?"

"I had no faith—only hopelessness—until Hank came and led me to freedom. We both owe our freedom to his compassion and strength. I have had to live a lifetime to come to a full understanding of the words, 'Wherefore, dispute not because ye see not, for ye receive no witness until after the trial of your faith.' It is now, in our old age, that we have finally received the witness of our faith. It is in these advanced years with failing eyes that we have a clearer vision of the truth of the principles that have guided our lives. It has been a good life, Maria. Thank you for sharing so much of it with me."

"You are welcome, Karl. It has been a blessing and a privilege. As I said so long ago, I could never be your Minnie, and you were not my Hank, but we have been good friends, and we have come to love each other—and we made a good, strong family."

The stars began to glimmer as if a distant lamplighter were at work, lighting them singly and in groups. They both dozed there in the pleasant evening air.

The warmth and brightness of what seemed like the sun on her face awakened Maria. As she opened her eyes, she could see someone walking up the path toward the house. She could not make out his features, but his long stride was familiar somehow. He was tall, broad shouldered, and dressed in buckskin. She stood to greet the man and invite him in for something cool to drink, but as she did so, recognition washed over her like a warm breeze on a cool day. "Hank. Hank, you are here!" she cried out.

He wore a broad smile, and he stretched his arms out to her. She hurried lightly over the steps that led off the porch—steps she had climbed or descended with great care for the past twenty years. The locket hanging around her neck glinted in the morning sun as she hurried to embrace him.

As she laid her face against his chest and put her arms around his waist, he encircled her with his arms and whispered in her ear, "Karl is sleeping. We won't disturb him. It's time for you to come with me."

When Karl awoke in the darkness, he reached out for Maria's hand, only to find it cold and lifeless. He sat without moving for a few minutes and then he whispered, "So you've gone home, Maria." He paused a moment and then added, "Give Hank my good wishes, and tell Minnie I'll be along soon."

#

Selected Bibliography

Arrington, Leonard J. "Mississippi Mormons." *Ensign*, June 1977, 46.

Bailey, John. *The Lost German Slave Girl.* New York: Atlantic Monthly Press, 2003.

Blockson, Charles L. "Escape from Slavery: The Underground Railroad." *National Geographic*, July 1984, 14.

Brown, John. *Autobiography of Pioneer John Brown, 1820–1896.* Salt Lake City, Utah: 1941.

Hartley, William G. "Gathering the Dispersed Nauvoo Saints, 1847–1852." *Ensign*, July 1997, 12–28.

Hurst, Frederick William. "Autobiography and Diaries." Vol. 3. 13 Nov. 1857–10 Jan. 1858. Salt Lake City, Utah. (In possession of Church History Library.)

Kimball, Stanley B. "Two More Mormon Trails: The Boonslick Trail; The Mississippi Saints' Trail." *Ensign*, August 1979, 49.

Kohler, Charmaine Lay. *Southern Grace: A Story of the Mississippi Saints.* Boise, Idaho: Beagle Creek Press, 1995.

Lay, Edward Leo. *San Bernardino: The Rise and Fall of a California Community.* Salt Lake City, Utah: Signature Books, 1996.

Roberts, B. H. A *Comprehensive History of the Church*. 6 vols. Vol. 3. Provo, Utah: Brigham Young University Press, 1965.

Stillitoe, Linda. "The World Moves In." *Pioneer*, Vol. 52, No. 2, 2005, 12–16. Published by Sons of Utah Pioneers. Salt Lake City, Utah.

_____, "From a Worthy Seed, Healthy Life Springeth: The History of the Salt Lake Stake." *Pioneer*, Vol. 54, No. 3, 2007, 2–8. Published by Sons of Utah Pioneers. Salt Lake City, Utah.

About the Author

Jean Holbrook Mathews was born in Ogden, Utah, of LDS pioneer progenitors. She met and married John P. Mathews while attending Weber State University, and they have three children. The Mathews family was transferred to St. Louis by John's employer, where they lived for thirty years. She received her B.S. from the University of Missouri–St. Louis. She spent ten years as a member of the Missouri State House of Representatives, during which time she received her master's degree from UM–Columbia. Her first love is history, with a special focus on Church history. *Escape to Zion* and her previously published novel, *The Light Above*, are focused on the hardships in the lives of the pioneers who shaped Church history.